ISLAND WOMAN

Bill —
Have a good trip
with Abbie!
Richard Sessions
5/10/01

ISLAND WOMAN

A NOVEL BY

RICHARD SESSIONS

Address inquiries to ARCH GROVE PRESS,
P.O. Box 2387, Lake Oswego, Oregon 97035.
Telephone: (503) 624-7811

Printed in the United States of America.

ISBN 0-9659402-0-9

Library of Congress Catalogue Number 97-61091

CREDITS:

"Reed College," from *Colleges That Change Lives* by Loren Pope. Copyright © 1996 by Loren Pope. Used by permission of Viking Penguin, a division of Penguin Books USA Inc.

From *Cannery Row* by John Steinbeck. Copyright 1945 by John Steinbeck. Renewed © 1973 by Elaine Steinbeck, John Steinbeck IV and Thom Steinbeck. Used by permission of Viking Penguin, a division of Penguin Books USA Inc.

From George Santayana, *The Last Puritan: A Memoir In The Form Of A Novel* (Cambridge, MA: The MIT Press, 1994) p. 242, 243.

From Gary Snyder, *The Real Work*. Copyright © 1980 by Gary Snyder. Reprinted by permission of New Directions Publishing Corporation.

Cover Art: R. E. Pierce
Book Design: John Rodal

Preface

What would you do if you found yourself, against your will, back in an unknown time? How would you cope if you had only your wits to help you survive, alone or among people completely foreign to you?

These are the circumstances in which Abbie Spence finds herself. But she is not without resources. Among them are a privileged upbringing by loving parents and a recent B.A. degree from Reed College, which Loren Pope, former education editor of the New York Times, calls "the most intellectual college in the country." Are these a help? Or a hindrance? Either way, Abbie must use her brains, cleverness and heart to navigate in a harsh, old world.

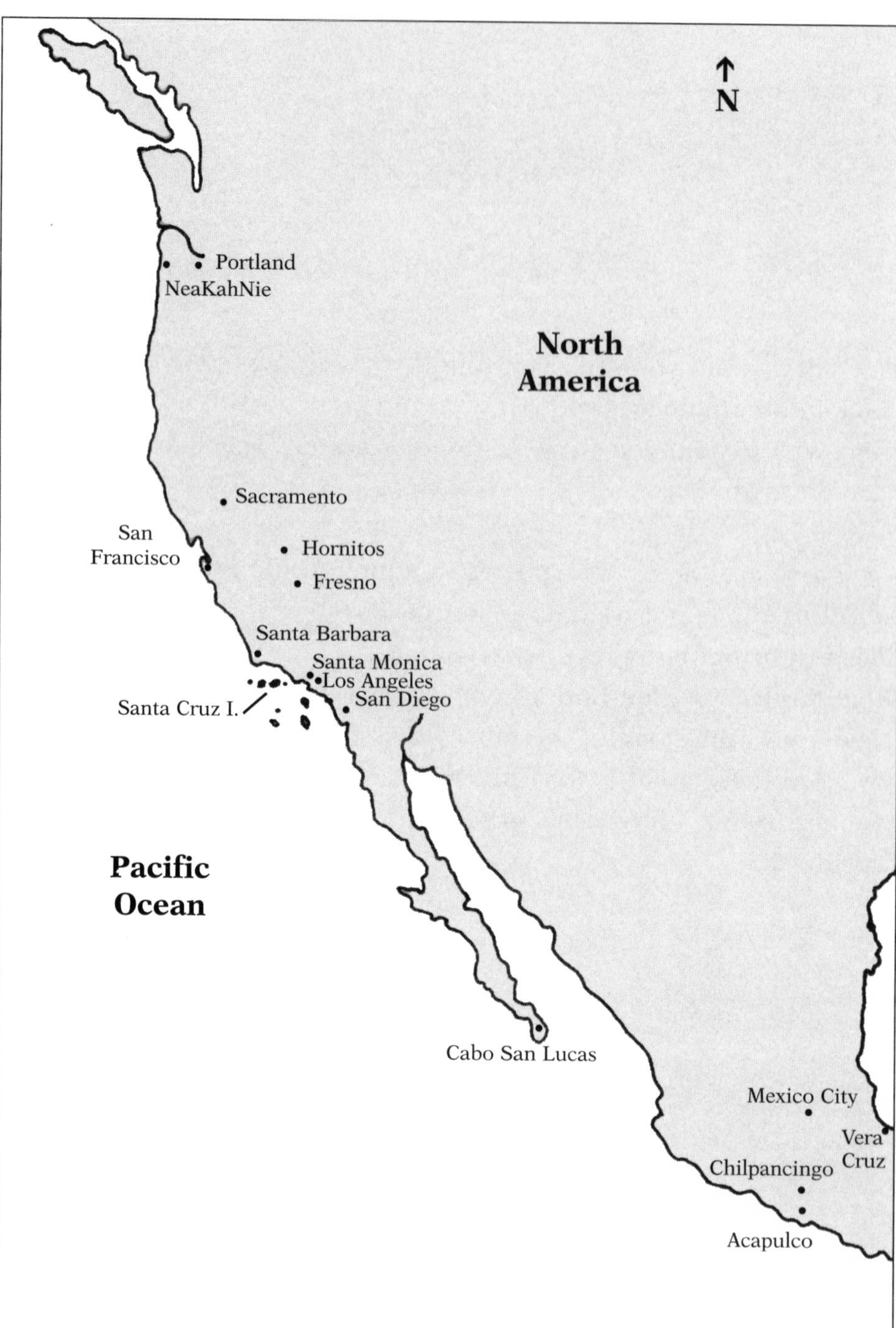
N
Portland
NeaKahNie
North America
Sacramento
San Francisco
Hornitos
Fresno
Santa Barbara
Santa Monica
Los Angeles
San Diego
Santa Cruz I.
Pacific Ocean
Cabo San Lucas
Mexico City
Vera Cruz
Chilpancingo
Acapulco

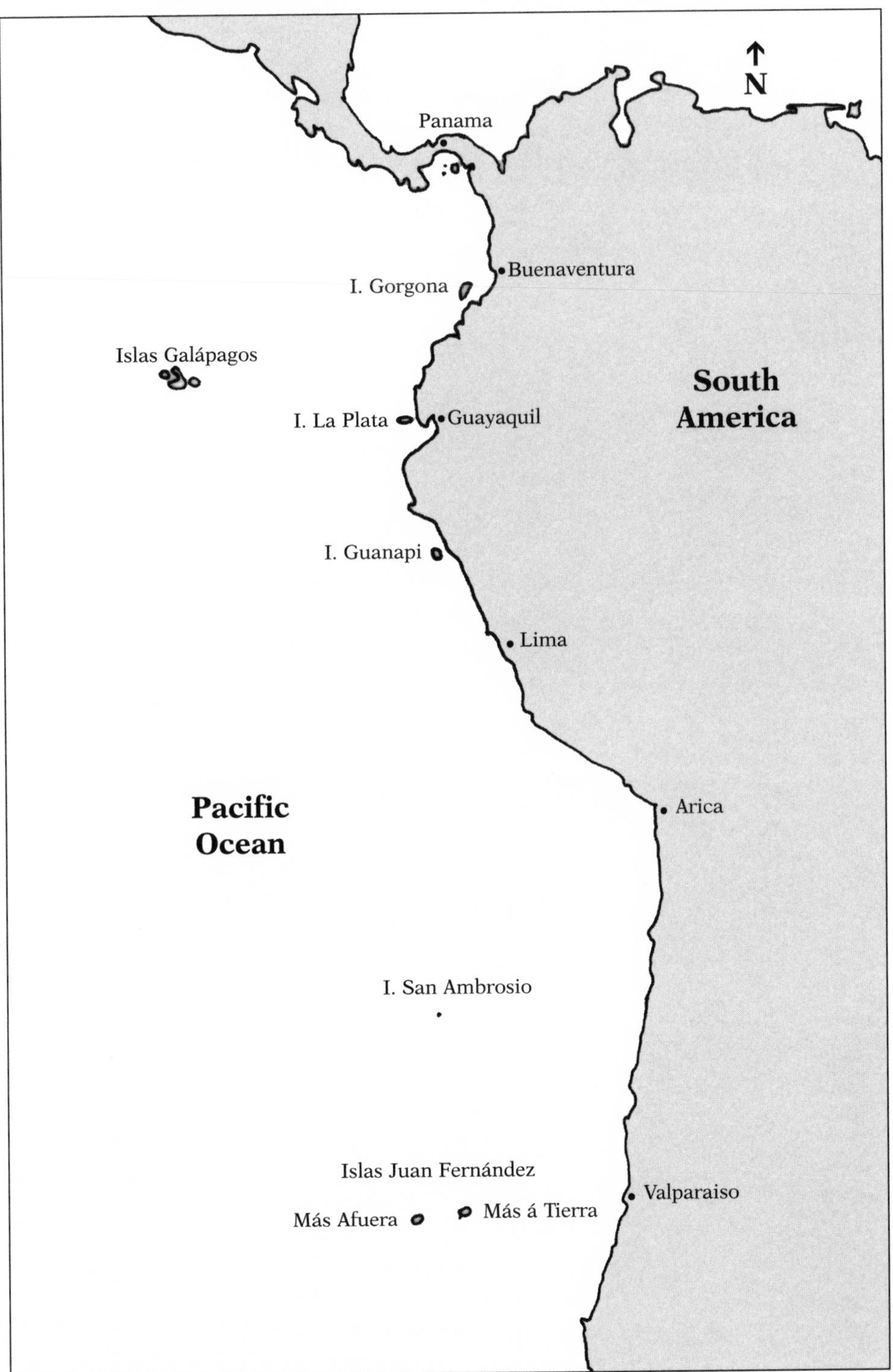
N
Panama
Buenaventura
I. Gorgona
Islas Galápagos
South America
I. La Plata
Guayaquil
I. Guanapi
Lima
Arica
Pacific Ocean
I. San Ambrosio
Islas Juan Fernández
Valparaiso
Más Afuera
Más á Tierra

I just want everyone to live out their lives and do the best they can for themselves.

James F. Kent

For my family and friends...

As a girl, I recall my father saying that astrology, miracles, psychic happenings, and all such stuff were hocus pocus. For him there was a scientific explanation for everything, even if science hadn't gotten around to it yet. You would expect this of a Professor of Mechanical Engineering. My mother, a social worker, although not superstitious, thought there were unknowables and forces and fates. She would talk about somebody's "life script." Up through high school I came down on my Dad's side of this.

At Reed College, I took a class in modern physics and learned something about relativity, quantum phenomena, and the grand unification theories. It was then I realized that physicists found the laws of matter quite mysterious. After all, how can one seriously consider that there may be twenty-some dimensions in the universe, as current string theory has it? I thought a lot about what these singularities might be—beyond the usual three space dimensions plus time—but I just couldn't imagine them. Cheeseholes in space? Too strange. During my college days I wished I could have talked with my father, but he was no longer living.

So, even though I shared my father's faith in science, I decided to keep an open mind to all of the inexplicable things about the world. I had moved cautiously toward my mother's view. That is one reason why, I think, I wanted to keep going to Gordon Bitterroot's meetings even though my girlfriend Crystal was having none of it.

"Abbie, Gordon Bitterroot is a kook. Why would you want to get involved with him? For a smart girl, I wonder about you."

We were talking on the way back from that first meeting.

"He's fun. Keeps you on your toes."

"That's one way of putting it."

"What bothered you—him or what happened at the meeting?" I asked.

"Well, the discussion about Mexican mysticism was OK. But, c'mon, that Madame Romanov—whatever her name—she was a case. No way did she move those cubes. Do they think we're dummies? It had to be magnets. All those people acting like it was real. C'mon."

"I just might go again."

"Well...it won't be with me, Abbie. Are you serious?"

I have always considered myself different from most girls. As a kid I remember that there seemed to be lots of boys in my neighborhood. I liked playing sports with them instead of dressing and undressing Barbie dolls. Mom said I was a tomboy, that I identified with my father. But don't get the wrong idea—I'm not masculine. Mom and my relatives said I was attractive. I always thought I was too thin for five feet seven. And, despite my blonde hair, too plain looking. Still, I got dates for high school dances, and I enjoyed dressing up and doing my face. Of course at Reed I never dressed up. Although I studied intensely in college I did find time for two boyfriends, including one who proposed to me when we graduated. But I was not interested in getting married. I believed it might happen in the future, but I wasn't inclined to guide my life so as to increase the probability of ending up that way.

"Abbie, where did you go?" Crystal said, flicking my hand.

"Just thinking."

"You're always thinking. Abbie Spence, Ms. Space Cadet."

"First I'm dumb, then I'm always thinking."

"I don't think that's inconsistent. Maybe by Reed standards." She chuckled. "Everything is inconsistent at that place."

After we graduated from Santa Monica High, Crystal went to Pomona College, and I took a scholarship at Reed. Four years later, with my diploma and Volkswagen, I returned to Santa Monica, even though my mother was then living in San Francisco. She had remarried, and I couldn't think of a convincing reason to live near her. Everyone was surprised that I took a job in a nursery, especially since I was not in the front office. I was watering the plants, hefting manure bags into cars, driving a truck to pick up supplies, and the like. I liked the menial work not only because I was outside, but because I could concentrate on ideas of great thinkers—you know, Kierkegaard or Camus or Plato. To me I was carrying on the Reed way of life. Ideas don't stay in the classroom but enter your everyday world.

I guess that working as a yard hand in a nursery is not what a combined literature-philosophy major is supposed to do. My relatives were especially critical of me. At a family gathering, an uncle once asked me what I liked about the job.

"I like having time to think. I believe people should consider basic philosophical ideas everyday," I told him.

"So who has time for that?"

"That's exactly my point," I said.

"Abbie, I don't know what happened to you up there in Oregon, but you need to join the real world."

"I'm happy. Why does that bother you?"

He just shook his head and went for another beer. He was totally into the American dream of getting ahead. I found it hard to believe he was my father's brother.

Crystal turned onto my street. In the middle of the block I could see my well-lit apartment building looming in the mist, like some off-shore oil platform on a foggy night.

"OK, Abbie, I'll see you later," Crystal said, as she dropped me off. "Take some free advice. Find somebody closer to your own age."

"Free advice, but worth its weight in gold."

"Yeah, I know, words don't weigh anything."

"Thanks for driving, Crys. I'll call you soon."

Why was Bitterroot interesting to me? Partly because he was English. Mostly because he was odd. I had enjoyed wayward souls at Reed, and I considered Bitterroot to be in the same vein. After the second meeting, when several of us went for coffee, I asked what he had done before coming to the States and opening the bookstore.

"Let's just say I was a history buff, Abbie."

"That's not an occupation, Gordon."

"I've been at it nigh on five hundred years. I'd say that is pretty occupying."

After making this statement, he laughed.

Crystal and I met Bitterroot and his friend Cliff Manssard at the Hollywood store one day when I was looking for a cheap copy of Rousseau's *Emile*. The window advertised the lowest prices in town on used books.

"Cor blimey! A young person who reads. For sure I thought you'd ask for cookbooks or old comics," Bitterroot said. He glanced at Manssard who was nearby, paging through a newspaper. "I just lost a bet to you, Cliff."

"Sorry," I said, chuckling.

"I think I have a copy, but why d'ye want Rousseau? He just titillated the bourgeoisie of Europe, didn't he?"

"Well...in a way, yes. But he was quite different from other enlightenment philosophers. I'd like to know more about that. I didn't get to read him much when I was in college."

"Aye, the noble savage, nature, that romantic junk."

"Romantic junk? I don't think so. Nature is the major issue of our world now, right?"

"I still say junk." And he got me arguing and laughing.

By the time we left, Bitterroot had reduced the book's price to ten cents. He then invited Crystal and me to come to a meeting at Manssard's house in the Hollywood hills where "people get together for intellectual discussion."

Bitterroot claimed he was from the western part of London, an ancient village named Wantage, and came to Southern California because there were more Brits here than in any other part of the U.S. He'd been here for about five years. His hole-in-the-wall place was hunkered in the middle of a decrepit building on Beverly Boulevard. Unlike Manssard, Bitterroot appeared to be poor, always wearing old, worn clothes. I guessed he was in his mid-to-late forties. He was broad shouldered, and his hands were gnarled and rough—not what you would expect in a book dealer. His face was tanned and lined but peaceful. Sometimes his pale, blue eyes had a depth that sucked at you, and they began twinkling the instant before that low rumble of a laugh erupted in a staccato crescendo. It made you laugh just to listen to it.

Looking back on it, I think the key for what later happened was my telling Manssard that my great great grandfather Spence had come to California on the clipper ship *Orion*. We were talking after the second meeting.

"So you like to sail, Abbie?"

"I love it. My Dad had an Islander 32 for many years."

"Uh huh. I have a forty-two foot ketch. She's down at Marina del Rey. Maybe you'd like to crew on her some day."

Manssard grinned, his teeth clamped on a meerschaum pipe that hung mostly unlit from the corner of his mouth. His gray and black hair ran in streaks straight back from his forehead. He was tall and wiry. Crystal had pegged his age at fifty-five.

"Sure," I said, imagining I would never set foot on the big ketch. I told him of my father's interest in nautical architecture, and I was pleased when Manssard said that the fascination had obviously rubbed off on me. Despite this conversation, I was completely surprised by Bitterroot's phone call a few days after the second meeting.

"I want to be sure you're coming Tuesday night, Abbie."

"Why?"

"We are going to re-live part of a passage taken by a vessel more than a hundred and forty years ago."

"Oh?" I hesitated. "What vessel?"

"The *Orion*."

When it came time to leave my apartment that Tuesday evening, I was surprised when my legs suddenly felt weak. I had to grab the door, but I gathered strength again as I went down the stairs. I knew I was of two minds about going. I had reread the letter my great-aunt Spence wrote about her father in 1876. It chronicled his arrival in San Francisco on May 6, 1850, and his trip, first by steamer to Sacramento and then by horseback to Mariposa County at the southern end of the Mother Lode. He panned and sluiced for gold near a mining camp called Agua Frio. Later he settled in the old town of Hornitos. There he opened a general store in partnership with another fellow and married my namesake, Abigail Snow. The sparse facts were lonely, and I had always wished for more details about this courageous man and the rough life he, Abigail, and the family must have suffered. Was I being offered the opportunity to see what he might have experienced aboard a ship enroute to California? It had to be a hoax.

I enjoyed being in Manssard's living room. There was a massive stone fireplace at one end. The fireplace and the huge, hand-carved ceiling beams gave the effect of a gentrified hunting lodge. An intricately woven Persian carpet in reds, purples, blues, and bright saffron covered the floor. Statuary stood on marble tables, and on the white plaster walls were large, European pastoral paintings in ornate brass gilded frames.

There were only twelve people in the room, fewer than before. Maybe this was because the program's topic was unannounced. The smaller circle made for more intimacy. A poet named Van Carli started the meeting with verse to help people relax. When the poetry ended, Bitterroot stood up and announced that the evening's program was an experiment. For those who wanted to go, there would be a journey to a clipper ship enroute from Boston to San Francisco via Cape Horn. The time of the voyage would be in January of 1850, and our narrator would be Cliff Manssard. Bitterroot encouraged everyone needing to make a stop at the bathroom to do it now as there would not be any breaks for the next hour. There were a few chuckles as Manssard's girlfriend, Claire, and I got up.

When we resettled on the couch, the room was already dark. Manssard stood before the fireplace, looking intently at some papers on a music stand, lit by a tiny book lamp. Bitterroot sat on a footstool in the middle of the group. His gold pocket watch was dangling in the narrow beam coming from a spotlight mounted on the wall. The watch's long, gold chain began swinging, and the watch flashed back and forth through the beam. Like a lighthouse at rapid tempo, there was darkness, a sudden flash, and darkness again.

"Watch the watch. Let yourself relax. We are going on a trip. Get ready to go. Relax and come with me. Concentrate on the watch." Bitterroot's voice was soothing.

I closed my eyes, wondering if I could let myself go and then getting angry at myself for wondering it. Then I heard Manssard.

"We see the bark *Orion* under the command of Captain Henry C. Bunker. She is a long, narrow vessel, close to 300 feet in length, with three tall masts and a large bowsprit jutting forward. She is in fine condition, only three years old, with a full complement of sails—royals and studding sails alow and aloft, port and starboard, staysails and a mainsail on the aft mast. The sails are pulling strongly, and she plows easily through the waves. Looking below we see a spacious cabin between decks, accommodating more than seventy passengers. There are two large houses above decks, also filled with passengers and there is an awning over the whole of the after cabin to ward off the sun."

There was a long silence, and then Bitterroot took up again.

"Watch the watch swing. The ship is a good clipper ship and we are going to visit her at sea. All of the ninety passengers are having a grand time, and we will drop in on them, maybe even see someone who looks familiar. Let yourself come. Relax and come with me, mates. You can see the bark *Orion* now ghosting in the night, with running lights and cabin lanterns glowing. Let's get closer."

I felt myself become drowsy. The picture of the ship became vivid, as if in a strong dream. If I got closer maybe I could see the people. I heard Manssard's voice again, but it was farther away.

"The *Orion* left Boston harbor on November 12, 1849, and stopped in Rio de Janeiro for supplies and water. She is now on her way south again heading for Staten Island on the eastern side of the Horn. It is getting cooler, and the wind is stronger. We see that only some of the sails are up, but still she makes good speed. There are whitecaps, but *Orion* rolls easily."

I could now see the ship clearly, even though it was dark. The sails and masts cast shadows on the deck from the moonlight. On the afterdeck, a man stood at the large wheel, moving it slowly one way and then the other. He wore a heavy, dark coat and a tight woolen cap. Then suddenly I felt Bitterroot pulling at my arm.

"You'll need different clothes, Abbie, and a warm jacket," he whispered.

I went with him into the darkness and changed into the clothes he handed me. I remember bloomers and high top rubber boots. The last to go on was a heavy, woolen coat. Wherever we were, it was getting cold. I now felt wind on my cheeks and heard the sound of waves.

He turned me and said, "Look, there's the *Orion*. Get closer to her, Abbie."

I could see the cabin lights and hear the creaking of wood and flapping of lines on canvas as she moved up and down like some giant sea animal. Suddenly I realized I was precariously situated, and I lunged and grabbed onto the wooden railing, wedging my feet into the gunwale. Cold, salty spray splashed against me. I looked down and saw iridescent foam rushing past the side of the ship. I knew I had to get over the railing or I would fall into the sea and be lost in seconds as the *Orion* sped on its way. The rail, in addition to being slippery, was large and difficult to grasp. I tried to swing my right leg over but the bloomer caught on something. The ship leaned toward me, and I almost slipped off. When it rolled the other way, I tried again. This time I was able to lock my leg over the rail, but I couldn't get leverage to lift my body over. Only by inching on each roll to the opposite side was I eventually able to straddle the rail and then ease myself down on the deck. I was now good and wet, the water having drenched my hair and face and run down my neck into my dress. The wind was chilling me.

Afraid to stand, I crawled aft over lines and around barrels and crates lashed to the rail, making toward the lights of the after passenger cabin. When I got there I looked into the first porthole. A large lantern moved on gimbals on the side of the cabin wall, the flame flickering slightly. I could see men on bunks, some sleeping and others reading or watching a card game in progress at a table in the center of the cabin. I saw no women. As cold as I was, I decided not to shout. Instead, I continued aft, thinking it better to approach the man at the wheel. As I got to the end of the cabin I could see the coxswain and another man on the raised afterdeck. The coxswain's face was dimly lit from the reflection of a light that was probably used to see the compass. I stood up, more sure of my footing now that my eyes were accustomed to the darkness, and I walked toward the men slowly.

When the lookout pointed toward me, I realized they had seen me, and I shouted, "Hello!"

The one who pointed screamed and started running around the other side of the aft cabin. The coxswain started blowing on a boatswain's pipe, making shrill sounds. I stood still, suddenly aware that I must have frightened them. Then some other sailors came up on deck. Some of the passengers were now behind me, talking excitedly. Was one of them named Spence?

"Somebody please help me," I shouted.

"It's a woman," someone said.

An older man with an officer's hat now walked toward me slowly, a frown on his face.

"I'm Captain Bunker. What are you doing up here, ma'am?" he asked, now just a few feet in front of me. "You're wet. Who are you?"

I was frightened. He now stepped closer, scrutinizing my face.

"You're not one of our passengers. Who are you? Answer me."

"I'm Abigail Smith, sir."

"How did you get on this ship?"

"Uh, at Rio de Janeiro."

"By whose authority?"

I heard indignation rising in his voice. This could only lead to trouble. I made myself shake.

"Captain, sir, I'm sick and cold. Please help me." My voice was plaintive.

There were two other men now standing with the captain. One was looking at me intently.

"She'd better get warmed, sir," he said.

"Take her below to Mrs. Bunker's cabin, Spence. Tell Mrs. Bunker to care for her. Johnson, go ask Mrs. Wheeler to help. See that some food is brought to the cabin."

"Oh thank you, Captain," I said. I noticed a flicker of a smile on his lips.

"We'll talk when you're feeling better, Miss Smith." Then he turned and headed up toward the wheel. The gathering of men made way for me as Spence led me down a narrow stairway and aft through a narrow passageway with doors on each side. As he knocked at one, he looked into my face.

"Do I know you, miss? You look familiar."

I was speechless. I knew I was looking at my great great grandfather. His face had a puzzled expression, but his eyes were searching my identity. I wanted to tell him who I was, to hug him.

An elderly lady opened the door slowly. She was in a nightshirt with a blue robe over it.

"Who is it?"

"Spence, ma'am. The Captain wants you to take care of this girl. We found her on the deck. Mrs. Wheeler will be coming to help."

She peered at me, disbelief on her lined face.

"Please help me, Mrs. Bunker. I'm wet, cold, and tired."

Her face mellowed. "Well, come in girl. Thank you, Spence."

The cabin was tiny, consisting of a single berth on one side under one porthole, a small writing desk with a chair, and a built-in closet.

"My lands. Look at you. Let's get you out of those wet clothes."

We tugged off my clothes, and I noticed she looked quizzically at my bra. She helped me into a flannel nightshirt from a drawer and then took a towel to my hair.

"What is your name, dear?"

"Abigail."

"And where are you from, Abigail?"

I could see that the certain barrage of questions would lead to problems, so I said I was very tired and could I get in bed.

"Of course, dear." She pulled back the colorful piecework quilt, and I crawled under it. I put my head on the pillow and closed my eyes, trying to breathe deeply. As I felt another blanket being pulled up over me, there was a knock at the door. This apparently was Mrs. Wheeler, and the two of them whispered about me while I wondered what I was going to do. After a long while, the lantern was blown out, and they left. I let myself relax. My body was exhausted, probably as much from the anxiety as from the physical exertion of the past hour. I became drowsy, and soon I was dreaming.

I don't remember how much time had passed, but I sensed that somebody, a man, was pulling me up in my half-sleepy state.

"Let's go back, Abbie," I remember him saying.

Next I was putting on my own clothes again. Then I walked across the quarry tile entryway into Manssard's living room. It was still dark and people on the couches had their eyes closed. As I sat in the same seat I had left, I heard Manssard's voice.

"A storm is brewing in the south, and gale winds will now drive the *Orion* southeast toward the Falkland Islands. This may be a good place to leave her. She will eventually round the Horn in one more month, encountering thirty-foot seas in places but making it without mishap."

"We are coming back," Bitterroot said loudly. "Let yourself come back. Release your concentration, everyone."

The lights came up. People rubbed their eyes and looked around, most smiling.

Claire stood up. "Thank you, Cliff, that was marvelous."

Her comment triggered applause from everyone but me and Bitterroot. He looked at me as if to see what I was feeling. I looked back into his deep eyes, and a shiver went through me. My right knee hurt, and under my blouse my bra was missing.

I didn't want to join Bitterroot, Cliff, and Claire for coffee that night. I just wanted to go home. I guess that along with my awe over what had happened, there was a bit of anger, too. My thoughts weren't clear, and I needed time to sort them out. Bitterroot reluctantly accepted this after I promised to meet him at the bookstore the next day. We would go for lunch.

As soon as I crawled into my bed I conked out from exhaustion. I slept soundly until my alarm woke me at the usual time. My leg hurt, and it was then I noticed the bad scrape, now scabbing, above my right knee. There was a splinter in my left hand, and one of my nails was broken. I called the nursery and asked for the day off, agreeing to trade a day with a boy who might come in to substitute. I slept some more, then took a hot bath and physically began to feel better over coffee and a muffin. Deep down I knew I had been on the *Orion* and knew I had been face-to-face with my great great grandfather. But how that had happened was what my reasoning could not accept. All kinds of questions hovered in my mind, and I wanted to ask them of Bitterroot. Then I had second thoughts. I should just stop all this nonsense right now. I wouldn't show up for lunch, wouldn't go to any more meetings, wouldn't see him ever again. Isn't it time to get serious about my life? Find a better job? Seek some new friends? Maybe I should go back to school, get a Master's degree in something useful.

Now my ego had recovered. But why couldn't I see him just one more time? What harm would there be in that? I would find out some answers to the questions, resolve the matter, and then turn over the new leaf. That sounded sensible.

Bitterroot had a broad smile on his face when I walked in. He squeezed my hands. When I hiked up my dress and showed him the wound on my leg, he laughed, although a little nervously. We went to a nearby restaurant for a roast beef and tossed salad combo. He ordered a Bass ale and two glasses, and when the waitress had filled them, he toasted me.

"To Abbie, a rare person. And to a marvelously successful first voyage."

"First and only voyage. Gordon, I could have been hurt if not drowned."

"Abbie." His voice was low and conciliatory. "I didn't mean for you to board her. I know I said to get close, but I didn't dream that you would lay ahold. I was just caught up in the excitement of seeing her. So fine looking, she was. But it turned out well after all, you must admit."

"It was scary."

"But you handled it perfectly. You have a good head on those shoulders. I'm proud of you."

He was working on me, I realized, and I looked away from the steely eyes.

"Where were all the other people?"

"They didn't come. Oh, they think they took some trip, but it was just imagination. They stayed in Manssard's living room. Abbie, bloody few people do what you were able to do. Take my word for it."

"You've done it before?"

"Aye."

"How come I was able to? Did you know that I would?"

He took a long swig of the ale and hesitated a few moments before answering.

"I didn't know for sure that you would, but I thought you were motivated to see your great great grandfather. You were open, so I did what I could. Neither of us alone could have made it happen, though."

His answer didn't really make sense, but I felt he couldn't explain the mystery any more than that. He seemed sincere.

"Gordon, why did I have to change into those clothes? And where did they come from?"

"Can you imagine what a fright for those nineteenth-century people to see a lady in twentieth-century clothes? It was bad enough that you appeared from nowhere with a Valley girl accent and then disappeared again." He laughed, and I had to laugh, too.

"Then you had the clothes?"

He nodded. "You can get any kind of costume you want in Hollywood."

I then remembered that he helped change my clothes, and I blushed. I decided it was best to leave that subject alone.

"What would have happened if you hadn't taken me off when you did?"

He shook his head slowly. "That's the tricky part. One has to be cautious with history. She can absorb little things but not big things. One has to be careful that little things don't become big things."

"What do you mean?"

"Well, let me give an example. Say that you had stayed aboard the *Orion*, and Captain Bunker the next day decided to stand into port and set you ashore. That might have delayed *Orion*'s time for gaining the Horn. Let's then say that a terrible blow hit at that later time, and the *Orion* was wrecked with a loss of all hands. Follow?"

"You mean...my great great grandfather would never have arrived in California?"

"And never have married and never have had children. Abbie Spence might be somebody different or not even exist."

"But..." The thought was mindboggling.

"Aye," he said. "History can be changed, but understand that people wouldn't know it had been changed. They would have grown up with whatever is different as if it were normal."

It was too much for me. Too preposterous. Crystal was right. Bitterroot was off the deep end. And here I was having lunch with him as if he were a regular person.

"Gordon, I'm not going to the meetings anymore. I just don't like this whole business."

"That doesn't surprise me, Abbie. I understand thee."

The tone was condescending, and suddenly I no longer wanted to be there. I hadn't finished my meal, but my appetite was gone. He must have detected my mood change because he finished quickly, and we left without any further conversation.

That afternoon I put on my swimsuit and drove down to Santa Monica beach and lay there listening to the breakers—the soothing sound of earth's metronome. Slowly I began to feel better.

The next morning, as I drank some hot, fresh-ground Starbucks and the sun flooded through the apartment window, warming my back, the enormity of having seen my great great grandfather set in. What an utterly priceless experience! I thought about the *Orion*, how it had been flying through the waves. I had been on a real clipper ship, underway in 1850. Unbelievable. I looked at the scab on my knee, touching its roughness. It was real. Then I thought of Bitterroot. He had given me this magnificent memory. He and Cliff had done this for me. I picked up the phone and dialed the bookshop.

"Gordon, it's Abbie. I acted badly at the restaurant."

"Don't apologize, Abbie. I think if anything, I owe ye one."

"No, no Gordon. It was a splendid gift—you and Cliff—I really appreciate it. It was just incredible."

"Perhaps we should talk, Abbie."

"Yes, I'd like to. It's going to be another nice day. I'm not working today—do you want to go to the beach?"

Bitterroot was only too willing to lock up his shop that afternoon. We met at Venice beach, not far from the breakwater at Marina del Rey. Bitterroot liked to watch the boats coming in and out, like seabirds at a common nesting ground. He was wearing faded, cut-off dungarees, a rust-stained shirt, and tennies with holes worn through the tops. His dark hair was uncombed. But his broad grin made up for all of this.

We lay down on my two beach towels. The sun was high and hot, and I could already feel some perspiration. Other people were picking their spots on the sand, but it was a weekday, so there would not be too much crowding. I gave Bitterroot a Henry's from my small cooler and took a bottle of pink grapefruit juice for myself. We chit-chatted for a few minutes about the weather, good beaches, and the boats going by.

"Gordon, tell me honestly, how did you make that happen?"

"The *Orion*?"

"Yes."

He frowned and looked out at the horizon.

"God has given me a gift, Abbie, that no one else I know has. I have the ability to tune in to certain frequencies of reality and slip into them. And once I'm into one of these pockets, I can slide down to another time and place and pop out again. I cannot explain it more than that."

I couldn't believe it. Yet, it had happened with the *Orion*. I knew it had. "Can anyone else do this?"

"There are other people that I've been able to move that way. But none have been able to move on their own without me."

"And I'm one of these you can move?"

"Aye, lass—the first woman. I didn't know for sure you could until you started slipping with me. Then I put you into the right clothes."

"But if I wasn't supposed to go on the *Orion*, why did I need the clothes?"

"Well...I wanted you to be in the right frame of mind."

He swigged the remainder of the bottle and took another out of the Igloo. Then he looked at me and smiled as he took off his shirt.

"Can Cliff go with you?"

"No. Cliff and Claire know I can go, and we've tried many times with them, but they have some blockage, like most people."

With his shirt off I noticed that Bitterroot had a lot of hair on his body. From a forest on his broad chest, it ran in a narrow swath down into his pants. I saw he had scars in several places, including a large star-shaped gash on the lower left side of his abdomen.

"You're looking at my pretty scar?"

"What caused that, Gordon?"

"A shot I took at Yorktown when I was with Cornwallis."

"What?"

He laughed harder than ever, and I joined him. He was such a joker.

"The year be 1781. I came close to meeting my maker that time. I had to catch a fast pocket out of there afore the wound sapped the life of me." He kind of smirked as he picked up sand in his hand and let it slowly drain out on the ground.

"Why on earth for? I mean...are you serious?"

"'Twas the decisive battle of the Revolution. I had brought a couple of others in to see if we could somehow help stop the Yankee rabble. But it didn't work. Washington carried the day. He deserves all the fame he's received. Without him, this land would still be under the crown, and so would Canada."

"Gordon, you are...you are..." I couldn't think of what to call him.

"But I've learned now that changing the historical tide isn't done by aiding in one battle or two. It must be more strategic. It has to bring on large change. More political. Has to galvanize whole masses."

I rolled my eyes. "But why even try? What's the point, Gordon?"

"Why not? Why is our present version of history the right one? There are many different roads we could have taken."

"Things are what they are, Gordon. You seem to have some crazy notion that things are not right."

He chuckled. "That be so, Abbie. And I have a plan that will be much better. Fantastically better. I call it my Southern Dreams."

I decided not to encourage any more of the nonsense.

"I'm going for a walk on the beach."

"I will join you." Then he laughed, eyes twinkling in the sunlight, and I laughed. He was incredible, that's all. And I couldn't help liking him.

Bitterroot pulled me up and kept my hand in his for a few long seconds as we walked to the ocean's edge. I felt excited strolling with him, not caring what people were probably thinking—old enough to be my father—as they watched us go by. Even though I felt an attraction, I'm not sure he did, which was fine.

Two days later Claire surprised me at the nursery. I remember the day, September 1st, my dad's birthday. Supposedly she was looking at azaleas, but from the way she came over to me, I suspected I was the object of her visit.

"What a surprise! How are you, Claire?"

"It's good to see you, Abbie."

"Can I help you pick out some azaleas? We have some nice ones."

"Well, I'd like two white ones for a shady spot—an indoor atrium, actually."

I wondered what her house looked like. Manssard had told me it was beautiful. We looked at the selection of plants, and she picked the two largest. I put them on a dolly and took them inside to the cash register. After she paid, I followed her out to her car.

"There you go, Claire. You picked a couple of good ones."

She smiled slightly, the wrinkles in her tanned face showing strongly in the sun, and the auburn dye of her hair glinting starkly. She was at the awkward age, still retaining some shape and beauty but getting close to menopause. I wondered what I would look like in my autumn.

"Well, thank you, Claire. Maybe we could have coffee some time."

She brightened. "I'd like that. Actually, Abbie, we might be able to get together sooner. I came to ask you something. Cliff and Gordon are talking about a week's cruise to Santa Cruz. That's one of the big islands west of Ventura. They want the two of us to come along. If you go, so will I. But I don't want to be the only woman."

"Well, what dates are you talking about?"

"I don't think they're set. Could you take a week off during the next month?"

"Maybe."

"Abbie, it would be a fun trip. You could have the forward cabin all to yourself. I would prepare frozen meals in advance. No telephones. Natural harbors. Beaches. And there is this painted cave on the northwest side of the island that is something to see, they tell me."

"It sounds lovely, Claire. Let me see if I can get away from the nursery. I have some vacation due. I'll see if my friend Crystal can take in the mail and water my plants. Give me your number, and I'll call you."

"Oh wonderful, Abbie." She hugged me, clearly excited about the prospect. She wrote her phone number on the back of one of Manssard's business cards. On the front with his name was a three-masted sailing vessel. Below were the words, "Sailing History Consultant."

The degree to which Manssard played the role of consultant was amusing. But he was interesting and would no doubt add to the enjoyment of the trip. Claire would be lots of fun, too. But I was most excited by the prospect of being with Bitterroot.

4

Early on a Tuesday morning we tossed the braided dock lines onto the deck and pushed *Ocean Gypsy* out of the slip. There wasn't even a whisper of wind to ripple the smooth, undulating carpet of ocean, so Manssard throttled up the Volvo diesel and we motored without sails westward along the Malibu coast. Million dollar beach houses glided by on shore. Behind them, cars sped along the Pacific Coast Highway, bearing drivers toward city jobs.

The sun moved higher over the Santa Monica mountains, brightening the glare on the water and heating the cockpit. To make the most of our self-generated breeze, I moved to the cabin top. As I lay on my stomach, my body succumbed to the vessel's rhythmic rise and fall in the swells. It was a sensual motion, like riding a mammoth porpoise, I imagined. The diesel's vibration added another dimension of physical pleasure. I was massaged from head to foot. But something was strange. I had been favoring my knee, but now it seemed just fine. I sat up and inspected the scab. It was gone. There were no signs of a bruise. I had never seen a wound heal so fast. But the strangest thing was that I couldn't remember how I got the bruise in the first place.

Before long the wind was up, meeting us head on from around Point Dume. Spray was in the air, occasionally spattering up to my spot. It was time for a change. We put up the sails and cut the engine, tacking southwest. A few miles out we tacked back the other way, clearing the point. The rest of the day was a "slog," as Manssard termed it, tacking up the coast against an increasingly strong wind. When late in the afternoon we finally pulled into Channel Islands Marina at Oxnard, we were beat. As soon as the lines were snugged on the cleats, Bitterroot poured us Beefeater and tonics, and Claire made cheese and cracker snacks. We were salty and sweaty, but it didn't matter as we rehashed the day's sail. Instead of cooking at the dock, we went to a restaurant called The Captain's Table, a seafood place not far from our marina. Everyone was being nice to me. Bitterroot was especially solicitous.

As we downed our seafood, Manssard said our next stop could be Prisoner's Harbor or Pelican Bay on Santa Cruz Island.

"Prisoner's?" I said. "Is there a prison there?"

Manssard laughed. "A prison colony—not now, but at one time. It was established in the 1800s to isolate criminals from the mainland."

"Aye, islands were cheaper than building prisons," Bitterroot said. He sounded disgusted.

"They had a real problem in southern California," Manssard continued, "because Mexico sent all kinds of people north to colonize the area after her independence in 1822. A lot of them were released from jails—murderers, thieves, prostitutes, and whatnot. A number of these people got a free ride to California and shortly thereafter a free ride to Santa Cruz Island." He laughed.

"What a waste of a beautiful island," Claire said. "In those days it was most pragmatic," Manssard replied.

"It was a shame, Claire," Bitterroot said. "Typical of the short-sighted colonial mentality. A prison colony wrecked the most beautiful island in the Pacific, Más á Tierra of the Juan Fernández group. The damn Spanish and later the Chileans kept it full of prisoners. A real waste. And to think we had the chance to colonize it." He shook his head.

"America could have?" I asked.

"America!" He roared with laughter. "I'm talking about the Spanish South Sea in the time of English privateers like Francis Drake, William Dampier, and John Clipperton. In those days the American colonists were still trying to find a way out of the Chesapeake."

Bitterroot looked to the others and smiled slyly, almost as if there were some secret among the three of them. I didn't know what to say. My ignorance of the history he was talking about was obvious.

"That was in the Pacific during the 1600s and early 1700s, Abbie," Manssard said. "At that time America was still concerned with the eastern seaboard."

"Well, enough of the past," Claire said, as she raised her wine high. "I propose a toast. Here's to Santa Cruz Island, as pretty today as ever. And here's to a fine trip on board the *Gypsy*."

"Hear, hear."

There was increasing silliness as the alcohol and food weighed upon us. That night not even the crackly barnacle sounds or the *Gypsy's* movements could keep me from a deep sleep.

In the morning Claire and I took showers on board and then the fresh water tanks were topped off. We got away from the harbor around nine in the morning. Again we powered northwest with our mainsail up for stability and then cut the engine when the wind came. Before noon we saw the rocky juttings of the small, closely joined Anacapa islands first. Manssard said the word "Anacapa" had evolved from the original Chumash Indian name, *Eneeapah*, meaning "everchanging."

"Are there any Indians left?" I asked.

"Oh no. The last ones on these islands were killed off in the early 1800s. The famous "Lost Woman of San Nicholas Island," further south of here, was captured in about 1853, I think. On the mainland the Chumash were centered in the Santa Barbara area and were mostly wiped out in the 1700s. I'm sure you've heard about how the good Mission fathers tried to convert and domesticate them and in the process gave them diseases."

"Yes, a shame."

"Well the Chumash were regarded as superior to many other California tribes because they had a higher level of technology in weaving, basketry, tools, and the like. They weren't a warlike people. On the islands they had a nice life, getting most of their food from the sea. They built canoes called tomols that could carry up to twenty-five people. They could paddle back and forth between the islands and the mainland."

"It's too bad that way of life had to end," I said.

Bitterroot looked at me, amused. "It wasn't that long ago. It could be seen again."

Manssard smiled at me and winked.

"It would be fabulous to see Indian life as it was in those days," I said.

Bitterroot nodded. "The only problem in going back and seeing those people is that they can also see you."

Soon we came up on the mountainous bulk of Santa Cruz Island. The peaks looked high and I learned some were 2500 hundred feet in elevation. I was struck by the diversity in the geography. There were rocky cliffs, expansive bays, and narrow inlets where beaches could be found. Large trees covered some areas of the island, and chaparral dominated others. We went past Prisoner's Harbor, where a long pier reached out into the wide bay and some structures could be seen in the interior. Following along the coast for some while, we suddenly came to Pelican Bay, a small horseshoe-shaped harbor surrounded by rocky walls. A few other small craft were anchored inside. We dropped our sails and went in, evading large growths of brown kelp, and let the anchor fall to a white, sandy bottom twenty to thirty feet down.

After the sails were secured and an awning was put up over the cockpit, Bitterroot and Manssard unfastened the dinghy from the foredeck and lowered it into the water. Bitterroot then took me aside and suggested he and I go ashore and leave Claire and Manssard to the privacy of *Ocean Gypsy*. I quickly got the idea, and we rowed off amid their goodbyes and promises to have dinner cooking on our return.

The only way up the cliff was to land the dinghy on a large rock and scramble twenty feet up crevices. Fortunately there were a few good footholds. Moving away from the edge of the cliff we came to an old fisherman's hut made from stone. It was on a rise in the middle of the ridge, overlooking the bay on one side and the ocean on the other. The structure was solid and venerable, and I pictured men inside sitting cozily around a fire, oblivious to a raging storm on a dark night. We hiked up the ridge from the cabin and soon were among tall pines. Bitterroot pointed to a bluff far up to our left.

"Let's go up there. We'll have a great view."

"It's a long way, Gordon."

"No more than twenty minutes I'd say. C'mon Abbie, it'll be fun."

He trudged with a slight hunch, water sloshing in the plastic container on his belt. I followed, feeling good to stretch my legs. When the path petered out we moved cross-county, down into a ravine with a dry stream bed, and then back up the other side to another higher ridge that led to the point Bitterroot had picked out. We were now out of the trees and the sun was warm. As we finally approached a large rock that would provide a panoramic view, we were startled by sudden movement in the brush. Several mountain sheep, one with well-developed horns, bolted from the bushes and soon disappeared around an outcropping.

"Are those wild, Gordon?"

"Aye. Descended from sheep put on these islands by the early explorers and buccaneers."

"Why did they do that?"

"Fresh food. By the time the ships got up this way from around the Horn, their scurvy-ridden crews were half dead. Mealy biscuits were all they had left and the water in their barrels was putrid. The fresh mutton and water from island springs saved them."

"Why couldn't they get provisions from the ports along the way?"

"In the early days there were no ports. One had to trade with the Indians who didn't have domesticated animals. Later the Spanish controlled the new world and fought anyone who came into the Pacific. Their ports were closed to all other nations. Spain didn't colonize or control offshore islands like these very well, and they became refuges for the English and Dutch."

The view made the hike worth it. The deep blue of the ocean, broken by occasional whitecaps catching reflections of the sun, spread out before me as far as I could see. On the horizon the water melded with a creamy overcast sky. Close in, waves surging from the west bent around promontories and rocky islets, coming sooner or later against the cliffs, and throwing spray furiously in all directions. Off the points and in the bays, seaweed danced in clusters. In the air, seagulls wheeled around. I sat enraptured for several minutes. Then Bitterroot noticed the tears moving down my cheeks.

"What's wrong, Abbie?"

"I don't know. This happens to me sometimes when I see beautiful scenery. I cried when I was on Glacier Point in Yosemite a couple of years ago."

"You are a romantic at heart," he said.

"In some ways, yes. It's odd, when I see vivid scapes I get to wondering about reality. You know, is this real or in my mind? What am I at this moment? What is all that out there? You know the philosopher George Berkeley? Well, I wonder if he was right when he said that visual perception is not of external things but just ideas in the mind."

He smiled. "If Berkeley's right, then what reality is there?"

"That's just it. I don't know."

"And you never will, Abbie. So we just have to proceed as if there is a reality, sometimes out there, sometimes our own, usually a mixture. And ultimate reality doth not matter."

I smiled at him. Sometimes Bitterroot was profound.

Then I felt him take my hand. His hand felt good, and I squeezed it. I kept my eyes on the horizon, but I could fell my heart beating.

"A spectacular view, Abbie. It's too bad it's marred by the man made. Just think how fine it would be, not seeing the boats in the harbor, the people down there, or the hut, or that rusty piece of sheet metal down near the shore. Just the natural island."

I followed where he pointed and nodded.

"We could easily have that view if you wanted to go back in time a little," he said. "We could do it for a few minutes."

I thought about that, imagining the boats, people and hut gone. It would be even more beautiful. Pristine. I wondered if the hazy horizon would be sharper.

"How far back would we go?"

"Oh, two to three hundred years should do it."

"Where would we go?"

"Nowhere. Just sit on this same rock."

"Would it be safe?"

"Sure."

That was comforting. I squeezed his hand again.

"OK."

He grinned at me and said, "Close your eyes, Abbie. Relax your body. We're going back. Going back to see this lovely island as its first European discoverer, Juan Rodríguez Cabrillo, probably did. Let yourself drift. We're going back, going back, going back."

His voice was low and soothing, and I found it growing more distant as I seemed to be drifting downward into a misty dark zone. It was slightly cooler as I moved lower. Then it was totally black. His faint voice now disappeared. I became frightened. I reached my hands under me and felt nothing. Then suddenly it was light, and I touched the coarseness of a rock and looked down to see that I could sit on the huge stone. Once situated I looked around. It was close to dusk and the reds, grays and browns of the mountains and cliffs resonated against the deep blue iodine sea. It was breathtaking. Far off in the distance I thought I could see the pale purples of mountains on the mainland. The waves were subdued, lapping the rocky shoreline. Tears welled up in my eyes.

"It's gorgeous, Gordon."

There was no answer. It was at that moment that I realized he wasn't with me.

The rock was the same one we had been sitting on. I went to the edge and looked down at the talus slope. God forbid that Bitterroot would have fallen. I didn't see him. Then I looked back along the ridge we had taken on our way up, but he was nowhere to be seen. He has to be somewhere around because he said we both would be going. Or had he? Now I wasn't sure what he had said. No, he probably just wanted me to enjoy the view on my own for a while, and then he would be along to take me back.

Pelican Bay was nestled peacefully in the arms of the surrounding rock. Then I saw three large pelicans with their low hanging chins winging close to the water. I hadn't noticed any when we came in on *Ocean Gypsy*. The pines on the low ridge were about the same as before, although they didn't stretch out as far toward the point. Of course there was no path.

My stomach grumbled. It was getting late and I hadn't eaten since lunch. I hoped Bitterroot would come soon. I peered again at the horizon. The mainland definitely could be seen, although in the beginning twilight it was fading into grayness. I looked at my watch. It showed four fifteen, but it had to be later than that. I felt in my pockets. My Swiss Army knife, matches, and hankie were in one, and my comb and compact were in the other. Nothing was missing. Even the Sierra Club cup was at my belt. I still had on the same clothes—blue corduroy shorts and a white short sleeve blouse and my new Topsider shoes. But I was shivering. It was definitely colder than before. And it was getting dark. Where was Bitterroot?

It then occurred to me that he might not come for several hours, and I would be better off away from the rock. He should be able to find me wherever I was. I looked around the sky but didn't see the moon. If I left immediately perhaps I could make it down to the trees before it was totally dark. I moved fairly swiftly back the way we had come, carefully watching my step. Angling down the side of the ridge, I came to the stream bed just as darkness fell. To my shock, my foot plunged into cold, running water. It was a small creek, about six inches deep and three feet across. I scooped up a cupful of water. Delicious. I drank quite a bit.

Why was the stream here now? It came to me that a lot could happen geologically in a couple of hundred years. Water tables shift; underground springs come and go. Or, maybe it's a different time of year, spring instead of fall? Maybe it had recently rained. I jumped the stream and felt my way up the opposite slope. At one point I slipped on the side of a rock and scraped my ankle. Near the top of the ridge I stepped heavily into some prickly brush, scratching my legs. I was so frustrated I felt like crying, but I was now in the trees. With luck I could find a soft, level spot among the pine needles. The hike had warmed me, and I realized that now sitting in the cool night air would be chilling. But I had no choice, so I huddled against a large tree, took off my wet shoe and sock, and piled needles over my feet and legs.

"Hurry up, Gordon," I said between clenched teeth.

After sitting there for a couple of hours worrying about Bitterroot coming, I finally lay down and closed my eyes. But I couldn't sleep because of the cold. The pine needles heaped over me for warmth pricked my bare legs and arms. The ground was hard. Little rocks and protruding roots stuck me. And most of the night I worried that Bitterroot would show up on the rock and not know where I was. When the sun finally rose, I got up, relieved that the endless night was over. But I felt lousy. My ankle pained me on every step. My clothes were filthy. My hair was tangled. Still, I eagerly scanned the high ridge and the rock for Bitterroot. I shouted a few times. But there was nothing. Walking aimlessly down toward Pelican Bay, I was suddenly ravenous. What I would have given for a latte and croissant right then. I thought about the first Starbucks I had gone to in Sellwood, a funky little community next to Reed College.

"OK, get real, Abbie." I would have to find some food. But what?

There were seals sitting on the rock where we had landed the dinghy. The large one roared at me before they slipped into the water as I climbed down the cliff. Seagulls and more pelicans were circling around, and a large black bird, maybe a cormorant, swam half submerged near the cliff. Otherwise, the natural harbor was empty. Where *Ocean Gypsy* had been anchored there was only a patch of kelp. I guess it all hit me at that moment because I sat down and wept.

"Gordon, where are you?" I screamed, when there were no sobs left.

But there was only the sound of the waves and the gulls in reply. Obviously, something had gone wrong. He had said just a few minutes. But I was way back here alone in time and he was somewhere else.

The hunger wrenched my stomach. Abalone. There was probably abalone on the underwater cliffs, and I could dive for them. But I would need something stronger than my fancy pocket knife for prying them off. After a search along the ridge I came back with a pointed, narrow piece of rock. Since there were no people around I shed all my clothes and eased into the cold water. I hadn't skinny dipped in quite some time, and the sensation was satisfying in its freedom. I drifted down and looked around. Large seaweed bushes swayed like hula dancers in the currents. Moving to the wall, I searched for the rounded shells and immediately found one about six inches across. Not far away were two others, and there were more below. At least I wouldn't starve. The first one I tried clamped hard against the wall, and it was impossible to budge after its foot had taken its grip. I worked faster and pried off a little one before he could cinch down. He fell to the bottom. I tried more, but it was strenuous, and I needed to come up for air in between each attempt. Finally I grabbed off a big one; he must have been close to ten inches in diameter. Taking a large breath at the surface, I swam down and gathered the shells off the ocean bottom. But as I turned to go up, my eye caught a large shadowy shape moving toward me. It was a shark. Adrenalin shot through me. I wanted to scream but of course couldn't. Instead I just put my arms out in front of me as if to hold the abalones in an offering. He came directly at me then turned slowly about five feet away. His beady eye glared at me for a moment before he turned again and lazily moved off, his tail sweeping slowly from side to side.

I let myself drift up for air and, not wanting to make a splash, dog paddled as best I could back to the rock, looking around every few seconds for a fin. Once out of the water I gasped for breath, my heart pounding as if it would burst. The seagulls' cries overhead seemed to indicate that they understood what had happened.

With all that expenditure of physical and emotional energy, I was even hungrier. I put on my clothes and climbed to the ridge. As starved as I felt, I was not about to eat Mr. Abalone raw, so I went up into the pines and gathered wood for a fire. I gouged him out of his shell, cut the foot from the innards, and pounded the tough muscle with a large rock until I could barely move my arm. I built a stone enclosure for the fire and stuffed it with dead pine needles and kindling in the best tradition of the Boy Scouts, which at one time I had wanted to join. I was determined to use only one match from my precious book. The flame flickered, almost went out, then slowly caught. Soon the fire was crackling. But as I stood up to get more wood, I heard a whirring sound behind me. A large black bird was grabbing the abalone foot off of the rock. I lunged and shouted. The abalone fell into the dirt as the bird squawked and peeled off down the ridge. Just then something jabbed my head, almost knocking me down. It was another bird. I felt the spot of pain and my fingers came away with blood. Looking up I saw several more of them whirling around me. Ravens! One was now flying off with the discarded abalone guts and here came another, hovering over the abalone steak again.

"No, that's mine!"

A rage took me. I grabbed a short, dead branch intended for the fire and hurled it at the raven, now rising with the meat. The stick struck at full force and with a screech and black feathers flying, the raven and abalone landed in a heap ten feet away. Scolding cries of the other attackers now filled the quiet in a discordant chorus as they drifted up to land in the high branches of the pines.

I dealt the thief several mortal blows before I realized in some horror what I had done. I had never heard of ravens attacking humans. I knew they stole eggs from nests and sometimes attacked other birds, but this was amazing. It was almost as bad as that Alfred Hitchcock movie, The Birds. Wait until I tell... The thought hung there. There was nobody to tell.

I picked up the abalone foot, now covered with dirt, and realized I would have to wash it in the stream. The fire. I ran back to the fire, but it was out. The episode had cost me a match. From the stream I carried back a cup of water and willow branches on which to skewer the strips of abalone. As the meat cooked, my hunger was strangely absent, but it came back with a vengeance as soon as the first bite was in my mouth. The meat was chewy and bland, but I ate it with gusto. I was still hungry afterward, but I decided to focus my efforts to two other pressing problems—how to start fires without using matches and how to stay warm at night. And it occurred to me that the two went together.

Again thinking about the Boy Scout manual I had read as a young girl, I set about carving a block of wood with a round hole in it. Next, I whittled a small stick to twirl in the hole. At the end of the day, despite an incredible amount of effort, no spark had ignited the tiny shavings near the hole. That night, at the cost of another match, I slept on a thick bed of pine needles next to red hot coals in my makeshift fireplace. I dreamed of Bitterroot only half the night. The other half was devoted to sharks and ravens. But they were all of the same kind anyway.

The next morning I again awoke hungry. This could get monotonous. Yesterday it had taken most of the day just to eat breakfast. Hopefully, I could do better today. When I was on the sea lion rock I had seen nesting gulls on the side of the cliff overlooking Pelican Bay inlet. Maneuvering on the steep wall was far more difficult than I imagined, but I managed to reach three nests and warm my pockets with little eggs. I felt guilty when I watched the screeching gulls return to their empty nests. But I needed food, and they could lay more. Two of the eggs were at a late embryonic stage, and I discarded them. The others were fine, and I scrambled them in my aluminum cup over the coals that I had kept going. It was the best meal since leaving *Ocean Gypsy*.

I decided to wash everything—my cup, my clothes, and myself—and I braved the cold running water of the stream. It was too bad there was no soap or shampoo, but at least I washed out the big pieces of dirt and felt better. I wrung out my clothes and spread them on bushes to dry and stretched myself bare on a flat rock for the same purpose. I thought about what I should do over the next couple of days. The most important thing, other than feeding myself, was to find shelter. The pleasant weather might not last. I had already concluded it was spring because of the new shoots budding on the bushes. It would be getting warmer, but there still could be storms. Should I leave this area? What if Bitterroot were to come looking for me? But then again, maybe he could not come for me because of some problem I didn't understand. Maybe he doesn't know what time period he put me in. Maybe he's looking in August and I'm in April. The whole thing was absurd.

I finally decided I should not count on Bitterroot. But that thought was, quite suddenly, depressing. Was I locked into a lonely existence on Santa Cruz Island until my death? What kind of life would it be but scrabbling hand-to-mouth for food, day after day? Nothing to read. No people to visit.

No hope for a reasonably human existence. The prospect was dreadful. I had the urge to blot everything out, to just scream "No" to it all. Perhaps that's what a nihilist feels. I had never understood the concept before. Nihilism rejects all knowledge and denies all truths and values. Does it also reject hope? Without hope there is no will to live.

But the nihilists in history were the young Russians of the middle nineteenth century. I remember someone in one of my classes saying that the Czars, the Church, and the Russian winter could make a nihilist of anyone. The Russian nihilists had fought all authority, first intellectually and then physically through the Bolshevik revolution. But the fact that they fought meant they had not lost hope. My lot was different. Who could I fight? Father Time? The sharks and the ravens? No, my situation was the opposite. Rather than anarchy, it called for structure. Rather than nihilism, I needed faith.

I hiked westerly along the ocean escarpment, looking for caves or large overhangs. It was rough going in places, and I needed to use my hands. This created a problem because I had to carry my yet-to-be-proven firemaker, a hollowed-out piece of wood for keeping hot coals, and my anti-raven club. I needed a way to tie the firemaker and club to my belt and to put a strap on the coal tote.

I thought about cutting up my socks or taking strips of cloth from my shirt, but decided that the nylon straps from my bra would last longer. In my situation I certainly didn't need to hold up my breasts for anyone anyway. The only concern was for my nipples. They might get cold. But if my maternal ancestors had done without bras, why couldn't I? I carved holes in the firemaker and club and tied them around my belt with the straps, using a bow knot so I could loosen them quickly if necessary. This arrangement worked fairly well, although I had to be careful of the loops catching on branches.

During the next three days—I was notching each day on my club—I stayed close to the shoreline because the mountains were steep and my food supply was in the ocean. I found plenty of driftwood to make fires for cooking and sleeping. My diet was abalone and gulls' eggs until on the third day I added lobster. I discovered them in rock crevices on ledges and at the sea floor, their antennae sticking out to detect movements of creatures they might prey upon. I found that by tapping their feelers gently, the lobsters would come out to see what was there, enabling me to pin them with a forked stick. Using my bra cups as protective gloves against their sharp edges, I could grab them around the thorax and get them ashore. Boiled in my Sierra cup or roasted, they were delicious. Lobster soon became my first choice in the ocean supermarket.

I was now several miles from Pelican Bay. I had left a rock cairn on the point where Bitterroot and I had parted company. Next to the cairn I had formed an arrow out of small stones, pointing to the west. That at least would tell him I was alive and where to go to find me. If, of course, he still existed.

On the sixth morning, the weather turned from sunny to overcast. By midday, thunderclouds had gathered. With each passing minute I became more concerned about having no shelter. A cold, moist wind came up, and soon my tanned skin broke out in goose bumps from top to bottom. Large waves began pounding the shore. If I didn't find a shelter soon to protect my matches, coals, and some firewood, I was in for trouble. As I climbed over a rise to view the terrain below me, the first raindrops began. Lightning flashed in the distance, and the accompanying rumble echoed in the canyon behind me. Then the rain came.

"Try not to panic, Abbie."

Looking out at the waves crashing into the jagged rocks, I saw some seals swimming toward shore. Even they knew enough to get out of the storm. But where did they go? I watched them cruise into an inlet between two rocky cliffs below me and disappear. The rain was now borne at a slant by the rising wind. Impulsively, I set out to find the seals.

Slipping on wet rocks, sliding on dirt becoming mud, and darn near killing myself, I moved down the slope, landing on the wet beach at the head of the triangular inlet. Over to my left I noticed a dark cave spanning both sand and water. I thought I heard occasional barking. I climbed over several boulders, now hearing thundering bangs and thumps. The waves were slapping the sides and overhangs deep in the cave, making it a huge echo chamber. The yapping of the seals was a disharmonious counterpoint melody, and the overall effect was eerie. I crawled on my hands and knees into the opening. Even though the light dimmed sharply, I was grateful to be out of the rain. My eyes accustomed themselves somewhat, but beyond about ten feet it remained hopelessly black. I needed to find dry sand to lie on, so I slowly felt my way into the darkness. The din from the waves and seals continued some distance away. But as I crawled up the beach, the odor of animals became stronger. It was a pungent smell, with a tinge of rotteness. Then my hand came down on something strange, like dried out leather and fur with an oily feel. I jerked my hand away and strained my senses for any movement or danger, but I could detect nothing. I slowly felt the thing again, and when my hand hit the shape of a nose and slits for eyeholes, I realized it was a seal that had died and decomposed. I shivered, but more probably from my damp clothes than the grotesque object under my hand. I slowly moved around it and crawled further up the sandy slope. I bumped into more fur. This time it was warm. The animal emitted a huffing sound but made no move to get away. I stroked its neck. The seal didn't have strength to move. If I were a predator it didn't matter. I hugged it gently. The fur was thick and silky. Then I remembered that Manssard had said the California fur seals had been killed off on this coast prior to the 1800s. The fact that there were fur seals here now meant that the time was in the 1700s or before. I moved around and then encountered another seal who at least lifted its head and hissed at me but who also stayed in place. Maybe this was their graveyard. It gave me an uncomfortable feeling.

I was shivering, but a fire was out of question. My coals were out, and my matches were damp. What I needed was a blanket. Then it occurred to me that the seals might not mind sleeping with me and lending their warmth. All they would have to do is stay alive until the next day. It would be a reluctant, ironic act by them toward an animal whose kind would commit genocide on their offspring. I moved down and gathered up the partially decomposed skin. Although it was stiff, I managed to curve it around my legs and feet. Then I pushed the higher seal down to within a foot of the other. I wedged myself between their bodies, curling around them for maximum warmth. After a few minutes I stopped shaking, and although parts of me were cold most of that strange night, my middle and back stayed toasty warm.

As soon as light appeared at the opening, I was up. One of the seals had died. The other was breathing laboriously. I gave this one a last hug.

"Thank you, little fur seal."

The storm had passed, but small cumulus clouds were still moving by. In the east the sun was peeking over the mountaintops on the mainland, promising to dry out the wetness that clung to the rocks. This lifted my spirits and helped me to brave the cold, choppy ocean to find some abalone. I used several matches before the shavings from the damp driftwood caught. But when the wood was blazing, the price seemed worth it. The fire allowed me to warm up after the chilly swim, enjoy a hot meal, and dry out my clothes. Life was going to continue.

"Crystal, where are you? Are you missing me yet?"

This was the day I was to be back. And yesterday my mother probably phoned. What would they do when they found me missing? Would Crystal try to seek out Bitterroot or Manssard? Would Mom call the relatives? Would there be a search for me on the island? I could only hope they would get help, somehow, some way.

I stayed near the cave for the next day just in case I had not seen the last of the rain. I busied myself with gathering driftwood and storing it just inside the entrance. I visited my seal friends at noon and discovered that both had gone to seal heaven. Maybe they were mates and they had to be together, in this world or the next. As I ran my hands through their thick coats it came to me to skin them and make a fur wrap. I thought back to a vague course and remembered that tannin was used in the old days to cure hides. It came from oak trees.

As I hiked west, excited with my new plan, I came over the crest of a ridge and saw a large expanse of water and green grass. Before me was a beautifully shaped half-moon bay, met by a plain that rose slowly into a wide canyon. On the floor of the canyon a good-sized stream tumbled down a rocky channel. Higher up in the canyon, oak trees stood in groups, staking out the territory like confident sentinels. Below the canyon on the alluvial plain, long grass billowed in the slight breeze. Willow bushes followed the stream down almost to the ocean. As my eyes caught the darting movements of blue jays feeding on insects out and around the willow branches, my eyes began to tear. The scene was dazzling.

Skinning the two seals was a bloody business, especially so with my undersized pocket knife. The task took the rest of the day. I thought about cooking some of the seal meat but felt it wasn't worth the risk if the animals were diseased. I let the skins soak in a quiet tide pool overnight, thinking the salt would be a preservative. The next day I gathered a lot of acorns and knocked bark and small limbs off the oaks. I found a sizeable hollowed-out area on a large rock not far from the mouth of the stream. The bowl-shaped indentation made me wonder if Indians had formed it. I filled it with stream water and put in the ground up acorns and bark. Finally, I dropped the seal skins into this strange soup. I worked them every few hours with my hands and added more acorns and bark each day for several days.

Indians! Maybe Bitterroot had left me here to see some Chumash Indians. But I had seen no evidence of them. If this had been his purpose, wouldn't he have put me close to a village?

"Just forget about Bitterroot, girl."

I made a new camp not far from the rock, next to a thicket of willows that helped shield me from the wind. For the first time I had the sense of settling in. I found abalone and lobster plentiful down off the cliffs that bordered the bay. I caught a lizard and experimentally roasted the tail. It didn't taste good. I also spotted tracks of a small dog near my camp. I followed them for quite a while before losing them in a rocky part of the canyon. Probably a coyote or a fox.

As I became more aware of the animals, plants, and birds around me, I realized how little I knew about my habitat. I thought of my favorite Reed alum, Gary Snyder, the Pulitzer Prize-winning northern California poet whose works had been the basis for my senior thesis. In *Turtle Island* and *The Real Work*, he had criticized people's reliance on modern technology and their failure to understand the natural ecology of the region they lived in. People should get in touch with the land, he said, and especially the Indian ways and myths of the area. I recalled an oral report I'd given on Snyder and one of the quotes I had memorized. "We are...an animal that was brought into being on this biosphere by...processes of sun, water and leaf. And if we depart too far from them, we're departing too far from the mother, from our own heritage."

So here I was, living as close to the earth and as far from modern technology as a human could if you ignored the fact that I had a knife, cup, and matches. But was I happy in a Snyderian way? No. I felt insecure and lonely —just the opposite of what Synder held out for the close-to-nature existence. But maybe I could learn to relax. Maybe if I approached the land and sea in the way an Indian might, if I learned to appreciate and live within the island's intricate ecology, I would come to know the spiritual joy and essential sanity of which Gary Snyder spoke, or will speak, if I was now a century or two ahead of him. This time thing was strange.

Two days later, with a strip of leather cut from one of the seal skins, I laced the two furs together. I was most pleased with my new cover. That night I slept the warmest and soundest of any night since I had arrived on Santa Cruz Island.

6

I cut up the seal intestines into thin strips and cured them as best I could. I tied the ends of the strips to each other to make a long line. From one of the bones I carved a fish hook with a large eye for tying onto the gut line. With worms dug from the ground and small pieces of lobster meat, I was ready to try my luck. I headed out to the cliff rocks with my new fishing gear, including a better abalone pry stone.

On the first cast I had a bite but lost whatever it was. I rebaited with the worms—actually tying the worms on with a thread—and tossed the line in again. In less than two minutes something struck, and it was big. I braced my feet and pulled hand over hand. As the silvery fish was about to break the surface there was a sharp twang, and the gut was limp in my hands. I discovered that the hook had broken where the shank started its curvature. I was deeply disappointed and allowed myself a few cusswords. Still, I was pleased that the line was going to work. I just needed to make some stronger hooks. That could be the afternoon project. Resigning myself to another abalone lunch, I removed my clothes and grabbed the pry stone. Glancing at my body, I felt a wry pleasure that the usual whiteness of breasts and buttocks was disappearing. How the girls of Venice beach would envy this!

I swam toward some outlying underwater rocks that had scores of abalone and spent a while diving and surfacing until I had three large reds.

Catching my breath on a big, flat rock only a foot below the surface, I sat perched like the little mermaid watching over Copenhagen harbor, the waves sloshing over the rock as high as my navel. Looking back across the bay, my heart suddenly missed a beat. A long canoe with about ten men in it was moving swiftly into the bay, heading toward the mouth of the river.

For a moment I didn't know whether to wave or hide, but an atavistic impulse seized me, and I rolled off the rock and submerged. I came up behind another rock that rose several feet above the surface, not far from the point of the cliff. Peering around a corner I watched as the canoe, powered by the paddling of six of the men, closed on the beach. One of the men had been looking in my direction when I first spotted them, but there didn't seem to be any commotion or arm pointing as I would expect if they had seen me.

They drove the canoe up into the mouth of the stream and beached it. Then they took out bows and arrows, spears, skin pouches and other objects I couldn't discern. They were naked except for a piece of leather that hung down over their loins. Their hair was black and their skin a dark copper color. I figured they must be a hunting party. What should I do? I was becoming tired and cold and I didn't want to be out in these rocks as the surf rose. The waves would be dangerous in another hour. But where could I go? The braves might be around for some time. What if they found my camp?

The answer to that question came quickly. They seemed to be looking at the ground and gesturing excitedly. Of course. The topsider shoe print was not like any game they knew. I chuckled at the thought of them being confused, but they didn't act that way. Soon a couple of them were moving up toward my camp, and others were moving along the beach, east and west. When the two found my camp they yelled and all of them gathered there. The seal pelts and firewood would not be of much interest but my cup and watch were there. If they opened my compact would they see a mirror for the first time? This is what must have happened because there were shouts and squeals and as much ruckus as ten sober people could make. I almost thought to swim in at this point and join the merriment. But soon they were fanned out again, obviously looking for the mysterious me.

My heart began pounding again when five of them launched the canoe and began heading out. I saw that one man was also climbing out on the cliff. He would no doubt find my clothes and fishing gear. It was time to flee. They had closed off any hope of my going back via the bay. I would have to swim out around the point. If I were lucky I could duck into the seal inlet just beyond the second outjutting cliff and hide in the cave. I submerged and breaststroked under the waves. After about forty yards I came up for breath and looked back. To my amazement, the canoe had covered one third the way between me and the beach, and it was closing fast. The paddlers dug the water in unison, throwing spray with each thrust. A man in the bow seemed to point toward me. They must have seen me after all. There was no time for stealth now, so I stretched into full racing crawl, heading for the point. I kicked as powerfully as I could. When I was even with the point I looked back again, hoping I was no longer in view. But in that moment the prow of the canoe rounded the rock where I had been, and I knew then that I could not reach the cave in time. The boat was incredibly fast.

I turned in toward the vertical cliffs of the point. The waves were hitting the rock and bouncing back. If I could somehow wedge myself in a niche, maybe they would be afraid to bring the canoe that close. I got next to a protuberance, looking for handholds, and I heard them shouting behind me. My knee scraped a jagged corner of an underwater rock, but pain was the last thing on my mind. Somehow I found a ledge to stand on and nubs to hold to prevent the waves from knocking me loose. I faced outward. The canoe was thirty feet away. The men, their sinewy muscles gleaming, were deftly backpaddling to keep the canoe from broaching against the rock wall. Slowly, however, the craft was inching toward me.

The man in the bow was giving instructions to the paddlers as he studied the rock dangers. He peered at me intently for a moment. I looked at his eyes and tried to decide what he felt about me, but the dark brown pupils were impassive, the jaw firmly set. Maybe I was just some sea mammal they were about to harvest. Then, as the boat edged to within five feet of me, the brave held out his arm.

I remember stories about how people behave in emergencies such as wartime or in natural disasters. Some people do heroic things without thinking; others shrink in fear, perhaps also without thought. It just seems to be a matter of individual character. I'd always wondered what I would do under the circumstances. A moment of truth was upon me. I confess that I did not think. Something in me said not to take the outstretched hand. And further flight was impossible. I crouched lower until my nose was almost in the water, but I kept my eyes on a spot on the side of the boat just aft of the man now about to touch me. I took a deep breath, sprang forward with all of my strength and grabbed the side of the canoe. As I went under I pulled down hard and it came with me, pausing for a moment halfway. Then weight must have shifted in the boat because it suddenly turned further, capsizing. Bodies splashed into the water and the canoe hit the rock wall. I was now swimming under water for all I was worth toward the open sea to get away. A foot scraped my back but I kept going. I could see the dark shapes of rocks and the foam and bubbles of the surf swirling around them. I kept pulling and kicking until my air supply was gone. I rose to the surface, emptied my lungs and took a deep draught of fresh oxygen. In the process I allowed myself a quick glance back at the cliff. The Indians were around the canoe, trying to push it away from the wall, shouting in strange syllables. Again I plunged and headed for the second point, around which would be the seal cave. I wanted to make it past that rock and out of their line of sight before my second breath.

When I was about to burst, I came up again. I was past the outcropping and I allowed myself several heaving breaths and turned to look back. I couldn't believe my eyes. They were in the canoe and heading for me again. My mind for an instant wanted to stop all activity, but somehow the adrenalin pumped once more, and I bent forward into my speed crawl. It was a race. I thought I would make it, but somehow they pulled even with me just twenty feet from the cave. There was a splash and somebody grabbed my foot. I tried going under and kicking away from his grasp, but he came with me, holding tight. Suddenly my foot was free, but in the next instant there was an arm around my stomach. He was very strong and the tighter he squeezed, the more air I lost. I kicked toward the surface and we both came up together. Before I could become oriented, someone grabbed my hair and pulled me toward the boat. My underwater assailant disappeared, and soon I was being towed behind the canoe by my hair. I had to grab and pull on the new captor's arm with both hands to stop the excruciating pain on my scalp. The boat speeded up, and soon my body was planing out along the surface, belly up, for all to see.

It had all happened so fast. Up to now I had just been reacting with no time to think. But the reality sank in as my arms began to ache. A fear, bone deep, enveloped me as I realized that I was heading for bodily harm. What hope did I have?

I heard shouting between the men in the boat and those on shore. We were closing on the beach. My body was numb from the cold, and my arms were about to fall off. It would be mentally easy to succumb. We were now in the surf, and the boat slowed. My feet began dragging on the bottom as the shouting increased. Two men grabbed my arms and my head was released. I managed to get my legs under me and stagger along as they brought me up on the beach.

All of them—there were nine—were crowding around, some actually jumping up and down, yelling and looking at me with excitement and wonder. Several held spears. I felt a body or something against my rear. At that moment, and I cannot tell you why or how it came to me, I decided to sing. It was an old camp song that crossed my mind first.

"Kookabura sits on the old gum tree,
Merry merry king of the bush is he,
Laugh, Kookabura laugh,
Gay your life must be."

At first my voice was shaky, but as I repeated the stanza, for I couldn't remember any others, I was louder and more confident. They had stopped shouting and were listening. After the third repeat I then switched to "Home on the Range." Now they were definitely calmer, watching me almost in awe. I noticed my clothes and the belongings from my camp piled some yards away. Still singing, I pointed to my stuff, and slowly walked toward it. They continued to crowd around but allowed me to make the twenty feet or so. Still singing, I picked up my panties and pulled them on. Next, I got my shorts on and then my blouse. Now, of all things, I was singing Madonna's "Material Girl." If Bitterroot were watching from somewhere in time, he had to be laughing. I sat down and put on my boat shoes. Then I stood and slowly picked up every item, smiling as I handed every man something and continued my singing. The next act of the show was critical. I stopped singing and pointed to the canoe.

"Tomol, tomol," I said, hoping that this Chumash Indian word would be understood. Then I made a motion with my arms that they should follow and I walked slowly to the boat. They followed and watched me get into the craft. I sat down near the stern. I motioned for them to put my things in the boat and to get in with me. Then I pointed out in the bay and mimed the act of paddling. I wished I knew their word for village. Would they make the connection? I began singing again.

"Me father was the keeper of the Eddystone light
And he slept with a mermaid one fine night.
Out of that union there came three,
A porpoise and a porgy and the other was me.

Yo ho ho, the wind runs free,
Oh for the life on the rolling sea."

Now they were talking to each other. One brave, the largest, motioned them toward the canoe. Soon all of the gear was stowed, and the men were carrying the boat into the surf. They timed their run perfectly to miss the breakers. In short order we were making fine speed, bounding over the waves in the direction from which they had come. Eight of the braves manned oars and the ninth had the task of bailing.

As I watched the paddlers glistening arms and shoulders move in rhythmic synchrony, I felt strange, like I was partaking of something forbidden. The blue of the ocean and reds and yellows of the cliff reflected the dazzlingly bright sun. There was a rush in my ears, and my eyes began to tear. I can't explain exactly what came over me, but like some banshee I started screaming. It was a joyful sound. The braves must have caught my feeling because they began whooping and hollering, and the rowers increased their tempo until spray was flying all over us.

When the yelling ended, and there were just the sounds of paddling and the bow hitting the waves, I thought about what had just transpired. For some reason my mind flashed to my father's study where he was helping me with my homework. I still remembered his words. "Abbie, don't just think about the answer, look also at the givens for the problem. Sometimes the answer is to change the givens. And that applies in life too." I saw a knowing smile on his face.

Dad's lesson would not have come from my mother, however. As a social worker, she was always trying to get her clients to gain insight and modify their behavior. For her, the world was a big given that could not be altered. In this model, Crystal was a striking success, although my mother had never quite said so. Crystal did things by the book. She joined the right clubs in high school, majored in something practical in college, took a position at an advertising agency, and would probably marry a businessman like her father, have two children, and live in Santa Monica, Palos Verdes or Encino. Of course, if I were more like Crystal, I wouldn't be here. I could now picture my mother's face. The lips were tight.

The voyage took about two hours, I guessed. We went westerly to the end of the island. When we left my home bay and at several other times during our voyage, the rowers stopped and the lookout stood up and scanned the horizon carefully. I wondered what they were looking for. Were there enemy tribes around, requiring that they be on guard?

The boat's hard bottom and the action of the waves made me sore. The tar used on the joints of the rough hewn planks got on my pants and legs, adding to my discomfort. I tried to focus my mind on the coastal scenery. In a few places I saw waterfalls coming down over the cliffs, runoff from the recent rains. I also saw an opening to a cave, large enough to take a sailboat in, mast and all. This must have been the Painted Cave that Claire and Manssard had talked about. God, that seemed long ago now. Could all three of them have known what was going to happen to me?

I had stopped my singing and shouting shortly after we hit the open ocean. I still wasn't able to get a good look at the braves because they were frequently watching me. I was leery of maintaining eye contact with them, so when I was not watching the coast I confined my gaze to the back of the rower in front of me. Nobody tried to talk or make gestures to me or to be familiar in any way. I wondered what was going through their minds. The odor of their sweat was strong. Fortunately the wind blew steadily. The only drawback to that was the periodic spray that was thrown inboard.

As we drew close to the west end of the island, I could make out another island farther north. I figured it was Santa Rosa, which I had seen on

Manssard's chart. As I watched this less-wooded land, one of the braves shouted. Another canoe had been sighted, and I could see it heading for us from around the large rock headland. The boat was similar to ours but smaller. It contained three men. From the motions and shouts I gathered that they were friendly. They began following us, and soon other canoes were converging on us. The end of the island was a high mountain with a low plateau at its base. There were many large rocks at the shoreline. I noticed piles of discarded abalone shells along the shore, most of the iridescence faded from the sun. I figured we were getting close to the village, and my heart began beating faster.

About a mile farther along, we rounded up on the other side of rocks forming a reef line and entered a sheltered bay. By this time there was an entourage of several canoes behind us. Men shouted between boats and the shore, which now contained quite a number of people with more arriving by the minute. In the background I could see many dome-shaped huts that made up the village. A couple were quite large. Smoke rose from what I guessed to be cooking fires in several areas around the huts.

We headed for a sandy place where several boats lay overturned up on the beach. Naked children who had been playing in the water now ran up on the shore to be with the adults, gathering more or less in a half circle around the spot where we would land. Most of the men wore leather coverings at their loins, but a few were naked. The women wore only short skirts made out of some grassy material. A couple of them held baskets.

Several men came down to help pull up the canoe as we glided onto the beach. The boatmen got out and gathered up my belongings. I stepped out and began walking cautiously toward the crowd. I saw a tall, robust man at the front of the group. He had on an elaborate, multi-tiered shell necklace, and white markings were painted on his cheeks and chest. The braves were placing my things in front of him. He looked at my clothes and for a few long seconds scrutinized my shoes. The crowd didn't appear hostile, nor were they afraid of me; their attitude seemed to be one of curiosity. I stopped ten feet in front of the large man and bent over stiffly in a bow of sorts. Then I pointed at my belongings on the ground. I continued to point as I moved slowly toward them, and the man and the crowd backed a few paces. I kneeled and sorted through the things until I found my knife. Then I stood again and held it out toward the brave I figured was the chief. "It's for you. Please take it." I smiled as friendly as I could.

He stepped to within a pace of me and looked at it, but didn't take it. To further entice him I slowly bent out each blade, the awl, screwdriver, and corkscrew and then folded them back. A smile came to his lips. Again I held it out to him. This time he took it from my hand as if it were a delicate piece of crystal. The crowd murmured. He examined it and pulled on the blades, successfully getting out the large one. Then he put it up against his tongue to taste it. It was at that moment that I noticed the silver cross underneath his necklace. A Christian cross. I was stunned. Was it really, or just some likeness in Chumash jewelry? He must have noticed me staring at it for he unhooked it and offered it to me. I examined it. It was silver, tarnished in the crevices, but shiny on the flat surfaces. On the back of the horizontal arm of the cross in small letters was imprinted "Ve con Dios."

There was no doubt. These island Chumash had had contact with the Spaniards. But how? My mind searched back in California history. Maybe the Spanish priests were already on the coast. Junipero Serra had come up and founded the missions. When was that? The late 1700s? Santa Buenaventura and Santa Barbara would be very close across the channel. If I could get over to the mainland I could probably find them. But then what? Would I want to live with these padres? I would probably be safe there, but it would be a hard life. These same Chumash would eventually be wiped out under Spanish harshness and the white man's diseases. How ironic for a Chumash chief to be adorned with a Spanish silver cross.

I smiled at the chief as he motioned for me to put the cross around my neck. It was to be a gift in exchange for the knife. I put it on, and he beamed. Then it occurred to me that he might think I was Spanish. I pointed to the cross and then held my hands out, palms up, looking around with my eyes. He didn't understand but knew I was asking something. An older woman now sidled next to him and said something, motioning at me. He then took the dull end of a spear and began drawing in the sand between us. The figure was unmistakable. It was vessel with two masts and square sails—a European sailing ship. He made some movements with his hands, but I couldn't figure out his meaning. Then he made a motion as if stroking a beard. So there were men with beards on the boat. Undoubtedly white men.

If the cross had come from such voyagers, it could mean a much earlier time than the 1700s. Manssard had said the Spaniard Juan Rodríguez Cabrillo had sailed up the coast around 1550, and he had definitely stopped at these offshore islands. Manssard had said that Rodríguez Cabrillo probably wintered at San Miguel Island where he broke an arm or a leg and died. He and his crew undoubtedly traded with the Chumash Indians of these islands. And there were later Spanish expeditions and voyages. The cross could have come from any of these explorers. So the year that I was in could be anywhere from the middle 1500s to the 1800s. There was hope, but no hope. The crush of discouragement settled into my body and my left leg began shaking. I felt exhausted and famished. I tried smiling at the chief, but he watched me with sudden concern. I mimed drinking and eating and he quickly barked and motioned to others behind him. Two women came up and grabbed me just as my knees gave way. I don't remember exactly what happened then; I might have lost consciousness. I recall bending down to go in the small opening of a circular hut. I was put down on a reed mat and water was given to me. Some kind of strange tasting mush and a couple of pieces of raw fish were put in my mouth. Somehow I got them down. I really didn't care what happened at that point. I must have slept for quite some time.

I awoke once in the night, needing to urinate. I vaguely remember one of the women taking me outside. She squatted next to me as if to show me how. I didn't need any coaching. I hadn't relieved myself since the braves first found me. After that I again slept soundly until morning. I've always been amazed at how moods and emotions can swing so strongly from one day to the next. My father once told me to be careful not to make important decisions during a high or a low, but to wait a day or two if possible. This thought hit me as I looked at the interior of the hut, the morning sun streaming in the door, the sound of children and other human activity outside. There were three women in the hut with me, two younger and one older. Compared to my despair in front of the chief the day before, I felt buoyant.

I scrutinized my surroundings. The older woman, her face showing wrinkles under the dark tan, her breasts hanging limply, was sewing a leathery piece of animal skin, sitting on her knees. The younger women were preparing food of some kind, probably the same mush I had had before, mixing it in large shells. There were a number of baskets, pots, mats, skins, and pieces of bone and other tools and utensils around the edge of the hut. The youngest of the women looked to be around twenty, her black hair wadded up on the back of her head. Her face was plain, the dark eyes set under lids with a slight epicanthic fold. The other woman was a few years older and had a scar across the side of her face tracing a diagonal line from her cheek bone up past her eyebrow. All three women wore only a grass cover around their hips that extended to mid thigh. Next to me were my belongings, all except for the Swiss Army knife. I had on my shorts and blouse, and the silver cross was still around my neck.

Perhaps my good feeling came from knowing I was with other people. Even though I had no idea whether these Canaliño Chumash meant good or ill for me, I was relieved to be with them. It was a deep emotional sensing, a kind of animal faith. And if one believed the evolutionary biologists, it had come from our origins during the millions of years of African descent. With the group, you were safe; out alone, you were prey to the big cats and other beasts. The youngest woman glanced my way and saw me watching her. She said something to the others. Then she came over and kneeled down to look at me. I smiled, and her shadowed face brightened, returning my smile. I sat up, pushed my hair back, and tidied my wrinkled apparel. Quickly the young one brought me breakfast, again the mush and strips of raw abalone. This time there was no gagging; I ate it all with a singular concentration that pleased my onlookers.

When I had finished I pointed a finger toward myself.

"Abbie, Abbie."

The young women caught on quickly. Soon I knew that the youngest one was Bowtu and the next in age was Lamikli. At least this is what it sounded like phonetically. The old woman kept to her sewing but appeared to be listening. I learned the words for hut, fire, fish, shell, water, man, woman, child, and some others. I was sorry not to have a notebook and pencil. It would be a difficult language to learn, especially mastering some of the strange pronunciations. But I decided I would have to try. It was clear that Bowtu and Lamikli were intelligent and very interested in me, especially Bowtu. When I went outside, they both followed, assuming an attitude of excited apprehension. Lamikli lingered ten yards behind, but Bowtu stayed on my elbow.

The people in the village watched us with great curiosity. There were more women and children around than men—the braves were probably off hunting and fishing. I counted about thirty huts and estimated the tribe's size at 70 to 100. More and more I found myself liking Bowtu. She was energetic and seemed to find me very humorous at times, and her high pitched laughter was infectious. In one instance we were both laughing together over a little crab that one of the young boys gave me, but Lamikli frowned, as if we should not be having such a good time.

It became apparent that my two acquaintances were also escorts. When I went beyond the edge of the village to relieve myself among some rocks, Bowtu and Limikli insisted on being with me. This guarding role became more obvious when I went for a swim. Both of them swam out beyond the reef with me, watching me closely. I also observed that two men and from time to time, the chief would saunter around to see where I was and what I was doing. I tried to show no outward concern about this but realized that the surveillance could be defensive on their part or could be out of a protective concern for me. They did not seem to indicate that I was a prisoner, but I wondered what they'd do if I struck off away from the village. I decided it would not be wise to test them.

In the early afternoon, the canoes began arriving as men came back with fish, lobsters, and various mollusks. One group had a small dead fox. In the weeks ahead I learned that the diet was mainly seafood, with an occasional seal or small land mammal or bird. Acorns and seeds were also popular and formed the main ingredients of the mush I had been given. Roots of certain trees and bushes also were eaten. The women dug them out of the ground with sticks. Fish was normally eaten raw, but meat was cooked on an open fire. When I insisted that all my seafood be cooked, they found this curious but not objectionable.

Gradually, the villagers' interest in me lessened, especially that of the women and children, but many of the men still behaved stiffly around me. I tried to fit in more by shedding my blouse and shoes, and tying my hair in a bun. I tried on a grass breech cover, but found it itchy and a little too immodest when sitting and bending, so I continued to wear my shorts.

On the second day, the chief came into our hut shortly after breakfast. I nodded deeply to him, which seemed to be what other women did in his presence. He smiled and looked at me in a friendly way. Then he went to Lamikli and spoke to her at length. At the end of his remarks he reached for her, grabbing one of her breasts and caressing a thigh. She smiled and they left the hut together. I didn't know what to make of it and tried my best to pump Bowtu, who acted as if nothing unusual was happening. The best I could gather was that the chief and Lamikli were a couple and were going to their hut. Not long afterward another woman, actually not much more than a girl, entered the hut. Her name was Meelop. She and Bowtu were quite friendly, and she ate with us and slept on Lamikli's mat that night. When I finally understood from Bowtu that Meelop and the chief were also a couple, it dawned on me that Chief Tooklaw, for that was what he was called, had more than one wife. I strongly suspected, and later confirmed, that Bowtu was also his wife. I also discovered that the chief alone was allowed multiple wives.

Later a small girl about five years in age came to the hut. She was

Bowtu's daughter by the chief. She, too, stayed the night. It took a lot of words, gesturing, and drawing with a stick on the sand that day to learn that the chief had two boys and a girl by Lamikli, who was his first wife, and the one daughter by Bowtu, who was his second wife. Meelop, his third and most recent wife, did not have any children.

During the next couple of weeks I explored the village. When Bowtu went to stay with Chief Tooklaw, Meelop accompanied me on my walks. I grew to appreciate the artistic and technical talents of these Chumash. The women wove beautiful coiled baskets of varying sizes out of grass and willow. Other baskets were ornamental, the grasses dyed with some kind of dark stain, perhaps iron, and woven in intricate geometric designs. I saw some wooden bowls with shell beads inlaid around the mouth, also painted with the lovely designs.

The men were equally talented. On a large rock with a vertical face a hundred yards up behind the village were painted pictographs in various colors—black, red, white, buff, and green. One day Meelop and I watched a large man paint a salamander-like figure among the motifs of sun, water, birds, and animals. His face was marked with white paint on his cheeks and chin. Around his neck were several rows of shell necklaces. The rock seemed to have some religious significance, and I guessed that this man was the tribal shaman. At one point when the shaman turned from the rock, I was struck by the fierceness of his expression. He did not look at us, but toward the horizon, sweeping his arms slowly several times before turning back. He was a little unnerving.

In addition to the canoes, the men's handiwork was shown by their weapons—bows and arrows and spearthrowers—as well as fish hooks, small rattles, and flutes. The reed and mud huts were meticulously made. Some were halfway underground, and one large one had no roof by design, but I didn't know what it was used for. Where two and three families lived together, their quarters were separated by large hanging tule mats.

I liked observing the children. Those too young to help their parents—boys in hunting and fishing and girls in cooking and domestic work—played freely about the village. I liked listening to their animated chatter; I imagined their Chumash conversations matched that of kids everywhere. My physical and psychological settling in to this new life went surprisingly well during the first two weeks. The only worry I had was that I was treated too well. When I tried to help in food preparation, cooking, cleaning the hut, or even fetching water from the creek, the women wouldn't allow it. The only work they didn't mind my doing was fishing off the rocks. Apparently this wasn't a primary female duty. I was clearly being treated as a guest. Fortunately, after about ten days, they allowed me to roam freely by myself in the village. This sense of freedom gave me a good feeling, as if I were truly being accepted by the tribe.

At the beginning of the third week, however, something happened that changed things completely. It was in the late afternoon when most of the men were back from their sojourns. I was fishing off a rock that formed the main reef protecting the inner estuary where the canoes were always beached for the night. My line was down on the seaward side, the waves surging against and between the barrier rocks. I had caught a large sea bass in this spot the day before and was trying to repeat my luck. As I looked out toward Santa Rosa Island a large tomol showed in the distance. Five men were in it, four of them paddling wearily toward the harbor. In watching them, a strange sensation came over me. One of the rowers looked familiar. As they rounded the end rock in the arm of the reef, I saw distinctly the short man in the far stern position. I stiffened and almost lost my balance. The deeply tanned brave looked exactly like Gordon Bitterroot.

When I had gotten over the shock, I was ecstatic. Bitterroot had come for me. He had planned it all along. He let me get a taste of this place, and now he would remove me. I shouldn't have doubted him.

I dropped the fishing line and hurried over the rocks back to the beach. The canoe landed in the estuary, and several village men and women came down to help unload the large baskets in the boat. A few children gathered to watch.

Running up the sand to the creek inlet, I felt physical release, as if my body had been taken out of confinement. I couldn't wait to talk to Bitterroot. It would be so wonderful to have coffee with him again in Hollywood.

"Gordon, Gordon. Here, it's me," I shouted as I approached the group around the canoe. Those working and watching all stared at me for a moment, then turned back to the unloading. Shell beads were being taken from one basket and placed in leather pouches. Acorns from another were being put in small baskets that had been brought down. When all of the cargo had been removed, the short brave lifted the paddles from the boat and, with the help of another, turned the vessel hull up. I drew a quick breath when I saw his pale blue eyes. I moved closer to him.

"Gordon, it's me, Abbie." He looked at me for a long second but no recognition whatsoever crossed his face. He and another man now lifted one of the large baskets and carried it and the paddles up toward the village, not looking back.

Then it dawned on me. Of course he couldn't let on that he knew me—not in front of everyone. I watched him walk. The gait was the same. But he was younger, perhaps thirty years old, and more handsome than the Hollywood Bitterroot. Although deeply tanned, his skin pigment was noticeably lighter than all of the others. However his speech, from the few Chumash words I had heard, sounded exactly like that of the other braves.

Lamikli appeared at my side, greeting me. "Where are the fish?" she asked.

Through a combination of words and gestures I told her a large bass had gotten away, and the fishing line was gone. She frowned. Then I pointed at the small, blue-eyed brave heading toward the outskirts of the village and asked his name.

"Biru," she said, also telling me he was the owner of the canoe.

Biru. I said it silently. Now there could be no doubt that he was Bitterroot. As we walked back to our hut, the thought occurred to me that Biru would contact me when nobody could observe us. Maybe he would come for me that night when everyone slept. I decided to move my furskin bed close to the door.

I was on pins and needles for the rest of the day. From the front of our hut I watched everyone who came in view, hoping I might get another look at Biru, but he stayed out of sight. That night I put all my belongings in a carrying basket and placed it just inside the entry to the hut, next to my furskin. I told Lamikli and Meelop that I would sleep better with fresh air. After a couple hours of wakefulness, I finally fell sound asleep only to be awakened by early morning light and the sounds of Meelop preparing breakfast. Biru had not come.

My first impulse was to find Biru's hut, but then I thought better of it. I needed to learn more about him. After breakfast I went for a walk with Meelop, who seemed to understand me better than Lamikli. I asked her about Biru and learned he was a trader. Unlike the other tomol braves who worked together in large trading groups, Biru was a loner with just a few helpers. He took shell bead necklaces, fish, and sea lion meat from our village and the nearby Santa Rosa villages and from Anacapa crossed the channel. At Hueneme, Mugu, and other Chumash villages on the mainland, he traded for acorns, seeds, tools, and other necessities. He was frequently gone for weeks at a time. As a tomol captain he had great skill and was highly regarded by the village. Meelop tittered slightly when she told me Biru had never taken a wife.

Did that mean he was homosexual, I wondered? All societies seemed to have such individuals, and it was possible there were a few within the tribe. If Biru had been a long time trader in the village, did that mean he couldn't be Bitterroot? That was puzzling.

I asked Meelop why Biru had blue eyes and light skin. This took some doing, since I didn't know the word for blue. But I found a bluish rock and eventually got my meaning across. Her answer, equally difficult for me, was that there were others with blue eyes. This was surprising because I had seen only brown-eyed people in the village. My doubt about her statement was apparently strong enough to lead her to prove it to me. She took me by the hand and we went to a hut in a back area of the village where I had not been before. She called a name at the entrance and soon an older woman came out. I judged her to be over fifty. Her blue eyes were set deep in her pale, wrinkled face. Her hair was a brownish gray, instead of jet black. Her nose was broad, but her lips were thin and her chin was sharper. Her features and coloring gave a European cast to her appearance, especially in profile.

Now I was less sure about Biru. Maybe there were recessive traits in the Chumash gene pool that produced light hair and light-complexioned people. Or, even more likely, maybe there had been sexual contact with the Europeans. I tried to ask Meelop about this, but she could not comprehend my meaning. She repeated several times the word Chup, which I had taken to mean the central Chumash God. To me a Caucasian non-god was more likely, either seafaring explorers—Spanish, British, Dutch, or maybe even Russian, depending on what century it was—or the good padres and vaqueros of the coast. The thought was both intriguing and unsettling. It meant that such contact could happen again soon, which could have uncertain consequences for me, if indeed Biru was not Bitterroot and I was not about to be transcended out of this fix.

Although my optimism was dampened by what I learned about Biru, deep down I still felt that he had to be Bitterroot in historical disguise. The looks and the name were just too coincidental. He was probably waiting for a moment of privacy for us. Maybe it was up to me to help arrange it, so I decided to try and find Biru.

After lunch I went swimming by myself and then meandered along the beach, watching the children. I walked by the estuary and noticed that Biru's canoe was still there. I headed up toward the village outskirts where I had seen him go. There were two small huts at the foot of a bluff that shielded the village from the prevailing wind. I suspected that one of these was Biru's. With no wife or family, he wouldn't require large living quarters.

There was no fire smoldering at the first hut, but there was at the second, so I went up to its entrance. I could hear a scraping sound within.

"Biru." I said it quietly so as not to attract attention. The scraping sound stopped. "Biru," I said again.

He suddenly stepped out. He had an arrow shaft in one hand and some kind of bone scraper in the other. He wore nothing. I couldn't help glancing at his genitals before I looked into the pale eyes.

"Hello Biru. My name is Abbie." I tried my best to pronounce the words in correct Chumash.

He stood staring and finally said something that I figured was "What do you want?"

"I do not speak well," I said.

To this he nodded, the stern expression unchanged.

I looked around and noticed that a woman down in the village was looking up at us, but no one else seemed to be paying attention, and nobody was close enough to hear what we were saying.

"Are you Gordon?" I asked in English, smiling.

There was no comprehension on his face, not even friendliness—just an alert wariness. Now I was feeling uneasy.

"Please, if you are Gordon Bitterroot, wink or say something. I want out of here."

His mouth seemed to relax, but still he said nothing, maintaining a stare that moved around on me.

"Can I ride in your tomol?" I asked in Chumash.

"No," he replied. Then he wheeled and entered his hut.

I stood there, feeling foolish. Had I been wrong to seek him out? Either he wasn't Bitterroot, or this was not the right approach. I turned and retraced my steps back to the beach. The woman who had watched me up at Biru's followed me with her eyes until I was within sight of my hut. Not long after I was back, Lamikli entered the hut.

"Why did you go see Biru?" she demanded.

"I wanted a tomol ride."

"You can't ride with Biru. Chief Tooklaw will give you a tomolo ride."

With this, she left. I found myself, somewhat embarrassed, looking at the chief's mother. She was weaving a basket. Apparently I had not behaved according to protocol.

In about twenty minutes Lamikli came back and motioned me outside. There, smiling, was Chief Tooklaw with two other braves behind him, all three holding paddles. Lamilkli and I were going with them.

The chief's canoe was quite large, but the three of them were able to move it fairly fast. Chief Tooklaw was in the bow, followed by me, another paddler, Lamikli who was bailer, and the stern paddler. Except for the seawater puddling around my bottom, it was a fun ride—almost as exciting as my first trip with the hunting party. As Chief Tooklaw turned to look at me from time to time, I made sure to give signs of my enjoyment by laughter and occasional squeals at the cold spray. I think he purposely headed into the wind and waves to get maximum effect, for he laughed when we were heavily bounced and doused.

Chief Tooklaw was one of the largest men in the village. His height and powerful physique gave him a commanding demeanor. Unfortunately his face didn't match the godlike body. Over most of both cheeks were pockmarks and his chin seemed cockeyed, as if it had been broken at some time. One eye bulged slightly, perhaps due to a thyroid condition. While he smiled frequently at me, he mostly appeared stern to others, even to his wives, and this made me wonder about his real nature. As the chief he undoubtedly had to wield authority, and although he seemed to consult a lot with others, perhaps a certain amount of ruthlessness went with the office by necessity. My intuition told me to be on excellent behavior in his presence.

Three days later, while musing over the Biru/Bitterroot paradox, I got my period, my first since joining the village. When it had happened previously at my camp, I used a piece of seal fur tied in position by a leather thong wrapped around my waist. I stayed near the bay to wash it out every so often. It was a fairly messy arrangement, but there was no better alternative that I could devise. What did the Chumash women do? Come to think of it, I had not seen any of them in that situation. So I asked Bowtu who was now back, having been spelled by Lamikli. She quickly packed my belongings and led me away without explanation.

We ended up at a hut that, to my surprise, was full of women who were menstruating. The hut was a place to sequester women during their menstrual time. No men or children were allowed except for nursing babies. Instead of furskin as a napkin, the Chumash women used dry fronds from some kind of wide-leafed plant. A large supply of the leaves was piled in a corner. Before I could object, Bowtu was fixing me up with the fronds. They were scratchy, but I felt I could not protest. She also found me a place on the ground for my fur bed in between two others. She then introduced me to the eight women who were there. Of course, they all knew who I was.

Even though everyone was very nice in welcoming me and trying to see to my comfort, I found myself wondering how this practice of isolation of menstruating women had come about. It would do no good to ask. For them, going to the women's hut was how it always had been. It was natural.

The only regret I had during this interlude, other than the chafing between my legs, was missing close-up a full tribal religious ceremony held by the chief—the first since my arrival in the village. I had been aware of some small gatherings where there had been music and chanting by the shamans, but not on the scale that now took place on the third night of my confinement. It was a command performance attended by everyone in the village but small children and those in the menstrual hut. We were about 50 yards away, watching from the fire area.

All of the activity took place in the large, roofless enclosure. A space was made in the middle and the chief, shamans, and elders had front-row seats around the circle. The rest of the villagers crowded around the outside of the low walls. Both men and women were painted, mostly on their faces, and wore decorative necklaces and bracelets on their arms and legs. The chief and his assistants had colorful headdresses and were painted in greater detail than the others.

After warm-up music with a syncopated beat—flutes and rattles playing pleasing notes that had a strange resemblance to modern jazz—the crowd began swaying and moving to the beat. The music stopped when Chief Tooklaw rose and talked for a short while, his voice loud and emphatic. Then the dancing started, two couples at a time, the men in loin cloths and the women in short colorful skirts. Their feet moved quickly to the beat of the music and their bodies were agile in jumps and bends. The crowd chanted and shouted encouragement as the volume and tempo increased. Excitement built steadily. Four sets of couples danced, each more accomplished than those before.

I noticed that things were being passed among the onlookers. The inner circle of shamans drew at some kind of pipe making its rounds. There also was drinking from containers that passed through both the inner and outer circles. After about an hour of dancing, the final act—provided by the shaman and his assistants—was dramatic, although I couldn't understand it. The shamans chanted, danced, shouted and made a great many symbolic gestures to the ground, the sky, and off in different directions. At one point the chief joined them for a while. The crowd enthusiastically responded with shouts and moans and laughter.

When it was over, the crowd dispersed. I asked one of the women near me what it had been about. She said something about the sun, the sea, Chup and the chief. She smiled broadly. Too broadly, I thought.

That night I did not sleep well.

9

In the morning my flow was all but finished, and one of the women said I could go to the ocean the next day. All women had to bathe in the sea after their menses. It was a ritual much like the Jewish mikva. The women had to cleanse themselves—all the nooks and crannies—to be fresh and clean for their husbands. Even unmarried women had to do it. I welcomed it, but I was amused when Meelop accompanied me into the surf to show me how.

Back in my hut everything went on as usual, and I mainly found myself thinking about Biru. I had not given up hope that he was Bitterroot. I wondered if I should try to see him again. I figured that he would probably go on another trading voyage soon. I began to think that I should try to go with him. Even if he weren't Bitterroot, it might be a good idea to get away from the village, just so the chief or any of the single braves, several of whom had looked at me with more than casual interest, wouldn't get any serious ideas. In the long run, maybe I would be better off with the Spanish, if I could find them, but the thought of spending the rest of my life with anyone in this time and place was depressing. I kept telling myself that I would be rescued sooner or later. I had to stay positive.

Late that afternoon, as I sat on my fur bed trying to carve a fishhook out of bone, a large shadow crossed in front of me. It was Chief Tooklaw, followed by Lamikli. I got up quickly and realized he wanted to talk. For some reason it was harder for me to understand the men than the women, so I listened as carefully as I could. It was something about the morning meal. I asked him to repeat it. Yes, he was asking me to take breakfast with him at the roofless hut.

I smiled and said I would be pleased to do so. What else could I say? Since he had been such a good host, it seemed the least I could do. A denial, I'm sure, would have offended him. So it was agreed. He smiled broadly, squeezed my arm, and left. Then both Lamikli and Meelop hugged me. Such physical contact with me had not been shown before, although I had seen them express feelings in a physical way with each other and with others in the tribe. However, as I thought more about the fact that the chief wanted to me to dine with him and that Lamikli and Meelop were unusually friendly, I began putting two and two together. It added up to the strong probability that I was the object of the chief's desire. I became very nervous.

That evening, as I stewed about it, I decided I would tell him that I wanted to be taken to the mainland. I would say that I needed to join my people, the whites. He should be able to appreciate this. I would not say that Biru should take me, because he might become jealous, but just that Tooklaw should arrange it. Of course, I would profusely express my appreciation for his hospitality. I'd tell him I would speak highly of him to the Spanish, whom he seemed to revere. I would do this before he did something stupid like propose to me. With this settled in my mind, I felt better and finally dropped off in sleep.

When I awakened I found all three of the chief's wives working busily in the hut. They were fixing the feathers of beautiful wraparound skirts. They intended for me to wear one to the breakfast with the chief. I dreaded wearing it because it would be uncomfortable and, due to its midthigh length, difficult to keep decent when sitting. My panties, previously worn out, had been discarded earlier. The only alternative was wearing my shorts, which were quite frayed and still stained with tar. They were not especially becoming compared to the multicolored wraparounds worn by the women on festive occasions. So I decided that this was one time when I should "do as the Romans do."

About midmorning it was time to go. As the four of us walked to the roofless hut, I felt more like a Chumash than at any other time since my arrival. It was due to the wraparound skirt and the white paint markings that I had allowed Lamikli to put on my tanned face, as well as the friendly looks and greetings other villagers gave us. I was clearly a part of the "in group," and I liked the feeling.

When we arrived, a crowd had gathered. Apparently the whole village was showing up for the occasion. Chief Tooklaw and the shamans were all painted and dressed in their finery, the same as they had been for the religious ceremony. In the middle of the enclosure on the ground was a beautiful rug made from strips of seal fur sewn together. The strips were of different hues of brown, making a handsomely striped pattern. Chief Tooklaw came up and took my hand and had me sit down next to him on the rug. Lamikli, Bowtu, and Meelop sat to either side of us. The shamans sat further out from them. They were somewhat solemn in contrast to the crowd, which was happy and talkative. My stomach began to flutter. Why was this breakfast so ceremonial?

When the village had finished gathering, the chief stood up and said something to everyone about the beauty of the morning and the happiness of our village. He also talked about children, but the meaning wasn't clear to me. Then he sat again, a satisfied smile on his face. The head shaman then rose and talked at length about Chup and places on the mountain, something about the sun and the sea, and about children and the chief's wives, motioning to Lamikli, Bowtu, Meelop, and also to me. Now I was getting scared. I decided I had better tell the chief about wanting to go to the mainland.

As soon as the shaman sat down I turned to the chief and said I needed to tell him something. As I did so, I noticed Biru standing off to the side of the crowd, separated from the others. He was watching us intently. It was the first time I had seen him since I had gone up to his hut.

"Now is not the time for talk," Tooklaw said. He motioned to Lamikli.

Lamikli was ladling some mush from a tightly woven basket into a large, pretty abalone shell. When it was full, she handed it to the chief, along with two bone spoons, one of which he gave to me. Now the crowd's murmuring seemed to stop. The chief took a large mouthful of the mush. It had the texture of hummus but was greenish gray in color, different from the kind I had seen before. He now offered the mush bowl to me. I took about half a spoonful. It was similar to the acorn mush we often ate in our hut, but it had an unusual tang. The flavor was like that of a green wheatstalk that you can pull up from grassy fields in springtime. It wasn't at all bad tasting. The chief took more and again proffered the bowl to me, and I took a spoonful. I realized I was quite hungry, having had nothing to eat that morning.

"Mot, mot, mot, mot..." The crowd began chanting in a cheerful way. Mot was the word for chief. I looked at Meelop, and there were tears of joy running down the young girl's cheeks. What was happening? Why were people so involved in watching us eat? Only Biru didn't seem to be smiling.

The chief clearly intended that we finish the entire bowl, so I matched him spoonful for spoonful. It was quite filling, and as we neared the bottom, I was no longer hungry. I looked up from the last bite, but something was strange. I saw black spots no matter where I looked. Something else was wrong. I was sitting on my feet, knees on the ground together to make sure my wraparound stayed down, but I was having trouble feeling my extremities. My legs seemed to be getting numb, with a prickly sensation moving up and down. It was different than just having the blood cut off. I touched my face and realized I couldn't feel it either. I looked up at the sun. Instead of its circular shape, it was changing shapes, from oblong to an hourglass and other asymmetrical forms, almost like a kaleidoscope. Now it was tinged with greens and blues. I vaguely remembered I was going to tell Chief Tooklaw about leaving, but as I turned to him, his face was already close to mine.

"You are now my wife," he said softly in his deep voice.

At first it didn't register, but then I realized that what had been taking place was somehow the village marriage ceremony. Only later was I to learn that when a man and woman take food from the same bowl, it signified that they were husband and wife. But at this moment I felt stunned and deceived. And, adding insult to injury, I was now aware that I had also been drugged. The mush must have contained the same hallucinogenic substance that the villagers had taken during the religious ceremony.

"No, no," I said, my words weak and slurred. "I'm not your wife."

But Tooklaw didn't seem to be listening. I felt a strange feeling and looked down to see that his hand was rubbing my legs. I tried to move my arms but they stayed behind my back. He had pinned them together with his left hand. I didn't have the strength to pull them away. Now his face was roaming on my neck and shoulders. I looked out at the crowd, which appeared to be swaying as people watched, but strangely I felt no embarrassment. It was almost like I, too, was in the audience watching in a rather clinical way as Chief Tooklaw paid me this physical affection. I looked up and saw the clouds moving around weirdly as if they were playing tag. Slowly I felt warm feelings lick inside me. I was becoming aroused. It was different from anything I had experienced before—quite intensely delicious, in fact.

Then after a few moments or minutes—I don't know which—the chief stood, bent in front of me and in a quick, almost effortless motion, slung me over his shoulder, my legs in front and head behind. He swung around and said something to the crowd, and they again began chanting "Mot, mot."

Tooklaw turned, his strong right arm holding me in place, and began walking away with me bouncing slightly at each stride. I knew we were heading toward his hut. As we passed the edge of the crowd, which was upside down to me, I again saw Biru. He was only a few feet away and I saw his face very clearly amid the waviness. Instead of a frown, there was now a slight smile on his face. No, it really was a smirk, and it was ugly and insulting.

With this realization, something deep inside me turned. In that agonizingly long moment, a fundamental idea flashed in the remaining gray matter not yet submerged in the dizziness of the mush. I could see Jean-Paul Sartre's saying, "I am my choices," on a chalkboard in my brain. I was free to choose; I had to choose. My existence was at stake. And from where I do not know, there came energy.

With all my might I twisted my body. Tooklaw stumbled as my weight shifted, and he went down on one knee. I slid off his shoulder to the ground, hitting on my hip but not feeling the impact. About five paces in front of me was Biru, suddenly looking alarmed. On hands and knees I crawled over to him and encircled his ankles with my arms. He tried to step out of my grasp, but my hands held tight to his legs and he fell. I moved up and locked my arms around his waist.

I heard the crowd gathering and talking animatedly. Above this I heard Tooklaw shouting. I buried my head against Biru's chest and held on as tightly as I could. Now Biru was trying to move as he talked to the chief. Tooklaw's shouts were getting angrier, and I felt a sharp kick against my back. The crowd became ugly, yelling and hissing. Dirt clods and small stones began to hit us. Someone yanked my foot and twisted it. Biru leaned over me, trying to shield me from the flying objects. Something very hard hit the back of my head, and I felt several kicks and jabs against my buttocks and legs. Sand flew into my eyes, and reflexively I closed them despite the fierce pain. My skirt was jerked off. Spit hit the side of my face and ran into my mouth. The din was incredible. I felt that at any minute I would die, but it didn't matter.

Then Chief Tooklaw was yelling something, and slowly the noise abated. The rocks and debris that pelted us stopped. The mob was going away. Within a couple of minutes it was quiet. I could hear the surf in the distance. It was over, and I was still alive. I let all my aching muscles relax, and as this happened, sobs began welling up from deep in my chest. Tears flowed, taking the worst of the dirt from my eyes. I released my grip, and Biru sat up and began brushing the debris from me. He slowly stood up. I could barely see him, but I could make out dark red blotches and lines on his face, shoulders, and arms; it was blood. He bent down and his powerful arms closed around me, hoisting me up slowly. My legs trembled involuntarily, and I could not have stood without his support.

"Come," he said.

I nodded. With his steadying arm around my waist we moved half stumbling down to the ocean's edge. I, too, had blood oozing from several wounds. Other places of my body began revealing their pain and my right leg was increasingly difficult to move. The water was friend and enemy both. Its initial bracing effect was sobering. Then the salt attacked the raw flesh and brought searing pain. I cried out. Biru threw water over me to get the dirt out of my wounds and did the same to himself. I began shivering violently and would have fallen but he saw me in time and lifted me into his arms and carried me up on the beach. I tried walking but my legs went rubbery, and I blacked out. I don't remember how I arrived in Biru's hut. The powerful little man must have carried me the whole way.

When I came to I was on a fur ground blanket. Something was painfully poking the wounds on my back, one at a time. I turned to discover Biru next to me, his tongue out like a dog's, licking each sore. I had to fight myself to avoid screaming and pulling away. It not only hurt terribly, it was distasteful to watch, so I kept my eyes closed and bore the pain stoically, only because I knew that saliva contains a natural antiseptic. By the time Biru had finished with the last bloody gash on my ankle I felt bound to repay his kindness. So I turned to him and licked all of his wounds with the remaining strength I had. Then I fell back and slept deeply through the rest of the afternoon and most of the night, kept warm by the fur and the body heat of Biru sleeping next to me.

I awoke with a fever. All my sores hurt, but I needed to relieve myself. I stood up but felt very lightheaded. My right leg was so stiff I could not bend the knee. But somehow I managed to drag myself outside to get rid of the pressure in my bladder. On the way back in I bumped into a pile of things. They were my personal belongings from the other hut. How did they get here? Did that mean that I was not going back there? I could easily understand that I was no longer welcome there. Was the marriage to the chief annulled? Most likely. We had not consummated it. He probably hated me now. I had embarrassed him terribly. Maybe I wasn't even welcome in the village. But I would have to sort these things out later. Now it was time to get well. I again tried to sleep but the fever allowed only fitful dozing, and this unpleasant state carried me through to the morning.

Biru, awake before me, had placed nuts and berries in a basket near my bed. My fever was down some and I ate, although without much appetite. There was also water in a large bone cup, and I downed it all. Biru watched me but turned away when I looked at him.

"How are you?" I asked.

"All right," he replied without looking at me.

Was he embarrassed? He asked if I wanted more to eat. I said I didn't. I could see in the dim light a couple of ugly cuts and bruises on his face and head and a bad gash on his shoulder. I vaguely remembered licking them. The one on the shoulder should have stitches, I thought. But who would do it? Scars were things of pride to the Chumash. Biru picked at his teeth with a sharp thin bone. He had been eating the meat of some kind of bird—a duck perhaps. What was he thinking about me? The million dollar question was why had he helped me? Why had he suffered for me? He obviously didn't have to. He could have turned on me like the rest, but he didn't. Would he be ostracized now? It would be impossible to get answers to these questions from him, I knew. A more practical question that I dared not ask was how long I could stay in his hut. That might become clear once I was healthy again.

When my sores began to scab over, I started wearing my shorts. I still felt uncomfortable without my bottom covered in front of Biru, even though we had gone through the most intimate contact conceivable to me. Seemingly in response he started wearing a breechcloth. That night he also moved his mat to the other side of the hut to sleep. That removed a slight worry in the back of my mind but at the same time was vaguely disturbing. Was it a sign of rejection? Did he have no interest in me as a woman? But why should I care about that?

The next day my leg felt better and I began moving around the hut, trying to be helpful. I made the same acorn mush I had seen fixed by the chief's wives and gave some to Biru. He seemed to appreciate my helping in food preparation, and I sensed that he was genuinely pleased that I was healing well. We didn't talk much. The only questions he would answer were factual ones, such as where utensils were kept, whether he wanted food, and the like. When I went outside, Biru told me to stay close to the hut. I soon surmised that we were persona non grata. People avoided eye contact and conversation. A couple of times I heard hisses. So that answered my question about whether I would have to leave Biru's hut. No one else would have me.

Apparently Biru was not as ostracized as I, or at least he felt comfortable going to the creek for water and to other places I couldn't observe. On the next day one of Biru's boatmen brought fish to the hut. He and Biru talked in low tones and I could not understand them. After the man, Gonim, had left I asked Biru what it was about, but he just smiled and said nothing. At least he was in good enough spirits to smile. It was more than I could do.

Later that evening after a dinner of roasted perch and berries, Biru talked to me more than ever before. He even used my name, which shocked me.

"Abbie, I am going on a trip in the tomol. I will be gone for many days. You stay here in the hut until I return."

"I want to go with you, Biru."

"You can't go. Wait here for me."

"Please, Biru, take me in the tomol. Please."

"No. I'm going. You must stay." He said this emphatically.

I could see there was no way to change his mind.

"How many days until you return?" I asked.

He looked pensive and then picked up his bone knife and began making marks on the ground. When he was finished I counted twenty. He was probably going on his usual trip to the mainland. I felt sad. He looked at me, and I nodded. More than anything else this seemed to indicate that he was not Bitterroot, for what better opportunity would there be to pull me away? The chief and the villagers probably could not care less about my leaving.

The next morning Biru was up well before daybreak. I got up, too, and fixed him breakfast. He was silent all during his preparations. I watched him gather his things in the dim predawn light. He told me Gonim's wife would bring me food while he was away and then walked out of the hut just as the sun was breaking above the horizon. When he realized I was following him down to the estuary he stopped and glared at me.

"Go back. You must stay in the hut."

So I couldn't even see him off. I was surprised to feel myself so emotional at his leaving. I looked at him unhappily and then quickly put my arms around him and hugged him. He didn't embrace me back, but put a hand on my face, patting it gently. In his eyes I saw some tenderness before he pushed me away.

"Bye," I said.

He nodded and left. I went back to the hut and lay down. I felt terribly depressed.

When I went outside again later that morning I found three abalones on the ground next to the hut's opening. They must have been left by Gonim's wife, whom I had never met. So I wasn't going to starve. I set about preparing them for the midday meal. But what about water? There was a day's supply in the hut. If that wasn't provided I'd have to fetch it myself from the creek. It would mean passing close to at least two other huts on the way. Fortunately, Biru's hut was at the westernmost back edge of the village, so that passage out and around most of the huts was possible. It also meant that I could go behind it to relieve myself without encountering other villagers unless they for some reason had come to that outlying area. I had noticed, however, that since the marriage fiasco few people came near our hut. It apparently was off limits.

I got up before daybreak the next morning and ventured to the creek with two large pots. Almost nobody was stirring in the village. Only one young boy saw me when I was on the way back. He quickly ducked back into a hut, appearing frightened. I heard loud words exchanged in his hut, but nothing else happened. No one came out, and I got back without incident. As I rounded the corner to Biru's hut, however, I immediately was face-to-face with a pretty young woman who was carrying a basket. I guessed it was Gonim's wife. I smiled and said hello as I set down the water pots. She looked at me hesitantly and took something from the basket and thrust it at me. It was a large piece of seal meat.

"Thank you. My name is Abbie, what's yours?"

"Piapa," she replied softly, quickly leaving before I could engage her further. She may have been surprised to find me up so early.

On the third day my confinement became unbearable. With nobody to see and no place to go I was stir crazy. I spent almost all my time trying to weave a basket, but it wasn't turning out well. If only I could go fishing and swimming, I thought, I might be able to survive until Biru returned. Would the chief and villagers allow that? I wouldn't know unless I tried. Nothing ventured, nothing gained.

I decided to try it midmorning when most of the braves were away and in broad daylight so there would be no appearance of stealth. I took fishing lines and hooks and slowly walked down to the ocean but away from the village on the outward side of the estuary. I made eye contact with no one on the way and picked my way out to some rocks in the surf that were hard to get to. With my knife, which had been returned along with my other belongings, I cut pieces of abalone for bait and cast out two lines. I watched to seaward with trepidation, expecting any moment to hear tribesmen behind me or to see a tomol full of braves rounding up in front. But nothing happened except for two bites on the lines at the same time. Anybody watching had to be laughing because I got a halibut and a sea bass tangled together, losing the bass. The next fifteen minutes was spent untangling the lines. I stayed out about an hour and then went back in the same manner I had come, but with three fish at my side.

The next day I was braver, swimming for twenty minutes after I fished. But this time I noticed two braves sitting high on the bluff watching me. I acted like I hadn't seen them, putting on my shorts as soon as I was out of the water and again going directly home, head down and eyes averted. The elders were allowing me some freedom but weren't going to let me do as I pleased, I guessed. When I got back I looked through my things and realized that the silver cross Tooklaw had given me was gone. Undoubtedly he had ordered it taken back while I was away. It was clear I wasn't being ignored. I wondered if they were watching the hut at night.

I found myself mulling a great deal over my predicament. If I had anything now, it was time to think. The question most on my mind was what my goal should be. If I believed, as I now did, that Biru was not Bitterroot, what then? Should I try to steal away from the village? If so, where would I go? Back to living alone somewhere on the island? Back to Pelican Bay where Bitterroot had left me? Or should I try again to get Biru to take me to the mainland to find the Spanish? Would that be out of the frying pan and into the fire? Or should I just stay here and try to be happy?

As I wrestled with the unknowables of the problem, I remembered readings and discussions at Reed on the meaning of truth and goodness. How do we know something is genuinely good—a right objective in life? Always in the middle of these basic conundrums was my favorite philosopher, David Hume, the old skeptic. After all, it was he who led me to reject religion. After reading his *Dialogues Concerning Natural Religion,* I didn't see how any thinking person could still believe in a supreme deity. Hume, true to form, thought we should maintain a healthy skepticism toward knowing anything with certitude. But that wonderful advice didn't help me here. I had to decide something about my existence. There were three options, and they weren't all equally good. One had to be the best for me at this time. How could I determine it?

I decided I would make the great distinction that western philosophy had settled upon, to separate desires from needs. Desires were what we acquired as individuals, but needs were natural desires of all persons, born of the requirements of our species. A good thing was what we needed, not necessarily what we desired. So I should want to do what I needed. Food and shelter were a basic need, but I figured I would have them whether I lived alone, with the Chumash or with the Spanish. These were not at issue. Health? It was very basic. Here I might do better by myself or among the Chumash rather than with the Spanish who carried many communicable diseases. Human contact? It was a very basic need that I wouldn't have off by myself. But what of the quality of human contact? Love and intimacy are an important part. Could I have it among the Chumash when there were such cultural and intellectual differences? Would it be better among the Spanish, culturally closer but still hundreds of years behind me? Children? I could probably have them in either society, but obviously not by myself unless I got pregnant and then went off to be alone. That didn't seem very wise. Security? Probably best among the Chumash, second best with the Spanish, and worst alone. What about knowledge and learning—a basic need the philosophers all agreed upon. All choices were sadly lacking here, but the Spanish at least offered the potential for western style intellectual discussion and books, even if only religious ones. Freedom? Clearly I would be the most free off alone. My life as a woman in Chumash and Spanish society would be proscribed, perhaps the most among the Spanish, depending on my status.

So where was I? I decided the weight of these needs ruled most against being alone. Giving up the freedom of a singular life was not as bad as being lonely for the rest of my life. So I would be better off among the Chumash or the Spanish than living in isolation. But among these two societal choices, I could not decide. Ideally, it would be best to try them both before making up my mind. I knew fairly well what Chumash life was like. I needed to find out about the Spanish, but in a way that would allow me to rejoin the Chumash if I so desired.

As I thought about this, the best means to achieve the goal was Biru. If I could get him to take me to the nearest Spanish settlement, such as the Mission Santa Barbara, perhaps I could not only find out what year it was, but what possibilities there were for life there or elsewhere among Spaniards. If Biru would leave me there for a month or so and come back to see if I wanted to return with him to the island, this seemed to be the best plan I could have.

Even though I arose early each day, I didn't see Piapa. Maybe the word had reached her that I was catching fish every day and didn't need the food she would ordinarily bring. So one day I didn't go down to the sea and sure enough she arrived early the next morning. I stepped out quickly to meet her.

"Good morning, Piapa. How are you?" I was cheerful.

"Good morning," she replied, handing me this time the hind leg of a fox already cooked.

"Thank you, but please don't go. Stay and talk to me, Piapa."

She didn't say anything but lingered with her eyes down.

"Did Gonim go with Biru?" I asked.

"Yes."

"Do you know when they will be back?"

"Five days maybe."

She began edging away.

"Piapa," I said firmly, "do they meet with the Spanish when they go over there?"

She looked puzzled. "No. There are no Spanish over there. The Spanish are on winged boats." With that she left.

I was shocked. There were no Spanish on the mainland. Junipero Serra had not come north yet from Mexico—or what would later become Mexico. That meant it was before the middle 1700s. Could Piapa be wrong? Her mate, Gonim, travelled with Biru all along the coast. They met with the coastal Chumash. He would hear whether Spaniards had been seen, and surely he would have told her. In fact, all of the village would know about such a momentous event. I had simply neglected to ask about it all this time. The Spanish seen by the tribe had come on ships—the early explorers. So it was earlier in time than I had thought and hoped.

That changed things for me. There would be no point in going over to the mainland, other than to sightsee. I would find only more villages of Chumash and other tribes to the north and south. So my best choice was to stay where I was, at least for a while. Within the village, I was stuck with Biru, for better or worse. But it could be worse; it could be Tooklaw. At least I admired Biru, even though he didn't talk much. Our relationship would be platonic, that of good friends. His roots didn't seem to be in this village. He would be away much of the time—which was probably a blessing. Maybe I eventually could travel with him. It would relieve the boredom of village routine. And if it came to it, maybe at some future time I could think about a serious mate and children.

I shook my head, not wanting to believe that my new plan was the reality I faced. But Bitterroot had not come and probably never would. Something had gone wrong, and there was no way out. I shivered, and my eyes teared over. I had admitted it—the cold, harsh fact that I knew was true. I let myself weep quietly, the face of Mom watching me from somewhere in my mind. She was sympathetic but couldn't help me. I remembered her saying once when I was crying, "So what are you going to do about it?" In her book, crying got you nowhere.

The day Biru came back was hot. The sun beat down from nearly straight overhead. I figured it was late June. It hadn't rained for over a month and our little creek had less water coursing down it than when I had arrived. I was very excited to hear from Piapa that Biru's canoe had pulled in. Forgetting my imposed isolation, I ran down to the estuary. Others arriving to greet the traders were eager to see what they had brought and paid no attention to me.

Biru saw me and smiled as I waved at him. It seemed to take forever for the boat to be unloaded. I saw that he had one basket that was destined for our hut. It was heavy, and he carried it while I carried two of the paddles. I could tell he was tired, but I hoped he was willing to talk.

"Biru, how was your trip?" I asked as we walked together.

"Good."

"Why was it good?"

"Good trades. Good weather."

"Oh, that's nice. You look tired."

"Yes, I need to rest now."

"I'm so glad you're back, Biru." I almost said that I missed him very much, but thought better of it.

"What's in the basket, Biru?"

"I'll show you."

In the hut Biru took the cover off the basket. There were carved implements, a couple of pipes, feathered skirts, arrows, soapstone, a pot of tar, and other wares. On the side near the bottom I saw some colored shells and lifted them. They formed a gorgeous, mother-of-pearl necklace, each piece matched in size and shape.

"For you, Abbie."

My breath sucked in noticeably.

"Oh Biru, for me? It's beautiful. How wonderful!" I'm sure he got my meaning even though I had lapsed into English.

Biru laughed loudly, delighted that I was pleased. It was the first time I had seen him laugh so. I didn't know who was happier. I threw my arms around him and then kissed him. That embarrassed him slightly, but he continued beaming.

"Oh thank you, Biru. Thank you very much. I like them a lot." I put them around my neck. They fell just below the top of my breasts. I found my compact and looked at myself in the mirror. The necklace was truly lovely. Any quality department store in Beverly Hills would have been pleased to have it in a showcase.

Wearing my new acquisition I proudly fixed some acorn mush and fish for Biru. He was hungry and ate it all. Then he took a nap while I looked through all the goods once again.

When later I went behind the hut to urinate, I noticed some spotting. I was getting my period. That put me in a quandary. Was I supposed to go to the menstrual hut, or would they not want me? Should I tell Biru? If I kept it secret and he found out, how would he react? How much of a taboo was it to stay at home with your period? I decided I'd better tell him. When he awoke it was dusk. After I was sure he was up and of clear mind, I broached the problem.

"Biru, I have my blood today. But I will stay here. OK?"

He looked sharply at me, as if he were chastising a child.

"Go to the woman's hut. You cannot stay here. Chup will not allow it."

"Will they let me in?"

"Yes, it will be all right for you there. You go now."

I was disappointed. Biru had just come back, and I wanted to be with him. But there was no choice; it was unlucky timing. I packed some things but decided I'd better leave my new necklace. I hadn't remembered any of the women wearing jewelry at the hut. I showed Biru what food was available and then left.

Not surprisingly I found the same women in the menstrual hut as before. While a few were cool toward me, others were friendly, which was gratifying. I received help with the basket I was weaving and after a couple of days was included in village gossip. The most surprising was that Chief Tooklaw would be taking a new wife. This could only help my situation, I thought. If the chief were happy with his new bride, maybe he would be less angry with me and I would be reaccepted by the village. Several of the women wanted to know if Biru and I shared the same food bowl. I'm sure they were disappointed to learn we did not.

When my period was finished I went down to the ocean and washed thoroughly. I took a long, refreshing swim far beyond the barrier, which made me tired but exhilarated. When I returned to Biru's hut, my mood was joyous.

Biru was pleased to see me. He set about boiling two large lobsters, and I made some mush. For dessert there were berries. He told me he had worked on his tomol for the past several days, putting new asphalt stickum in the joints. He had already heard of the chief's betrothal. Biru was surprisingly talkative. I guessed he was finally becoming comfortable with me. Later, at my suggestion, we walked to the beach and watched the sunset. The deep golds and pinks against purplish clouds were so spectacular my eyes watered.

That night as I bedded down I almost was willing to thank Chup for the good feelings that had come to me. As I lay there, waiting for sleep, I could hear Biru still stirring. Then I realized he was moving his ground mat over by mine. I was now alert. What were his intentions? Should I move away or say something? I decided to wait and see. But my fears were for nothing. Soon he was asleep, and I followed.

In the middle of the night I awoke, somewhat uncomfortable. It was quite warm. Then I found that Biru was up against my back and his arm was around my waist. I tried to move away but his arm tightened around me. I knew he was awake, too. I lay there quietly but my heart began to pound. This was more than the platonic relationship I had planned on. Did he want me? Did I want to be wanted? I could feel his chest move ever so slightly against my back and a tingling sensation came over me. It had been so long since I had been held. His hand now moved slowly on my front. It felt nice. My breathing increased. I caressed his arm with my hands, moving it slightly higher, until his fingers met my breasts, so eager to be touched. The fire starter was now ignited. I felt him move closer, his lips grazing my neck. His arousal was obvious and contagious. Now his hand moved all over me, leaving a trail of excitement wherever it went. There was no stopping now. I turned in to him. The coals were all aglow. I didn't even mind that Biru wanted me from behind. It had all happened so fast. I had not made the decision—my body had.

Proof that a mind-body duality exists.

I lingered in bed with a good feeling the next morning, dozing in and out of sleep. By the time I got up, Biru was already out. It was just as well. I was unsure what I would feel when I looked him in the eye. For me, making love always changed the relationship. It was as if the act released chemicals in my body, coloring my feelings about the world and about my lover for days to come. It also caused an unspoken understanding, as if the physical enjoinment created an intimacy that was more than itself.

I don't confuse this with romantic love, which I have distrusted ever since I learned it sprang up during the Middle Ages. Before that time it didn't exist in European culture. Henri Bergson claimed that love was conceived through the religious emotion created by Christianity. Love was brought into the world by that religion. The problem, according to Bergson, is that the nearer love is to religious adoration, the greater the disproportion between lover and love object and the deeper the disappointment when imperfection comes to light, as it must.

For me, Biru was not someone who would be my first choice as a mate, but he was a good man. Certainly I could do much worse. And as I thought more about my situation that morning, I decided that I was very lucky to have him. By the time he came back at midday, I was filled with wonderful feelings toward him, and I hugged him warmly. His responsiveness showed that he had no reservations about what had taken place.

That night and for the next several we again slept together, making love numerous times. My appetite had been whetted, and I was enjoying our new attraction immensely. Only after several days did I have thoughts about where this would lead. I knew that my safe time would be over soon and that to trust to chance after ovulation would be asking for it. I didn't want to get pregnant. Could I refrain? Probably, if he would cooperate. Would he? I didn't know. Although it would be difficult, I decided to talk to Biru about it.

Our conversation, while walking on the beach at sunset, was like two people talking past each other. The differences in culture and time were never more apparent to me. Biru acted like not having sex was like not drinking when thirsty. Once a couple had begun it, then it always was. Only during menses was it taboo. I almost came to believe he did not understand that his seed made a baby. I think he really did understand this but refused to comprehend that it could or should be prevented. The concept of prevention did not exist for the Chumash. That night the beauty of our lovemaking was haunted by the beginning of my worry.

I learned that Biru would be leaving on another voyage in ten days, but that was not soon enough to avoid some days of my most fertile time. My solution was to get sick—not really, but for Biru. It was a time-honored lie only slightly more sophisticated than the headache. Biru accepted it and did not force himself on me. The one exception was the night before he left when I was my own worst enemy. I had told him I was better that day. I must have unconsciously wanted to make love before he left. Our lovemaking was wonderful that night—he even enjoyed me from the front—but I paid for it with days of anxiety until my period came again. Chup was with me.

I was in good spirits—keeping myself busy— while Biru was away, but I was eager for his return. Believe it or not, I felt happy in my new role as hut mate to Biru. I looked forward to seeing his trade goods and having a worry-free time of lovemaking. It is amazing how one can adjust to the excitements of the simple life. Gary Snyder was right. I even began wondering what kind of ceremony Biru and I would have if we decided to eat from the same bowl. This after only a month and a half of being together! In my more reflective moments I knew this was crazy. I was not a Chumash and never would be. But what else could there be? I did not want to think about my mother or Crystal or my life at Reed. Such thoughts could only depress me. I did not want to think about possibilities with explorers from Spain or other countries. How could being with them be good for me? The village was now my existence. Better that I was enjoying it for what it was.

Two days after Biru was back, braves in tomols returning from fishing expeditions that day said they had sighted a winged ship. The word spread like wildfire from hut to hut. Soon everyone was standing on the high ground behind the village, peering out at the horizon. Biru and I shielded our eyes from the low sun and looked where others were pointing. We could make out the brown-colored sails of a distant vessel heading toward Santa Rosa Island from the east. The white gods had come again. Everyone buzzed with the news.

Chief Tooklaw immediately called a meeting of all the elders, men and women, and they talked for quite a while. When Biru came back, I asked what had happened. He said they decided not to go to meet the ship today since it would become dark before they could get back.

They would watch where it went and then strike out for it in the morning. Biru clearly was excited, as were all of the villagers. I felt an internal vibration that something momentous was going to happen.

That night I couldn't sleep. Many thoughts crossed my mind. Were they Spanish? Probably, although English, Dutch, and other nationalities had explored the California coast, too. Would they come to our village? If they did, should I see them? They would know I was not an Indian. What would I say if they asked where I had come from? What if they saw my modern possessions—especially Topsiders, watch, and knife? Should I try to hide these things? Should I tell them I was from the future? This would probably not work. They would think I was crazy or engaging in witchcraft or something.

If they were Spanish, would they think me English and therefore the enemy? Would they want to take me with them? To where? Shipboard life would be horrible. There would be rats and vermin. The sailors might have scurvy and other diseases. Old wooden ships frequently sank. On the other hand, it would be interesting to talk to the explorers, even if only to learn what year it was and what historical things were happening. But my intuition told me I would be better off not attracting their attention. Although I had taken Spanish at Reed, my facility with the language was limited.

With all of these thoughts I don't know how I slept, but somehow I managed a few hours before Biru was up. Even though dawn had not yet arrived, the whole village was awake, working to make the tomols ready for the voyage. I helped Biru prepare baskets of nuts and berries. He was not very talkative, but I learned they would go to the large bay on Santa Rosa Island across from our village where the winged ship was believed to have anchored. All of the canoes—about fifteen—were readied except for one, which was under repair. They all left within a minute of each other, bearing the strongest braves and their weapons and a great deal of food to use for trading. The men who stayed and all the women and children waited patiently that day, watching to the west for the return of the braves. Eventually the canoes came, straggling in by two's and three's, late in the afternoon. Chief Tooklaw and Biru's boats were the last to arrive.

The hubbub of conversation in the village that night was amazing. The ship was Spanish and held eighty men. There were two large poles, which I assumed were the masts. The ship carried two canoes on its back. There were many fireholes, which I guessed to be cannon. The sailors were friendly and had traded willingly. Some braves sported trinkets, little toys, and figurines, made mostly of clay, wood, or glass. These were passed around for all to marvel over. But Biru had none of these. He instead presented me with a silver cross similar to Tooklaw's but about one half the size. Biru apparently thought I was sorry the Chief's cross was taken from me and was now pleased to replace it. I was quite taken with his thoughtfulness, even though a cross was not something I would have sought. But Biru was proud to see me wear it. Now I had two pretty symbols of his affection.

Of most interest to me was the report that the Spaniards were looking for other winged ships. Biru didn't know why, however. The other bit of news that excited all of us was that the Spaniards would come to our village during the next day or two in one of their winged canoes. So the entire tribe set about gathering as much food as it could in preparation for trading.

Three days later the Capitán of the Spanish vessel arrived with three sailors in a sloop-rigged boat about twenty feet in length. They anchored it in the estuary close to shore and were landed in the Chief's tomol. The whole village came down to watch, forming a large circle around the bearded visitors. I had decided to go native, wearing only a Chumash skirt and tying my hair on the back of my head like the other women. I wanted to blend in and not attract attention.

The Capitán wore a black hat, white shirt with ruffled sleeves, and tight, faded blue breeches with tarnished brass buttons. From the way he gave orders to the others, there was no mistaking that he was in command. The two sailors who came ashore wore dark blouses and dungarees that ended just below the knee. All of their clothes were soiled and wrinkled from many days at sea. The two sailors on shore had flintlock pistols in their waistbands. The sailor who remained on the boat had a long gun laying across his knees. The Capitán had a sword in a scabbard strapped to his left side. I guessed his age to be about thirty-five. One of the sailors appeared to be about the same age as the Capitán, possibly a few years younger, but the other seemed quite young, in his late teens. The young one carried a canvas bag that contained the trinkets for trading.

The visitors toured the village first, accompanied by Chief Tooklaw and a few of the elders. They stopped and drank from the stream and went up to the high ground and looked out at the horizon. On the way back, the party broke through the crowd quite close to where I was standing next to Biru, and the Capitán stopped and stared at me for about a half a minute. Then he stepped to within a few paces and smiled.

"Buenos días, moza."

I smiled back but said nothing.

"Do you speak English?" he said with a heavy accent.

I was surprised at this and must have betrayed myself in some small way because his eyes got bigger and his lips pressed together firmly.

"Dime," he said, almost shouting. "Eres inglesa?"

"Qué decís?" I stammered.

"Hablas español, muchacha?" he asked.

"No se que decis, Señor," I said, looking away from the smoldering eyes.

I told him I didn't understand, but he didn't believe me.

He shook his head. "No te creo! No mientas, muchacha."

There was another long group of sentences from him as he stepped even closer. I could smell his stale breath. I figured he was asking how I had learned Spanish.

"Qué, Señor?" I said, shaking my head.

Finally he looked around at the two sailors who stood behind him and he started laughing uproariously. He might have said something about Spanish seeds among the Indians. They joined in the mirth. Chief Tooklaw and the other elders now smiled, for up to that point they had shown considerable concern about what was happening. The party now moved on, heading for the large canvas bag that sat on the beach. I realized I was shaking. I looked at Biru, who had been watching me closely the whole time. I thought I saw a smile playing at the corners of his mouth, but otherwise he showed no emotion. I hoped I had not embarrassed him.

After much gesturing with sign language between the Capitán and Chief Tooklaw, the villagers began bringing out baskets of food. The Capitán inspected the contents and seemed pleased. He began pointing at people in the circle. After some apparent confusion, Tooklaw again conferred with the elders. He and another went around the group, talking to various braves and women. The conversation became heated at one point but finally stopped. Chief Tooklaw then took the hand of Umea, a young, barely pubescent girl, and led her to the Capitán, who nodded approvingly. One of the sailors led her back behind them and had her sit down. The crowd murmured at this. Then the chief called out for Meelop. She walked reluctantly through the gathering and bowed in front of Tooklaw. The Capitán nodded. Meelop sat down with Umea behind the sailors. Chief Tooklaw now pointed at the canvas bag, but the Capitán shook his head and held up three fingers. Tooklaw shook his head.

"Tres," the Capitán shouted now, again holding up three fingers. Tooklaw, appearing exasperated, turned to look at the crowd. Then he looked at Biru.

Suddenly I was being pushed forward. I screamed. Biru had his arm around my waist, and half lifting me, walked me down toward Tooklaw and the Capitán. I tried to dig in my feet but couldn't get my weight down. Instead my toes just kicked up sand harmlessly.

"No, Biru," I yelled in Chumash. "Please, no!"

It was to no avail. I tried to twist out of his grasp, but now the sailors had grabbed me. I ended up on the ground at the foot of the Capitán. As I looked up at the Spaniard, I saw him smiling lasciviously and nodding. I looked at Biru, but he would not meet my eyes. Before I could think of what to do, the sailors dragged me around next to Meelop and Umea. I began thrashing, trying to break their grasp, but they sat on me, twisting my arms. A rope was tied around my wrists and around my ankles. I was now prone on the ground, my face pushed into the sand. I felt my legs bend and realized they were hog-tying me. I couldn't move. I heard the crowd talking loudly with excitement as the canvas bag was pulled toward them and opened up. The deal had been made.

"Don't fight, Abbie." It was Meelop. She helped me to lie on my side and brushed the sand out of my nose and mouth. I looked back to see Chief Tooklaw taking trinkets out of the bag and handing them to the villagers, who were jumping around with glee. Other braves were helping the sailors load the food baskets on the boat, which had been brought up to the shore. When that was done, Meelop and Umea were helped into the deckless sloop. The sailors untied my feet and prodded me toward the boat. I climbed in quickly to avoid their hands, which were also groping me. Then, to my surprise, I saw Biru coming to the boat with a small basket. He placed it next to my feet. I could see that it contained some of my belongings, including both necklaces. He then kissed me on the cheek.

"Good trip," he said, saying the Chumash word that the traders commonly used when they set off on their long voyages.

"Why, Biru?" I said. Tears were streaming down my face. "Why?"

"It is better," he replied, turning away quickly.

The Capitán now jumped aboard, and several of the braves pushed the long boat out into deeper water. The sailors made the lines ready and prepared the sails for hoisting. One of them took the helm. Once the boat was heading in the right direction, the Capitán said "'Hora," and the sails went up. The wind filled the rust-stained canvas and quickly we were moving toward the open ocean. As I tried to make myself more comfortable, I felt something in between the toes of my right foot. It looked like a small piece of paper folded several times. The villagers were now waving from the shore and shouting. Meelop and Umea waved back, stoically. I motioned to one of the sailors to untie my hands. The Capitán gave approval.

As soon as I was free, I moved to one side of the boat and surreptitiously extracted the paper from my toes. Observing that the Spaniards were preoccupied with maneuvering the boat around the rocks, I leaned to the side and unfolded the small scrap of parchment. It had dark ink handwriting on it in an old English style.

Fear not. We will have our Southern Dreams.

Wear the Cross for safety. Destroy this.

I wadded the message into a little ball. Glancing around to be sure no one was watching, I dropped it over the rail into the swirling foam. Then, overcome with emotion, I put my face in my hands. It was as if every single cell in my body sighed at once. After all this time, Bitterroot had communicated. I was not totally abandoned.

But who had given me the note? It must have been Biru when he kissed me. Was Biru really Bitterroot, as I had originally thought? Could he have written it? But if he were Bitterroot and knew English, why didn't he just talk to me? No, Biru probably had not written it. But he had brought my belongings, including the cross that I was now instructed to wear. He had obtained the cross the day before. Somehow he had a connection to Bitterroot. What was it? Did it mean that Bitterroot was over at Santa Rosa? My heart fluttered. Had he arrived on the Spanish ship?

"Southern Dreams." Those were the words he had mentioned during his craziness at Venice beach. Oh, no. Was I part of Gordon's idiotic plan to change history, which he had never gotten around to telling me about?

"You conniving son of a bitch," I said softly. How dare he not ask me? Anger welled up. When I see him he's going to take me out of here—no ifs, ands, or buts.

The note said I was not to fear. But if so, why the warning to wear the cross for safety? Was the Capitán somehow a part of this? If so, why had he let his sailors manhandle me? Why even the note? I felt like screaming with the frustration of it all.

I thought that Biru had really become fond of me. We had made love. If he were just a messenger, what did he really feel toward me? Was it all a ruse? A pang of anger swept through me at the same time that tears filled my eyes. I could not sort it out. But no matter what it all meant, the most immediate question remained: Was I moving toward safety or danger?

I felt a hand on my face and looked up. It was Meelop.

"Do not cry, Abbie." She stroked my cheek.

I tried to smile at her and suddenly felt terrible. Tooklaw had traded her like a basket of abalone. Her marriage to him meant nothing.

I looked up and saw the sailors all watching us. I realized from their stares, that they were enjoying our seminudity. Suddenly I felt vulnerable. Would I be safe pretending to be a native? Or would it be wiser to pretend to be European? If there was safety through the cross, then religion would be more believable in a European. But I could not be Spanish because I didn't know the language. I couldn't say I was a colonist on this side of the continent. My best disguise was as an Englishwoman, but would I then be considered an enemy? How honorable were these Spaniards? Could I even pull off some explanation for my presence on Santa Cruz Island?

I examined the contents of the basket. In addition to the necklaces I found my shorts, blouse, comb, compact and handkerchief. Missing were my Topsiders, watch, Swiss Army knife and Sierra cup. I hoped that Biru had kept these things, especially the knife. Perhaps it was vain, but I wanted him to remember me. The knife, at least, would be truly useful to him.

I took a deep breath. I lifted my old faded shorts from the basket and pulled them on under the grass skirt. Then with an equally deliberate motion I donned my blouse, buttoning it as high as it would go. It felt rather confining after all the weeks of being topless. I fastened the silver cross around my neck, leaving it out where it would show. I untied the Chumash skirt and put it in the basket. That quick I had become someone else.

"Capitán!" the oldest sailor exclaimed.

The Capitán, who had been standing a few feet forward, holding onto the rigging as he watched ahead, stared at my transformation. His eyes narrowed with suspicion. He almost lost his balance, recovered, and then cursed loudly in Spanish. He made his way back and sat on a thwart opposite me, scrutinizing the cross and particularly my clothes. Then he reached out and felt the material of my shorts.

"Quién sois vos?" he asked quietly.

"My lord captain," I said slowly in English, "I am a Christian and a Catholic. Please help me." Then I touched myself in the Catholic symbol of the cross. He reflexively crossed himself.

"You are English?" he said, this time in his heavily accented English.

"I will talk to you later about this," I said. "I need proper clothes when we get to your ship." I didn't know if he understood me for he didn't say anything for nearly a minute, just looking a me as if he were trying to comprehend something unbelievable.

"I will give you new clothes," he said finally. "Tell me where these clothes came from."

"I will explain later." I was hoping I could have time to think through my explanation between now and when we arrived at Santa Rosa.

His eyes narrowed and he reached out and took my hand quickly and before I realized what he was doing, he had my index finger folded and pinched in his strong grasp, inflicting increasing pain in my knuckles. I couldn't pull away.

"Tell the truth, Señora. Are you English?" The words were harsh, spoken through clenched teeth.

"Ow! Stop, please. Yes, I am English." I was squirming with the pain. He loosened his grip but still held on.

"How did you get here?"

I didn't know what to say. With my left hand I grabbed the cross around my neck and brought it to my lips.

"Por Dios, Capitán! Por caridad!" I cried.

He quickly dropped my hand and sat back, surprised. He looked around at the sailors and then stood up. He said something quickly in Spanish and I caught the verb "to talk" and "Santa Rosa." Then he made his way forward again.

I was uneasy. I had made him feel guilty about hurting me. I guessed that he wasn't sure how to treat me. I hoped he had not been humiliated, especially in front of his men. I looked at the sailors, two of whom were reclining in the bottom of the boat. I realized that they could see up under my companions' skirts. The youngest sailor grinned at me. I turned my back on them. Meelop and Umea turned also. I looked at Umea and caught a thin smile. A maternal feeling came over me. What was in store for her, I wondered. How could her parents have given her away? I decided I must not worry about her or Meelop now. I had to concentrate on my own dilemma. Soon I would have to give an accounting to the Capitán.

I had told the Capitán that I was English and a Catholic. Was that a contradiction? When had the English Catholic church broken off from the Pope? I couldn't remember the history. Chances were that my English Catholicism might not cut it with these Spaniards, but it certainly was better than being a Protestant or a heathen. And the note had instructed me to wear the cross.

What could I say about how I got here? That was the crux of my immediate problem. If I said I didn't know, they would not believe me, but a story that was vague and inconsistent would certainly cause suspicion. They might force me to tell the truth, which would be completely incredible to them. Spain was notorious for the Inquisition and sadists such as Torquemada, and torturing enemies was common. Those terrible times probably had not taken place in the not-so-distant past. Even Junipero Serra was reputedly a member of the Inquisition, although probably a benign one. I would have to be very careful. I would have to think through a convincing story. My life depended on it.

We were heading into a strong wind and had to tack several times to cross the channel. It took most of the afternoon. While I worried that the Capitán might try again to question me, something happened to distract him for the rest of the trip. A sail was seen on the northeastern horizon. The vessel seemed to be heading our way. Using a hand telescope, the Capitán watched the newcomer much of the time. Every now and then he would say something to the crew who were also very interested in the vessel. From their conversation I gathered that this ship was also Spanish and one that they knew about. As we drew closer together, it was apparent that the ship was heading toward the very harbor where we were going and would arrive there before us. By the time we arrived, there were two sailing ships anchored in the bay about one hundred yards from each other. One was half again as large as the other. The smaller one was closer to shore. The large one had just arrived. We would pass it close by. I could now see sailors getting into a boat, readying to go ashore.

Both ships had huge, boxy sterns that curved up high, just like old ships I had seen in illustrated history books. The sterns of both vessels had windows up high, and the large ship had a couple of gun ports below these. Sails were wrapped up, but not too tidily, on hefty yardarms. Hundreds of ropes draped down and across the large ship. Now I could see barrels and boxes lashed to the deck. There was a row of twelve square openings along the side below the deck rail, apparently for cannon. Men were working about the deck. The colors were vibrant and the air was so clear. The scene was like something out of a Cecille B. DeMille movie. My eyes began to water as I took in such unreality. How in the world could I be here to see this?

Several men now came to the rail of the big ship to watch us. Soon more came, and they started cheering and whistling. The Capitán doffed his hat, and the sailors in our boat waved, yelling things I could not make out. The comments must have been funny, for there was laughter on both sides. As we went by the bow, I saw the vessel's name carved and painted in green on the side—*La Reina de Cádiz*.

We were heading for the small ship, which I guessed must be the Capitán's. I could now make things out on shore. A number of tents and lean-to's were clustered in an area high on a shelf above the beach. Smoke was rising from several campfires that sailors were tending. I could see some men swimming in the low surf while others lay on the sand. Off to my left, perhaps three hundred yards away from the camp and on higher ground, I could make out Indian huts, no doubt a Chumash village. Directly below the village near the mouth of a creek were a number of canoes. Between the two encampments were groupings of Indians and sailors together, probably trading.

The smaller ship was not as finely made as the large one. There were no carvings on the stern cabin cornices. It carried only four cannon ports on a side. Whereas the big ship had three masts, this one had only two, and it rolled more noticeably in the late afternoon surge. It looked to be about sixty five feet in length and because of the shorter length, the demarcations between the raised foredeck, low midship and high rising afterdecks made its lines less graceful. It looked more like a small cargo vessel than a warship.

There didn't seem to be any sailors on it. But after some shouts by our crew, a couple of men came to the side to help tie us up and tend the rope ladder that hung down. It took all our sailors to keep the sloop from crashing into the side of the ship while we went up the ladder, Capitán first, women next.

On deck I heard a bleat and turned to discover a goat in a large wooden crate next to me. There were also chickens in cages. Looking forward I was struck by the size of the bowsprit, which jutted forward about twenty feet. There was a swivel gun mounted on the rail. Lashed to the base of the bowsprit was a massive iron anchor, the flukes fashioned with sharp points that were heavily rusted. From the main deck a door led into the forecastle. Looking aft there were two doors, one to the lower cabin and one to the upper. There was a large tiller and a binnacle in front of it. To my eye, it was older than La Reina. I wondered where and when it had been built.

"Venid, Señora." The Capitán motioned me to follow him.

We went up some stairs and through the door to the upper aft cabin. I looked behind and saw that Meelop and Umea were not following. They were going with the sailors to the forecastle. My heart jumped. I didn't want to be separated from them, but it was too late. The passageway was narrow and dark once the door closed itself by means of some kind of weighted strap. A small side door opened into a cabin with light streaming in from two open portholes. The Capitán motioned me in. There was a narrow bunk with rumpled bedding on one side, a small table and chair centered under the two portholes, and a chest in one corner. Over the table a gimballed lantern swung as we rolled. The ceiling was only two inches over my head, and there was scarcely room for a person to turn around. It gave me a claustrophobic feeling.

The Capitán turned the chair out for me. I sat down and put my basket on the trunk. He sat on the edge of the bunk.

"Now what is your name, my English Señora?" he asked quietly.

"Abigail Spence."

"Abigail Spence," he repeated. "My name is Capitán Bartolomé López de Torres." His eyes were dark and piercing.

"I am pleased to meet you, Capitán López de Torres."

He nodded slowly. "And tell me how old are you, Miss Spence."

I hesitated for a moment. "Capitán, I will be most happy to tell you all about myself at dinner. But now I need to see to my privacy. I would like some cloth and thread to make a dress. I would also like some soap and water to clean up, please. May I use this cabin?"

His mouth tightened for a few seconds before he broke into a smile. "Yes, you may use my cabin. I will have cloth, needle and thread brought to you. And soap and water. We will have dinner in two hours. This you agree?"

"Yes. Thank you very much, Capitán López de Torres." I then crossed myself.

He got up to leave, but I stopped him with one last question.

"Capitán, can you please tell me what year it is?"

"The year? The year? Dios mío, Señora!"

"Yes. I have lost track of the year."

There was amazement in his face. "Señora, estamos en el año del Señor de mil setecientos cuatro."

1704.

"Gracias, Capitán," I said, trying not to show emotion at this revelation. "I look forward to dinner." I smiled. He smiled back and closed the door.

I reclined on the bunk, exhausted. The emotional strain of all that had happened, not to mention the wind and sun on the water all afternoon, had sapped me. So far Bitterroot had not appeared, and the Capitán had not mentioned him. But I shouldn't be impatient. I was pretty sure he was somewhere close by. Things would all work out in due time. Maybe he'd be one of the sailors or one of the tribesmen in the village. I tried to think what 1704 might mean historically. The industrial revolution started in the early 1700s. English literature blossomed. There were wars in Europe. Other than that, nothing came to mind.

I could feel the motion of the boat. I sat up on the bunk. The movement, the closeness of the walls, and the smell—a combination of soiled clothes and mildew—made me feel nauseous. I went to one of the portholes and breathed deeply as I looked out on the harbor. I could hear men shouting. A small boat, out of my range of vision, had come alongside, thumping against the ship's hull.

Suddenly I realized my hand was resting against something strange, and I started. It was a wooden crucifix fastened to the wall. The figure had spikes showing in His hands and feet. The leaves and thorns of the bramble on His head were carved with precision. There was a worn spot on His chest, suggesting a history of touching fingers. I stared at the revered object for a few moments, wondering what Jesus would really think if He knew all of the history that had followed in His name.

The queasy feeling passed, and I could see better in the dimness. On the table a large leather-bound book lay open, and above it sat a feathered quill and corked ink bottle in a well. It was a ship's log. Line upon line of handwritten entries were scrawled next to dates in black ink. I couldn't read the cursive Spanish, but I could tell from the numbers that much of it included bearings, distances, estimated speeds, and so forth. There were small shoreline sketches, too. The last date was 5 Septiembre. I turned up the front part of the book to look at its leather cover. Inscribed in large gold lettering was *"Guadalupe"* and below that

"Acapulco." So this ship was the *Guadalupe* out of Acapulco.

There was a knock at the door. I put the log back as I had found it and wheeled around.

"Sí?" I said.

A young sailor entered cautiously with a bundle in his arms. He was barely over five feet and his clothing was not like that of the sailors on the deck. As I got a good look at him I realized he was a boy of around twelve or thirteen. He had peach fuzz on his face.

"Hola!" I said, cheerfully. "Hablas inglés?" I hoped that my Spanish lessons would start coming back.

He looked at me strangely. "No," he said, dropping his head in embarrassment. Then he thrust the things onto the bunk, mumbling "Con su permiso, Señora" and something else I couldn't understand. He left without making further eye contact.

As I shut the door I discovered a keyhole in it. Looking around I found a small iron key hanging by a leather thong on a small hook on the wall. I tried it in the lock and heard the latch move. The door was locked. Then I turned to the things the cabin boy had left for me.

There was a large piece of roughly woven tan-colored cloth about the size of a tablecloth. It was made of handspun cotton or flax. There were several long pieces of rawhide. I could maybe use these for a belt. In a small sack I found white thread wrapped around a stick, an iron needle stuck in the thread, and a funny looking knife, somewhat like a pitting knife. It was very sharp. Also on the bed were a pair of black high top shoes with leather laces and a pair of black cotton socks. I put a sock on my foot and tried on a shoe. It was slightly large for me, but laced up tight all the way, it was a pretty good fit. Better too loose than too tight.

I wrapped the cloth about me, measured for an A-line skirt, and cut the piece so that it would reach the tops of the shoes. Then I cut little straps and sewed them at short intervals down each side to keep the skirt closed. I sewed on belt loops, and then I put it on. It didn't hang right in a couple of places, but I decided this was the best I could do in the time available. With the remainder of the material I made a shawl. I cut it so that it wrapped around my shoulders, hanging down to just above my elbows. I sewed ties to the front so that I could fasten it just below my neck and over my breasts. I was pleased that the ends draped down my front, past my waist and over the top of the skirt. I tied the leather belt pieces to one side, letting the ends dangle several inches at my hip. I thought of my mother who had taught me how to sew. Not bad, huh Mom?

As I was looking for a mirror there was a knock at the door. Again it was the cabin boy, this time with a large tin bowl of water, a cake of black soap, and a threadbare towel.

"Muchas gracias, muchacho," I said. "Cómo te llamas?"

He looked at me with astonishment. I repeated my question.

"Pablo. Con su permiso, Señora." And he was gone.

After the door was locked again, I stripped down and, using the corner of the towel as a washcloth, did my best to scrub off the salt and sweat. I wished I could wash my blouse and shorts, but that would have to wait until some other time. Then I set about shampooing my hair with the cold water and rather sudsless soap. I dried my hair with the towel and, with the comb from my basket, spent considerable time getting the knots out. My hair was now fairly long, reaching to my shoulders. I pulled it back into a ponytail and tied it with a strip of cloth that I fashioned into a bow. Not knowing how much time had passed, I lay down and napped, awaiting the call to dinner.

A knock at the door woke me up. I had been dreaming about Meelop and Umea in distress and calling me. It seemed so real.

"Señora Spence." It was Capitán Torres calling from the other side of the door.

"Yes, one minute, Capitán."

I hurriedly put on the new outfit. I put the cross on over the shawl as the final touch and unlocked the door. Capitán Torres came in and stared at me for quite a few moments.

"You look very nice," he said finally.

"Thank you Capitán Torres." I had a thought to tell him to call me Abbie, but decided against it. The more formality there was, the better.

We walked aft down the narrow passageway. There were other doors off of it, each similar in shape to the door of the Capitán's quarters. At the end we came to a bigger door with square designs carved in relief. The brass door knob was heavily worn. The Capitán held the door open for me. My first impression of the salon was the light and airy feeling caused by the large square windows in the stern. It was a spacious room, stretching from beam to beam. A globe in a wooden frame stood to one side near a slanted chart table. At the other side of the room was a large dining table with padded chairs. Two men rose to greet me. The one with the officer's uniform was smoking, and the strong aroma of tobacco filled my nostrils. The other man, florid and balding, was a priest in black robe and white collar.

Capitán Torres spoke directly to the men, apparently introducing me, for I heard my name. When he stopped speaking and I felt their stares, I decided to curtsey like a proper Englishwoman. When I met their eyes, they were smiling.

"Señora Spence," the Capitán said, "may I introduce Capitán Tomás Ortega Vazquez and Father Ignacio."

"Buenos días, Capitán Vazquez y Padre Ignacio," I said slowly, trying to keep my accent as proper as I could. "Lo siento, pero no hablo español. Hablan usted inglés?" I hoped they too spoke English.

"No," said Capitán Vazquez, chuckling. Father Ignacio shook his head, a querulous expression on his face.

"They do not speak English," Capitán López de Torres said. "I will translate."

I nodded and smiled at them.

"Por favor, Señora." Capitán Vasquez pulled out a chair from the table next to him and gestured that I should sit down. I looked at Capitán López de Torres who nodded approval. Then I moved across and sat down, careful to smooth my skirt under me. Then all three of the men sat down, positioning their chairs in a small circle in front of me, slightly away from the table. When I discovered that I was fingering the cross nervously I forced myself to take a deep breath and appear calm. Father Ignacio was now looking at the cross, frowning slightly. Then he spoke to Capitán López de Torres who turned to me.

"Señora Spence, Padre Ignacio asks if it's true that you are a Catholic. Were you baptized?"

So here it was, the questioning. It was bad enough to have to answer to one man alone, but I had three interlocutors, one of them a priest, no less. By the deference paid to him, Capitán Vazquez appeared to be senior to López de Torres. Vazquez looked to be in his forties, with dark hair and a moustache. I figured he was the captain of *La Reina de Cádiz* and must have come over in the boat that arrived while I was in the cabin. He was likely the commander of the expedition. I could see from the corner of my eye torn tufts sticking out from the braided epaulet on his shoulder.

Looking across to Father Ignacio I could see sharp eyes but a tired body. His nose was slightly bulbous with tiny red veins showing. Turning my gaze to Capitán López de Torres, I noticed that his eyelid was twitching spasmodically. Suddenly a surge of womanly pride calmed me. Don't be daunted. How could three men from antiquity, no matter how imperious, be a match for a modern, well-educated American woman? And a Reedie, no less. From some remote area of my brain appeared the cigarette slogan, "You've come a long way baby." I had to fight against laughing out loud. The situation was as sublime as it was dangerous.

"Yes, I was baptized as a baby in Dublin, Ireland. That was where I was born. My mother and father were both Catholic."

As Capitán López de Torres translated I could see on their faces the information sink in and new questions arise.

"So you are Irish? Why did say you were English?"

"My real father died from the pox when I was only nine months old. We were living in London at that time. My father was a linen merchant. My mother remarried my new father, an Englishman, Robert Spence. So I took his name."

When that was translated, Capitán Vasquez looked irritated. He spoke at length, looking back and forth between me and Torres. Finally Torres nodded and turned to me.

"Señora Spence, you are in a precarious position. You are in Spanish territory. We demand to know how you arrived on these islands and from where. Please speak slowly."

"Well, I went with my mother and father when I was seven years old across the ocean from England to Virginia. We settled in Jamestown colony. My father worked for the governor tending his lands. When I was eighteen, we decided to resettle in Jamaica. My father had saved some money and heard that land with good crops could be obtained in Jamaica. So we left Jamestown with another family on a ship bound for Port Royale. But just before we arrived, some pirates captured us and took over the ship. During the fight they killed the captain and my father and Mr. Johnson. That was the family who went with us. And they sailed us to some islands where we stayed for a while.

"The pirates fought amongst themselves, one group wanting to stay in the Caribbean Sea and the other group wanting to go around the horn. So the pirate captain Jean LaRue—he was a Frenchman—commandeered the ship we were on and took some of the crew and me and my mother as prisoners. My mother and I had to do the cooking. We sailed through the Magellan Strait and came to the South Sea. My mother got sick and died, and I was the only woman left. We stopped at many islands and came through the hot latitudes. Some of the crew became ill and died. We captured two Spanish ships. When we got here, I decided to hide on the island and not go back on the ship. There was too much sickness and not enough to eat. I decided I would rather die on the island.

"The crew searched for me but couldn't find me. When they left, I lived alone on fish until the Indians found me. They took me in, and I lived with them until Capitán López de Torres came."

Capitán López de Torres now took a long time translating what I had said. At times Vazquez asked him questions. Lopez de Torres answered them but then turned to me again.

"What was the name of the vessel? How large was it? How many men were on it? How many guns?"

"The name of the ship was the Providence out of New York. It was about the same size as this ship. When we started out around Cape Horn there were 22 pirates and ten prisoners. When I left the ship about three months ago now, there were only 20. The captain and about half the crew were French. The rest were English, Dutch, and other nationalities. The navigator was Portuguese. The ship had only four large guns below decks on each side. There were little guns on the bow and stern like on this one."

After this translation, Vazquez asked what islands we had stayed at. I told him I didn't know their names except for the Galápagos. There were a number of others, especially south of here. Then he asked where the Spanish ships had been taken. I told him one way south and one around Panama somewhere. He asked about the Spanish prisoners from these ships, and I said they had been released ashore or in their own ships after the cargo was taken. Vazquez then wanted to know if we had captured any towns. I said no towns were attacked except for a small Indian village some time after we left the Galápagos. It was raided for food. I didn't know the name or where.

Vasquez and López de Torres then talked for a while. Finally López de Torres asked more questions.

"Where was Jean LaRue going next, Señora Spence? You must know that."

"I don't know, Capitán López de Torres. They never discussed their plans with me."

"Did they ever talk about our galleon from the Philippines?"

They both were looking at me keenly. I realized this knowledge must be very important. I knew I must answer fast and convincingly.

"Yes, now that I think about it. I remember Captain LaRue talking about a Spanish galleon. He would mention it whenever the crew was tired and wanted to turn back. But I didn't know any more than that." I hoped to God I had given the right answer.

López de Torres smiled and repeated it to Vazquez who nodded demonstrably and struck the table with his fist. Then they talked for a while. Finally Father Ignacio started talking to López de Torres who again asked me questions.

"Padre Ignacio wants to know if you married an Indian."

"No, I have never married," I replied.

"Didn't you live with one of the Indian braves?"

"I took shelter in the hut of a trader named Biru, to get away from Chief Tooklaw who wanted to marry me against my will. Biru was just a friend."

Capitán López de Torres looked at me dubiously but translated to Father Ignacio who said something else and watched me carefully as Torres translated.

"Have you been pure in heart and body for our Lord?"

I made my face register surprise. "Sí, Capitán. Tell Padre Ignacio I am pure in heart and body. Although captain Jean LaRue was a pirate, he was also a Catholic, and he protected me. And of course my patron, St. Francis, also protected me." Then I crossed myself and brought the silver cross up to my lips.

After the translation and a brief exchange with Father Ignacio, López de Torres asked if I would do confession with the Padre. I said, of course, I would like that, but I could only speak English if that was all right. After the translation, Father Ignacio smiled at me and nodded.

Apparently I had passed the first inspection because López de Torres now rang a small bell, and soon Pablo appeared with a tablecloth and silverware to make the stout, rectangular table ready for the evening meal. On his second trip he arrived with some kind of liquor in a decanter. He poured the amber liquid into small silver snifters engraved with rams' heads on the sides. Although some was offered to me, I declined, thinking abstention better for the image I was trying to portray. Also, I would need a clear head for further conversation.

The sun was setting, and the mellow rays gave an orange tint to the salon, now collecting darker shadows in the corners. On the table, handcrafted silver forks and knives lay next to pewter platters on which were large soup bowls. Small wine goblets were also set. The place settings were attractive with the cream colored linen.

First there was soup, a thick broth with chunks of meat and pieces of some kind of vegetable, perhaps a root obtained from the Chumash. The soup was highly seasoned with a strange tasting spice I couldn't recognize. A main course of barbecued goat was brought out, and it was quite delicious. A loaf of stale bread was also served. A dark red wine was opened and poured. I tried some but found it vinegary. Oh, for a Napa Valley Cabernet or a Willamette Valley Pinot Noir! The men ate with gusto, not taking much time to talk. Their table manners were lacking, reaching for things without asking, dropping food on their laps, chewing with their mouths open. They took numerous helpings of the meat. The dessert, consisting of berries and sweet biscuits, was served by Pablo without removing the main dishes. The biscuits were hard and similar in taste to oatmeal. I had more than my share. Finally the dishes were cleared and a strong, dark tea was brought.

Toward the end of the meal the conversation had picked up among them, and occasionally a question was directed my way. These queries were miscellaneous and varied; for example, the kind of crop my father wanted to have (some kind of nut trees), the kind of fish I ate when I was on my own (mainly abalone and lobster), where Jean LaRue was from (France), where I had learned the little Spanish I knew (from a trader who lived near us in London), and so on. I realized that although these questions seemed casual, they were potential pitfalls for me. If what I said was implausible or incorrect, my credibility and therefore security would be at risk. So I decided to try to change the focus by asking López de Torres a question.

"Capitán, could you please tell me why your ships have sailed up here? Surely you didn't come up just to rescue me."

López de Torres stared at me for a moment, as if my daring to ask a question were an act of impertinence. But then he interpreted and there was serious discussion among the three of them. Then Vazquez shrugged and spoke slowly and with feeling, staring at me the whole time.

"We came up here," Torres interpreted, "to espy and capture any foreign sea dogs that we find. We will have revenge against pirates who capture our ships, attack our towns, torture and kill our people, steal our riches and our food, sail in our seas or set foot on territory rightfully granted by the Pope, belonging to His Majesty, King Philip of Spain. And you, young woman, are going to help us find Jean LaRue so we can hang him. He will not take our galleon or any more Spanish ships. We will give him the bloody party that Francis Drake deserved instead of the knighthood that your treacherous Elizabeth bestowed."

It was obviously a statement I should not reply to. I just looked at him, nodding slightly, wondering what was going to happen next. Vazquez then roared with laughter and the others joined in. They raised their wine cups and toasted, gesturing me to join them. I raised my cup and Vazquez shouted words that I think were "Death to LaRue." When they had downed their cups they stood up. Vazquez said through López de Torres that it was a pleasure to meet me and I was a beautiful woman, even if I was English. He looked forward to seeing me again. Father Ignacio said that later in the evening he would come by for me to take confession. He and Vasquez left together. Capitán López de Torres then took me back to the cabin.

"Señora Spence. You stay here. Do not walk around the deck after dark. It is not safe." With that he started to leave.

"Capitán López de Torres," I called. "I want to see Meelop and Umea now, the two Canaliña girls who came over with us."

He came back into the room and spoke softly but intensely.

"Señora Spence, you cannot see them. You are not to fret about them. They are heathens and of no concern to you."

I couldn't believe my ears. I was so angry I couldn't talk. But before I could gather my thoughts as to what to say, he left, taking the key with him.

What a quandary I was in. My story had been so convincing that they now were going to chase an imaginary pirate. And I was to help them. What a tangled web I had woven. But on this web I was not the spider. I was the fly—a prisoner—although that had not been stated in so many terms. Probably they thought I was glad to be with them, happy to have been rescued from the infidels. I was, at least so far, receiving civilized treatment. Meelop and Umea were probably not so fortunate. The thought of them made me feel like crying. God only knows what they had been going through up in the forward compartment. Somehow I had to find out about them.

And what of Bitterroot? Where was he? There had been no mention of him by the Capitáns or Father Ignacio. So that meant that if Bitterroot were around, he was incognito. But he must know of me here. How else could I have received the note? When would he make contact? Certainly he would not let me be taken away by these Spaniards. But this thought rang hollow in my mind.

I sat on the bunk and tried to think. The sun had set and it was getting dark. There was an oil lamp on the wall, but I had no matches to light it. Was I to sleep here? Why had López de Torres taken the key? Did he not want me to lock the door? Father Ignacio had said he would come by for confession. Was that for real? He wouldn't be able to understand me. What would I confess anyway? That I had yearnings for Biru? I just couldn't stay here at such loose ends. But what could I do? Escape was out of the question. No doubt there were sailors on watch. Should I try to find Meelop and Umea? Going on deck against the Capitán's orders would change things—my prim role could be undercut. Maybe I could feign seasickness. As I worked up my courage to peek out the door, I heard footsteps in the companionway, followed by a knock.

"Con su permiso, Señora."

It was Pablo's voice. I opened the door and found him holding a small flame on a stick.

"Vengo a encender el farol, Señora."

Not looking at me, he deftly moved into the cabin, unfastened the glass chimney, and lit the wick. Friendly yellow light now crept out across the room, the shadow lines swaying ever so slightly with each slight roll of *Guadalupe*.

As he turned to leave, I stepped in front of the door to block his exit. I would make him talk to me.

"Sientate, por favor. Quiero hablarte," I said.

He looked at me, alarmed. I sternly pointed to the chair, and he finally sat down on the edge of it.

"Dónde están las canaliñas, Pablo?" I hoped he would know by the term, canaliñas, I meant Meelop and Umea.

He just sat there looking puzzled.

"Por favor, Pablo, dimelo. Dónde están las Indias."

Now he understood.

"Se han ido a tierra, Señora."

They had gone ashore. But to where?

"A dónde, Pablo?" I asked.

He shrugged. "No lo sé, Señora." Then he stood up, obviously wanting to leave. I shouldn't frighten him any more, I thought.

"Gracias, Pablo."

He caught my eye, and I smiled at him appreciatively. There was a flicker at the corners of his mouth as he passed by me and out the door. The black smoke from his torch, smelling like pitch, lingered in the cabin.

There were two possibilities. Meelop and Umea were either with their kind at the Indian village or at the makeshift camp with the sailors. The thought of them at the mercy of the sailors was abhorrent. But what could I do? The priest. He was my best hope.

After a short time I again heard someone walking slowly and heavily in the companionway. He stopped and softly called my name. I opened the door to find Padre Ignacio.

"Buenas noches, Padre. Entrad os lo ruego."

"Gracias. Como está su merced?"

"Bien, gracias, pero quiero hablar con las Indias, Meelop y Ume—mis amigas." I had decided to ask him about Meelop and Umea immediately.

He moved over and sat in the chair next to the table, rubbing his forehead. He had understood and was thinking how to answer. I sat opposite him on the bunk.

"Comprende, Padre?"

"Sí, mi hija." He looked me in the eye for several moments, a serious expression on his face.

"No es posible." Then he spoke at length in Spanish, most of which I could not grasp, except for occasional words as compassion, Catholic, Indians, correction.

When he had finished I shook my head. "No le entiendo, Padre. Dónde está el Capitán López de Torres? Yo quiero hablar con el Capitán en inglés." By asking for Capitán Torres I felt I perhaps could head off the confession.

"Lo siento, mi hija, pero el Capitán ha ido a tierra. Yo he venido a oir su confesión." The Capitán had gone ashore and I was now to make the confession.

The harsh look on Ignacio's face made me realize he was ordering me and would not be diverted from his mission. Defying Father Ignacio's religious authority was probably not at all wise. So I crossed myself, nodded and lowered my head. He put his hand on my head for a moment and said something about God, then turned himself away so I could not see his face.

"Te escucho, mi hija," he said. He was listening.

A lump rose in my throat. What should I say? Would he even know or care what I said in English? Something inside me said to play it straight. It just might be possible that someone who could understand English was listening.

"I need forgiveness, Father Ignacio, for I may have sinned. I have become close with Meelop and now consider her a friend, just as I would a Christian. I also have great sympathy for the young girl, Umea. I know they are heathens and have no grace from God. But Meelop helped me when I was in the Indian village. She seems so nice, so human to me. I have come to believe she should not be ill treated by anyone. I fear that the sailors are physically abusing her and Umea against their wills. I cannot help thinking this is wrong and contrary to God's wishes. I believe God wants us to love and be kind to all people and creatures. I believe the Indians have rights to be respected, not to be enslaved. These are my heavy worries right now. I want to go to Meelop and Umea and help them. I ask you to help me to help them. Please have God forgive me if this is wrong, Father."

There was a long, silent period.

"Has acabado, mi hija?" he asked. Had I finished?

"Sí, Padre."

He turned around to face me. His countenance was now different. His eyes looked rather sad.

"Sí, San Francisco de Asís es su protector, mi hija." He again put his hand on my head and with the other made the sign of the cross toward me. He prayed softly and quickly, mentioning God and Jesus. Then he stood up and nearly tripped on his robe as he tried to maneuver toward the door.

"Padre Ignacio, quiero volver a tierra," I blurted, hoping he might take me ashore. I then picked up the washbasin and placed it on the floor. I squatted over it backwards to mime going to the bathroom. He at first stared in disbelief, then laughed.

"Por favor, padre, vamos a tierra," I said, hoping the light moment would sway him.

"No," he said firmly. "Su merced se queda aquí."

"Gracias, Padre Ignacio," I said as he left me.

Within a few minutes Pablo was knocking on the door. He had two things—a short wooden stool with a large hole in the seat and a bucket half filled with seawater. He set the bucket, which had a long rope attached to the handle, on the floor and placed the stool over it. Only then did I realize what it was, and I burst out laughing. I guess I sounded almost hysterical. It was like some kind of pent-up emotional release. Maybe the absurd practicality of this in my bizarre situation struck me deeply. I just howled. Pablo started laughing, at first a somewhat embarrassed chuckle, then a full-blown belly laugh. We must have laughed together for several minutes when the door opened, and an older sailor looked in to see what was going on. Pablo regained his composure quickly and hastily left with the scowling man.

"Muchas gracias, Pablo," I called after him.

After the door was closed I lounged back on the bunk. I felt a great deal better. Maybe it was the laugh. Maybe it was the confession. Or maybe it was just getting through the events of the day with body and soul intact. As I relaxed, I realized I could easily fall asleep. I forced myself up and inspected my new contraption. It was filthy. There were hairs and stains on it. My mother definitely wouldn't approve. So, using the remaining wash basin water, I scrubbed the seat and frame all over with soapy suds, getting off the goo and smell. No squeamishness was allowed, but at the end I struggled against nausea. No sooner was I done than I felt the heavy call of nature. My long dress worked perfectly. If anyone would have come in at that moment, they would have thought I was just sitting normally on a stool, my dress down all around, hiding the real business going on. Afterward, I stretched out on the bunk, leaving the lamp lit. The now gentler motion of the ship and the cool wafts of breeze through the portholes conspired to knock me out. Let the dragons of night come. I couldn't care.

I slept soundly for several hours. What woke me was a solid bang, something hitting the ship. I jumped up and went to a porthole. I could hear men's voices. A boat was alongside and they were coming on board, but I couldn't see them. I couldn't understand the Spanish, but one voice, giving orders, was that of Capitán López de Torres. There was exaggerated laughter. They probably had been drinking. I could feel the vibrations of feet on the deck. Soon I heard footsteps in the companionway. They stopped outside the door. Then I heard a key turn in the lock. I stood up looking for any object to grasp for defense and found a spyglass in the drawer of the table. But nobody came in. Footsteps went further aft and I heard a door open. Then there was silence except for the usual creaking of the timbers and the lap of water against the hull.

I went to the door and turned the handle slowly. López de Torres had locked it. Why? To keep others from disturbing me? In concern for my safety? Or to keep me locked in so that I couldn't try to escape in the wee hours? I decided to think positively about it. I lay down again and did not wake until daylight crept in.

With the light prying at my eyes, I stirred, not wanting to let go of the dream. I was with Bitterroot at the restaurant in Hollywood where we went after the meetings. I had said something about the 1600s giving way to England's golden era of Empire. "Yes," he said, "the golden era—oh for the days of Empire again. If only I could be there to expand the glory of Britannia, if I could turn the tide on one close sea battle or plant the flag on one little island." I was now laughing at him. Silly chauvinistic dreams. "But Abbie, I will have my Southern Dreams. Our Southern Dreams." His smile grew wider and wider and wider like the Chesire cat's. And I woke up.

Immediately I started scratching my side and my leg. Oh, no. Bed bugs. I hadn't even slept under the covers. I stood and shed my clothes. Large red bites, in a line over my rib cage and on the back of my leg. My scalp itched, too. I had probably picked up lice as well. But how could you get rid of them without Quell? I turned my clothes inside out and brushed and shook them. The bedding needed cleaning and the cabin needed Lysol. I put my clothes back on and started pulling off the bedding. I wouldn't sleep another night on those dirty covers. I checked the door, but it was still locked. I needed to get out into the fresh air.

I went over to a porthole. The ship was lying in a direction allowing me to see the sailor's camp. There were several men up and tending morning fires, probably making breakfast. The thought made me aware that my stomach was empty. Off to the side of the camp I could see some bare-chested people sitting next to a log. One was lying down. I got the telescope from the drawer and pulled it out to full scope. The magnification was excellent, but it was hard to keep the glass steady. I could see eight Chumash women. They were chained by their legs to the log. One of them was Meelop. She had her head on her arm, lying against the log. I could easily see that she was unhappy. I looked at several other faces, all of them young. One was in obvious pain, grimacing. The one on the ground was nude. Her eyes were closed. It was Umea.

A rage came over me. I ran to the door and started yelling and pounding on it with my fists. I screamed for someone to open it. Soon there were footsteps in the hallway. I heard the key turn in the lock. The door opened and López de Torres stood there in a nightshirt, sleep still in his eyes.

"Qué pase? Qué pase?" he yelled. He looked all around inside the cabin, then at me.

I grabbed his hand and led him to the porthole.

"Look, Capitán, the Indian women are chained up over at the camp. Why? What have your men done to them? They are in pain. Meelop and Umea are over there. We must help them."

He looked out for a few moments and then back at me. His alarmed expression slowly turned into a fierce frown.

"The Indians are all right. They have not been harmed."

"Why are they chained up?" My voice was still high pitched.

"They were chained so that they would not walk away and fall off the cliff in the night. It was for their safety. Do not worry about them, Señora Spence." He said this with barely controlled anger.

"Will they be released to go back to their villages?" I asked more calmly.

"They will be released when we decide to release them. And you are to be quiet about this matter, or I'll have you chained up too." He glared at me so intensely that I had to look away.

"Capitán López de Torres," I said, finally meeting his look again, "I need to walk around outside. I need to wash my clothes and air out this bedding. Will you please arrange a boat to take me ashore?"

His gaze now fell to my breasts and then to my hips.

"Did you make a confession with Father Ignacio last night?"

"Yes."

He nodded and smiled. "Good. Well, Pablo will bring you some breakfast. Later I will take you ashore. Now please be calm until I come."

"Yes, thank you, Capitán. One more thing. I would like some trousers to wear. Can Pablo get me some?"

"Sí. Maybe it will be more fitting for you, Englishwoman. Good day."

14

The breakfast brought by Pablo consisted of two hard boiled eggs, thick bread with orange marmalade, and fresh, strong coffee. It was filling and quite good. As I ate I could feel vibrations from activity on the deck. Large things were being moved about and pulleys drawn until they squeaked. Pablo took away the bucket. When he brought it back with new seawater he also handed me two clean pairs of blue denim pants. Then he opened the trunk and pulled out a high button shirt of white silk with roomy raglan sleeves.

"Para su merced, de parte del Capitán López de Torres," he said. So this had come from the Capitán.

He opened the built-in drawers, put all of the Capitán's clothes into the trunk and towed it out and down the hallway. On his last trip he took away the dishes, the logbook, and the spyglass. With that, the cabin was all mine.

I tried on my new outfit. The pants were tight around my hips and loose around the waist. I would need a belt. The rawhide straps from my dress worked serviceably, even though the waist was bunched. The pant length was fine. The shirt was long and baggy under my arms, but it felt smooth on my skin. I turned up the cuffs. I would need to sew on another button to keep it closed. For the time being I tacked it with a piece of thread. Did men wear such fancy silk in this day and age? Probably for nice occasions. The Capitán could have given me an ordinary denim shirt. He obviously intended this as a nice gesture.

Before long Pablo was again at the door. This time he handed me a cloth bag.

"Para su ropa, Señora."

It was a clothes bag. I nodded and put my dirty things in it along with the soap and towel. Pablo grabbed up all the bedding and tied it with a cord and motioned me out the door.

When we stepped out into the sunlight, the ship seemed under siege. Sailors were everywhere at work. Somebody was shouting orders. A large sail was draped across the rail and an old man sewed on patches. Ropes hung here and there while men pulled on them. A yardarm was being hoisted onto the after mast. Several men were aloft. Gradually the activity halted as they saw Pablo and me move down the ladder to the main deck. It was suddenly quiet. I felt as if I were on stage. Some of the men were quizzical, some smiling. Most of the faces were covered with dark beards. All of them stared at me.

"Buenos días, Señores," I said loudly.

That nearly brought down the rigging. They shouted greetings and exclamations, some of them whistling, and they talked and laughed among themselves.

"Silencio!" The shout came from the bow. It was Capitán López de Torres. He bellowed something else and soon all the sailors were at work again. Quickly the Capitán came down from the forecastle deck to meet us.

"Good morning, Señora Spence. I must ask you not to talk to the men again. Understand?" It was an order.

"Yes, Capitán, I understand. And good morning to you. I want to thank you for these clothes. This shirt is beautiful."

He smiled. "I'm sorry we don't have your size. But you look very good. Are you ready to go ashore?"

"Yes. It's so nice to be out in the air. I thank you, Capitán." He smiled broadly, obviously pleased by my appreciation.

We climbed down into the ship's boat. Pablo went down first and settled in the bow, the bedding beside him. I sat in the middle behind two sailors who manned the oars. López de Torres sat in the stern. Soon we were off, not heading directly to shore, but toward the windward point. I looked at the Capitán and, as if anticipating my concern, he leaned forward to explain.

"There is a fresh water creek just this side of that point. It will be good for washing."

Looking toward the sailors' camp, now behind us, I was surprised to see that most of the tents were down. Men were dismantling the remaining ones and packing up. I looked hard at the log but could see nobody around it.

"Capitán, why are they breaking camp?"

"We are leaving with the afternoon wind. We are going to find Jean LaRue." He grinned broadly at that, his crooked teeth white in the sunlight.

"But where are the Indians?"

"We let them go, Señora Spence. I told you that no harm would come to them, no?" With that he winked.

I felt a sudden ambivalence. I hoped it was true that Meelop and Umea were free and safe, but now I was worried about me. Obviously López de Torres planned to take me on the *Guadalupe*. If we were leaving this afternoon, I might not see any of my friends again. The Capitán's remark was unctuous. Undoubtedly he knew what had taken place with the women captives. He probably had been a part of it, if not the instigator. After all, it was he who traded to get the women.

"I am glad you released my Indian friends, Capitán. They are nice people."

To this he shrugged, "They are heathens, Señora Spence."

As we approached the shore I saw a narrow cove that had not been discernible from farther off. We rowed into it and into the mouth of the creek that flowed into the cove. Except for a small sandy place where we could beach the boat, the shoreline was rocky. The stream bed led up into a narrow canyon. The cove was choppy, and all of us got wet as we disembarked. Once the boat was hauled up into the rocks the Capitán told the sailors and Pablo to wait with the boat. Pablo started beating the bedding on the rocks.

"There are some pools for washing up in the canyon," López de Torres said to me, pointing up the rocky slope. "Follow me."

"Capitán, I want to go alone."

He turned and faced me with raised eyebrows. "No. Women cannot be alone. I will go with you."

"Why can't women be alone?"

His face flushed red. "It is not done, Señora. Certainly you know that!"

"But Capitán—I want to take a bath."

"All the more reason for me to stand guard, Señora. I will not look."

This time I blushed. What could I say? I was dealing with values and a code that I couldn't argue against. Women's liberation was two and a half centuries away.

"Or would you rather go back to the ship?" He said this in a sneering tone.

I almost agreed just to spite him, but I couldn't bear not having the time ashore.

"Very well, Capitán, I will follow you."

After picking our way about a quarter mile up into the treeless canyon and well out of sight of the ocean, we stopped at a deep pool of clear water headed by a small waterfall. Moss clung to the orangish rock walls that were adorned by ferns around the edges of the pool. It was a small oasis amid the rockiness. With Capitán Torres sitting behind me on a rock, I slowly washed my clothes. Only the sounds of the falling water and occasional chirps of birds could be heard. I felt myself relax, as if the contact with the water grounded the electrical tension of my body, draining away the bad vibrations of the past few days. I let myself get lost in a kind of reverie of hand motions. When I had finished I laid out the clothes on sunny rocks. All during this time Capitán López de Torres had not made a sound. But now he cleared his throat.

"Señora Spence, I know you are not whom you say you are."

The anxiety all jumped back into me.

"Why do you say that? I am me. What gives you the idea I am not me?"

He smiled. "No woman who has been with pirates is pure. No woman who travels with pirates is honest. There is something about you that is strange. The way you act with men is improper. The Spanish you speak is like none I have ever heard. Even the English you speak is not like what the English speak. Your story is not believable. I think you made it up."

"It is the truth, Capitán. If I am strange, it is because I was with the pirates too long. One cannot be normal with them."

He shook his head slowly. "We could make you tell the truth, Señora. You know that."

"Capitán, I suffered so much with the pirates. I am now grateful to be with civilized people who treat others honorably."

He chuckled. "You are very smart, Señora Spence. I don't want to see you harmed. No, I will protect you because I like you. But in return, I want you to like me." His eyes burrowed into me. "You like me, don't you?"

"I like you, Capitán López de Torres, because you are an honorable man. I know you are not like the pirates."

He stood up, looking down at me. I remained seated, looking at his boots. Suddenly he squatted down to eye level and took my hand in his.

"Señora, you are pretty. I will protect you on the ship. I will see that you have good food and nice things to wear. I will see that you have a pleasant voyage." Now his hand moved up my arm in a caress. For a moment I was entranced with its movement.

"Your eyes are like jewels, shining in the sun. I would love to care for a lady like you." The voice was soft and deep. Now his hand touched my cheek and moved slowly down my neck.

I stood up. "Capitán López de Torres, thank you for these compliments." I did my best to smile at him. "This is not a good time to talk. I need to have a bath. You must understand that I feel very dirty. Will you please give me privacy now?"

He stood up, watching me carefully, looking for the meaning of my body language, the sound of my voice. I felt like a rabbit in front of a cobra.

"Yes, I can understand this is not the time, Señora Spence. I will stand away to protect you. Please go ahead and take your bath." He smiled broadly, then moved over the rocks down the canyon slightly and out of sight. I took a deep breath. Somehow he had misread me, I knew. He must have thought that only the timing was wrong. I gritted my teeth. I would have to set him straight later.

I waited a few minutes and looked to make sure he wasn't watching. Then I took off my outer clothes and waded into the water in some men's shorts that Pablo had provided me for an undergarment. The water was cold but delicious. I took off the shorts and washed them with the soap and rung them out. Then I sat on an underwater rock and soaped all over, finally slipping in to scrub and rinse. Next I washed my hair, even though the soap left it stringy. Then I wallowed for a while. When I was ready to get out I noticed a slight movement above the waterfall. It was López de Torres. He was watching me from behind a rock. I should have suspected so. Should I call him to account or ignore him? I decided the latter course would be less risky. I would pretend I didn't know. I toweled off and dressed quickly with my back to Torres.

"Are you ready, Señora Spence?" he called from above.

He knew that I was, but I would surprise him.

"Not yet, Capitán. Un momento, por favor."

Gathering my things and stuffing them in the bag, I now started down the canyon as fast as I could walk over the rough terrain.

"Señora, Señora." Torres was on his way down too, about fifty yards behind me. "Wait, Señora."

I kept moving fast, jumping from rock to rock, careful not to lose my step. He was gaining on me little by little, but in a few minutes I would be over the ridge and in view of the sailors.

"Señora Spence, please stop."

I couldn't help laughing. His voice had such a bewildered quality. I reached the cut where the canyon emptied out on the side of the slope.

"Ahhh." His cry was urgent. I looked back but could not see him.

"Capitán?" I shouted.

"Help, I am hurt Señora. Please help me."

The cry had seemed real, but could have been a ruse. I decided to keep going.

"Wait, I will get help for you."

"No, please, you come."

I headed down the slope. When I reached Pablo and the sailors, they looked at me curiously, peering up the canyon for the Capitán. I was able to convey that he needed help, and they all hurried up to the cut. Then I realized that I was alone. I could go off. The boat was too heavy to drag to the water single handed. The only other routes were to pick my way along the shore, either around the point or back toward the sailors' camp. Either way would be slow going, and I would be visible to the ships. Somebody in a dinghy could easily catch up. The idea was exciting but pointless. They might treat me badly after an attempted escape. I sat down on the boat and waited for my macho Capitán to be brought down by his men.

He came down under his own power, limping slightly. He glared at me.

"Are you hurt badly, Capitán? I got the men as quickly as I could. I was very worried."

"It is only a small injury to my ankle. It will heal fast."

He ordered the men to launch the boat and soon we were back next to the *Guadalupe*. When the Capitán climbed the rope ladder I did not notice his favoring a foot. On the deck he walked normally.

Pablo escorted me to my cabin and put the aired-out bedding on the bunk. Later he brought me lunch of cold chicken, bread, and pickled cabbage slices. I decided to nap for a while but was disturbed by Pablo once again.

"Es la hora de la Santa Misa, Señora. Venga su merced."

It was time for mass. I accompanied Pablo to the main deck and saw all of the men sitting in rows. In front were Capitáns Vazquez and López de Torres and the first and second mates from the *Guadalupe*. Standing in front with his black robe, facing the gathering, was Father Ignacio, a bible in his hand. I was instructed to sit to the side with Pablo and a handkerchief was provided to cover my head.

The mass lasted about thirty minutes. Much of it was in Latin, but I also heard Spanish from time to time. I understood very little. One of the prayers seemed to be about the impending voyage, and I also heard the term "piratas." I was impressed that the men could sit so solemnly. It was clear that these men believed in their Christian God wholeheartedly. I tried to do as they did, mouthing words during the prayers, kneeling forward, and crossing myself at the appropriate times.

When it was over Father Ignacio asked how I was and if I were looking forward to the voyage ahead. I said I was, but that I would not like to be locked in my cabin. I wanted freedom to come on deck to see things. I wasn't sure he understood, but he nodded. I wondered if I dare ask to be transferred to *La Reina de Cádiz* with him. Increasingly I found myself trusting the old Padre. And the situation with Capitán Torres was bad. Would he would tell of his suspicions about me to Capitán Vazquez and Father Ignacio? Probably, if I gave him reason.

Now López de Torres and Vazquez joined us.

"Señora Spence," López de Torres said in a most friendly tone, "Capitán Vazquez would like you to join us for some coffee before we get under sail, if you please." Capitán Vazquez nodded and smiled at me.

"Yes, of course. May I just freshen up in my cabin first?"

Pablo escorted me to the stairway, amidst several of the sailors who were making ready for hoisting sails. One particularly handsome man with a long moustache smiled and winked as I went by. I held my natural urge to smile back. As I was about to enter the second level companionway I glanced at the men around the large sweep tiller on the afterdeck. A short man with dark hair but no beard, was staring at me. He looked to be in his early thirties. He had powerful shoulders, rough hands, and pale blue eyes. My heart jumped. He closely resembled Bitterroot. I wanted to say something to him—he was only ten feet away—but I was inexplicably tongue-tied. Pablo was holding the door for me to go in.

"Pablo," I said, pointing to the short sailor, "cómo se llama aquel caballero?"

He looked at the man who now turned away and began coiling a line on the deck.

"Se llama Abirrute, Señora."

Abirrute! With a roll of the r's. So here he was again. Bitterroot had somehow cloned another version of himself—this time Spanish.

When my cabin door closed I slammed my hand against the crucifix. His countenance did not change. Why hadn't Abirrute contacted me? Was he just another quiet Biru? Could he get a message to Bitterroot? Maybe he hadn't talked to me because there was no opportunity. But with the ship heading to sea now, there would be less chance to find a moment of privacy.

The purpose of the meeting with Capitán Vazquez was to find out if I could tell them anything about Jean LaRue that would give clues as to his whereabouts. They were especially eager to know about the pirate's armaments and tactics. They clearly wanted to be ready for battle. In response to their questions I mostly said "I don't know" or "I didn't pay attention to that."

I learned through the discussion that they believed LaRue was laying for the Manila galleon. Apparently the yearly treasure ship's route was east from the Philippines to the California coast at the latitude of San Francisco until the land signs—the señas, as they called them—were seen. Thereupon the vessel turned south and followed the coastline to Acapulco. The galleon—sometimes there were two each year—usually sailed between these islands and the mainland. Therefore it was logical for a pirate to lie in wait here to intercept this huge, lumbering ship. The biggest problem was timing. The galleon didn't leave until around July and could take six to eight months or longer for the passage, depending on the weather. But Capitán Vazquez thought the galleon might pass through here around mid-November. So LaRue being up here at this time was not coincidental.

I also learned why my existence was so alarming to them and why I had to be taken seriously no matter how incredible my account. English privateers had gone after the Manila galleon before. Sir Francis Drake had sought it in 1578, and Cavendish successfully captured it a few years later. Another attempt had been made by an Englishman named Marborough in 1670. The attacks had usually taken place off the tip of Baja California, a prominent landmark for the galleon to round before heading into Acapulco. But for pirates to be hunting their prey so much farther north and out of the Spanish zone of protection was major intelligence that had to be verified and reported to the Viceroy of New Spain.

When they figured I had no other information to impart, the discussion turned to where I should be located during the trip. The question originated with Father Ignacio and apparently surprised López de Torres, who hesitated in his translation.

"Señora Spence, Father Ignacio asks if you are comfortable on my ship. You are comfortable and happy, no?"

Ignacio and Vazquez were watching me closely.

"Do they want me to go on *La Reina*?" I asked, stalling to sort out what I should say.

"Yes, you could go on that ship if you want. But on mine you will be well treated and we can speak English to each other."

I thought of Abirrute. Was he worth my staying on the *Guadalupe* and putting up with López de Torres?

"Yes, Capitán López de Torres, I would rather stay here, but under two conditions."

"What are those?"

"That I can go on deck whenever I want and also that I can change to *La Reina* later on."

He beamed and translated. Capitán Vazquez said something in reply, mentioning Pablo.

"Yes, you will be given permission to go on the afterdeck whenever you want, but always in the company of Pablo."

"Can I move to *La Reina* later?"

"Oh sí. It will be a long voyage, and there will be opportunities for you to change later."

Before we broke up, Father Ignacio said a prayer and we all crossed ourselves. Capitán Vazquez said, "Viva el Rey."

Once I settled in my cabin again, I puzzled over the sailor, Abirrute. Was he related to Bitterroot? When I had asked Biru about his father, he had said he didn't know him, and he wouldn't discuss it further. Here was another Bitterroot look-alike. I wondered if there would be any opportunity for contact with Abirrute when I was up on deck. López de Torres would undoubtedly tell Pablo not to let me converse with any of the men.

These Spaniards were different from what I had expected. The strength of their commitment to Catholicism was especially surprising. No doubt such faith was a major part of their dynamism as a people. I recalled that historian Eric Vogelin said the history of western civilization owed itself to two basic developments—the Hellenic philosophy of self awareness, and conversion of the Israelites to a God who could not be seen. This Judaic idea of an outer Cosmos inseminated the development of Christianity, which in turn brought a revolution of thought—a "de-divinized" daily world and a new spiritual world. With powerful new symbols and social-ordering myths, Christian societies were energized to take over the merely existing civilizations. For Vogelin, the essence of history was the revelation of God's way with man. I didn't appreciate Vogelin's theory much when we had discussed it in one of my history classes. But when I saw Spanish Catholicism firsthand it seemed to make sense. Spanish society was a world unto itself, carrying powerful symbols and concepts to interpret existence and social reality, and thereby to know the truth of things. These New World explorers and conquerors clearly felt they had just such truth.

The two ships were towed out of the anchorage and the sails were broken out. Slowly *Guadalupe* made way to the north as each sail billowed and then was trimmed to the westerly wind. *La Reina de Cádiz* was several boatlengths in front, the high stern rolling. She was like a giant shoe, skipping along gracefully to the dance of the waves.

Capitán Torres arranged some canvas and pillows for me to sit on while on the afterdeck. In the back corner at the foot of the railing, I was at one of the highest places on the ship and could see everything well. Pablo sat a few feet away, probably happy not to have to do work but perhaps chagrined that he had to stay with me. Any of the other men would have given a month's wages to trade places with him, but Pablo was too young to appreciate the situation.

Usually there was only one sailor on the afterdeck, the man who worked the large tiller. In rough weather, however, others helped him. Every so often the Capitán, first mate, or second mate—whoever was on duty—would come up to look at the compass to make sure the coxswain was steering the right course. They also used their glass to scrutinize the horizon or, with a handheld device, took bearings on a landmark. The watches changed every four hours with the sound of bells. They knew to change the watch when all of the sand ran out of a four-hour glass.

The intended direction was westerly, but because the ships could not point very close to the wind, we would have to tack a great deal to make a westerly course. From the top of the mast, the lookout could see as much as twenty miles in daylight, but at night often the only warning was the sound of the waves against the shore, which too frequently meant disaster in such hard-to-maneuver ships. So the ships would head away from land at night.

I soon found out that even in rough weather, I was better off on deck. In my cabin or anywhere below decks, I quickly became seasick unless I was lying down. This made dinner a problem. It was served in the salon to me and the two officers not on deck. I would go there with an appetite, but by the time the food was put before me, I was no longer hungry. Fortunately, breakfast and lunch could be taken on deck. Sometimes this meant that I was on deck while Pablo was still below, which the Capitán did not like. But after a while, nobody seemed to care very much about this. The men behaved well toward me, and my intuition told me they were trying to show the inglesa Señora how professional they were. Spanish pride was at work. I also noticed how well they responded to the Capitán. Contrary to what I would have thought, they seemed to like him a great deal.

One afternoon while I was on my pillows on the afterdeck and Pablo was below getting our lunch, the watched changed. To my surprise Abirrute took his station at the large tiller. He immediately moved far back on the tiller toward me, but kept his gaze ahead.

"Señora Spence. Please listen, but do look at me." Although there was a Spanish accent, he spoke English. The inflection was similar to Bitterroot's.

"Are you Gordon?"

"Keep your voice low, and do not look at me. I am not Gordon. I am in his service."

"In his service? What do you mean? Where is Gordon?"

"Shhhh. He cannot come on the ship. It is too dangerous."

"Can't he come at night?"

"There are lookouts. He is an English enemy, and the Spaniards might kill him."

"Well, can you take me out of here?"

"No. Only Gordon can do that. He will see you when there is an opportunity. He wants you to stay alert, but to try to relax. Enjoy the scenery."

"Relax? Relax? He has to be kidding!"

"Shhhh. Gordon will talk to you later about the Southern Dreams plan."

"This is crazy, Señor Abirrute. I don't even know what that plan is. I don't want to stay any longer. Not one day. Do you understand?"

"You will be an important personage in the plan."

"What plan? What plan?"

"Shhhh Señora. The plan is to bring a large expedition of English man-o'-wars and settlers to the South Sea. Gordon will explain it. No more talking now. Pablo's coming."

Pablo came on the afterdeck with bread and stew and sat next to me. I tried to eat some, but my stomach was in knots. Abirrute's bizarre conversation kept echoing in my mind. There were so many things I wanted to ask. But, thank God! At least Bitterroot was aware of my situation, bastard that he was. Southern Dreams. What craziness!

With night having fallen, the wind was strengthening and the seas were up, making *Guadalupe* pound up and down. From inside my cabin, the ship was very noisy as all manner of things banged and creaked and groaned. I was sleeping fitfully, thinking about Abirrute and Bitterroot's idiotic plan. Around midnight something startled me. I bolted up in the darkness to realize a man was sitting on the edge of the bunk. He spoke just in time to head off my scream.

"Do not be alarmed, Señora Spence. It is me."

"My God, Capitán López de Torres! You scared me."

"I am sorry. I wanted to see that you are satisfactory. It is very rough tonight."

"Oh. Well, I am fine. Thank you for checking, though."

Through the covers I felt his hand rub along the top of my leg.

"Are you staying warm, Señora?"

"Yes, I'm quite warm, thank you." I doubled my legs under me to escape his touch.

Now he moved over and sat right next to me. I tried to scoot back, but I was against the wall; my legs were pinned down by the covers. His hand found mine and squeezed it.

"Señora," he said softly, his face very close, "please let me taste your lips."

His arms went around me and pulled me toward him. I turned my head away. He began kissing the back of my neck.

"Please, Capitán, I am not feeling well."

He continued and his hands now moved to my front. I pushed them away sharply and got up on my knees.

"Please don't, Capitán. I'm sick. Please leave me alone."

"Señora, it has been such a long time. And you are so beautiful. Relax yourself. I will be gentle."

He slowly but strongly pulled me down against him and his mouth found mine momentarily before I was able to turn away. But his arms went around me, keeping me off balance as he kissed my cheek and neck. Eventually I managed to get my legs under me again. Then I shoved him as hard as I could, and he slipped off the bunk onto the floor.

"Please!" I yelled. "Don't you understand 'no'?"

He stood up slowly, then suddenly hit me open handed on the side of the head. My face stung, and my ear began to ring. His voice was low and tight. "I think you need to understand something...to learn some appreciation. That's what I think."

He left without another word. Then I heard the key turn in the lock. I began shaking. I crawled under the covers. The wind howled and the ship rolled ominously. I would not be sleeping for quite a while.

Some time in the night the weather abated, and I fell asleep. When I awoke again the motion was steadier, and I realized that it was daybreak and we were sailing well. Again I dozed. By midmorning I was hungry, and I dressed. It was odd that Pablo had not knocked. I checked the door. It was still locked. I pounded on it loudly, yelling for Pablo, but no one came. I did my ablutions and then tried yelling some more. But it was to no avail. My worst suspicion took charge. López de Torres was punishing me for last night. How long would it last? I waited.

I could tell by looking at the sun through the porthole that it was afternoon. I saw an island off in the distance, probably San Miguel. The ships had split up the previous morning. Capitán Vazquez had taken *La Reina* down the Santa Barbara coast. *Guadalupe*, more maneuverable, was to search San Miguel and then the south sides of Santa Rosa and Santa Cruz. We were to join up again at the eastern end of Santa Cruz Island in several days. If either ship discovered the pirate vessel they were to engage. Vazquez thought that either of the Spanish vessels could take the enemy in his weakened, undermanned condition. So until the rendezvous, I was stuck on the *Guadalupe* with López de Torres.

By evening my hunger pangs had eased, but my thirst was now very strong. Again I beat on the door. But instead of calling for Pablo, I yelled "help" many times at the top of my lungs. Maybe my distress would be heard by the crew and prove embarrassing to the Capitán. Would they just accept my being locked up? But even if they wanted to help, they would not be able to challenge Torres. The pounding and yelling was tiring. Already I could tell that without food my condition would weaken.

"Gordon. Mother. Daddy. Crystal. Anyone, please help me." I said this softly as tears slowly ran down my face.

I knew they couldn't help me. My father was not going to slip down from the heavens with that blue-eyed wink, the relaxed smile, and a ready comment on how I might solve the problem. How do you change the givens now, Dad? My mother would not have wanted me to shout. She did not like conflict. But how do you social work a guy like López de Torres, Mom? What would Crystal do? She who always had the right moves? She would say I shouldn't have gone sailing with people I didn't know. Great, Crys.

I had gotten into this fix and nobody but me was going to get me out of it. Whatever happened, I suspected it would involve more pain.

16

An hour or two after nightfall I was awakened by the door opening. It was Pablo. He had a candle, a half cup of water, and a piece of biscuit. I took a gulp of the water first and then ate the biscuit quickly. After that I finished the water.

"Pablo, me voy contigo," I said as I stood up to go out with him.

"No, Señora. No es posible. El Capitán López de Torres ha dicho que no." His eyes were sad as he told me I must stay.

"Yo quiero más agua y mas comida, por favor, Pablo." I needed food and drink.

"No hay más, Señora. Lo siento mucho." There is no more. With that he left, not bothering to take the bucket, which needed changing. Again the lock was thrown.

I felt pain in my stomach. I needed more food. I lay down and brought my knees up to my chin to try to lessen the hollowness in my middle. The night seemed to go on forever. I dozed between stomach aches. At one point I awoke from a dream where I was drinking from the slop bucket. In another dream I was having sex with Capitán López de Torres while he put chocolate candy in my mouth.

When the morning light came through the porthole I felt tired but more clear headed than before. I would simply have to get someone to help me. This barbaric treatment must stop. Abirrute. Should I call his name? Why not, it was an emergency. It might force Bitterroot's hand. I started pounding on the door, yelling, "Help, Pablo, Abirrute, anyone." I did this for about five minutes. During the periods of listening, I heard sounds but no one came to assist me. I shouted out the portholes. No one seemed to care. I lay down again, demoralized. What could the Capitán have said about me that would keep normal people from coming to my aid?

After some time of dozing, I heard considerable activity along side the ship. I went to the portholes. I could see that *Guadalupe* stood off the sandy, half-moon harbor of an island, probably San Miguel. Two of the ship's boats were heading for shore. There were several wooden casks in each. They were going for water. The bright sun glinted off the azure bay and highlighted the low-lying greenery with orange and pink splotches of wildflowers waving against the rock-brown cliffs. As the strong scent of seaweed came through on the breeze I found myself tearing. I should be going ashore on one of those boats. If I were on good terms with Capitán López de Torres, no doubt I would be.

Why had I resisted him? I was no virgin. I was not saving myself for anyone. Womankind down through the ages had learned to accommodate. Wasn't that our evolutionary script? Wasn't that our strength as a sex? Why fight it? It was 1704, so who would know anyway? Not even my dad was around to care.

I began sobbing. My dad was such a kind and principled man. Although he did not show his affection much, I knew he loved me. Guiding me in my homework all those years so that I really learned something rather than just the answers. I narrowly missed being high school valedictorian and felt I had failed him. But he had said how proud he was at my achievement. All the outings as a family. The friendly advice in different ways—respecting people, appreciating ideas, knowing and accepting yourself, standing up for your beliefs. The major shock in my growing up and learning about men was that very few were like my father. Far more were like Bartolomé López de Torres than were like Robert Spence.

By midday I was ravenous. My mouth was dry, and I began thinking seriously of wetting it from the slop bucket as long as I did not swallow it down. The idea was repulsive, considering what all was in the bucket, but I was past the stage of worrying about niceties. I got my determination up and moved over to lift the top pan. The door opened. It was López de Torres. He was wearing his Capitán's hat and carrying a tray of food and beverage.

I was speechless. I could only look at the several pieces of cooked chicken nestling on the plate next to pickled cabbage. A bottle of ale and two glasses were also on the tray. My saliva returned and my stomach wrenched as the aroma filled my nostrils. I could have leapt like a cat to get the chicken. He looked at me warily and put the tray on the desk and stood between it and me. There was a bemused expression on his face.

"Good day, Señora Spence. The crew and I have been sad about your being sick and delirious. Are you feeling any better now? I brought you some food to see if you are finally able to eat."

He then tapped the side of his head. "But before I give you this, I want to know if you have done any thinking. Have you gained any appreciation about your circumstances? Eh?"

I wanted to charge him, knock him down and smash that nasty mouth with my fist. I wanted to pull his hair and gouge his face with my nails. The dirty bastard. Adrenalin was shooting through my body, and my lips were quivering as I stared at his eyes. I wiped my mouth with the back of my hand. His expression changed slightly, and he stepped slightly to the side.

"Please sit down, Señora Spence, and I will give you this plate."

He lifted it up and slowly extended it to me. My knees went weak. I grabbed the plate, fell back on the bunk and began wolfing down the chicken. I didn't look up until I had finished two of the three pieces. Capitán Torres was now holding out a glass full of amber ale. I took it and drank it down in a few gulps. Then I went at the third piece of chicken and the cabbage.

"Eat slowly, Señora. It will be better for digesting."

He filled my glass again, and I downed it. The plate and bottle were empty.

"May I have more?" I asked.

"Not now. You should go slow."

"May I go up on deck?"

"Perhaps later. I think now you should rest to get back some strength. Why don't you stretch out under the covers?"

He came over and pulled back the covers. I scrutinized his face up close and shivered. How near I had been to doing him bodily harm. Never before had I experienced such a rage. It was frightening.

"Señora Spence, let me help you. Why don't you take off these clothes?"

He sat down next to me and slowly and gently began unbuttoning my shirt, watching me closely. I sat there in a kind of suspended animation, now feeling the ale, observing his fingers manipulate the buttons. I knew what he was doing and what would inevitably follow. And I allowed it. I had no will or energy to resist. Next my trousers came off and my shoes and socks. Then my underwear.

"Go on," he coached, smiling as he lifted the covers.

I turned and slid into bed, facing the wall. I heard him undress and felt him move in behind me. Slowly his arms enclosed me and I felt his kisses on my shoulders. My heart was not willing, but still it happened. It was painful, physically and emotionally, especially when it was over. Bitterroot, you are a first-rate bastard.

That evening, after spending a couple of hours on deck with Pablo, I had dinner in the salon with Capitán López de Torres and the first mate, Filipé Obregon. The Capitán was cheerful and especially solicitous toward me. Fortunately Obregon was there and López de Torres did not try to make intimate conversation.

Obregon was a taciturn man who, while not friendly, was always correct with me. He was wiry in build and had thinning dark hair combed straight back, which made his wrinkled, leathery face more stark than it needed to be. It was difficult to tell his age. Whereas the Capitán was demonstrative, affecting an almost swashbuckling style that the crew seemed to love, Obregon was stern and commanded a kind of fearful respect. I often wanted to know what he was thinking when his hollow eyes fixed upon me. The only time I saw him smile was when the mainsail boom fell down and knocked a young sailor to the deck. Obregon had gone to the man quickly, but when he found the seaman had only a bruise and injured pride, Obregon returned to the after deck with a huge grin.

I ate extra helpings of the goat which was carved up and roasted on deck while *Guadalupe* lay at anchor in San Miguel harbor. Even to this day I think it was the finest tasting meat I've ever eaten. No doubt my previous starvation had had something to do with it. I also consumed what seemed like a gallon of water and several glasses of wine.

That night I did not sleep much. I lay awake listening for the key in the lock, fearful that the Capitán would come. *Guadalupe* had left San Miguel, and we were now hove to south of Santa Rosa's west end, waiting for daylight to come so that we could inspect the island's shoreline for signs of Jean LaRue. But López de Torres did not come, and after sleeping late into the morning, I arose with optimism that my fortunes had turned. Maybe he just had wanted to conquer me and teach me a lesson.

I spent a most pleasant day, watching the sailing skills of the officers and crew. The boats went into many bays and inlets. Indian villages were seen in a few places, and several tomols came out to greet us. We traded for fresh seafood and roots. That evening we enjoyed a dinner of lobster and abalone.

At dusk *Guadalupe* again headed away from the island, keeping on duty only a two-man crew, the forward lookout and the tillerman, who kept her moving slowly until daybreak. The next day we searched further along the coastline of Santa Cruz Island. This was the opposite side from Pelican Bay where I had arrived on *Ocean Gypsy*. That seemed such a long time ago, yet it was only three months. It was still hard for me to believe how my life had changed. I had gone from being a happy, free, modern woman with hope in my heart to living with fear and danger and little hope for any future other than a squalid if not tortured existence—unless I was rescued. Where on earth was Bitterroot? When would he see me? As I lay in the bunk, dark thoughts crossed my mind. I forced these self-pitying thoughts away from consciousness. "Abbie, you must continue fighting."

Fortunately I slipped into sleep. But something brought me to alertness about three or four hours later. The ship was quiet except for the usual squeaks and groans of rigging and timbers. I had heard a sound in the hallway. Now a key turned in the lock of my door. In the darkness I could barely make out the door opening slowly and a human form coming in.

"Who's there?" I called, my voice quivering.

"It's me. I'm glad you are awake, my Señora."

Capitán López de Torres came over and sat on the bed.

"I cannot sleep, Señora Spence. I can think only of how lovely you are. I must be with you. Have you been thinking of me?"

"Yes," I said truthfully.

He reached out and took my arm, caressing it up and down.

"How are you feeling, my beauty?"

"I feel fine, Capitán."

"Good, good."

His hand now moved over my face and slowly down my neck and lightly across my breasts on the outside of my nightshirt. My nipples firmed, and a sudden distaste came over me. He kissed my face and then shed his clothes quickly and pulled back the covers.

"Capitán, you please get in first and let me have the outside. That will be nicer for me."

"Of course." I could tell he was grinning.

I got out of the bunk and let him crawl in against the wall. When he was down I ran to the door. It was locked but the key was in it. I fumbled, but was able to get it open.

"Espera!" he cried, jumping up. It was an order to halt.

I ran down the hall and out onto the companionway. I pulled the nightshirt up above my knees and climbed the ladder to the afterdeck, my bare feet picking up splinters along the way. There was a dim, flickering light at the binnacle, and I could make out the shadowy shape of a man, his hands on the large tiller. I said nothing and ran to the corner where I sat during my daytime stays. There I crouched down. The man looked in my direction but did not say anything. My big toe on my right foot was in pain from a splinter that had been driven under the nail. I worked on it, trying to pincer it with my fingernails.

Then I heard fast footsteps up the ladder. They stopped on the afterdeck. I could see Capitán Torres looking dimly around. The man on watch saluted.

"Dónde está la Señora?" I heard López de Torres ask the tillerman.

I heard no reply but the Capitán started slowly in my direction. He had on pants and shoes but was bare-chested. I stood up. It was cold, and I began to shiver. There was no escape. He had me cornered. Even if I tried to go around the binnacle and up forward there was nowhere to run. Now I could see the twisted smile.

"You still have not learned, Señora Spence."

"Capitán, I needed some fresh air."

"Do not lie to me." His arm went up quickly and smacked me on the side of the face. I gritted my teeth and closed my eyes, expecting another. Now he seized me, shoving me against the railing. He grabbed my hair in his fist and shook my head vigorously. It hurt terribly, and I took his arm, trying to lessen the pain.

"Don't ever run from me again, Señora, or I will tear your hair out, handful by handful. Do you understand me?" he hissed.

I nodded meekly, but a ferocious feeling began building inside me. It was pure rage. And it took me completely when his hands tore the top of the nightshirt and reached down inside to fondle me. I exploded with unbelievable energy. I stooped down as his hands moved on my breasts, reached my arms around his legs and locked my hands below his buttocks. I brought my knees together and lifted with my legs as I used to do with bags of fertilizer. He rose in the air, flailing wildly as I leaned him toward the stern and toppled him over the railing. There was a surprised shout, and his fingers clawed at the railing, momentarily holding on with his left hand. With a sudden reflex I pushed his fingers. His grasp failed, and he disappeared into the darkness. I heard his shoes scraping the stern planking as he went down. There was a double thud followed by a splash. He must have hit the rudder before going into the ocean.

I stood there astonished. I felt a scream coming. But no sooner had it started than there was a hand over my mouth and another grasping my upper arm tightly.

"Shhhhhh," I heard in my ear. "Be quiet."

I looked into the face. It was hard to make out the features in the darkness, but I knew it was Abirrute.

"Go down to your room. Go to sleep. Act like nothing has happened. If anyone asks, you were never up here. You were in your room all night. Understand?"

"But we must try to save him."

"No. Not after what you did. Your chance to live is bad now, but it would be worse if he came back. Quick. Go."

He pushed me forward, and I limped all the way into my cabin. The pain in my foot was excruciating. After I locked the door I went to a porthole to see if I could hear any cries. There was only the sound of the waves. As I crawled into bed, I was trembling from the pain, the cold, and most of all from the shock of what I had done. Abirrute had seen it all. And he wanted to protect me. This showed that his loyalty was to Bitterroot and not to his Spanish superiors. He clearly was taking a great risk on my account.

My mind whirled the whole night. At one point I jumped up in anguish. I quickly grabbed the Capitán's remaining clothes and shoved them out a porthole. Finally I dropped off to a fitful sleep, exhausted from the worry of it all. When I awoke the sun was coming in the portholes. For a second or two the day seemed normal, until everything from that terrible night came back. I had killed a man. I had caused Capitán López de Torres to die by drowning. I had thrown him overboard. When there still might have been a chance to recover him, I had gone down below to bed. Not someone else, but me. Now I would have to face the consequences. Tears began slowly rolling down my cheeks. How could this have happened? What rights did I have? Probably none. Who would care about the Capitán's transgressions? The crew would only know that I had killed their beloved leader.

Abirrute had said for me to say I was in my room all night. Should I do that? I had always told the truth. Truth is always the best policy, my dad had said. But telling the truth now meant certain punishment, probably death. Could Abirrute save me? Apparently he would lie for me. If only he could take me out of here, out of this time and back to my own. The unknowns swirled in my mind. I decided I'd better get dressed. Thankfully, my toe felt better.

No sooner had I tied my shoes than there was a knock at the door. It was Pablo. He came in and looked around the room.

"Señora, dónde ésta el Capitán?"

"No lo se, Pablo, no lo se." I shrugged and gave him a bewildered look. I asked nonchalantly when I could take breakfast.

"Más tarde, Señora. Primero tengo que encontrar al Capitán." Pablo left in a hurry, concern embedded in his face. The boy was going to look for his captain.

Even from my room I could tell that a thorough search was underway. Doors banged, and shouts and earnest conversations were taking place. The whole crew was involved. Once again Pablo came into my cabin, this time with first mate Obregon. They scrutinized everything, looking behind the desk, and even pulling out the long drawer under the bunk. Then they excused themselves.

In about thirty minutes Pablo came and took me to the salon. There, seated at a table, were the first and second mates. The Capitán's logbook and other papers were in front of them. An ink well and quill were at hand. Several seamen stood in front of the table, including Abirrute. The high tension was visible in everyone's expression.

"Buenos días, Señores," I said.

"Buenos días, Señora," Obregon replied. He then looked at a seaman named Bustamante and said something.

Bustamante looked at me and began speaking in heavily accented English.

"Señora, Capitán Torres is missing. We have searched the ship and cannot find him. We are trying to learn who saw him last. You please tell us when you saw him last."

"Oh, I hope nothing bad has happened to him," I said with great feeling, bringing my right hand over my collarbone as if suddenly shocked.

"We fear he may have fallen into the sea. Please, when did you last see the Capitán?"

I took in a sharp breath. "I...well...I saw him when we had dinner last night right in this room with Señor Obregon." I pointed to the dining table and looked at Obregon as I spoke.

"You did not see Capitán López de Torres later in the evening?" Bustamante asked.

"The Capitán escorted me to my cabin after dinner, and that was the last I saw of him."

"He did not come in your cabin later?"

I caught Abirrute's eye momentarily before looking directly at Obregon. "Of course not," I replied with indignation.

After some period of interpretation, Obregon asked something of another sailor who was standing next to Abirrute. The young man gave a lengthy reply, only part of which I understood. I gathered that he had been the one on duty last night as the bow lookout. My heart beat faster.

"No, no," Abirrute now interrupted, shaking his head. "No hay nadie."

There was quick exchange between Obregon and Abirrute. The young man spoke again. Then Abirrute spoke at length, glaring at the sailor. As I watched Abirrute, I could see that while there was a resemblance to Bitterroot, especially the eyes and forehead, Abirrute's nose and mouth were distinctly different.

Obregon spoke to both of them and then looked at me.

"Señora," Bustamante said, interpreting Obregon, "the lookout last night claims he heard people talking on the aft deck after midnight. He says he heard a woman's voice."

"Well that was not me, Señor. I was asleep. I did not go on deck last night." I looked him in the eye and turned to meet Obregon's penetrating stare as the interpretation was made.

Obregon and the second mate conversed at length. Again there were conversations with Abirrute and the young sailor, this time initiated by the second mate. Abirrute was shaking his head. Suddenly Obregon became angry and stood up and shouted at Abirrute, who now crossed himself and stated a reply quietly. Obregon glared for a moment and then shouted at the young sailor. The man became flustered and stammered but appeared to restate his testimony. He, too, crossed himself.

Obregon then dismissed Abirrute and the young sailor. He said to me, "Gracias, Señora," and told Pablo to escort me to my cabin.

I followed the lookout and Abirrute out the door, with Pablo following behind me. There were only a few steps to my cabin door. Surreptitiously I hooked my finger in Abirrute's belt loop as he walked in front of me. I tugged it, slowing him, and leaned next to his ear.

"Abirrute," I whispered strongly, "tell Gordon Bitterroot that I demand to get out immediately. And that I refuse to participate in Southern Dreams."

He reached around and jerked my hand away from his belt loop and continued on without turning. But I clearly saw his head nod twice before he disappeared.

After the door was closed, I peered out the porthole but could not see Santa Cruz. It was probable that we were heading out, perhaps retracing our course in an attempt to find the missing Torres. So who would they believe, I wondered, Abirrute or the young lookout? Abirrute, being older and more experienced, was probably more believable. On the other hand, the young sailor's testimony gave something to go on. Without it, there was just the Capitán's inexplicable disappearance.

One thing in my favor, I decided, was that nobody would suspect that I could have lifted López de Torres' bulk over the side, so the suspicion would fall on Abirrute or someone else if they thought there was foul play. The disappearance would boil down to whether it was an accident or not. My guess was that they would find it hard to believe that the Capitán could fall over in relatively calm seas unless he was drunk. I hadn't smelled anything on his breath.

The key to my safety was Abirrute, just as I was now essential to his. If only I could talk with him secretly. But that would be foolhardy. Our credibility depended on our not knowing each other. I wished I had not called out his name when I was being starved.

Abirrute was an enigma. What was his relationship to Bitterroot? Had he signed aboard before the ship sailed from Acapulco months ago? If so, did he or Bitterroot know or plan that far back that I would end up on the *Guadalupe* when I was deposited at Pelican Bay? That suggested predestination.

Determinism—the age-old controversy about free will. I remembered part of a quote from one of the Greek Stoics, perhaps Aurelius: "Whatever may happen to thee, it was prepared for thee from all eternity...". Could it be true? I had always felt I made my future happen, for better or worse, by my decisions and actions. But somehow Bitterroot knew I would end up with the Chumash because Biru was there. He knew I would join the Spanish, and be on the *Guadalupe* because Abirrute was on board. I could have asked to go on *La Reina Cádiz*. If I had, Abirrute would not have been there. Neither would Capitán López de Torres. Events would have been different. I would not be a murderer. What happened had happened. Was it destiny?

I remembered from my physics course that physicists never understood why time doesn't flow into the past just like it does into the future. Newton and Einstein's theories give no explanation as to why time goes only one way. Maybe it does go both ways. I am in 1704, but I have knowledge of the twentieth century at the same time. That particular future is already set down. So determinism is right. But if it is right, why does Bitterroot think he can change history? If he can change it, determinism is not right. I was totally mystified.

When Pablo brought me bread and meat for lunch, I asked to go on deck with him. He was hesitant but finally agreed. As I walked out on deck the mood of the crew was sullen and heavy. There were no greetings or smiles toward me as in the past, only glares or heads turned away. As we took our usual place on the afterdeck, I realized the ship was still back-tracking. There were two lookouts in the crow's nest instead of one and men were searching the water from the port and starboard railings. The loss of their Capitán was weighing heavily on the men, and I began to feel a horrible remorse.

After an hour of misery I went back to the cabin. As I stepped into the companionway from the deck, I heard a sailor shout something. It sounded like "bruja," pronounced the same as the first two syllables of brouhaha. I turned back to see if someone was talking to me, and while I found a couple of men staring at me, they didn't seem to be trying to communicate.

"Pablo," I said as we stood at my cabin door, "cómo es bruja?"

He looked at me fearfully and shook his head slowly. When I was inside, he locked the door.

That evening I took dinner in the after salon with the first and second mates and the sailor, Bustamante. All of them were rather stiff. I did not try to make conversation, and the meal passed in an awkward silence. The ship had hove to in the darkness and now rolled heavily in the westerly swell, which had been building all afternoon. It was difficult to keep the plates and glasses from sliding on the table. At one point Obregon's cup of water slid across the table and against my plate. I reached it at the same time that he did, and our hands touched. He jerked his hand back quickly, as if burned. When I looked at him, I saw fearfulness in his eyes. I began feeling very uncomfortable. Something strange was in the air, and it was more than the sense of loss and mourning for Capitán López de Torres.

After a dessert of dried apples, Obregon spoke to Bustamante and mentioned my name. I waited for the interpretation to be sure I understood.

"Señora Spence," Bustamante said with difficulty, "Primero Obregon requests you not go on deck unless you obtain his permission. Do you understand?"

"Sí. But why?"

He interpreted my question, and Obregon's dark eyes flashed. He said something rapidly.

"You are not to ask why. You are to do as he says. Do you understand?"

"Sí. Yo entiendo." I met Obregon's firm look.

After dinner I was again locked in my room.

The next morning I could see through the portholes that we were heading back to Santa Cruz Island. The search for the Capitán had been given up. Pablo brought me breakfast in my room. I tried to engage him in conversation, but he was distant and curt. When he brought me lunch I told him to tell Primero Obregon that I needed to go on deck badly. I was located on the seaward side and could not see the land through my portholes unless *Guadalupe* came about, which happened only occasionally. I was bored all morning and felt it would end up as another claustrophobic day. But in the early afternoon Pablo and Obregon appeared at the door. They would allow me to go on deck but only for a short while. I was surprised to see that both of them had flintlock pistols in their waistbands. Obregon had two. I asked Pablo why they had the guns but received no answer.

Although there weren't many sailors on deck, my appearance caused a commotion. Several shouted "bruja," and many became agitated. Obregon shouted them down, and they eventually went back to work. But I could see them steal glances my way from time to time. As I sat in my usual spot, Pablo stood at the rail forward of me, watching the main deck. Obregon stood in front of the binnacle, alert and wary. I now had my answer as to why my freedom had been curtailed. I had become a curse. Whether I was involved in the Capitán's loss or not, my presence on board was bad luck. I guessed that bruja probably meant witch or the like. For the men I was the inglesa bruja, something to be hated and feared.

Before long I saw the ship's longboats coming, the oars moving up and down in unison. As they pulled up close there was shouting between those on deck and the men in the boats, many of whom were bare chested in the heat of the sun. A low-pitched squeal arose, and I saw a couple of men pointing to a large, wild boar laying on the bottom of one boat, his legs tied together. The men gave him wide berth as he thrashed and kicked. His curved tusks were several inches in length. Jokes and laughter now filled the air as the men jubilantly bantered about the fortunate catch.

A large net was thrown down into the boat to hoist the pig from a boom swung out over the side of the ship. Several men pulled the line through a block and tackle on deck, while the pig thrashed furiously in the net as he was hoisted up. The mate had ordered ale broken out, and already some of the crew were swilling the dark liquid. It was clear what we would be having for dinner, and the celebration was starting.

The boar was unwrapped from the netting by two of the sailors. Another was holding a sword for the coup de grace. Suddenly one of the sailors holding the net cried out as the pig shot out between his legs. The ropes around the pig's legs had come loose, and the ferocious little beast was running wild on the deck. Several men tried to catch him, but the pig charged them directly, gouging their legs with his tusks. Two men went down screaming. Now everyone was shouting, mostly trying to get out of the way of the dangerous incisors and tusks. Staying clear was difficult, as the boar kept changing directions rapidly. The man with the sword bravely lunged, sticking the pig's hind end and bringing a loud squeal, but the frightened animal seemed only to move faster after this. Another hapless sailor went down. Obregon moved down to the middeck with pistol in hand. From a distance of about eight feet, he fired. The boar was hit but not stopped. The noise and the blow apparently spooked the animal, for he headed directly toward the boarding gate and disappeared overboard. His trajectory carried past the longboat below and into the sea.

Everyone quickly went to the rail to look and several sailors went down the rope ladder to man the boat. Obregon was shouting orders. The pig was swimming erratically and getting farther away from the ship, his snout above water, eyes wide with fear. When the boat was untied and began heading for the pig, he was roughly sixty yards off. From our vantage point on the stern, Pablo and I had the best view, and Pablo pointed and gave instructions to the boat's crew. But as I watched the pig I suddenly saw something else moving near it. It was a triangular fin. Pablo saw it too and yelled. The crew doubled their effort. The fin now disappeared. Just a few seconds later the boar screamed and went under the surface. Then it bobbed up in the roiled water. I could see dark coloration around it—blood. Men were shouting from the ship. The boat was now within fifteen yards, and one of the sailors raised an oar to smack the water. But the pig was hit again hard from below and raised up out of the water momentarily, then went under again. This time it did not come up.

The men in the boat circled the spot, pushing their oars deep to locate the pig, but to no avail. After several minutes the conclusion was inescapable. The shock, disbelief, and disappointment was reflected in everyone's face. Bitter comments and cursing were heard all about the deck. Attention was slowly given to cleaning up the mess. The three injured sailors were carried below so that their wounds could be tended.

"Bruja." Now a group of men were crowding together on the main deck, looking and pointing at me. "Bruja, bruja," they chanted angrily. Others joined them. Obregon turned to Pablo and shouted that I should be taken below. He then yelled at the men on deck. But when they saw me walking with Pedro toward the stairway, they became incensed. "Bruja, bruja, bruja," they hollered in unison.

Several now started up the bottom stairs toward us, yelling and gesturing menacingly. Obregon ran down the stairs to block them at the first level, drawing a pistol. He motioned for Pablo and me to come behind and get into the companionway. As I followed Pablo I looked down at the mob, now bunching at the bottom stairway and pushing the leaders forward. I was shocked to see that the first one was the tall, handsome sailor who had smiled and been so friendly during my first time on deck. His face was contorted in rage. Beyond the crowd I saw Abirrute, standing by himself next to the mainmast. His face was drawn in apprehension as he watched.

"Quietos todos!" yelled Obregon, planting himself in front of the onrushers and pointing his pistol at them. The second mate appeared with a gun.

In a few more steps, Pablo and I could turn into the companionway and open the door, but the men did not stop. They pushed forward and began grappling with Obregon. I heard a gunshot as I turned the corner. The shouts and grunts were loud. A hand grabbed my foot, and I fell. Pablo was holding the door open, but I couldn't get up. I pulled my leg with all my might. The shouting became a din. I was in pure panic. So this was how it would end for me. Then suddenly my foot broke loose and quickly I crawled on hands and knees into the companionway and the door swung closed. I heard Obregon shouting again. There was another shot. I ran to the salon and shut the door behind me. I propped a chair up against the doorknob. Then I lay down on the floor in a corner. I was shaking violently. I expected any second to see the door battered in. My life was over. The only question was how badly they would hurt me before they put me to death.

But after a minute the noise seemed to subside. The door remained intact. After about ten minutes I heard a knock.

"Señora Spence, soy Pablo."

I went to the door cautiously. "Pablo?"

"Sí, Señora. Abra su merced."

I let him in. He had his pistol in his hand, but there was nobody else in the hallway.

"Vamos a su camara, Señora," he said. He led me to my cabin and locked the door behind me. I collapsed on the bunk and pulled the covers over me. God had given me a reprieve. Only Obregon's brave action had saved me. One clearheaded man between me and bloodthirsty animals.

My mind flashed to my Reed freshman days when I was intensely interested in finding the Truth. I had read and read in my effort to quench this strange craving. I believed that somewhere in that library I would eventually find Truth written, perhaps in one of the ancient volumes deep in the stacks. But I had finally stopped the futile search after reading the words of the Vicar in George Santayana's *The Last Puritan*:

> The Truth is terrible thing. It is much darker, much sadder, much more ignoble, much more inhuman and ironical than most of us are willing to admit, or even able to suspect.

After that I no longer wanted to find the Truth. That thought had struck me as truth enough. Now on the *Guadalupe*, Santayana's words were especially compelling. How fitting that Santayana was a Spaniard.

I must have dozed a while, for I awoke to the sound of a great deal of activity aboard the ship. I looked out a porthole and saw the shore very close. The *Guadalupe's* boats were in the water and heavily manned. They were towing the *Guadalupe* into anchorage.

When the anchor was down we swung slowly around. *La Reina Cádiz* came into view riding easily on her manila hawser. I could now see Capitán Vazquez, his first mate, and Father Ignacio embarking in a boat to come over. Somehow they must have heard about López de Torres for their faces were dour.

When I heard the party come down the hallway I thought for a minute they were stopping at my door, but the footsteps continued aft toward the salon. No doubt they would want to talk at length with primero Obregon. There would be much to discuss. From the traffic to and from the salon, it appeared they were bringing in others from time to time.

Tick, tickety tick. As I lay on the bunk I heard a strange little sound on the hull outside my cabin. It was as if something—a small rock—were bouncing on the side. It happened again. I went to the porthole, and the sound was next to me. Then a bug seemed to pop through the porthole. It had white wings. I jumped back. Then I saw that it was a folded up paper on a thin line. Tied below it was a square nail, rusty from age. I unknotted the line and carefully removed the paper, unfolded it and turned it to the light. The handwriting was similar to but not the same as that of the note I had received after leaving Biru. This note read:

Stay with the account you gave. Our mortal lives depend on it.

Keep patience. Gordon will visit you later. Destroy this immediately.

I wrapped the note around the nail and tied it tightly with the line. Then looking out the porthole to be sure no one was around, I threw it out and watched it disappear into the depths with a plop.

The note had come, obviously, from Abirrute. He had to have lowered it from the afterdeck. That was risky. But he must have felt it was worth the risk.

"Our mortal lives depend on it." I felt palpitations.

I looked out the porthole. The cove had massive cliffs surrounding it, making for a formidable landing. A boat had made it, for I could see sailors walking along the rocky shore. They were enjoying themselves, but I was totally without joy.

Under any other circumstances, it would have been nice to see Father Ignacio and Capitán Vazquez, but our greeting was rather stiff. Pablo helped me gather my things into a sack. I was being transferred to *La Reina de Cádiz*. The sailors standing around on the deck were sullen as they watched me go. I knew they were thinking "Good riddance." At the boarding gate Primero Obregon nodded slightly but showed no emotion as I said goodbye and thanked him for saving my life. Only Pablo seemed to get moist in the eyes when we exchanged an "Adiós," and I kissed him on the cheek. As I put my foot over the edge onto the first rung of the rope ladder, I glanced forward at some of the sailors who were watching. There to one side was Abirrute. As our eyes met, he smiled slightly and raised the fingers of one hand in a subtle wave. As I tried not to smile back, unsuccessfully, tears came to my eyes. I moved down the ladder quickly to get out of view.

With us in the longboat was Bustamante. Apparently he would be our interpreter. The trip over to *La Reina* was short but wet from the spray kicked up by the wind. *La Reina* had a slower motion than *Guadalupe*, and it was almost like stepping onto land by comparison. My reputation among *La Reina's* sailors must have preceded me, for the men watching me arrive were unsmiling and wary, even as they scrutinized me with fascination. Capitán Vazquez allowed no chance for topside exposure but moved me quickly up into a companionway. Soon we were in the Capitán's spacious quarters.

There was a chart table and desk, and in the middle of the room was an oval dining table. Six cowhide chairs surrounded it. A single bunk was built along an interior bulkhead. Handsome cabinets with carved designs covered much of the interior walls. The room was in the very stern of the ship, and two large square windows provided a lovely view of the cliffs. In the hull on each side were four large portholes, now open, providing fresh air.

There were five of us in the room—Vazquez, the Padre, Bustamante, *La Reina's* first mate who was called Jíminez, and myself.

"Sientese su merced," Vazquez said, holding out a chair.

After I was seated the rest all followed, each looking at me with suspicious interest. Vazquez took charge of the conversation. Bustamante interpreted.

"Señora Spence, there has been much trouble on *Guadalupe*. Capitán

López de Torres went over the side and is probably dead. Three men were injured by a boar. Two men have injuries from pistol shot. All these happenings are not accidents. Please tell us what you know about such terrible things. What part did you have in them? And tell the truth, or we will force the truth out of you."

Suddenly it was stifling in the room. I could smell the sweat on the men's bodies. I could smell my own perspiration, too. I had not taken a bath since leaving Santa Rosa Island. I wanted to thrust my nose into an open porthole.

"Señora?" Vazquez began tapping on the table with his fingers.

"Capitán, I had nothing to do with the accidents. It is terrible these things happened, but I was just a bystander. I know nothing more than what everyone else knows about them."

Vazquez, on hearing the interpretation, tightened his jaw. He glared at me skeptically.

"Decid la verdad!" he shouted angrily, accusing me of lying.

"I can tell you nothing more," I said softly.

After the interpretation his face became red. He stood up swiftly, and marched around the table. From behind he leaned over me and shouted. I hunched over not knowing what to do. My hands were shaking. Then his hand moved to my head, and suddenly my ear was in excruciating pain. He was gouging my ear lobe with his thumbnail and pulling it down. I screamed, and my eyes began tearing. I grabbed his large fist but could not loosen his grasp. After a few more shakes, he let go. Again he shouted something. I was cowering.

"No, no. Por caridad, Capitán!" I cried, looking up into the fierce eyes.

"Hable su merced!" he shouted.

"Tell us the truth," Bustamante said. "What happened to Capitán López de Torres?"

"I don't know what happened to him," I said softly. "After going to my cabin after dinner, I went to sleep. I did not hear anything about the Capitán until the next morning."

Bustamante interpreted my statement, and Capitán Vazquez replied.

Bustamante said, "A man heard a woman's voice on deck late that night. It had to be you."

"No, I was in my cabin all night."

After the interpretation was made, Vazquez lunged at me. His left hand found my breast and he pinched my nipple between his thumb and forefinger. It was horribly hurtful. I yelled and tried to pull away, but his other arm came around my neck, locking me against him. I yelled and half bawled. Then, suddenly he let go, only to grab my other ear lobe and pinch it. I felt my hair being pulled at the same time. I almost lost consciousness, it hurt so much. When he finally let go, I slipped off the chair and found myself sobbing on the floor, throbbing with pain. Vazquez grabbed my arm and jerked me back up on the chair, yelling at me.

"Hable su merced! Quiere más? Hable!"

I hunched forward on the table holding my hands over my ears, crying. I don't remember what happened exactly, but the men were talking to each other. I heard Father Ignacio's voice and heard the word "confesión." After a few minutes the chairs shuffled and I heard footsteps heading for the door.

"Señora Spence." It was Father Ignacio. I felt a hand on my shoulder, shaking me gently.

"Señora Spence."

I looked at him through blurred eyes. I was moaning. He talked slowly and softly. After a minute I was able to compose myself and began listening to his words.

He said it would go easier for me and I would feel better if I unburdened myself to God. His large, gentle hand moved over my head, smoothing my hair back. He looked into my eyes and spoke some Latin and made a sign in front of me. Sudden feelings came over me in a way I had never experienced before. I had a vision of my father and grandfather joined as one before me, consoling me, making my hurts all better. I leaned over onto his legs and put my arms around his waist and cried. I felt the healing hands on my head and shoulders as he spoke soothing Spanish phrases to the Niña on his lap.

As I calmed down, I realized that while I considered what had happened torture, it was in the normal course of events for Capitán Vazquez and his men. Even Father Ignacio who was being so nice, was not really of a different cloth. His techniques were different, but not his objective. He wanted my confession. So my position was grave. It would be so simple to tell the truth about what happened to López de Torres. Could I just do it and trust in God for the consequences? I wanted to. But what would happen to me? What would happen to Abirrute?

If I stayed with my story my fare would likely be more pain. The main course would be worse than the appetizer I had been served. I knew I could not stand much of it. They would get the truth, and they knew it. Wouldn't it be better to yield the painless way—to their God? Wouldn't they be more inclined to offer forgiveness? Perhaps spare my life? Abirrute had thought not.

"Stay with your story." Was that because they might go harder with him? He had purposefully decided not to try and save López de Torres. Was his concern for me? Or for Bitterroot?

"Padre, quiero confesarme." I was resigned. The residual energy drained from my muscles. I would give in. I could see no other way.

"Bueno, mi hija. Cuándo quiera su merced."

I sat up and looked out the back window with its large mullions in the panes, the latter with small bubbles and other imperfections.

"Capitán López de Torres was not a nice man, Padre," I began in Spanish.

As I paused to choose my words carefully, I heard shouting on the deck. At first there were a few voices, then more joined in. What were they saying? "Piratas, piratas!" The ship's bell began clanging. Father Ignacio jumped up and ran out of the room, leaving me alone. Something important was happening.

Fate is definitely strange. A ship had been sighted from the mast top. Of course, they all thought it was that of Jean LaRue, the pirate. *La Reina* and *Guadalupe* began gearing up for battle. The cannons were being made ready. The decks were cleared. The anchors were raised. All the sails the ships could hold were hoisted so as to overtake the enemy, who was heading south down the middle of the Santa Barbara Channel. It would have been amusing if it were not so tragic. Shakespeare would have loved it. But what did it mean for me? Obviously the ship was other than Jean LaRue's. But what ship was it? Would Vazquez shoot it up, thinking it to be the nasty pirate I had described?

I was told to stay in the Capitán's cabin. It was as comfortable and hopefully as safe a place to be as anywhere. If the enemy came broadside to *La Reina*'s stern I might be in trouble. Shot and cannonballs could easily come in the windows. It would be an hour or two before the engagement. Meantime I could watch *Guadalupe* sailing off our aft quarter, leaning heavily to starboard, sails straining, the bow nosing up spumes of spray.

After about an hour, we slowed. I could distinctly hear cheering. *Guadalupe* in the distance began to reduce sail. What was happening? I opened the Capitán's door to try to hear better. Men were shouting and laughing. "Galeón, galeón." The feared ship was the large galleon coming from the Philippines heading to Acapulco. Excited, I ran down the companionway and up on the afterdeck. Men were laughing and frolicking. Rum had been broken out, and the joy was infectious. Some yelled and waved their hats at me. Capitán Vazquez saw me and came over, a large grin on his face. I couldn't help smiling back. He pointed forward off the bow and there it was—a gorgeous sight. The galleon was huge, with full sails up on the tall masts, lumbering downwind like some leviathan out of a fairy tale. A small flag, the colors faded from the sun, flew from its top. I could make out men in the crow's nest. It was so eerily beautiful, that I began tearing.

Vazquez threw his arms around me and kissed me on the mouth, then lifted me high and danced around in circles. I could taste the rum from his mouth. When I was put down, other men gathered around and hugged me. I felt like a bean bag being tossed from one to another. Someone gave me a mug of rum. Everyone was shouting, and I couldn't hear myself think. After several swigs of the powerful brew I, too, was laughing absurdly. It was a marvelously unreal time. I didn't even mind the stray hands. It was a celebration for the great treasure ship. As several men rode me around on their shoulders, I almost forgot the misery I had experienced. Janus had turned.

As we closed on the big ship—her name was *Rosario*—she dropped all her sails except a fore staysail to keep her weigh on. *La Reina* also reduced canvas. Capitán Vasquez spoke her with a megaphone and soon after both ships dropped boats as they drifted downwind fifty yards apart. To my surprise, Vazquez ordered me to get my clothes. I was to be in the boat with him.

The two longboats met between the vessels. The sailors drew the boats together with lines but kept them from bumping by holding poles between them. The galleon's captain was Señor Fermin de Salavarría, a veteran of several passages both to and from Manila. He and Vazquez, sitting in stern thwarts, talked at length. I tried to catch the conversation but it was difficult to hear up where I was, even though I was understanding the language much better. Much of their communication was about the nature of the passage over on the *Rosario*, the condition of the crew, the status of food and water, etc. I gathered that conditions on the galleon were unusually good. Vazquez told of their search for a pirate and of finding me on Santa Cruz with the Indians. Then I think he said something about warships being no place for a woman. I gathered from the nodding of de Salavarría that I would be going on the *Rosario*.

And so it was that fate completed its trick on that November day of 1704. Soon I was climbing up the long rope ladder on the side of the massive Manila galleon.

18

The galleon was easily three times the size of *La Reina de Cádiz*. With its large superstructure it was like a floating hotel. It contained men, women, children, animals, fowl, plantings, and untold treasures in its hold. It was a community of rich and poor.

I was put in a section below decks where women and children were quartered. I was assigned a berth in a small room next to a Filapina named Flora Villalobos. Only later did I learn that her previous bunkmate had died of a fever two weeks out of Manila. There were crosses and Virgin Marys hanging about the berth to ward off evil. God only knows what the disease was. Perhaps typhoid or malaria. I was fearful of sleeping there but they assured me that the good Virgin would not let anything bad happen. I didn't ask why the good Virgin had neglected the previous occupant. But there was no other open berth, so I hoped the bacteria, or whatever, had disappeared in the long stretch of time. I scrubbed the bunk and aired out the straw pallet.

Except for that worrisome beginning, my sojourn on *Rosario* was like a vacation. I slept a great deal the first few days. My only activity was going up to the waist—the main deck at the middle of the ship—for mandatory mass and to the passengers' mess for meals. The latter were hardly worthy of the name, being mostly heavy soups, chicken, biscuits and occasional dried fruits that were carefully rationed. The best parts of the meals were chocolate, which the Spaniards craved, and cinnamon flavored tea. The people were a motley group, mainly Spanish and Filipinos, but quite a number of Chinese and other Asians and a few Indians. I sat only with Flora, who took me under her wing. She was only slightly older than me and spoke Spanish slowly. This worked out well, for I had a spurt in learning the language and soon could hear and speak it almost as well as English. Flora and I would sit up in the passengers' deck area and chat for hours at a time. I just had to be careful when she asked certain questions.

"Abbie, where will you go when we get to Acapulco?"

"I am meeting someone, and we'll be traveling in-land. What will you do, Flora?"

"I am going to a hacienda. I'll be with a family and help take care of the house. I'm excited because I will be with young children. They tell me it is a large house, and the countryside is beautiful."

"That sounds wonderful, Flora." She had never married and I knew that being around children was important to her.

There clearly was a caste system on board the ship. At the highest level were the priests and ship's officers and any of the Castillian Spanish. Next came the native born or Creole Spanish and below them the Filipinos. The Chinese and other Asians were next. Last were the native Indians of New Spain, some of whom appeared enslaved. Women, of course, were secondary to men in any of these categories. As a foreigner, I didn't fit into the hierarchy very well. I tried not to associate with any particular group and was mostly left alone, which suited me fine.

The priests were all of the Franciscan order. There was one young priest named Escovar, who talked with me from time to time when I was up on deck. He asked me where I had come from, and I was careful to tell him as little as possible. He seemed educated, and I enjoyed learning about the passage from him. At one point I almost blew it, though.

"Padre, on the trips east from the Philippines, do the galleons ever stop at the Hawaiian Islands?" Obviously I was not thinking and realized it too late.

"What islands are those, Señora?"

"Oh...some little islands off California," I stammered, "north of San Miguel."

"I haven't heard of those. Are you sure?"

"Maybe I'm mistaken."

I then remembered that Captain Cook had discovered and named the Sandwich Islands. Despite the hundreds of trips from Manila to California and Acapulco to Manila, the Spanish captains must have never seen the Hawaiian chain.

The navigation and piloting was fairly routine for the galleon's officers. Escovar told me they had "portolani" to follow, which were detailed directions giving all the coastal islands and landmarks and the bearings to sail by the compass. An astrolabe was used for siting bearings on various objects. At night they used a device called a "nocturnal" for telling the time of night by the relative position of the guards of the pole star on any day of the year. Latitude was found by a seaman's quadrant, which fixed the degree from the north star.

Their navigation worked well for the galleon route going east. All they had to do was see land signs near the California coast, and then head south, following the shoreline south. Ocasionally storms took them off course, like the time they shipwrecked on the northern Oregon shore. I remember this from a Reed College expedition to the coast. We had stopped to see some beeswax candles with Spanish insignia that had washed up on the beach at Manzanita, just south of a coastal head called NeahKahNie. There was an Indian legend that some of the ship's treasure had been buried ashore. But the treasure has never been found.

Escovar, who had sailed the passage before, proudly pointed out the major islands and headlands that we passed.

"Señora, that large island coming up is Santa Catalina. On my last voyage, there was a storm with hot winds from the east, so we moved to the other side for protection."

I nodded with appreciation, having taken similar refuge from the Santa Ana winds in my father's Islander 32. I wondered what Escovar would think if he could know about the huge oil tankers, hundreds of pleasure craft, and ever-present airplanes that would frequent these waters and airspace in three more centuries.

"Padre Escovar, do you think humans will ever fly?"

"What a strange question, Señora. But of course not. God did not give us wings."

It was a warm and rather lazy voyage as we sailed downwind with the following sea rhythmically tipping us forward and slightly to port, and then back again. For relief from boredom the crew seemed constantly to be engaged in gaming. They would bet on everything from dice throws to the weather. The major excitement came from the cockfights, which were held every two or three days up forward. The women, of course, did not get to watch these. Our entertainment was restricted to sewing, talking, and overseeing the children's play.

Interwoven into all social activity was the Church. At daybreak a priest sang the Te Deum. After sunrise, several masses were given. All of the officers, crew, and passengers attended, except those on watch. In the afternoon, following the Salve Regina, miraculous stories were read and discourse given on religious matters. On Sundays there was added to the above a sermon by one or two of the priests. At odd times, too, the religious aspect was evident. One morning when I was sleeping after mass and breakfast, a woman stuck her head into my room and sang out:

"Death is certain, the hour late, the Judge severe. Woe unto the slothful. Do now that thou canst do before all is done and thou diest."

An apostolic fervor permeated the ship. If any non-Catholics had boarded the *Rosario* in Manila, they were soon converted, even the most uneducated natives—they especially, for proselytization was the Spanish crown's raison d'etre, other than accumulating wealth. That the priests would brook no tolerance from their way was shown one week after I had boarded. In a ceremony observed by all, a sailor was brought before the mast.

"Father Escovar, what has the man done wrong?"

"He has committed blasphemy."

While everyone watched, two priests aided by sailors burned a hole into the man's tongue. His offense was swearing on two occasions.

"Isn't that penalty too severe, Father?"

"No Señora, blasphemy against God is not allowed, for the fate of our ship is in God's hands. His wrath should not be provoked."

The event was accepted righteously by nearly everyone. The piercing cries of the poor man echoed in my ears for days.

The *Guadalupe* and *La Reina de Cádiz* accompanied the galleon until one day the *Guadalupe*, after speaking with both the *Rosario* and *La Reina*, headed in toward shore. The talk on the deck was that her leaks had become worse and required her to limp into San Diego bay for repairs. *La Reina*, however, stayed with us the rest of the voyage, triumphantly leading the way into Acapulco bay. *Guadalupe's* departure made me wonder if I would ever see Abirrute again. Were the needed repairs part of Bitterroot's plan? But I refused to think about that any more. Life was momentarily pleasant, and I wanted to savor it.

Only at one point on the trip was there worry about enemies. This was near Cabo San Lucas, the tip of baja California. Escovar told me that the Cabo was where the pirates had lain in wait in times past to attack the galleons as they rounded the corner. Both the *Rosario* and *La Reina* had their guns readied and manned as San Lucas approached. But their vigilance was not to be tested this time. It was clear sailing past the Sea of Cortés and southeastward down the mountainous coast into the hot and humid latitudes of New Spain.

December 8th was a holiday of sorts with colorful celebrations on the deck. People wore silks and fineries and engaged in singing and dancing. I wondered if it was because we were getting close to Acapulco.

"Flora, why are they celebrating?"

"It is the Day of Conception of the Blessed Virgin. Surely you know this."

"Oh yes. I did not know that this kind of celebration was allowed on the ship."

"Yes, it is encouraged."

Immaculate conception. A miracle—one of those strange events that defy critical analysis.

For me our impending arrival brought solemnity, because I didn't know what would become of me. Might they forget about me and allow me to go my own way? If so, what could I do? I had no money or means of support. Would Bitterroot make the predicted appearance? I was pessimistic. Abirrute was back on the *Guadalupe*, and there was nobody to ask for help, save Flora. What help could she be? I thought of asking Father Escovar for advice, but something told me I should not invite any official attention. Better to wait and see what happens.

"Don't worry, Abbie. I will help you," Flora said, sensing my anxiety.

"Thank you, Flora. You have helped me so much already."

As we approached Acapulco, which literally means the "mouth of hell," the cannons from the fort protecting the harbor began firing to announce our coming. The lookouts on the ridges and mountains to the north had known of us for days and had sent word. Our arrival was the big event of the year, and the town's population was swelling to more than twice its normal 4000 inhabitants. The people would welcome the big ship and try to partake of the riches from *Rosario*'s hold.

We followed *La Reina* into the bay around the island of Boca Chica, which sat at the mouth of the entrance. The harbor is nearly surrounded by precipitous mountains and the extraordinary landscapes gave a sombre and wild feeling. The wind stopped immediately, and a stifling heat reflecting from the rock walls enveloped the ship. The reason that Acapulco was the finest harbor on the west coast was due to it being almost hermetically sealed from outside winds and waves. The sky was strangely bronze and vaporous.

Whiffs of putrid odors made my eyes water. Acapulco was aptly named.

Three boats of rowers were lowered to tow *Rosario* to the north end of the bay, where the town splayed around the water's edge at the foot of a steep mountain. The large bow anchor was let go in the cove in front of the town. To my surprise, they tied the stern line to a tree on the shore, positioning *Rosario* only forty feet from a wooden dock where the unloading would take place. Small lighters were tied up there for traversing the span between the ship and the dock.

A couple of other small ships were anchored nearby, including a "filibote," a floating hull for hauling supplies down the coast with the prevailing wind. *La Reina* anchored further out from the town to stand guard for the galleon. This probably was not necessary, since the fort's large cannons could easily sink any enemy ship trying to come in.

People were now crowding on the deck, shouting to the gathering throngs along the shoreline. Soldiers surrounded the dock, keeping it clear and protected from the townspeople. Booths, tents, and awnings were going up in the street along the shore. It was like a fair being set up—wares and food and all manner of things would be sold, along with, no doubt, some goods from the ship. A festive spirit began to infect everyone.

I stood with my bag next to Flora, planning to disembark with her and tell the officials that I would also be going to a hacienda for domestic work. Already the King and Viceroy's galleon magistrates and the town constable were aboard discussing clearances and procedures with the Capitán. The passengers would be allowed to go ashore in the order of their caste ranking. All needed to be cleared by the local authorities, who had set up an office for this purpose on the far end of the dock.

Father Escovar came by to chat while we waited, not caring to take advantage of his privilege to disembark before us.

"Where are you going when you go ashore, Padre?" I asked.

"To the Monastery of Saint Francis. It is at the edge of the town, Señora. Then the next day I will go on a wagon across the country." Escovar smiled broadly. I could tell he was very happy.

After the people were ashore, the inventorying and unloading of the ship's hold would be done under strict supervision of the galleon magistrates and their assistants. The King and Viceroy would make sure that all merchandise due them would find its way to the guarded warehouses for shipment by mule train across the narrow continent. There were large numbers of black stevedores on the dock. They would do the backbreaking work of unloading the *Rosario*.

It took an hour before our turn came to ride over to the dock. On the dock I followed along with those waiting to be cleared. As I stood in line, sweat was dripping off my nose. It was stiflingly hot, and I was nervous. Flora kept telling me not to worry, but that did no good. Little did she know. When I was finally in front of the desk, the uniformed man looked at me suspiciously.

"Your name, Señora?"

"Abbie Spence, Señor." I had difficulty getting it out.

"What is your destination?"

"A hacienda to seek work."

He told me to wait and went over to where some men were standing. He began talking to one whom I recognized as Jíminez, *La Reina*'s first mate. They looked at me, and Jíminez nodded. The officer came back and said I was not free to go. I was under arrest until some questions could be answered. He motioned and another uniformed man of lesser rank came over. I was to go with this man to some place and stay until tomorrow when the alcades, the municipal magistrate, could see me. As we left I waved at Flora, who had been waiting for me, and she started crying. The poor dear could not believe that I could be in trouble.

As the guard led me through the merrymaking crowds—the well dressed, the working folk, and the paupers—I felt horribly depressed. Would it be death or hard labor? Were all of my troubles coming to an inglorious end in this stinking town in a back eddy of history? So where was that bastard, Bitterroot? When would the *Guadalupe* arrive? Obviously it would be too late. Abirrute would come ashore to find that the inglesa bruja had been dealt with sternly as was appropriate for witches. The Inquisition knew just what to do with the unGodly and the English enemies. This one doubly deserved purgatory.

We passed shops in the town's center, including the Royal Apothecary's Shop, and came to houses, mostly adobe with tiled roofs, eventually arriving at the outskirts of the town. The officer led me to a mud-walled house with a thatched roof. A chicken coop was out back. He knocked on the door, and an older woman with graying black hair appeared. He spoke to her quickly, and she nodded several times, eyeing me carefully.

"You are to stay here until tomorrow when I come for you. Do not leave at any time. Do whatever the Señora tells you. There will be a guard outside of the house." And he left.

The Señora, María de Esquibel, showed me to a tiny room with a dirt floor. A low bed of rough planks with a mat on it was the only furniture. A piece of cloth hung over the window. The room felt only a little cooler than being in the sun. I could hear hens clucking outside and a dog barking not too far away. I lay down on the mat and closed my eyes. I felt miserable.

Later Señora de Esquibel brought me a small earthenware pitcher of good-tasting water and a couple of pieces of cooked chicken. She said the water came from a chorillo, or little stream, off the mountain. She smiled at me but apparently didn't want to talk, despite my asking her questions. Maybe she was forbidden to befriend prisoners. The food cheered me somewhat. She showed me an outhouse near the hen yard where I could relieve myself, but accompanied me to be sure I didn't slip away. I wondered if there were really a guard around. I was struck by the poverty of her existence. It was far worse than the shipboard life on the galleon. As there was only one candle, which she used, I went to bed at dusk.

I slept fitfully for several hours. I don't know what woke me, but I detected something outside the window. All of my senses strained to fathom what it was. It was dark, but I had no idea of the hour. Then I heard a slight sound as if a foot had moved on the ground. I sat up and stared at the cloth over the window, my body now tense. Then I heard a whisper.

"Abbie. Abbie. Can you hear me? It's me."

My heart jumped, and I gasped.

"Abbie, wake up. It's me, Gordon."

"Yes, I'm awake, I'm here," I whispered back. "How did you get..."

"Shhh. Don't talk. Hand me your things and come. Be very quiet. We don't want to wake the dogs."

Without time to think, I quickly gathered up my things and handed the bag through the window to a gnarled hand. Then I pulled the curtain to one side and pushed my legs through, dropping softly to the dirt. There, standing one foot in front of me, grinning in the moonlight, eyes shining, was Gordon Bitterroot. Shock, ecstasy, rage, chagrin—it all swirled inside me as I stared at him, saying nothing.

19

I followed Bitterroot noiselessly up past the chicken coop and into the trees. There was a small path that could be discerned in the moonlight, leading through the brush. Glancing back as I reached a break in the trees, I could see the bay, the pale moonlight reflecting off the water. The ships riding at anchor were like tall ghosts casting long shadows. There were flickering lights on the galleon and the wharf. Oil lamps could be seen in houses around the town. Music and boisterous parties could be heard. Far off a dog was barking. Some nearby crickets added accompaniment.

We hit thick bushes, and it became darker and harder to pick our way along. As we slowly climbed in altitude I felt a sense of elation come over me. It was hard to believe that soon I would be in Los Angeles in my time. The mountain was steep, but knowing the fear and suffering soon would be over gave me great energy. So Bitterroot had not forgotten about me. He was a bastard, but just now a wonderful bastard. I only needed to get out, that's all that mattered.

"Gordon," I hissed, "isn't this far enough?"

"Just a bit farther, to the top of this ridge," he hissed back.

We climbed for what seemed like another twenty minutes before reaching the top of the ridge that came down from the large peak to the northeast. We went off the path and eventually came to a flat-topped rock that provided a vista not only toward the bay but also the interior. One could see dimly a valley, other ridges, and mountains.

"Oh Gordon, if you only knew what I've been through. How badly I want out. Please let's get back, and then we can talk." I couldn't help the tears streaming down my face.

"I do know what you've gone through, Abbie. You've done well. I'm proud of you. Except for Capitán López de Torres, it couldn't have been done any better. You're a star pupil."

Something churned within me. There he goes again, talking like he was in charge of me. But I held my tongue.

"Gordon, just beam me back. Now, please. I'm ready."

He stood up, looking out over the bay. "We're not going back yet, Abbie. We have to push on with the plan."

It was like a punch to the stomach. Then the ground began moving. I felt like I was losing my balance. The scrub tree in front of me began shaking.

"Gordon, what's happening?" I shouted.

"Get down," he commanded, crouching down himself. The mountain was moving back and forth. After about thirty seconds it stopped.

"Just a tremor," he said. "This is one of the worst fault areas in the world. The plates continually rub here."

I sat up, still trembling. But more shattering than the tremor was the statement I had heard just before.

"Did you say we're not going back?"

"It's not time to go back. The important work is still to be done."

"I don't care," I yelled. "I want to go back now! Now! Do you hear me?" My screaming voice echoed.

"Shhh. Keep it down, or someone will hear us," he said softly. "I know you are tired and want to go back, but we are getting close to our Southern Dreams. There is no turning back now."

"Gordon," I said, trying to control my rage. "You have no right to keep me here, against my will. Take me back now. I'll even discuss your crazy Southern Dreams—the men of war ships, whatever—when we're back there. So let's just go now."

"No Abbie, we have to push forward. It won't be hard from now on."

Something in me broke. I flew at him and started flailing at his head. I wasn't in control. I was so angry I could have ground him into hamburger. As he defended with his arms, I scratched and clawed and kneed and pounded. It went on for several minutes until I became exhausted and began crying. He had my wrists in his hands and slowly released them when he saw that the storm was over. There was blood on my hands. I must have gouged him badly before he gained control of my flashing nails.

Nothing was said between us for quite some time. I felt both ashamed and gratified. It was childish, but he more than deserved it. I wouldn't have cared if his eyes had come out. Then, as my anger subsided, all I could think of was, why me? Why did he want to do this to me?

"Gordon, just tell me why," I said softly. "Why are you doing this to me? What did I ever do to you? Why me?"

"Because, Abbie, only thee can do it."

"Do what, for God's sake?"

"Turn history around. Get the Spaniards out of the Americas."

"Get the Spaniards out of America? What on earth are you talking about, Gordon?"

"Spain doesn't deserve the New World. History has shown that Central and South America have been a disaster under Spanish culture and the Catholics. First Cortés and Pizarro pillaged the finest Indian societies in all of history. They stole their artifacts, melted down their beautiful gold and silver artwork, murdered and enslaved their people, and gutted the mineral resources. The Spanish way of life, the authoritarian government, the imperious church—either treating people like children or terrorizing them with the Inquisition—the mean-spirited and lazy values brought over, the closeting of the women add up to the worst possible heritage that could have come to this beautiful land. Look what has happened. In three hundred years all of the Latin countries have become economic and social basket cases. The populations are mostly uneducated, poor, and indolent. They multiplied beyond control because Catholicism said it was good to have babies. How will they ever recover from this exploded population bomb? Look at Mexico City—it's an abomination. Now the beautiful rainforests are being destroyed with terrible loss of habitat and species. All for what? No, Abbie, it shouldn't have happened, and we can turn it back. You and me."

I stood up slowly, stretching away the hurts in my arms and legs from the tussle. "You're crazy, Gordon. I knew you were weird. But it's more than that. You are psychotic."

"Abbie, open up your mind. You know what I'm saying is true. Spanish control over the New World was a major mistake—a cruel joke of history. Here was a pint-sized country already on the decline by the 1600s. Here was a corrupt and stupid religion already reformed in form and substance by the leading societies of Germany and England. At a time of the flowering of science and the Enlightenment, who was selected by default to influence more than half the Americas? Ignorant Spain and the Catholics." Here, Bitterroot spat loudly.

"Abbie, Spain and its uneducated peasants did not even know what the Enlightenment was. They did not understand the concepts of freedom and equality. Right now in 1704 Hobbes, Locke, Bacon and Decartes are unknown to these people. In the next few decades, they will not even hear of Rousseau or Voltaire. Even by 1900 more than half of their population will still be illiterate. No, they bought into authoritarianism early and kept it late. They had Franco, a dictator, up until the 1970s. Their Catholicism thrived on illiteracy and ignorance. This is Spain. And these were the people allowed to spread their cultural cancer to more than half of the New World. Incredible!"

"Gordon, that cultural cancer gave the world Picasso, Greco, Miró, Cervantes, Goya, and Segovia. It produced literature and music, Mediterranean architecture, some of the best laid out cities, and rational government. It gave the world brave explorers and compassion for the poor. It gave us one of the major and lasting empires. You are talking about Spain and one of the more romantic, colorful, and energetic peoples of Europe. What would the European tradition be without Spain?"

"Europe and the world—especially the New World—would have been a lot better off. All those bullfighters and priests should have stayed home. They knew not what seeds of misery they were planting."

"You are so arrogant! So who should have colonized South America by your book? England and its infantile kings?"

"Any of the forward looking countries at the time would have done a far better job—England, France, Germany, or Holland. Germany, one of the more intelligent and inspired countries, unfortunately, was not a sea power. Holland was too small and caught up in its mercantilism and the East Indies. France was torn between Descartes and Rousseau. She had not yet dealt with her Catholicism and feudalistic monarchs. France was focusing internally, getting ready for her revolution. The only country that could have taken—and will take—the New World away from Spain is England. And the time to do it is in the late 1600s or early 1700s. England has superior sea forces. Drake and his Golden Hind showed that the Spanish Main is vulnerable. But it takes more than hit-and-run privateers. It needs commitment from the government. It needs a major military force to wrest away key strategic locations, and it requires its own people to come and hold the captured lands and to settle. It needs the imagination of the English population to be captivated with the idea. It needs a galvanizing event. That's right where we are now, Abbie. That's where you come in."

The hair on the back of my neck was standing up. He was off the deep end, for sure. Holding conversation with him was ludicrous. He actually believed what he was saying. What was I to do? I was dealing with madness.

"Gordon, why don't you get someone else to do it? I'm really not up to this. Why don't you get Biru or Abirrute or whoever those guys are. Are they real?"

"I need a woman, Abbie. You are the first I've been able to find. My historical friends can still help—Abirrute because he speaks Spanish—but only you can do what is needed."

"What exactly do you need me to do, Gordon?" I was trying a new tack, talking seriously with him.

"I can't tell thee now."

"Why on earth not? How could I do it if you don't tell me what 'it' is?"

"You must not know, lest the Spanish get it out of you, as they can so easily do. Only when the time is right must thee know. Meantime, we'll put you in position."

"What position? Where?"

"Further south. First to Panama. Then further south. To a strategic island."

"And how do I get there?"

"First you will go on the filabote that will be leaving in two days, taking goods to Panama. Abirrute will be on it to help."

"But why don't we just beam me down there? Why waste time?"

"Because your mind is not right now. Also, the timing with other events has to be just so."

"What's wrong with my mind? Is it that you don't think I want to go there?"

"I know thee, Abbie."

"Yes you do, Gordon. And you must know that I'm not going on the stinking filabote. I quit right now. Right here. You and your Southern Dreams can go to hell. If you won't take me back to Los Angeles, then I'll just stay here and die. You won't help me, so I won't help you. How do you like that, my friend?"

"Abbie, that would be a grave mistake. If you go on with me, I warrant that you not only will be famous in history, but that you will get back to Los Angeles. It will have a different name of course. But you will have immortality. If you don't go for the Southern Dreams, you will rot here and no doubt be horribly mistreated by your beloved Spaniards if you even live very long."

"You would really abandon me?" My voice was almost a squeak.

"It is thee who will choose."

I couldn't believe what I was hearing. I stared at a piece of his skin on my fingernail for a minute. Then I found my voice again.

"You are a first class brute, Gordon. You say the Spanish are brutal, but just look at you now. You have kidnapped me, lied to me, allowed me to be tormented and tortured, and now you are ready to callously cast me to a terrible fate. You are a sadist. And a chauvinist. Don't talk to me about the Enlightenment. I hope the Spaniards catch you and run you through. I'm going no further with your cockeyed plan."

I thought I saw Bitterroot actually wince. He turned away and looked out to the bay for a minute or two before facing me again, his jaw set.

"So be it, Abbie. Then let me help you avoid further harm. At daybreak, make your way down this ridge to the east and to the river at the bottom of the valley. There you'll find the road. Wait there and hail the morning mule train that will be going inland. Your friend, Villalobos, will probably be on it, and you can join her. I will go back to the house and hold María de Esquibel incommunicado so that they don't know you have escaped for quite a while. By then you will be out of the area. Chances are they will search only locally and not go after the wagon party."

He actually meant it. I was at first dumbfounded, but then my anger rose again.

"Fine. It's a little late for favors, Gordon, but as you say, so be it."

"Lie down in the leaves and try and get some rest. You'll need it, Abbie. I'm going back to the house. Faretheewell. So much for the Southern Dreams."

And then he chuckled.

There was nothing funny. I stood with a horrible feeling in my stomach. But I would not flinch.

"Goodbye, Gordon."

He slowly made his way back the way we had come and I listened as the sounds of his footsteps faded. I looked up at the stars. I suddenly felt like praying. "Oh God, if you really are there, I need you more than ever. Please, please help me." After a few minutes of complete silence, I lay down on the ground.

I didn't sleep much the rest of the night and was groggy when dawn finally came. It was hard for me to start east, down into the canyon. I thought seriously about retreating to the house where Bitterroot was. I could have breezily told him I changed my mind, that I would go on the filabote. But it would have put the lie to my whole being. If I did that, I would stand for nothing. I would have allowed his intimidation to work. He would have won. And besides, I had seen enough of smelly vessels for a while. So with reluctant determination, I made my way down the steep side of the ridge toward the river, which fed into a large lake that I now could see—probably Lake Papagayo that Escovar had mentioned.

I was calling Bitterroot's bluff. Something in me still felt that he would not allow me to be stuck in this place and time for the rest of my days. Deep down I did not believe he was totally ruthless. I told myself that once he realized I would not participate in the Southern Dreams, he would take me back.

I thought about his thesis—that Spain had not been the right colonial power for the New World. There had been, to be sure, a lot of excesses. The conquistadors had terribly mistreated the Indians. But the English had also mistreated the North American natives. Spain always had varying racial and ethnic groups in its background—Arabs, Moors, Jews, and other Mediterraneans. So, culturally, it was easier for the Spanish to work alongside the Aztecs and the Incas. The Spaniards had come for riches and empire and did not bring many women. Thus the Spanish men intermarried with the Indians. New Spain was bound to become heterogeneous—a mestizo people with an amalgamated culture derived from both the Spaniard and the Indian.

The English were different. They were settlers seeking religious freedom. They wanted to have their own communities, and they had come, men and women, for new lives. Although there were missionaries, most Protestant settlers did not care about converting the heathens, as the Catholics did. They pushed the Indians westward and did not fraternize. The only good Indian was a dead Indian.

Thus the North American colonies became much more English in race and culture than New Spain became Spanish. Is this English approach one that Bitterroot wanted? A more purified colonization? If that had happened and the Catholic church had not been dominant, as it wouldn't have been under English rule, then there would have likely been a far smaller and more racially separated population in the central and southern new world. The Europeans would have had their communities and the Indians their reservations. The idea sounded preposterous.

Besides, how in the world could one woman make a difference in all this? Gordon was out of his gourd.

It began to warm up, and the humidity was high. I was tired and hungry. I could now see the dirt road, and this kept me going. The foliage thickened as I got closer to the bottom. At one point I grabbed at a drooping tree limb only to see a small, green snake coiled on a branch just inches from my hand. I screamed and jumped, falling back on my rear. The snake, frightened, slithered higher among the branches. I wondered if it were poisonous.

The road was narrow where I met it, with many hoof marks and wagon wheel tracks gouged into the dried mud. During heavy rains it was probably impassable. I found a good place to lie down and watch for anyone coming up the road from the west. Soon I was snoozing. The sound of hooves woke me about twenty minutes later. But the wagon was coming from the east. I scrunched back into the bushes. Four mules were pulling a long wagon with seven people in it—four men, two women, and a young girl. The men had wide-brimmed hats, and the women wore colorful scarves over their heads. As they went around the bend and out of sight, I surmised they were heading for the galleon fair. Soon after, another wagon full of people followed by a couple of men on horseback came through from the same direction. Several people, heavy loads on their backs, also passed on foot. At least the road was well traveled.

In less than an hour, I heard a wagon coming from the west. When it rounded into view, I scrutinized it and saw the white robe of a priest among the passengers. I jumped out into the road and waved my arms; the driver reined in the six-mule team, and the animals stopped twenty feet from me, wary-eyed and heaving. The man next to the driver grabbed a musket, jumped down, and came up to me cautiously.

"Who are you?" he asked in a Spanish that almost had a drawl.

"My name is Abbie Spence. I want to talk to one of your passengers. Please mister." I hoped my Spanish was understandable. I felt I was getting the idioms down.

Several of the passengers including the priest had stood up in the wagon to see what was going on. I recognized Father Escovar, who was staring at me.

"Father, it's me, Abbie."

He jumped quickly to the ground. I also could see Flora now, smiling and waving.

"Señora Abbie, how is it you are here?" Escovar had an astonished look about his face.

"It's a long story. I'm tired and hungry. I want to come with you on the wagon, Father."

"But of course. We can't leave you here."

He turned to the driver, the man with the musket, and another who had gathered around us and told them he knew me, I had been on the *Rosario,* and I should be allowed to join them on the journey to Chilpancingo. Soon I was in the back of the wagon, sitting on a gunny sack of grain next to Flora and Father Escovar and eating a banana. A large cloth awning held up by posts at each of the wagon corners provided partial shade. There were seven of us altogether, the driver and his sidekick, and five passengers. The wagon was heavily loaded with supplies and baggage. I saw several rifles and pistols. Two riderless horses tied behind trotted along, swishing their tails to keep away the flies.

The road followed the river up the canyon, occasionally coming within a few feet of the bank. The driver stopped every so often to let the animals drink and rest. Pulling the heavily burdened wagon ever higher into the Sierra Madre del Sol was grueling. I felt sorry for the mules which often felt the lick of a whip when they lagged.

Flora and Father Escovar pushed me for an explanation of how I had come to meet the wagon at that place on the road. I told a half truth. I said that I had been taken to a house of decrepit condition and could not stand staying there, so I had left quietly in the middle of the night and had lost my way in the mountains behind the house. After answering a few questions, they seemed to be satisfied.

I then learned of their destinations. Father Escovar was going back to Spain as an envoy bringing news about the Philippines. First he would stop in Mexico City to brief the Viceroy and then he would travel to Vera Cruz and embark on a ship headed for Spain. There he would be seeing the king's ministers as well as church officials. It sounded quite important, and it was clear that Escovar was very proud of his mission. Flora would be leaving the wagon in two days at Chilpancingo, the highlands where a large hacienda owned by Don Eduardo Mendoza was located. She would take up domestic duties for Don Mendoza's wife, Doña Margaríta.

I enjoyed the scenery as we climbed higher. There were still coconut trees to be seen, but mostly there was thick, junglelike growths of trees and bushes. This verdure was mainly in the river canyon where there was water.

On the mountains and ridges there was little growth. We saw a skunk cross the road, which caused the drivers to rein in. On a tree trunk I saw a large brown bird the size of a chicken, which pecked the bark like a woodpecker. Escovar told me this was the Herrero bird. They were good to eat. Several more wagons passed us on their way down to the galleon fair.

It cooled off some as we reached a place near the river where we would spend the night. The humidity was still high and sweat formed on faces of anyone doing the slightest amount of work. I ended up helping Flora cook for the whole group after the men had set up the camp and made a fire. We had beans, tortillas, corn, and chicken. The women's sleeping area was sectioned off from the men's by a large blanket tied to a line strung between trees. My bed consisted of a reed mat and one blanket. It would be a difficult night, but at least the amenities were better than the night before.

After dinner clean-up, again done by Flora and me, Father Escovar joined us for conversation down by the water's edge.

"Father, what is Don Eduardo like?" I asked. "And how is it to live on a hacienda?"

"Don Eduardo is a descendent of one of the original conquistadors who came with Cortés. The conquistadors were given land grants from the crown as a reward for their glorious achievement, and these have passed down from son to son. Don Eduardo's hacienda is one of the orginal grants."

"They say it is beautiful, no?" Flora said.

"Yes, it is beautiful. But the beauty is marred by the problems."

"What problems," I asked.

"The treatment of the Indians on these lands is not good."

Escovar was critical of the way the Indian lands had been expropriated. Fields used by various tribes for crops had been destroyed when the rancheros brought in huge herds of range cattle. Worst of all was the establishment of encomienda, the law that all Indians on the granted land became the slaves of the landowner, who could treat and work them as he pleased. The Indians became the peons to work the mines and ranches under harsh and often brutal conditions. Indians were sold in slave markets, and the women were frequently taken and maltreated by the Spaniards and Creoles. Village and family life of the Indians was drastically altered by the Spaniards in their effort to pursue riches and Catholicize the heathens. Escovar was especially critical of an influential Spanish writer named Sepulveda, who at the time had justified the maltreatment of the Indians, categorizing them as inferior beings whose evil ways had to be changed.

The encomienda laws had been revised in the last century. Many of the landowners had become more enlightened in their treatment of the Indians, who were freed from the worst subjugation even though carryover of old attitudes still existed in places.

"I know Don Mendoza is very rich and respected. His is a successful rancho that covers much land. He has a young and vivacious wife and three lovely children."

Flora beamed. "He sounds brave."

"So what are your plans, Señora Spence?" Father Escovar asked.

In that mental moment before I spoke, my heart told me a secret. I wanted to go with Father Escovar on his exciting journey. The draw was not just to faraway lands, but the attraction of the man, as impossible as that seemed. It was everything about him, his gentleness, smiling eyes, educated speech, concern for the Indians. If Gordon had met Escovar, he would have to change his mind about the Spaniards and Catholics, or at least one of them. And if there was one Escovar, there had to be more.

But my heart was not rational. Escovar would be shocked by my thoughts about him. He would recoil from my touch. His life was given to Jesus and to the Church. He could not travel with a single woman. He would stay at monasteries. I had no money to be put up at inns. No money to pay for board. No money to pay for coaches and horses. I had only one change of clothes. There was no way to even propose going with him. It would be embarrassing even to express the idea to the gentle man.

"I would like to go work at Señor Don Eduardo's hacienda. Do you think they would take me?"

"Oh I'm sure they would," Flora said. "You are so smart. They would take you if they take me."

"Yes, I'm sure they can find a place for you, Señora Abbie," Escovar seconded. "I will speak to Don Eduardo myself about it."

He smiled benignly, and my heart saddened at how easily my fate had been sealed. But there really was no alternative. One bright spot was that I would be with Flora. Maybe I would like the new life. It had to be better than my miserable existence on the *Guadalupe*. And to hell with Bitterroot, too.

I awoke just before dawn when I heard one of the men stirring. Flora and I had to get up and make breakfast. My socks were especially ripe, but I put them on and slipped first one foot and then the other into the leather shoes I had obtained on the *Rosario*. When my left foot went into the shoe, I felt something in the toe. It began moving. It was unhappy. I jerked my shoe off but not before I felt something sharp stab my big toe. I screamed and threw the shoe several feet in front of me.

"Aieee," Flora yelled.

My toe was on fire and beginning to swell. The pain was so overwhelming, I could not speak. Several of the men gathered around me. One of them stepped on something near my discarded shoe.

"Escorpión!" he shouted. A scorpion.

The pain shot up my leg. I screamed more. They leaned me back on my bedroll and one of the men brought out a knife. I couldn't watch. Flora held my leg, and I jerked and yelled as he cut on my big toe and began sucking at the poison. He could have been cutting my toe off, the pain was so intense. Soon I became feverish and they put a blanket on me.

Flora held me. "They think you will be all right. Just try to rest."

I moaned while they carried me to the wagon. Underway, the motion and bumping on the road added to my misery. I curled into a ball on top of some gunny sacks under an old wool blanket and whimpered for a couple of hours under Flora's watchful eye. She made me drink lots of water. I began sweating profusely, becoming delirious. I don't remember what happened the rest of that day. By evening when we had camped again, the pain and fever had lessened. I was able to eat, but I felt very weak. I fell asleep early and was unconscious until daybreak.

When I opened my eyes, Flora was there, smiling.

"That is the hard way to get out of making breakfast and dinner," she said.

For the first time in twenty-four hours, I gave the hint of a smile.

The mountains grew steeper and the pitch of the road made the load too much for the mules. Supplies were tied onto the horses, and all of the men walked except the driver. I felt guilty staying in the wagon, but I still was not in shape for strenuous walking. I looked out three hundred and sixty degrees from my perch. The bare, rugged mountains were like a watercolor with hundreds of purplish shadings.

I didn't know the elevation, but breathing was less comfortable. Escovar said I would get used to the thin air. We made Chilpancingo just before noon. The village square consisted of a store, stables, and a small adobe church with a rounded belfry dominating the facade. Pigs were rooting off the street. Indian women in faded, geometrically patterned clothes stood and talked in front of the store, some holding sacks from their shopping. Children yelled and ran around the buildings. Although the air was cooler up here, the sun beat down, making it intensely hot in its direct rays.

The driver parked the wagon near the store so that some of the goods could be unloaded. The mules, now shuffling in gait, were unhitched and taken to the stable to be watered and fed. Flora and I followed Father Escovar to a small house behind the church amid some high trees. A severely limping priest came out on the porch to greet us, the bell on the swinging gate having announced our arrival. The older man and Father Escovar embraced warmly and chatted for a while before Flora and I were introduced.

We all sat on the porch in chairs made from branches while our situation was discussed. Father Antonio scrutinized me as Father Escovar explained who I was and that I wanted to work at the hacienda. It was clear from the old man's facial expression that I was puzzling to him. I gave him my best smile, and he warmed to me.

"What knowledge do you have Señora?" he asked.

"I can teach mathematics and geography, Father."

"She is very intelligent," Escovar said. "Her language is improving rapidly."

I blushed as Father Antonio smiled and nodded.

"If Don Eduardo is not out on the range lands, we might expect to see him in two hours," he said. A rider had already been dispatched to the hacienda.

I became nervous and excited. Slowly the prospect of living on a Spanish hacienda in 1704 was sinking in. Butterflies were flying around in my stomach.

The road from Hacienda Mendoza to Chilpancingo comes down a hill. The cry of approaching horses went up in the village long before one could recognize who was coming. But there were at least three riders and a surrey. One of the ridden horses was white. Father Antonio said it was the steed of Señor Don Eduardo Mendoza. The surrey belonged to Doña Margaríta. Excitement spread through the village. The fabled Don and his lady drew attention as if they were royalty.

The Don was the first to pull up. He wore a white, long-sleeved silk shirt adorned with black buttons, each appearing like polished obsidian. The tight black pants had decorative stitching in silver and gold down each leg. His black boots, with filagree designs and patent-leather shine, rose almost to his knees. He wore a wide-brimmed hat, also black leather.

Don Eduardo sharply reined, causing the panting horse to dance backward. A grin of white crooked teeth opened on the Don's darkly tanned face. Despite the splendor of the man on the horse, I was shocked. He was scarcely twenty-five years old.

Doña Margaríta pulled up in the surrey, her driver clucking at the roan mare to maneuver the coach so that it was sideways to the tiled walk in front of the church where we all stood. Don Eduardo helped her climb down. She was not more than five feet in height, but she had an amazingly narrow waist that made her ample hips and breasts stand out voluptuously. Her near perfectly featured face was milk white, made starker by her black hair and dark eyes. She wore a full dress, tan in color, with full length sleeves and white gloves. The dress had many folds and bulged out in the back with some kind of bustle. Over her head was a lacy white silk scarf that was fastened under her chin with an intricate gold pin. On her feet were dainty tan shoes that accentuated her small ankles. Gold buttons ran down the side of each shoe. Except for the imperious look, she could have been a high school student dressed up for a costume party.

Don Eduardo grasped the extended hands of the priests and began talking loudly while Doña Margaríta smiled prettily as she eyed Flora and me standing to one side. The men's conversation went on at length, and neither Doña Margaríta nor Flora and I were included. Finally, the men came over and introductions were made. I followed Flora's example and curtsied as best I could to the Don and Doña. I felt embarrassed about my rumpled clothes and could not help thinking I was not making a good impression. The padres beamed at us as we were scrutinized by our prospective benefactors. Doña Margaríta asked Flora about her life in the Philippines and what kinds of household work she could do. The Doña seemed satisfied with the answers. I became self-conscious as Don Eduardo stood close to me and looked me up and down.

"Muchacha, what subjects could you teach our children?" he abruptly asked.

I swallowed hard.

"Señor Don Mendoza, I could teach your children mathematics, geography, history, and philosophy...and the English language if you so desired."

He eyed me curiously. "Philosophy? What philosophy?"

"Well, Greek philosophy—Aristotle, Plato, Socrates..."

"No, I want them taught philosophy only by the church. And I don't trust any Englishman's history, either. You will instruct in mathematics and geography only."

"Yes sir," I said. "How old are your children?"

Something was suddenly wrong. A scowl came across his face. Doña Margaríta had just come up and was now looking at both of us.

"Don't you know to speak only when spoken to?" he asked with contempt. "We will ask the questions."

"Yes, I am sorry," I said, bowing my head slightly. I looked away from his stern gaze to Doña Margaríta.

"Can you clean rooms, moza?" she asked. Moza was a term for servant.

"Oh yes, Doña Margaríta," I replied, trying to smile at her.

"And empty bedpans?" Now she smiled, but not with warmth. I felt a sudden visceral aversion to her.

"Of course."

"Bueno, moza."

"Bueno," Don Eduardo echoed. "You may get into the coach now, muchacha."

I looked up and saw Flora being helped into the front seat of the surrey. I looked over at Father Escovar who smiled at me. It was happening so fast. I ran over to Escovar almost startling him.

"Adiós. May God be your guard, Abbie. Que El te acompane," he said, gathering his composure.

"Father, no, I think it's a mistake for me to go. Can I stay here?"

His face wrinkled. "There's no place for you here, Abbie. You're just nervous. You will do fine. Don Eduardo and Doña Margaríta will treat you well. Please do not worry. Do not keep them waiting."

"Please Father, could I go with you instead?"

"No, Abbie. No. Please, now get in the carriage."

I realized there really was no choice. I took in a deep breath.

"Adiós, Father Escovar." I couldn't stop tears from coming.

"Adiós. Vaya con Dios, Abbie."

I slowly walked to the coach. Hands pushed me up into the front seat next to Flora. Doña Margaríta was in back behind us. There was waving as the harness tinkled, the leather creaked, and the coach began moving. I felt sick. How had this happened to me? Flora put her arm around me and began dabbing at my eyes with a hankie. I don't remember much of the trip to the hacienda except that it was dusty. I do remember Flora's arm around me and her talking to me in encouraging tones. Thank God for her. But by the time we entered into the center courtyard, my dignity and composure had returned. If Flora could take this like a woman, then so could I. Damn if I would give them the feeling that I was intimidated. Where was my pride, anyway? I was an educated, competent person. These were uneducated, immature kids playing dress up. So as I stepped down, I stood tall and looked Doña Margaríta in the eye.

"What a beautiful hacienda," I said. "I'm going to like it here."

For a moment a flash of fear crossed her eyes. Then she gave her ingenuous smile. "Sí moza, you will like it, and so you will work hard, no?"

"Sí, Doña Margaríta."

"Listen carefully, moza. You are not to look at Don Eduardo. You are not to speak to him. You are to stay away from him. Do you understand me?"

"Sí, Doña." My optimism left as quickly as it had come.

The hacienda was a quadrangle with a tiled inner courtyard covering part of it. A shallow pond with fish and plants highlighted the middle of the courtyard, and not far from this was a well encircled by a stone wall. A large tree, somewhat like a weeping willow, stood to one side. Several flowers I couldn't identify were in bloom. Wooden chairs and benches provided a place to sit, some in shade, some in sun. Above the tiled roof of the house I could see the rugged peaks. The setting was truly beautiful. It was like being in the walled garden of Shangrila.

A large, friendly dog came up and nudged my hand. At that moment the children burst into the yard. There were three of them. The oldest was a boy of about seven. He had dark hair and piercing brown eyes. A girl of about five, with lighter colored brown hair and fair skin like her mother, came to stop with the boy just a few yards from Flora and me, staring. While they glanced at Flora, they seemed mostly fixed upon me, as if I were some weird animal. The youngest was a toddler who went up to hide in the dress of her mother, peeking around the folds. Bringing up the rear was an older woman. Her face was heavily wrinkled though she was only in her late forties, I guessed. She was dressed in a flowing calico skirt and red silk blouse. Her dark hair was coiled in a bun on the back of her head. If these were Doña Margarita's children, she must have had them very young. She had either been a child bride, or she was older than I had guessed.

"Niños, this is Abbie, and that is Flora," Doña Margaríta said in a firm voice. "Abbie will be your new teacher." The older boy looked warily at me but did not flinch or smile. The girl behind him put her thumb in her mouth. The older children's names were Juanito and Rosetta. The young one was called Dulcíta.

"Mozas," Doña Margaríta continued, "this is my mother, Dueña Carmela. You are to obey her as you obey me."

We returned Dueña Carmela's smile and nod. There was one immediate difference I saw between mother and daughter. The smile of the older woman was sincere.

The beginning did not seem auspicious. Even though there was the festivity of Christmas upon us and I received presents of shoes and a shawl, I had a feeling that Scrooge would have felt comfortable in that house. There was an unfriendly atmosphere that the holiday spirit could not overcome.

21

The servants quarters were in the back of the house, farthest from where the family lived. There were two other female servants, both very young, probably in their teens. They shared a room. Flora and I were put in a room together next to them. The room was stark, with only two beds and a small chest of drawers. The window had a piece of heavy cowhide hanging over it. This cover was rolled up during the day except in bad weather. My bed was a frame of planks with horsehair matting and a cotton cover. There were two wool blankets.

One of the servant girls took care of the family wash, which was done in large metal tubs out behind the house. Cold water was used from the well. Washing was an arduous duty, and I was glad not to have this responsibility. The other girl was the cook, but she was also helped in the kitchen by a young man who lived in the stable behind the house. He kept the fires stoked, lifted heavy things, and maintained the pantry. I learned that there had been an older servant woman who had died about four months ago. She had supervised the others. It was clear from the other girls and from Doña Margaríta that, even though she was the eldest of us, Flora was not to supervise anyone.

My role was rather strange. I was to instruct the two older children and to help Flora clean the house. I was also responsible for emptying the chamber pots for all family members several times a day, as needed. As this job was looked down upon by the other servants, I seemed to be lowest in the pecking order. However, the teaching role was a respected one, which put me a cut above the servant category. No doubt Doña Margaríta had planned this combination to be sure I remained suitably humble.

The family's quarters were luxuriously appointed. The furniture was a combination of teak and nara wood, ornately carved, probably obtained from the Philippines by means of the galleon. Beautiful silks and brocades hung over the windows. The tile floors had leafy designs painted on them and were brightly polished.

There were five fireplaces, one in the living room, one in the kitchen, and one in each of the family bedrooms. These were the only sources of heat, except for oil lamps and candles. Cooking was done in the kitchen in large kettles and skillets that could be swung over the fire on hinged wrought iron hooks. There was a large bathroom with a high sided copper tub. Hot water was heated in the kitchen and brought in by the servants. The water in the tub was made just the right temperature before the bather was called. The good sized dining room had a refectory style table with carved legs. This room was used only by family members and guests. The help ate in a small room off the pantry after the family had finished their meal.

Don Eduardo was seldom home during the day. The servants normally spent evenings in their rooms after kitchen clean-up, so I did not see Don Eduardo much. And due to what Doña Margaríta had said to me, I was afraid to see him. However, a few days after my arrival he sought me out and took me to the library to show me the books I could use in teaching the children. There were several religious books, two of them the catechism. There was one small atlas showing maps of Europe, Spain, and the New World. There was a book on Spanish history, a book on etiquette, a book on mining, and a Spanish dictionary. There was nothing on mathematics. There were no novels or poetry books.

"You can teach with these, Señora," Don Eduardo said proudly.

"Sí, Señor Don Eduardo. These will be good."

"You are to spend most of your time with Juanito. Do not worry about Rosetta."

I simply nodded, trying not to reveal my intentions. His directive made me want to only spend time only with Rosetta and to hell with Juanito. But some deep sense of fairness made me pledge to myself that each would get equal attention and instruction.

Doña Margaríta came up to me after my meeting with Don Eduardo.

"Moza, go scrub the outside patio. Use this only." She handed me a small handbrush.

"Sí, Doña Margaríta." I knew that my meeting with Don Eduardo had inspired this back-breaking task.

The lessons with the children were to take place in the library, which had a nice table and good light coming in the large windows. I decided to make the first meeting simply a get-acquainted time to learn about my new charges. I thought that holding the first session outside might be less intimidating to the children and I told Doña Margaríta of my plans. She became anxious and said we could go out only if Dueña Carmela accompanied us. As it turned out, Carmela stayed at a distance, leaving us on our own, which pleased me.

Juanito was aggressive but fairly well mannered. He came alongside me without hesitation and chattered about special places on the grounds. Rosetta hung back for a while, mainly listening to us. By the end of an hour, she was the one alongside me while Juanito ran out and about. I warmed to her immediately; perhaps my maternal instincts were stimulated because I sensed she needed love. Maybe her parents had given too much attention to Juanito and left her shorted.

"Were you on the galleon, Señora Abbie?"

"Yes, Juanito."

"What was it like? Did they fire the cannons?"

"No they didn't fire the cannons, but there was a lot of treasure in the hold."

Juanito wanted to know all about ships, but I told him there would be plenty of time at future meetings. The first session ended with both teacher and pupils excited about each other. I felt very good, but the feeling was shortlived. Upon my entering the house, Doña Magaríta told me to empty the chamber pot in her bedroom, and I was to be quick about it. I had never met anyone who seethed with so much jealousy.

At the next session, I introduced arithmetic. I started with rudimentary facts, since the only symbolic concept the children knew was counting. Juanito could add small numbers on his fingers, but that was about it. So we began learning addition and subtraction and how to do it with paper and pencil. It went slowly, but I tried to make it humorous by using funny examples.

"If you have a momma pig and she gives birth to four piglets, how many are there? Draw them and count them."

The children were able to do this correctly.

"All right, if one of the piggies is bad and runs and hides behind the barn, how many are there now?"

"He will come back. He will come back," Rosetta kept saying.

"What bad did the piggie do?" Juanito wanted to know.

I soon realized I was dealing with bright, inquisitive children who would tax my skills, but I welcomed it and looked forward to our sessions.

The variety of food served at the hacienda was not great. There was mainly beef, chicken, turkey, pork, and beans. I was concerned that there weren't enough green vegetables in the diet, but how could I explain vitamin deficiency? I gathered that I should be thankful for having food because many of the peóns, especially the Indians, were starving. But my fears about the diet increased when I realized that the life expectancy was around forty.

Carmela, whom I had thought was in her forties, turned out to be in her early thirties, scarcely older than I. She had not aged gracefully. She had married at thirteen and had given birth to Doña Margaríta at fourteen. Her husband, a vaquero, died from an unknown disease at age twenty-six. I learned that diseases and fevers occurred frequently and took a heavy toll. This made me worry about the water supply. With all the cattle around, I suspected that the water was polluted. Cholera could be endemic. Also there were mosquitoes. They could easily transmit yellow fever. The closest doctor was in Acapulco. But with the state of medical knowledge in 1705, for we had passed into the new year, that was probably for the better. He most likely did more harm than good, practicing bloodletting and other remedies of the day.

If I stayed long at this "Shangrila" I might live only ten or fifteen years, even if I did not catch a deadly disease. As if to underscore the point, I soon came down with a bad case of Montezuma's revenge. It layed me low for several days. Flora, thank God, helped me, but Doña Margaríta thought I was shirking and made nasty comments to me. During the worst of it, I kept thinking about my mother, wishing I were a child again so that she could soothe me. But I recovered and got back into the routine of teaching and taking out the foul smelling pots. My new life was starkly symbolic of fun and drudgery, beginnings and endings.

Perhaps the most depressing thing about my new existence was the confinement. Even during our free time on Sundays, we servants were not to go anywhere beyond the outer perimeter of the hacienda without permission. Whenever I asked, I was denied.

"It is dangerous, Abbie," Carmela said. "There is nobody to protect you from the men and the Indians."

"But I am willing to take my chances. Please let me take a walk. I am bored here."

"No. Don Eduardo will not permit it."

The family went to church in Chilpancingo every Sunday morning, but only one servant was allowed to go each time. I only rarely got a turn. I knew Doña Margaríta was behind this. On occasions when I did go, I was not allowed to talk to any of the men attending the service, other than old Father Antonio. Of the women I met, most treated me rather strangely. Still, I found the trip exhilarating if only because of the things to see along the way. About a quarter mile down the road from the hacienda were several barns, corrals, and bunkhouses. Don Eduardo's vaqueros lived and worked there. When we passed by these men, they looked at us but never waved or showed signs of familiarity. I asked about this and learned from the other servants that Don Eduardo Mendoza was a tyrant. He frequently ordered men to be whipped. He maintained the loyalty of his key lieutenants by providing them houses and upping their wages and keeping them fearful of him. On the other hand, his herds had expanded and the produce of the hacienda had continually increased. Of course, he had extended the rangelands by viciously destroying Indian villages that were in the way. But people and officials outside the hacienda admired the brave and energetic Don.

The situation reminded me of an excerpt I had once used as the basis for a paper in a literature course at Reed. It was from John Steinbeck's *Cannery Row:*

> "It has always seemed strange to me," said Doc. "The things we admire in men, kindness and generosity, openness, honesty, understanding and feeling, are the concomitants of failure in our system. And those traits we detest, sharpness, greed, acquisitiveness, meanness, egotism and self interest, are the traits of success. And while men admire the quality of the first they love the produce of the second."

This seemed to fit the young Don well.

I suspected that the reason that Don Eduardo did not permit his family or servants beyond the fence around the house was because he had enemies. Maybe some of the Indians and vaqueros would find it only too easy to take revenge if given the opportunity. By associating with Don Eduardo, I probably had enemies I did not know.

I did not encounter Don Eduardo's infamous anger until I had been at the hacienda about two months. However, I have to admit that I brought it on myself through my own stupidity. It concerned my teaching of geography to the children. The map of North America in the seventeenth century Spanish atlas was obviously wrong in many respects. California was shown as an island broken apart from the mainland. The northern area of Canada and Alaska was left open and undefined. Florida and New England were greatly misshapen. So from memory, I drew a modern map for the children, putting in the major bays, rivers and mountain ranges. I showed the Great Lakes and included islands such as Vancouver, Manhattan, the Aleutians, and the Florida Keys. I even showed the Bering Strait and how close Asia was. I did not put in any modern place names, thinking that without names the map would be innocuous.

Unfortunately, Juanito proudly showed the map to his father after dinner. Flora and I were in our room when a heavy knock came. Flora opened the door to a stern faced Don Eduardo.

"Muchacha, come immediately." He motioned me to go out with him. "Yes, Don Eduardo?" I said, quickly walking behind him.

"Into the library."

Once there, he shut the door and wheeled on me, his face red with anger. From the table he snatched up my drawing of North America.

"Did you draw this?" he demanded.

"Yes, sir."

"This is not correct. Not correct." He then grabbed the Spanish atlas from its shelf and flipped to the old map.

"This one is correct. Where...why did you do this one differently?" He shoved my map almost in my face, shaking it.

"Well...well..." I stammered. I did not know what to say.

"Where do you have the idea that California is not an island? It is most definitely an island. Our explorers have shown this. Are you a crazy inglesa? Do you just make things up?"

"Answer me!" he shouted, when I did not respond.

He advanced on me, his face livid and getting closer and closer. I put up my hands to keep him away while I backed up. But now I was up against the wall. He grabbed my hands in each of his and squeezed them with great power.

"Answer me, inglesa, or I will have you whipped."

I thought he might hit me. I realized I had to answer, or he would be driven to more frustration.

"Could we please sit down, Don Eduardo, and I will explain?"

"No," he shouted. "Answer me, now." His hands pressed harder, and I was amazed by the pain he could cause just by squeezing. His fingers were very strong. There was something else. I felt strangely submissive, almost wanting his power and the physical contact. Then a loathing came over me. I suddenly hated myself for liking his strength. I had to get out of his grasp. The macho way was just stupid. I had been around the submissive servants too long.

"Don Eduardo," I said slowly, keeping my eyes on the window behind him, "I learned the shape of the Americas from teachers in Jamestown. That map is what I was taught."

The pressure lessened.

"But our Spanish explorers know more than the English. We have been up in that territory and mapped all that is known so far."

"I think some of the English trappers have been farther north than the Spanish. The trappers have gone across the land from ocean to ocean. California cannot be an island or they couldn't have done this."

He looked at me, weighing my words. Slowly he let my hands drop.

"No, I do not believe it. You are to teach Juanito only what is in the atlas. Nothing else. Do you understand me?" He crumpled up my map and put it in his pocket. "Do you understand, muchacha?" he repeated louder.

"Yes, sir, Don Eduardo. I promise only to teach what is in your books. I promise."

"Very well, then. If I hear of you teaching anything more that is wrong, I will have you beaten and turned over to the men."

"Yes, sir," I said, nodding contritely.

As he turned to leave, we both saw Doña Margaríta standing in the doorway to the library. She glared at me. I knew then I would pay double for my mistake.

That evening I had nightmares. In the middle of the night I woke up sweating but excited and realized my dream had been sexual. Several large men, all unrecognizable, had overpowered me and repeatedly taken their pleasure.

As I listened to the distant lowing of cattle, letting my body relax, I wondered why I hated authoritarian people so much. It had to be my upbringing. Neither of my parents had been strict with me. There were clear expectations for my behavior but I had never been spanked, and only rarely had I been spoken to sharply. Reasoning was their method of approach and reproach. Tolerance was the watchword. My parents were disciples of Dr. Spock.

Would I have been better off with more parental authority? Would this have made me more adjusted? Crystal's father was more authoritarian than mine. She seemed to have accepted it. I smiled as I remembered her recounting the battles over using her dad's car, and coming in late. Unlike her, I had never been grounded. Maybe my folks had done me a disservice by being so easy. What did it matter? It was too late now.

Life became more miserable after the episode with Don Eduardo. It was as if his attack on me gave license to the others. The two servant girls and Dueña Carmela spoke very little to me. Doña Margaríta became meaner and assigned me horrendous amounts of work. The children seemed to pay me less attention. Even the chamber pots were more nauseous if that were possible. Only Flora remained friendly. I began to hate passionately the hacienda and everything and everyone in it except her.

I thought about trying to escape, but I realized I would be easily caught. I was too different from the people in the countryside to meld in. Who would dare help me and risk the wrath of Don Eduardo? If I tried to escape and were caught...I hated to think of what he would do to me.

So what was my fate? To remain and live a miserable existence until I caught some disease and died? I remembered a Russian poet, Tatyana Tolstaya, who was in fact a descendent of Tolstoy, saying that Americans were not used to suffering. If we are unhappy we run to psychiatrists. But, she had said, Russians never did because they felt that when they were miserable their souls were growing. Maybe that was my problem. I did not appreciate that with my suffering my soul was growing. But what good is a magnificent soul if you are a vegetable?

One day Doña Margaríta became irritated because I had not emptied her chamber pot while she was at breakfast. She ordered me to take it out immediately and then followed me out of the house.

"Moza," she shouted.

I turned around and saw the flash in her eyes. Behind her I saw Dueña Carmela coming out the door.

"Inglesa estúpida!" Doña Margaríta spit out. "Don't ever make that mistake again."

I stared at her but did not say anything. This must have made her angrier, for she suddenly grabbed the pot in my hands and dumped the foul-smelling contents down the front of me. The pot fell and broke. Then she swung, trying to slap my face, but missed.

I grabbed her, crooking my elbow around her neck. She clawed at my face with her fingernails.

"You bitch," I screamed in English as I put my leg behind her and shoved her down. I kicked her in the rear. She squealed and rolled over for protection. I was about to kick her again when I felt a hand seize my arm.

"Stop." It was Dueña Carmela. "Abbie, go wash yourself at the tubs immediately." She looked down at Doña Margaríta who was now sobbing. "Margaríta," she said sternly, "get up and go in the house. I'm your mother and you are still a child."

After this incident, Doña Margaríta tried to avoid me. That was good, but I became more depressed even so. I thought of Bitterroot and how I had proudly rejected his offer. How different that decision looked now. Chances were that I would never see him again. He probably had recruited some other fool to do his unGodly Southern Dreams. Ha. But the only fool in all of this was me. I had to fight a retching reflex in my throat. A small amount of bile came into my mouth and tasted horribly bitter. I swallowed it down again. Martin Heidegger had said there were two basic anxieties. One was being in this world, and the other was not being in this world. I had always thought that not being in the world was the one to worry about. But now, being gone from this daily madness was beginning to look attractive.

It is strange that when things are going well, we take them so for granted. You only miss things when they are gone. Trite but so true. I was now missing my future in America. I hadn't thought about it that much, but I really did want to meet someone special, fall in love, and have a family. I also wanted a career. I guess I felt I was one of those women who could manage it all. But it was not going to happen. Family and friends in Los Angeles had probably forgotten me already. I must be an unexplained missing person.

I knew the family hated me when nothing was done for my birthday.

The only recognition was from Flora. She brought me a biscuit with jam on it late on the evening of February 10th. I handled it stoically, but I was hurting inside.

The days droned on. I felt as if I were in a tunnel. The sun was bright, but it was dark for me. I was not taken to church anymore. One day the whole household went to a bullfight at one of Don Eduardo's corrals. I had to remain with Carmela, who wasn't feeling well that day. But I wasn't disappointed, for I had come to expect nothing.

Then one day another servant showed up. She slept in the stable instead of the house. Paya, as she was called, was beautiful in a slim, gaunt way. She had high cheek bones, deep dark eyes, and coal black hair that was always coiled on top of her head. She was an Indian, probably in her early twenties. Paya was strangely morose. She averted her eyes whenever I looked at her. She didn't talk to anyone or answer verbally. She only nodded or shook her head. Despite her distance, for some reason I developed an affinity to her. Maybe it was her patient silence. Or maybe she seemed to be suffering like me.

One day out in the yard I heard the children around the corner of the house. They were talking softly. Then I heard a stranger's voice. There were just a few words spoken and not distinctly. I stepped around to look and saw Paya touching a doll that Dulcíta was holding. Paya looked at it sadly, as much as sadness could appear in her implacable face. When she saw me, she straightened up and walked away.

Later in my room I mentioned to Flora that I had heard Paya speak. Flora was surprised.

"I heard something about Paya today," she said. "Her village was trampled by a cattle drive a month ago. Her husband who was village chief went crazy. And he took their two small children."

"What happened to them?" I asked.

"They went for the sacrifice."

Sacrificio? The word with its knife-like finality tumbled around in my brain.

"What do you mean, Flora?"

"They are dead, the husband and the two small children."

"How terrible!"

"Sí, Abbie," she said, crossing herself.

"But what about Paya? Why did she not go with them?"

"Nobody knows. She should have gone."

I had heard that sacrificial killings and suicide still took place among some of the Indian tribes. It was a hard-to-believe custom. But suddenly it was real and close. That explained Paya's tragic demeanor. She was consumed with grief and, no doubt, guilt. The thought of the suicide of her husband along with his sacrifice of their children made me shudder. It was such a pure act.

Paya did not eat with the servants. She took food from the kitchen when she retired to the stable after her dishwashing chores. The night after Flora told me about Paya's family, I watched her leave the house and walk down the path. Her posture was so erect that a plate on her head would not have fallen. As I watched, I felt for her and decided I should try to talk to her. After everyone retired, I slipped out the back door. Flora was to let me in when I quietly called outside our window. There was a full moon, and I had no trouble following the path to the stable. Paya stayed in a small room on one side of the large structure. It had a door to the outside and a window, from which lantern light flickered around a makeshift covering. I peeked through a slit and saw her sitting on her bunk. She was using a small kitchen knife to carve a wooden figurine of a man. On a crate next to the bed were two more figurines, those of children, along with the empty clay dish from her supper. I tapped lightly on the door.

She opened it and stared at me vacantly.

"May I come in Paya?"

At first I thought she would close the door, but then she went back and sat on her bunk, leaving me at the open door. I sat on the bunk a couple of feet from her. She gave me no look but continued some finishing touches on the man. The figurines were rather crude, with arms and legs straight and close to the body. The faces were definitely Indian, but the expressions were emotionless.

"Those are nice, Paya," I said softly. "Are they your husband and children?"

She looked at me as if surprised, but did not show any emotion. Then she looked down again, nodding.

"I was very sorry to hear what happened." Again she looked at me, as if wondering how I could have known. Then she moved her gaze away from me and toward the wall. A couple of minutes passed quietly except for the sound of a horse snuffling somewhere in the stable.

"Do you want me to leave you alone, Paya?"

She picked up the two child figurines and held all three in her hands, fingering them.

Then, almost inaudibly, she said, "I take these to them tonight."

I felt a strange tickling sensation on the back of my neck. The moment seemed almost sacred, and I felt I shouldn't even breathe. I wanted to ask so many things, but my voice would somehow be wrong. As I thought about it, there was really nothing to say. I simply nodded slowly, not knowing whether she noticed.

After a few minutes, she took a shawl hanging from a nail on the wall and wrapped it around her narrow shoulders. Staring as if oblivious, she went out the door, the figurines clutched in her hands. After a moment I went out and watched her move down a narrow path to the west, away from the hacienda and the stable. For some reason—a causal impetus that seemed not a part of my own self—I started after her.

The night was chilly, but the walking soon warmed me. I kept about 50 yards behind her, trying not to make noise. I don't know if she knew I was there or not; she never looked back. The small path through bushes and trees eventually joined a larger trail that ran along a ridge forming the edge of the plateau. Farther west, the mountain dropped steeply amid rocky outcroppings. We passed through a fence that kept cattle from venturing to the precipitous cliffs. There were large stone buttresses jutting outward at places. It was eerily beautiful in the moonlight, reminding me of an Ansel Adams photograph of Yosemite at night.

After another twenty minutes, the trail came to a point in the cliff that swept out into the air, culminating in an overhanging crag. Paya made her way toward a large flat place on the crag, scrambling between boulders. I followed carefully, trying to keep her in sight. The flat part of the rock, much like a large platform, jutted out, providing almost a 270 degree view of the deep canyon. Beneath the platform was a vertical drop of probably close to a thousand feet to a rocky talus below. Seeing Paya on the platform made me tremble.

As I moved quietly closer, about 15 yards from Paya, I could see her sitting lotus fashion, facing outward to the canyon. She began to rock, sometimes to and fro, sometimes side to side. I heard a low wailing sound, her alto voice moving up and down in a rhythmic pattern of several disharmonic notes. The starkness of the scene and the wails of the Indian woman struck a deep chord in me, and I began to silently weep. I felt a magical bond building between us and among all womankind as vague pictures of women from different settings came up on the screen behind my eyes. The intensity grew and was almost painful. We were in unity. I could now feel that we were all of the same soul that permeated throughout the universe, through all time. Amid my tears I could see Paya standing and raising the figurines toward the heavens. Now she made staccato-like statements between the notes of her chant, as if talking to a god. They were poignant descriptions of her children and husband. I was sobbing, trying not to make noise. Then she began removing her clothes, letting them drop behind her. Her statuesque beauty soon was fully revealed, the moonlight playing on the surface of her nude body. Slowly she undid her hair, letting it drop down her back. Picking up the figurines again, she began chanting louder and soon was almost screaming, standing on tiptoes. My tears now flowed so heavily that I could hardly make her out. Suddenly there was a blur and I dimly saw her running, figurines in hand, toward the abyss.

I rubbed the tears from my eyes and Paya was gone. There was nothing but silence and her clothes laying in a rumpled pile on the platform.

"Please be good to her, God," I mumbled. "She's come for the serenity she deserves."

I felt a warmness. We were all together, all sisters. And I wanted to be with her, to tell her how lovely it had been. There was nothing to return for, only reasons for going forward. I, too, could join in eternity, and be welcomed. I could see my father.

I stood up stiffly and walked out on the platform and sat down in the same fashion that Paya had. I rocked to and fro and side to side. It felt good. The chant in the same tones seemed to come effortlessly. It was as if I were already there. I could see outstretched hands just beyond the edge of the rock. Now I was up, shedding my old clothes, balancing on the balls of my feet, shouting. I could feel warmth all over. I could see them just beyond. I was yelling to them, and they answered. Come on, Abbie, the voices called. Come forward, Abbie. We're here. Now. I tensed slightly and felt that moment just before going off a diving board. Come, Abbie.

"Wait, Abbie."

Come on, Abbie. Come on. I closed my eyes and ran. My arm jerked and suddenly I spun and fell. The rock was hard as I hit my nose and knees. Where were the hands? There was only one, and it grasped my wrist. I was still on the platform.

"Has it come to this, lass?"

The voice. It was his voice.

"Abbie, get up and put on your clothes."

I got up slowly and turned. There he was, old clothes, the moonlight making dark crevices in his wrinkled face. He was smiling at me.

Something in me went berserk. This evil man had just made a sacrilege of truth and beauty. And us. He had thwarted me yet again. And the devil was grinning.

I rushed him with fingernails flying, gouging at his face as he tried to protect himself with his hands. I threw a knee strongly into his crotch, and he doubled over with a strange groan. I slugged and kneed and pushed and he fell backward. There was a heavy thump. His head had hit a rock. He lay quiet and rumpled, the only movement being that of his chest cycling in and out. I stared at him for a few minutes, my adrenalin still pumping and my breath short. Then I saw the blood. It ran down the rock from the back of his head.

As I stood there transfixed, strange thoughts came to me. I could throw him over the cliff. I could go over, too. Nobody would know or care. It could all be ended now. History would not feel so much as a blip. The universe would go on. God knows Bitterroot deserved it. Live by the sword, die by the sword. My life was really expendable at this point. Why not?

As I watched the oozing blood, I knew I could not bring myself to push him over. It was killing. When I had done it on the *Guadalupe*, it seemed like an accident. I wasn't rational. This would be murder. My upbringing was too strong. I saw my mother looking at me, her finger held up. I couldn't push him over. But Bitterroot would probably die on his own. The blood, showing no sign of abating, in an hour or so would ebb his life away. I would have to do nothing but go over on my own. In this lawless land, nobody would mind. There would simply be a shallow grave over in the dirt that in the matter of a few months would be hooved over and forgotten. Could I do it?

Again my mother's finger wagged at me. You know better, Abbie.

It was getting cold. I folded my arms about my breasts and squatted down to try to conserve warmth. It was no use. I could not just wait. I had to do something. Slowly I put on my clothes. I tore some long strips from Paya's shirt and bandaged Bitterroot's head. I was able to stop the bleeding. I made him more comfortable, covering him with the rest of Paya's clothes. Then to keep him warm I lay close to him, holding him, trying to save the man who by all rights deserved the worst, who had so mistreated me, who...had saved my life.

Bitterroot stirred after about an hour. He tried to get up but was too weak.

"Just rest, Gordon. You had a bad fall, and your head is hurt. You've lost a lot of blood."

"Is that thee, Abbie?"

"Yes."

"My head hurts mightily."

"It'll be OK. The bleeding is stopped."

"You pushed me, Abbie. You hit me."

His voice, low and husky, was matter of fact.

"Don't talk, Gordon. It won't be long before the sun is up, and we'll warm up. Save your energy."

"We must talk, Abbie," he said slowly. "I'm going to leave. You must decide if ye want to come with me. Our job is not done."

Oh God. The man is barely coming back from death, knows I almost killed him, and yet is ready to carry on as if nothing happened.

"Where would we go?"

"To Panama."

"In what year?"

"Same as today."

"Is that where I have to do my deed in history?"

"No, from there you board a ship and go to an island called Juan Fernández, a ways off the coast of Chile."

"Is that where I do my deed?"

"Aye."

"So why don't you just put me there now? Why go to Panama? Why do I have to go on a ship? For that matter, why did you put me on Santa Cruz with the Chumash?"

"It was necessary."

"Why?"

"I said it was necessary, Abbie."

"It was necessary for me to be raped by Torres? Gordon, I could jump off this place right now. You saw that I was willing to do it. I could also pick up a rock and smash your head. Only out of misguided principle did I decide not to let you die. If you want any cooperation from me on your crazy mission, you are going to confide in me. You must tell me your plan in all its details. Is that clear Mr. Bitterroot?"

He remained silent for a minute.

"Gordon?"

"I'll tell thee, lass. But please roll me on my side first. Something is sticking in me back."

On his side Bitterroot cleared his throat and his voice became better modulated. "That's better, thanks. I couldn't put you directly on Más á Tierra of the Fernández group, because I did not know thee. I did not know how you would be. You needed tempering, to see action, so to say. I put you at Santa Cruz with the Indians so that I could watch you."

"Did you know ahead of time what all would happen?" I couldn't keep astonishment from my voice.

"No, no," he chuckled. "One never knows. Most times it's been botched. One I lost, poor devil. Never could get him back. If only I could predict."

"You mean, Gordon, you've put others back in time like me?"

"A few. But none has been as capable as you, Abbie. You're the best. All the others were men, and you're twice the man of any."

I was amazed...and amused.

"The reason you must go with the Spaniards to Juan Fernández is that I must get their ship's log saying that you escaped on the island. When the Spanish captain's log is stolen in Valparaiso and sent to London, it will make most good reading for the Admiralty and Parliament. Can you imagine the public storm when they learn an English lass is holding land on the Spanish main for England? Singlehandedly? It will galvanize them, it will." He laughed merrily and then broke in to coughing.

"Aye, Abbie, they'll do what they should have done long before. Send ships of the line, soldiers and settlers to colonize and safeguard the island. Juan Fernández will be the South Sea toehold for England. It'll be the Gibraltar of the Pacific. We have Jamaica in the West Indies, and we need an island on the other side. From there, we'll be able to take other islands, and then take over ports and make settlements at key points in New Spain and South America. Once England has opened it up, the Dutch will help. Spain will slowly lose to superior forces, at sea and on land. Like the changing of the tide. If Henry Morgan and his small band could capture Panama, think how easy it will be for our navy and soldiers. I can taste the victories."

"What lands would you settle in?"

"We would settle in what is now Chile, Ecuador, Peru, Columbia, and Panama. Later their descendants and more settlers would push up into Mexico and California."

"But couldn't the Spaniards push these English out?"

"No, because we will have superior naval power, and Spain has no armies over here. They are tied down in wars in Spain. Besides, the terrain over here is mostly impossible for cannon to traverse. We will gain the loyalty of the Spanish slaves and natives because we will treat them better. They will join us in sea battles against the Spanish settlements."

I could only think of myself among his grandiose rantings. What did it mean for me?

"Gordon, how could I escape on the island? What would keep the Spaniards from searching and capturing me?"

"I have a plan for that. I know of a hidden cave where they won't find you."

"How could I survive there by myself?"

"Easy, that one. There are fish, fruit on the trees, even bread growing on trees. There are goats. And you can grow almost anything in the ground. It will be twice as easy as living on Santa Cruz. It's a paradise by comparison, Abbie."

'It will be,' he had said. Forgone conclusion in his mind. I shook my head.

"Don't fret, Abbie. Compared to what you've done, it will be like a vacation."

"How long will I have to stay there?"

"Only until the first English vessels arrive. You will greet them gloriously. Not long after, I will bring thee back to Santa Monica, whatever its new English name. And we'll share a glass of champagne."

It could easily be a year before they arrived, I guessed. A whole year. Then L.A? Could it be true that I'd ever see my wonderful city again? Would it be the same?

"Why would the Spanish take me on a ship out of Panama? How could that be arranged?"

Bitterroot's eyes closed for a moment and he groaned. "Hot. It's damn hot. I have a plan for that. But why don't we get out of this God-forsaken place. My head needs a poultice. Let's get down there, get comfortable, and I'll tell thee more. Are ye game, Abbie?"

I looked at him and found myself nodding. What the hell else was there? It was the only way out alive.

"Tha's a good girl. Now, you remember how to concentrate with me? Close your eyes. Let your mind go blank. We're going on a trip. Let yourself drift. We're going on a journey. Take my hand. We're going together."

He then whispered, "We're beginning to move. Relax and come along with me."

It became very dark. I was suddenly in total blackness. I was drifting but could not see where. Then quickly it became light again.

"We can see the river now. There is the hut we're going to. And there is Carlos waiting. Come along, girl."

The first thing I saw, other than the trail we were standing on, was the man in front of us. He was Abirrute. He smiled broadly but then became concerned when he noticed Bitterroot's weakened condition. I was aware of the stifling equatorial heat. There was the deep churgling noise of a river nearby. I could see bamboo, tall trees, and thick foliage. Then I heard chattering. I looked up into the treetops and saw dark shapes moving about. Monkeys. And there were red and blue colored birds flying between lower branches, cawing. They looked like small parrots.

"Gordon, what happened to you?" Abirrute said in English but with the Spanish accent I had heard so clearly that dark night on the *Guadalupe*. He came up to us.

"Hello Abbie. I'm happy to see you again."

"Oh, I'm so glad to see you, Abirrute." I hugged him like a long lost friend. He kissed me on the forehead.

Abirrute put his arm around Bitterroot.

"Qué pasa, Gordon?"

"I banged my head, Carlos. Help me to the hut. I need rest."

As I saw them together, I could see more clearly the resemblances and differences. They had to be relatives. My guess was father and son. Bitterroot's surprises no longer surprised.

I followed them as they turned off the main trail and onto a path that led to a thatched hut nestled in a grove of tall trees that looked like cottonwoods. The floor was dirt but surprisingly clean. Clothes hung on the walls. There were a couple of trunks below an open window. There was a table and four low bunks. On the table were jugs, plates, cups, utensils, papers, a large leather pouch, candles, and some things I could not recognize. Even in the hut's shade it was hot. I wanted to talk to Abirrute, but he was now tending Bitterroot, who was stretched out on one of the bunks.

"Carlos, fetch the Cacique and get his medicine man to make me a plantain poultice," Bitterroot said softly, his eyes closed. "You know where the village is?"

"Yes, I'll go right away. Abbie, you stay with him. There's water in the jug."

I gave Bitterroot some water. I felt his forehead and realized he had a high fever. Now I was worried. The wound may have become infected. I could see perspiration flowing in rivulets down his neck. His breathing had become noticeably heavier. I pulled off his shoes, pants, and shirt. How could this have happened so fast?

"Gordon, how are you feeling?" I asked, just to see if he was still alert.

"Goddamn swamp sickness," he muttered. "All these years coming and going and now it hits. Where's the Cacique?"

"He's coming. Abirrute's getting him. Try to rest."

A terrible feeling came to my stomach. Bitterroot was seriously ill, and I had caused it. Was he in danger of dying? A fear came over me.

Bitterroot was sweating profusely and almost gasping when Abirrute came into the hut followed by four naked, bronze-colored men. They were about five feet tall and had well-proportioned, sinuous bodies and black hair, high foreheads, and large eyes. One of the men had greenish markings painted on his face and body. He went directly to Bitterroot and began speaking strange words with occasional pidgin Spanish phrases. Bitterroot did not seem to be listening, however. The man inspected Bitterroot's body, paying close attention to the wound on his head.

I now noticed that one of the Indians held a large rolled up leaf, about one and a half feet in length. It was dripping. I wondered what was inside. Soon the man with the markings, whom I guessed was the chief or Cacique, was directing that the poultice be wrapped around Bitterroot's head. Once tied up it was like a fallen wreath on Bitterroot's head, with the main body of the poultice against the wound.

"Bueno, bueno," Abirrute exclaimed. The Indians all smiled. I felt dubious about the achievement. But this was nothing compared with the next event. One of the Indians carried a small sheath from which he now withdrew a tiny bow, not more than a foot in length, and even tinier arrows, each about four inches long. The tips of the arrows were sharp, needle-like reeds. To my amazement, the Cacique took Bitterroot's hand and held his arm out full length while the Indian with the bow drew an arrow on the string and shot it into Gordon's arm. It must have penetrated an inch, hanging down from its own weight. Blood began oozing from the wound.

"Bueno," Abirrute said.

The Indian mounted another arrow.

"Stop," I shouted, jumping—to the shock of everyone—between the bowman and Bitterroot. "You can't do this. He needs his blood to fight the fever."

Abirrute stepped up to me. "Abbie, stand aside," he said sternly.

"No I won't."

The Cacique and his men were becoming nervous, lifting their legs up and down, staring at each other.

"Abbie, please."

"No." I pulled the arrow out of Bitterroot's arm carefully and stopped the bleeding with my shirt. Then I folded his arms on his chest and turned around and glared at the Indians.

"Carlos, surely you know that bloodletting is not a curative. It is harmful. You know that, right?"

"It works, Abbie. Gordon needs this to heal."

I was taken aback. For some reason I had assumed Abirrute was a modern man put back in time like me.

"Carlos, how far into the future have you gone?"

He looked at me strangely. "Gordon says eighteen hundred twenty-two."

"Where was that?"

"Madrid."

"I see. Well, I have lived in times 160 years later than you. There have been many advances in medicine that you have not heard about, and the practice of bloodletting was stopped because it was not good for health. So you are going to have to trust me on this. Do not let the Indians shoot any more arrows. If Gordon were conscious, he would bear me out."

"But he is my father and what I say goes," Abirrute stated, his lower jaw thrust out.

"He is your father?" So I was right. If Carlos was Bitterroot's son, then Biru probably was, too.

"Sí."

But why hadn't Bitterroot taken his son to the 1990's?

"Well, I see. Look, Carlos, I didn't realize Gordon was your father. But,

I'm really telling you the truth. I do not like Gordon right now, and there have been times I'd just as soon have seen him...anyhow...". Tears came to my eyes, and I quickly looked away from him. When I turned back, he was motioning for the Indians to go, which they did rather reluctantly. As he looked at me, I could see his anger had gone away.

"I want him alive as much as you," I said quietly. "You do what you have to do, but I know that those arrows would not be good for him. They could cause additional infection."

"I believe you, Abbie," he said. Then he bent over Bitterroot and checked his heart and his breathing. Surprisingly, his gasping had lapsed into heavy breathing.

"If he continues getting better, I will not have him bled," Abirrute said.

I felt relief. Within an hour it was clear that Bitterroot's fever was breaking. He was on the mend. It seemed like a miracle. Thank God for the Cacique and his men. Bitterroot had known what he needed.

Abirrute and I sat in a corner of the hut, finally able to rest now that we knew Bitterroot was going to be all right. We talked some, and I learned that Abirrute had left the *Guadalupe* in San Diego bay, coming here by tunneling with his father, just as I had done.

"Did you know I would be coming down here with Gordon?" I asked.

"We expected it."

"Did you know I left Gordon at Acapulco and refused to go on that filabote?"

"Yes, my father told me."

"How did you know I would come here then?"

"My father usually gets what he wants."

"So you know all about me and the plan?"

"Yes."

"Do you think it was all right for him to do this to me? Against my will?"

Abirrute smiled thinly. "I don't answer that kind of question. I just help my father."

"Why do you help him?"

He shrugged. "My life has been extended because of my father. Otherwise I would be in a grave."

"When were you born?"

"1790."

It was incredible. To think that in my time he would be long deceased, and yet here both of us were, way back in history, talking as if it were normal.

"Where is your mother, Carlos?"

"She is buried in Madrid, along with my half brothers and sisters. Only I had the ability to travel through the years, like my father."

"I see. Do you consider yourself to be Spanish?"

"Yes."

"And yet you agree with Gordon's Southern Dreams idea, that the New World should be colonized by the English?"

He looked at me penetratingly for a few moments, and then said, "That is another question I don't answer."

As I gazed at him, I felt sympathy. The son was loyal to his father. How had Bitterroot come to meet Carlos's mother and have the child who became the man in front of me? I guess it didn't really matter. Suddenly Bitterroot and Carlos became more human. The man I was ready to kill only a short time ago on the precipice was, thank God, recovering. Why was I now feeling positive toward him?

The Indians returned, bringing food. They had raw fish, cut up in bite-sized morsels, and a great variety of fruit, most of which I couldn't recognize. The Cacique sat down with Bitterroot and slowly fed him. I had the feeling those two had a relationship that went way back. It was touching to see the devotion in the old Indian's eyes. There was plenty of food for Carlos and me. Some of the fruit was delicious, and other kinds ranged from bland to repulsive. Carlos tried to tell me what I was eating, and a few of the names were rather exotic—macaw berries, mammee pears, sapadillo's, calabashes, and plantains. I was ravenous and downed it all.

By late evening, when Carlos and I were tired, Bitterroot was sitting up, alert. He wanted to talk. His fever was all but gone, yet he kept the poultice on his head. The three of us talked for some time, mostly about my experiences. Bitterroot especially liked the story I had made up about myself, and how the Capitáns had decided to look for Jean LaRue. Then Bitterroot said it was time to talk about the next part of the journey.

"Abbie, you and Carlos will leave tomorrow morning in order to get to Panama by the afternoon. We can't delay another day. The ship could leave in two or three days and both of you must be on it. Getting clearance to embark will depend on how convincing you both are. Abbie, failure could cause thee to end up as a slave and land Carlos in irons. So listen carefully to the plan."

I had a deja vu feeling, as if I were back at the meetings held at Cliff Manssard's house. Bitterroot was his old commanding self.

"Wait, Gordon," I interjected. "If something goes wrong in the plan, you must agree here and now that you will come get us and take us away."

He looked at me for a long while. "Of course, Abbie."

It was obvious how hard it was for him to say this. I considered it a moral victory.

"Now," he said, continuing, "you, Abbie, are a Virginian, just like before, who was captured by the pirate Jean LaRue, but you escaped ashore on the island of Hispaniola and made your way to the town of Santo Domingo. The local authorities found that you were Catholic and educated, and that you could be a teacher. Señor Carlos Abirrute, here, was looking for a teacher for the school in Valparaiso. Carlos was commissioned by the Mayor of Valparaiso, Señor Echevarría, to conduct a search. Carlos heard about you, interviewed you, and convinced you to take the position. You were willing to do anything that would help you stop grieving for your family, which was killed by Jean LaRue. A small sloop was employed to take you to Porto Bello. From there you crossed the isthmus of Darien to Panama, where you are to take the next ship to Valparaiso. Señor Abirrute is to accompany you the whole way, seeing to your safe arrival."

"But will anybody believe that?" I asked.

"Carlos has official letters from Señor Echevarría and from the Porto Bello mayor, certifying both of you for travel to Panama. The documents are convincing. It is you who must be believable. Carlos will do most of the talking to the officials and soldiers you meet, but you may be questioned, too. You must bone up on the story with Carlos so that you know the details of your travel from the time you came ashore near Santo Domingo. You already have the story of your upbringing in Jamestown and the business with LaRue."

"But what about clothes and money? Do we just hike to Panama? How far is it? Is it safe? Who do we meet there? What ship do we go on? How can I do this, Gordon? I really don't like the way it sounds...."

"Calm thee down, Abbie," said Bitterroot, laughing. "Carlos and I have spent a lot of time on this. It should work. Carlos has Spanish ducats and can pay for everything. The vessel is a Spanish merchantman converted to a warship. Due to all the English privateer activity, it is making a patrol south along the coast and to the islands offshore, looking for foreign ships. Juan Fernández is its last stop before Valparaiso. Abirrute will sign you on as a special passenger and serve as a deck hand. And no, you don't have to hike to Panama. There is a mule and wagon ready. We have clothes for you and everything you'll need to be accepted for what you are. The rest is up to you. But knowing thee, Abbie, you'll do well. Just don't kill any more Capitáns." Again he laughed.

"But what if they have heard about López de Torres? What if they know about me?"

"They don't. *La Reina Cádiz* was lost with all hands in a storm off San Jose de Guatemala. The filabote and a couple of small ships came to Panama, but the Creole and Indian hands manning these vessels did not know about you. The Spanish travelers went to Mexico City. It will take a while before officials come to Panama. Most of the King's commerce heads to Vera Cruz. Besides, they don't care much about a crazy inglesa."

Bitterroot's confidence somehow depressed me. I felt tired and did not want to think of the enormity of it all.

"Gordon, do you really think this will work? It just seems impossible to me."

"I know in me bones it will work. England is so ready. She saw the Scottish boldly try but fail to settle Caledonia Bay on the Darien coast scarcely 50 miles from here. That was just a few years ago. The Spaniards didn't bother with them. Those Scots were fools and didn't know how to run a settlement. Imagine that there was no appointed leader! They were doomed. But England's appetite is whetted. We have the wherewithal to make such colonies prosper. We just need the political will and an event to start it. Queen Anne will support it, I know. So while you're on your way, I'll be checking every last part of the plan and beginning the arrangements in London. Abbie, you will be one of the most famous women in history. Books will be written about you. Believe it, lass."

"I'm going to sleep."

24

As the mule pulled us up over the last hill, I could see clearly the coastal savannah, the town, the blue gulf beyond with islands grouped together. There were rivers running down on either side of the town, the sun reflecting from the water. There were cultivated fields, houses with tile roofs, barns, and animals in pastures. The densest part of the town, on the edge of the ocean, was the walled in portion protected by lookout turrets at each corner. The scene was so pastoral and delicate that I couldn't help crying.

"Is anything wrong, Abbie?" Carlos asked.

"No, it's just seeing civilization for a change. It's gorgeous."

We continued down the well-traveled road, politely waving at horsemen and wagons passing by. So far, Bitterroot was right. Nobody seemed to look at us twice.

It had seemed strange leaving him. I had hugged him. Despite all of my feelings toward him since we met—intrigue, attraction, excitement, disdain, disgust, hatred—I still wanted to believe him. He seemed to care about me, to want me to be happy joining in his Southern Dreams and becoming famous. At least, I wanted to believe that he cared about me. If everything went according to plan, it might be a year before I saw him again. Maybe two years. Such a long time. Already I had been on this odyssey for eight months. Would it ever end? Would I ever go home? Thomas Wolfe's dark adage that you can never go home again came to my mind. Wolfe had better not be correct.

The full dress I was wearing, a pollera, was like the national costume of Panama, and, according to Bitterroot, of gypsy origin. It felt strange to be well dressed with combs of gold and pearl placed in my freshly washed and brushed hair. It was important to distinguish myself as a lady and not look like the slaves, Bitterroot had said. "Act dainty and proper, as if you are comfortable in polite society." I looked at Carlos, who flicked the whip expertly to keep the mule from tarrying. Carlos was handsome in tight black pants, black hat, and a white silk shirt. I felt a sense of pride and excitement that passersby possibly thought we were a married couple returning to town from a ride in the country. But it was too hot for a pleasant ride. Maybe that was why we did not see anyone like us. Already I was perspiring heavily.

We passed a group of black men at the side of the road, making a rock abutment where the roadbed had washed away. Most were shirtless and several had rags around their heads. I noticed that they were chained together by their feet. Two Spanish soldiers with rifles stood nearby, barking orders. The laborers glanced at us surreptitiously as our wagon passed.

"Were those slaves, Carlos?"

"Sí, there are many slaves in Panama."

My heart was suddenly heavy, feeling for the hot, tormented men. God, this is happening. Slavery is going on now in the southern colonies of America, too. Cheap labor is needed in the new world, so slavery flourishes, and all the insidious ideas about inferior races are brought forth to justify it. That legacy will continue for another two centuries. The suffering that had been caused and would to be caused was unthinkable. I felt a wave of nausea, disgust, and anger.

After about two hours, close to the town's outskirts, we came to an arched stone bridge over a river. A hundred yards downstream I saw several children swimming at a bend. Just this side of the bridge was a gated checkpoint where incoming traffic was being stopped. Armed men in uniforms were talking to each driver. Sometimes they demanded to see papers before allowing the traveler to cross into Panama. We pulled up behind a wagonload of hay probably destined for some stable in the town. My anxiety level went up, but I made a conscious effort to look calm.

The soldier on duty approached, a curious but respectful expression on his face.

"Please state your business, Señor."

Carlos gave his name and said that we had travelled from Porto Bello and were scheduled to meet with the Governor in Panama. Then he pulled papers from his pouch and handed them to the soldier, who was now nodding and showing deference. After looking at a letter with a wax seal, the young soldier gave us a sign to continue on and bid us good day.

"Who is the Governor?" I asked as the mule clopped over the bridge.

"Marques de Villa Rocha, President of the Royal Chancellery, Governor and Capitán General of Panama."

"Will we really see him?"

"No. He is too busy, either with business or with the intrigue of politics. His position is so powerful and so sensitive that the King does not allow him to marry, just to reduce the amount of influence. The Governor keeps himself closely guarded. We will probably see one of his aides."

We went by a large cluster of buildings bustling with soldiers, horses, and wagons. Small cannons on large wheels could be seen under a canvas-topped structure.

Carlos saw the awe in my look and answered an unspoken question. "New Panama is much different from the old town that the English buccaneer Henry Morgan sacked. It is well fortified now. There are more than 2000 soldiers."

We came to little streets with small houses. Many of them were wooden shacks. Some children could be seen but not many adults. The men were probably working somewhere, and the women no doubt stayed inside to keep out of the searing sun. Soon we came to the boundary of the inner city and followed the stream of vehicles going through a narrow opening in the wall, which looked to be ten to twelve feet high and several feet thick. The inner city was built on higher ground, almost to the height of the walls. Inside there was more activity on the streets than there had been outside. The houses, some of them behind their own little walls in the nicer areas, were older and closer together. Palm trees and plantings softened the Mediterranean architecture. Even though it was more dense, the desirable place to be was within the walled city. This was where the aristocracy lived.

We came to a rectangular plaza surrounded by shops—grocery, butcher, bakery, leather merchant, barber, fruit stand, clothier, blacksmith, cabinet maker, apothecary, almost everything. The heat did not seem as bad here because ocean air wafted in over the seawall. A number of people were shopping at the stores. Goods were being loaded onto and unloaded from wagons and carts. The sounds of the marketplace—wheels squeaking, trunks scraping on the walkway, vendors calling out their wares, horses whinnying, and the general hubbub of voices—made up a strange symphony. The people were diverse, some appearing well dressed and some in rags. They ran the gamut of race and ethnicity, ranging from Castilians, Creole Spanish, Asians, blacks with light skin and dark skin, Indians with different features—even a white-pigmented one—to strange admixtures I could not categorize. As we passed the bakery I noticed a gray-bearded Caucasian man with a small log chained to his leg. He had a wire basket of bread loaves on his back and dragged the log along as he hawked the bread to people going by.

"Don't catch his attention, Abbie. He is the only Englishman in Panama—a survivor captured ashore after a shipwreck near Porto Bello. The baker bought him at auction and brought him over the mountains. The man would love to speak to you, but you must avoid giving the impression you are an inglesa."

My breath caught at the thought of the poor fellow, but I looked straight ahead as we passed only a few feet from him. I knew his eyes were on me. Then I heard from behind me in quiet but unmistakable English cockney, "You 'ave a pleasant day, Ma'am. And may God 'elp you. Cause I am sufferin' bad."

The words lingered in my mind as we left the plaza, driving past the church, the cross on its belfry pointing to the heavens with righteous aim. Yes, many people had been enslaved in the new world—blacks, Indians, Asians, English enemies—whoever could be bought, coerced or beaten into submission, anyone whose enslavement could be justified. I thought of the blacks we had seen working on the road. What wrong had they committed? None. They just happened to have been born at the wrong place and time. Another people with superior force who believed in enslavement had happened by and taken them. Same with the Indians, although they had not been forced into captivity as often. Once snared, most slaves were trapped in misery for the rest of their lives. They were at the mercy of their owner. They would be lucky if their master was not cruel. But torture and cruelty were commonplace. And there was no redress. No hope.

Reading of slavery was one thing. Seeing it now firsthand was quite another. "Barbaric" was a word I had seldom used in the 1990s, because it had always seemed archaic. But here, in 1705, it had real meaning. My stomach suddenly turned, and I couldn't stop the retching reflex. I leaned off to the side of the wagon and spewed out the offending contents just as we pulled up in front of a stately building flying the Spanish flag. Soldiers standing at attention on either side of the door stared at me, uncertain whether to leave their posts and provide aid.

"Abbie, Abbie." Carlos had run around to my side of the wagon and was offering a handkerchief.

"Thank you, I'll be all right," I said, gathering my composure after a minute. "Maybe it was the heat or all that fruit I had this morning."

A young man, perhaps a clerk, came out of the building and approached us. There was a smirk on his face.

"Does the Señora need assistance?" he asked of Carlos.

"I think she'll be all right now."

"Yes, I am feeling better. I'm very sorry," I said.

Carlos offered his hand and I stepped down from the wagon, trying to be as ladylike as possible so as to recover whatever I could of my already compromised image. The young man had a perplexed look on his face, as if trying to figure out who I might be. My accent no doubt confused him. I looked at the building, with its graceful curvatures. A couple of people were staring at us from the windows.

"We are here to see Presidente Marques de Villa Rocha," Carlos said. "I am Señor Carlos Abirrute and this is Señora Abbie Spence. Is this the correct place for an audience?"

The young man stared at Carlos, surprised, then slowly nodded. "Sí, Señor. You can follow me, if you please."

The domed ceiling of the building's main room was high, with crisscrossing arches. Each section between the arches had painted frescoes of scenes in Spain, with the largest showing a royal couple in their finery. The floor was made from large diamond-shaped tiles of a rich coral color. We were directed to a seating area where several dignified people were waiting. The clerk disappeared into a hallway after taking the documents from Carlos. Guards with rifles stood on either side of the hallway door, impassive but watchful.

We waited nearly an hour, I guessed, before the same clerk came out and called, "Señor Abirrute." We were ushered into a spacious office in the back of the building. A tall, dark-haired man in tight, kneelength pants, silk shirt, and a black leather waistcoat with intricate silver designs in it rose from behind an ornate desk and greeted us. He was Señor Don Ramón, First Lieutenant Governor of Panama. I guessed his age at about 35 years. He had a light complexion and was one of the few blue-eyed

Spaniards I had seen.

"Are you feeling well, Señora Spence?" he asked.

I felt myself blush. So the news had spread all the way to him. "Yes, I am much better, thank you."

We all sat down in comfortably padded mahogany chairs with tall backs. Don Ramón spoke with a practiced air. "I have read your petition, Señor Abirrute, and I must say that the timing is uncanny. There is indeed a vessel that will be leaving for Valparaiso in a few days. It is a man-o-war, however, not a merchant. This is a rather unusual situation, and I will have to speak with the Capitán of *La Santa Rosa* to see if he would be willing to accommodate a lady. I'm sure he will gladly accept a practiced seaman such as yourself, Señor Abirrute, but a lady presents a number of problems, as I'm sure you both can understand." He smiled broadly, his thin moustache curving upward.

"We do understand, Señor Don Ramón, and we are willing to abide by whatever stipulations the Capitán may make," Carlos said. "I am commissioned also by Señor Echevarría, Alcalde of Valparaiso, to pay an above-normal fare for the passage of Señora Spence. The need for a teacher at the school in that city is very great."

Again the quick smile from Señor Don Ramón. "Indeed, Señor Abirrute, if there were not such a need, and if Señor Echevarría were not such a important friend of the Governor's, we would not hear of this request. But I will pursue the matter promptly. Now tell me, Señora Spence, as a Virginian, are you not loyal to Queen Anne of England, enemy of Spain, and the country that now wars against us?"

The question was not wholly unexpected. Bitterroot had warned me I might be challenged in this way.

"Well, Señor, Jamestown is an English colony, but we Virginians feel more loyalty to the Americas than to England. Also, I am Catholic."

"I see. If, God forbid, you had to help defend Valparaiso against attacking Englishmen, would you do so?"

I hadn't expected this question. I hoped I did not hesitate too long.

"Of course. The taking of life or property is wrong no matter who does it. Self defense is justified."

Señor Don Ramón smiled slowly, nodding. "And Señora, how did you come to be a teacher?"

"I studied in Jamestown with my mother who was a teacher before she married."

"And you know mathematics well?"

"I think so."

"Good. Then maybe you can help me. My son, who is eleven, asked me a question and I did not know the answer. Perhaps you would allow me to present it to you for your view of it?"

"Yes, please do," I replied, now aware that I was being tested by this suave man.

"Ricardo, my son, asked me how much all the numbers from 1 to 100 would add up to. I did not know and did not have time to add them up. Perhaps you can tell me."

"The sum is 5050," I said, thankful that I recalled one of my dad's math shortcuts.

Don Ramón was surprised. "How did you figure that out so easily?"

"If you write the numbers from 0 to 100 in one row and from 100 to 0 in another row, you get 101 number sentences that each add up to 100. Multiply 101 by 100 to get 10,100. Then divide by 2 to get the sum of one row." I showed him on a piece of paper. "It is a mathematical trick. You can show it to Ricardo yourself."

Amazement spread across Don Ramón's face. "That is very clever, Señora Spence. I can see you will be a good teacher."

"Thank you, Señor. Now would it be proper for me to ask your advice about a geography problem?" I hoped I was not pressing my luck. "If I can help, of course," he said.

"The question is whether California is an island. The Spanish geography maps show it this way. However, I had heard in Jamestown that English trappers had gone all the way across the continent to the Pacific Ocean and did not find California as an island. So my question is this. If I were teaching Spanish children about geography, what should I say about California?"

Don Ramón frowned. "Yes, I see. So you tell me what you would want to teach."

He had slyly turned it back on me. "Well, I guess I would teach that it may or may not be an island, that Spanish explorers think it is but that English explorers think it is not. How's that?"

"That is wrong, Señora," he said, smiling. "Spanish children need to know what Spanish people think, not what others think. That is an important lesson for you. Understand?"

I nodded. "I understand fully."

"Good." He chuckled, pleased with himself. "Señora, where are you going to stay until the ship is ready to depart?"

Carlos interjected that we would stay at the Panama Inn.

"That lodging is all right for you, Señor Abirrute, but I think Señora Spence should stay in a home. It would be only proper. I would like to offer my house. We have an extra room. Doña Ramón and our children would enjoy her company, I am sure. Would you like that, Señora?"

It was a sudden problem that did not fit with the plan. I looked at Carlos, who twisted uneasily in his chair.

"Well..." I said.

"That would be fine," Carlos said, finally. "I'm sure you would have a pleasant time."

"Good, then it is settled," Don Ramón stated, beaming.

I was worried. Having to stay with Don Ramón's family was an unexpected turn of events. Don Ramón seemed friendly enough, but he was clever. He might find me out and expose me. I could be enslaved just like the Englishman. And it might be worse if he suspected Carlos and I were up to something against Spain. But what could I do? There was no way to back out. It probably was morally wrong for me to stay in a hotel as a single woman. Bitterroot's research had not been perfect. So what if I were found out? Maybe it would be a blessing in disguise. If I were exposed as an imposter then Bitterroot would have to rescue me. That was our agreement. But was Bitterroot paying attention? He said he would be in London arranging things. Carlos said he could not communicate with him. Carlos had previously confirmed that, like me, he could only move through time by means of his father. So I would have to keep in character. My fate was in my hands.

Don Ramón's carriage pulled up in front of the white, single-story house. A polished brass gate stood before an arched doorway. No sooner had the wheels stopped than the inner door opened and a giant black man, white teeth gleaming in an oversized grin, came out to greet us. He was Dionisio, the butler. His cheerfulness was infectious, and soon I was chuckling at the repartee between him and Don Ramón. Before long I was meeting Doña Ramón, an exquisitely beautiful woman. Her flawless skin was the color and smoothness of white jade. How did she avoid the sun? I met the children, Ricardo and Concepción. They were well behaved but not shy. They acted quite friendly toward me.

The slaves were perhaps the most surprising thing about the household. They seemed to be part of the family. Benancio, the black cook, was married to Benancia, the white maid who waited on La Señora. They had a small child, Machinga, who was played with, and virtually looked after by Ricardo and Concepción. Manuela was in charge of the linen and washing. An older woman, Mama Chepíta, was like a grandmother to everyone. Jose Antonio Paez took care of the stable and gardens and also saw the children to school. Others of lesser station helped in myriad ways.

In a matter of hours I felt fully accepted and comfortable, as if I were a long-lost family member. The household was apparently used to guests, and I was just one more to be taken in and enjoyed.

After I had settled into my room, Doña Ramón invited me to bathe. It took no great perception to know I needed this after the long, dusty ride. The idea was wonderful. She said she would join me, which was puzzling. Did they have a tub large enough for two in the house?

The side-by-side marble tubs were sunk into the ground in the backyard. They were surrounded by a well-tended flower garden and screened by large vines. Flat tins of water, provided by the servants, had been warmed by the sun. Jasmine and roses floated on the surface to provide perfume. There was also a pleasant smell of burning incense. All this—along with the dainty soap made of almonds and goat's milk and the low, yellow sun casting shadows across the setting—lent a luxuriant ambience that I had never before experienced

"This is a wonderful place you have, Doña Ramón."

"Thank you, Señora. Life in Panama has its difficulties, but also its rewards. The rewards are close friends, strong family life, and for us, a nice home."

Doña Ramón told me about all the plants and flowers in the garden and the climate of Panama. I was amazed that we could hold such an interesting and friendly conversation for so long without getting personal. It made me appreciate the fine tradition of hospitality to which she held. By the end of the bath I liked her very much.

The wash basins and most of the dishware and utensils were made of silver. A silversmith regularly stayed with the family to make needed objects on site. Everyone had a jarro, a red clay cup with silver cover for water. They were kept in small openings in the masonry walls to keep the water cool.

Dinner that night was surprisingly formal. Carlos had been invited.

There were roses and hibiscus on the satin tablecloth between the silver holders of the homemade tallow candles. Don Ramón had on a lace ruffled shirt and wore shiny leather shoes with silver buckles. Doña Ramón had on a silk dress with many folds and a lace scarf. Concepción's hair was done up in curls, with gold and pearl ornaments and ribbons.

The first service consisted of soup and fish. The second course was roast meat, tamales, salad, and vegetables. Before the third course, the tablecloth was changed while we stretched our legs and relaxed in the living room. We returned to new fresh cut flowers and a dessert of arroz con cacao, rice cooked in coconut chocolate served with coconut cream and grated native cheese. This was accompanied by coffee liqueur. By the time the meal was over I was wonderfully sated. It was one of the finest meals I had ever eaten.

I'm sure that my enjoyment of the dinner was partly due to my relief that the dinner conversation was not taxing. I had been afraid that I would have to handle difficult questions and watch what I said. This did not prove so. Don Ramón did much of the talking, and the topics were the politics of New Spain and Panama, commerce, local people and events, the Indian tribes of the area, the children, and the family. Only once did someone ask about our trip to Valparaiso and what I would be doing there. But my answers were accepted seemingly without concern.

"Señora Spence, what do children do in Virginia?" young Ricardo asked.

"They go to school like you do, help harvest the crops, and milk cows. Sometimes the boys hunt turkeys with their fathers, and the girls sew quilts with help from their mothers. And of course they play a lot with other children."

"I would like to go hunt turkeys," Ricardo said.

"Gobble, gobble," Concepción said, to laughter.

After dinner we all took a pleasant walk around the city walls, saluting the sentries and meeting friends of Don and Doña Ramón. The women exchanged formal salutations—"Ave Maria Purisima" or "Buenas Noches de Dios a Su Merced." We arrived back at sunset just as the call to prayer rang from the cathedral tower, and we retired to the living room where Don Ramón led a prayer that even Carlos knew.

Following this, many candles were lit. Carlos and I were invited to join the family and favorite household slaves in the drawing room. The children recited poetry. Doña Ramón sang some French ballads. Then several of the slaves were requested to dance, which they did with relish, accompanied by drums and rattles, while onlookers clapped to keep time. One dance called the Punto involved intricate steps that the women danced alone. The Tambarito was a favorite of the children. The woman would move in graceful contortions while the man pirouetted, hat in hand, pretending to embrace her, but she would spin away at the last second. One slave dance was called the Cumbia and was done by a solid ring of couples facing each other. The women held lighted candles. If the audience liked the way the person danced, they got more candles. It produced great excitement as members of the audience tried to get their favorite dancer to end up with the most candles.

After the dancing Mama Chepíta sat on the floor in the middle of the room and told of deeds of the Spanish conquest and recited fairy tales of Arabia and India, the latter her country of origin. Finally Benancia and Dionisio brought in bittersweet chocolate crisps. At nine o'clock every member of the household had to be present for prayers. The Señora gave litanies in Latin and the Señor led prayers in Spanish. The ceremony ended with a blessing to the Master of the house.

That night I could hardly sleep. The bath, the dinner, the walk on the wall, and the evening of dancing and entertainment had been utterly enchanting. I could not think of a finer time in all of my life. It was hard to believe that people lived in this period with such devotion, cheer, and grace.

The next day I was able to spend time with the children after they came home from school. I learned the main areas of their instruction: penmanship; speaking French language; music, singing, and dancing; prayer and catechism; and learning good manners and respect. Only a small amount of time was spent on history, geography, and arithmetic. The girls were also taught to do fine needlework. Talking with Ricardo and Concepción was fun. They were interested in anything I said. I knew they would be a joy to teach.

My good impression of the family's life was tempered that night when I heard occasional screams in the slaves' quarters. Carlos later told me that people were superstitious, especially the slaves. They were afraid of the dark because they thought that departed friends might return. Carlos also told me there was little privacy in the community. The Old Town Hall was a gossip den as children's nurses and others gathered there to trade information on everyone else. The Panamanian officials often went there to hear the latest about people's wrongdoings. And there was always the oppressive midday heat.

On the third day of our stay in Panama, Carlos came to see me shortly after noon. We sat out at the far end of the patio. He spoke in low tones, so that the slaves doing washing on the porch could not hear.

"Everything is arranged with the Capitán of *La Santa Rosa*. We will embark tomorrow morning. Capitán Avila is charging more that I expected, but your quarters are very good. It seems to be a good ship with competent officers. You and I will be treated well."

Hearing this, I felt like I had as a little girl when it was time to go to the dentist. I knew it was coming, but I dreaded it. Being in close quarters on a smelly old ship again brought back feelings of claustrophobia and seasickness.

"How long will the trip to Juan Fernández take?"

"One to two months, depending on the weather. We will stop at several places along the way."

One to two months. It would seem like an eternity. Then I would be stuck alone on an island for God knows how long. The whole prospect seemed horrible. Juan Fernández. Even the name sounded bad.

"Carlos, do we have to do this? Even you know that your father's plan is crazy."

"Abbie, there is no alternative. We cannot stay in Panama. It seems good now, but let me warn you that it would not be so in the future. We have to go on the ship. We have to stay with the plan. Unless my father shows up, there is no alternative. I will come for you in the wagon at eight o'clock tomorrow morning."

There were no guests at dinner that night. The conversation during the meal went on as usual, but everyone could see that I was quieter. Don Ramón must have known that I was scheduled to embark on *La Santa Rosa* the next day. I expected him to mention it at the table, but he did not. After dessert, he asked me to join him and Doña Ramón in the sitting room, which looked out on the backyard. I could see from their expressions, enhanced by the flickering candles, that the conversation would not be light. Surprisingly, Doña Ramón led off.

"Señora Abbie, we know you are to leave tomorrow. We know also that you are not happy to leave. Forgive me, but I could not help hearing you cry in your room this afternoon. I have talked to Don Ramón about this. We would like you to stay with us. Please stay in Panama. This can be your home. We like you very much."

I was overwhelmed with her simple statement and how she looked at me so directly. Once again I had to keep back my tears.

"Thank you, Señora...I..."

"Señora," Don Ramón interrupted, seeing me struggling, "in all honesty, I do not think you will like Valparaiso. If I am permitted to say so, there are many more cultured people in Panama. I can tell that you are educated, and you like this way of life. You won't find it anywhere else in the new lands. We could use another teacher at the school. I have talked with the head instructor, and he would like to have you teach mathematics. I also would like you to tutor Ricardo and Concepción in other topics that you seem to know about. You will be a member of our family with your own room. You would have no labor like the other slaves. No one in this household wants you to leave. So please, stay with us."

Don Ramón smiled so genuinely that I realized my original concerns about him were wrong. He was a true gentleman and a family man. But he had said,"...like the other slaves."

"Don Ramón, would I be a slave if I stayed?"

He cleared his throat in an embarrassed way. "You would be a slave in name only. No English persons can be in Panama unless they are slaves. It cannot be otherwise. Henry Morgan, that English butcher who set fire to our city, made sure of that. But you would not be treated as a slave. You would belong to us and be a favored member of our family. I have the power of the Governor behind me, and you can be assured of full protection."

"But what if something were to happen to you? What if you were transferred or lost your appointment? What then?" Doña Ramón looked at him as he again cleared his throat.

"If we were to move, you would go with us. If you could not go, I would see to it that you would be given to a fine family who would treat you as we do. I give you my word. But we are here to stay. We have no plans to go."

"Abbie," Doña Ramón said, "the voyage will be dangerous. There may be sea battles. You may not make it. Here you will be safe. Our soldiers protect us. Consider that. Here you will be secure, with a home and family."

"Thank you both very much. I am deeply touched by your offer. My time here has been happy and I know I would enjoy it if I stayed. I like you and everyone here. But I must have some time to think before I give you an answer. Please allow me to sleep on it."

After the candles were out, I did not sleep. I did not want to go on the ship. La Señora was right, the ship could sink or any number of dangerous things could happen on the voyage. The dangers would continue on the island. What if pirates, the Spanish, or any other nation's ship came to the island? I might be captured and maltreated or even put to death. There was no civilized law. At best, I would be terribly lonely. How could I sit on that island for a year knowing the life I had given up in Panama? I might go berserk.

On the other hand, something told me it would be a grave mistake to be enslaved. Life was too unpredictable in this society to entrust myself to one man. The previous governor had been the victim of a palace revolt and was imprisoned for years. If there were any change in Don Ramón's status, what chance would I have as an English slave? I could be seized and sold into hard labor or encounter worse misery, despite the family's best intentions. If I stayed in Panama, would I ever see Los Angeles again? Would Bitterroot ever come for me? This time he might let me stew in my own juice out of vindictiveness of being thwarted.

I tossed and turned most of the night. I slept through breakfast. I was awakened by a loud knock. I threw on a dress and opened the door. It was Carlos, and behind him I could see Don and Doña Ramón. We went into the living room, and I gulped as I looked at the three expectant faces.

"You're not ready, Abbie," Carlos said.

"Are you staying?" Don Ramón asked.

I felt I should make it quick.

"I have decided to go on the ship. Thank you so much, Don and Doña Ramón, for your wonderful hospitality. It is difficult leaving you. Please give me your prayers." I kneeled and kissed their hands while they stood there not wanting to believe what they had heard.

The decision had come around four in the morning, and once made, I had been released into sleep. It was basically simple. I just could not be a slave—legally, intellectually, spiritually, or physically. I was choosing liberty. And very possibly I was also choosing death. Still, this felt better than choosing slavery, however sugar coated. Most importantly, I was choosing the only chance I had to get back to my twentieth century life.

26

As the rowers pulled heavily on their oars, taking Capitán Avila, Carlos and me out to the waiting *Santa Rosa*, the houses slowly blurred in the distance. The pungent marine smells, the cries of seabirds, the shimmer of sun reflections, all collided in my senses, underscoring the poignancy of the moment. Though I was sad, I knew my decision to leave had been the correct one.

During the shipboard journey to Juan Fernández Island, I had to be private and secluded as much as possible. There could be no familiarity with the officers or men as had happened on *Guadalupe*. I was strictly a passenger, not much different from cargo in the hold. I could do nothing that would attract attention. At my insistence, Capitán Avila agreed that I would not dine with the officers. I would eat at the officers' table during odd times. On occasion, when his watch schedule permitted, I would eat in the company of Carlos. When I was up on the afterdeck, I would be in an area curtained off so that nobody could see me.

La Santa Rosa was similar in shape to *La Reina de Cádiz* but larger. She appeared newer, had 32 gunports, and seemed more shipshape. As we approached, the anchor capstan was being turned by a group of sailors chanting lilting verses. The sailors increased their volume when we came over the gunwale, as if to show their pride. Sails were hauled up as soon as the shout came that the anchor had broken the surface. As the sails filled to the breeze, the ship bore away slowly to the south, clearing the leeward side of a nearby island. It was clear that the crew was well disciplined and in good spirits. They were ready to engage the enemy. Our track south would follow what would become the Columbian, Ecuadorian, Peruvian, and Chilean coastline, where we would look around the inlets and offshore islands that South Sea intruders were known to frequent. Our first destination was Gorgona Island.

Some Spanish school books had been given to me by Carlos as part of my disguise as a teacher. Out of boredom I spent much of my time reading during that first ocean passage. If nothing else, my Spanish would improve. There was also plenty of time to reflect on my situation. Freedom. How I had taken it for granted. I could now understand why this powerful idea had revolutionized the world. But the ironic thought occurred to me that while I had chosen not to be a slave in Panama, I was a still a slave to Gordon Bitterroot.

Somebody said that he who controls history controls the future. Bitterroot was planning to demonstrate that in a big way. What he planned would eliminate whole populations and their forbearers and give birth to new and different generations, all in an instant if you were in the 1990s. Day by day, year by year, if you were in this time. It was more than frightening. It was kind of like a retro-generational holocaust. It was...there wasn't even a word in the English language for it. And I was to be an accomplice. It was a shuddering thought. Every time I thought about it, I had to get it out of my mind.

After several days we sighted Cape Corrientes, which is so high that at first it looks like an island. From the charts that Carlos showed me, I realized this was part of what would later be the country of Columbia. We coasted south to the Bay of Buenaventura, looking closely at an island named Palmas at the mouth of a river. A tropical rain fell on us, and we headed westerly. Spaniards sluiced for gold at the mouths of the many small rivers we passed. The next morning we came to Gorgona, a heavily wooded island about six miles in length and several miles off the coast. We anchored at the west end in a sandy bay, and I was happy to be able to go ashore and hike around with Carlos. I especially enjoyed drinking from a fresh spring and watching the many seabirds who nested on the cliffs.

"Carlos, what if we find an enemy ship?"

"We will take over their ship and send it to a port with a prize crew. If they resist, we will engage it with arms and cannon."

"What happens to the enemy crew?"

"Some will be used as crew on the prize—those who are not troublemakers—and the rest will be imprisoned on this ship. Some might be killed if they are not careful. Those taken will ultimately be enslaved."

Two days later, at the island of Gallo, we found a ship anchored, and Capitán Avila sent a boarding party. It was a small Spanish vessel that was taking a cargo of brandy, sugar, flour, and cordage up the coast from Guayaquil. It had stopped to repair its rigging. The captain of the ship reported seeing no foreign vessels on his way up. When the crew came back, they had a wild monkey in a cage and a large, so-called lion lizard on a chain, both native species to the island. We inspected many more bays, seeing Indian settlements, and eventually passed the Island of Plata, so named because Francis Drake had anchored there with a captured Spanish prize. The ship had been loaded with silver plate, and Drake had divided the booty among his company.

We chased down a number of sails, all Spanish, on the way to Guayaquil, which I knew as a seaport of Ecuador. We had now passed the equator. The heat was nearly unbearable when the wind dropped. Guayaquil was a major port. The town had nearly a thousand houses and five parish churches. The port was well protected with two forts, one at the south end and one on a hill. There would be no enemy ships here, but Capitán Avila wanted to show the flag and pay his respects to the Governor. Only the officers went ashore, which made the crew and me unhappy. We left port just a few hours after arriving, having taken on some supplies. We found ourselves in very boisterous winds off Cape Blanco, but this was to be expected. The Spaniards have a proverb that "the stoutest Man of War must strike to Cape Blanco."

We now sailed away from the coast. The heavy land winds, no doubt influenced by the snowy Andes that could be seen far inland, and the strong northerly current, which I knew was the Humboldt current from Antarctica, made southerly sailing along the coast extremely difficult. We tacked back in to look at the islands of Guanapi and Clao near the river and the isolated town of Santa, where we later anchored and took on fresh fruit, water, and other necessaries.

We put in at Callao, and Carlos and I visited the thriving city of Lima. It was the City Royal for the Empire of Peru and the seat of a Viceroy and Archbishop. I was told that there were 17,000 Spaniards plus a far greater number of non-Spaniards, many of whom were probably slaves. Numerous ships were loading or unloading in the harbor. They were well protected by the castle fort which had seventy brass guns, all of them forty-eight pounders. Carlos and I went to several of the many churches and saw beautiful gold and silver ornaments and precious stones in the altars. One could find almost anything in the shops, and I only wished I had money. I did persuade Carlos to buy me an alpaca coat decorated with embroidery. He said I would need it at Juan Fernández, which was in a cooler climate and could be stormy.

The walk in the city allowed me to talk with Carlos without the worry of anyone overhearing, so I took the opportunity to find out things that were still puzzling to me.

"Carlos, who is Biru?"

"I've heard of him, but I've never met him. My father has recruited a number of people to help in different times and places."

"So Gordon has been at this a long time."

"Yes."

"How old is he?"

"He told me he was born near London in 1577."

I was amazed, but somehow I was not surprised.

"So how has he lived so long? And you, too?"

"When I'm on trips, I do not age. It is the same with him. When they're over I go back to where I was. I can remember the trip for only a day or two at most. They are totally erased from my memory, and I lose all physical evidence. Occasionally, though, I have strange dreams that I think come from the trips. But my father remembers all of his trips, and he seems to carry the effects."

"Like the scars?"

"Yes."

From Lima we tacked with great difficulty down to the port of Arica where Chile begins. We hailed several ships on the way, but they all were Spanish. Arica is the embarcadero for most of the mining towns of Peru. It was a pretty port, but only Capitán Avila and the primero went ashore. From Arica the Capitán decided to stop fighting the wind and current and sail out to San Ambrosio Island, several hundred miles to the southwest. From there we would go almost directly south to Más á Tierra of the Juan Fernández group. Both would be long passages.

Four days out, an ordeal that I had dreaded began with the cry, "Sail ho." At first the sighted vessel tried to run from us to the west, but as we slowly overtook him after a few hours, he turned to engage. The ship flew no flag, and when we got close, her cannons fired, followed by small arms.

I could hear shot going fast through the air overhead. A large spar on the foremast suddenly sagged. Men ran to man the lines to keep the sail from tearing. *La Santa Rosa* answered with a broadside of cannon, shaking the whole ship. The smoke from the gunpowder was acrid. Orders and curses were flying about. Several more broadsides took place. Then our ship wore away from the enemy, and I could feel the gun carriages being rolled on the gun deck. After the first gunfire, I was sent to the officer's galley below to help the steward prepare food. I think they mainly wanted me out of the way and out of danger, insofar as that was possible on an embattled ship. But I was strangely excited and would have stayed on deck to watch if I had been allowed.

After some sailing maneuvers, more cannon fire took place. The steward said our guns were bigger than the enemy's, so we could stay out of their range and still reach them. After a couple of hours the firing stopped. My ears were ringing so loudly I could hardly hear myself think. I learned that the enemy ship was fleeing, and we were trying to catch her. Obviously the Capitán's battle strategy hadn't been effective. A gale had whipped up, and the seas were becoming rough. Unfortunately the foremast rigging had not been successfully repaired and under reduced sail, we couldn't make our usual speed. Night came and the enemy ship was lost in the darkness. Still Capitán Avila kept on the same southerly bearing, making the best speed possible all through the night in hopes that the unknown ship could be seen in the morning. When daylight came, the high lookout on the mainmast reported no sail visible.

Surprisingly, only two men had been injured in the fight. One had taken a shot in the shoulder at the first broadside. The second had a crushed leg caused by an enemy cannonball coming through a gunport. The ship's surgeon was tending the miserable fellows. They needed medical attention in port, but rather than turn back to Arica, Capitán Avila decided to head for Juan Fernández Island where he thought the pirates would go to tend their wounds and make repairs. If they were not there, then *La Santa Rosa* would head for Valparaiso.

Fate is strange. Perhaps if more men had been hurt or if we had captured the pirate vessel, we'd be heading to Chile or Peru. Juan Fernández would be dropped from our itinerary. The Southern Dreams plan would be thwarted. But here we were heading there anyway. Why was the luck always with Bitterroot?

It took several days for us to sight Más á Tierra. The island first appeared like a deep blue hummock rising up out of the sea. As we got closer, the size and ruggedness of the high peaks became defined, and slowly the rich greens of the forests and vegetation came alive. The island was exotically beautiful and inviting. My heart began to palpitate as we drew up to the main harbor, Cumberland Bay, guns ready and officers straining at telescopes to see if our prey was holed up there. It was not.

We sailed around the island. According to the map Carlos gave me, it was shaped like a miniature Sicily. But Más á Tierra, which meant Nearer Land, was not really triangular; the three points were elongated and the middle squeezed. The island was about six miles at its maximum length and about two miles at its maximum width. The highest peak, El Yunque (the anvil), was more than three thousand feet high and was bare of vegetation at its top. It had steep sides. There were a few bays on the island, these on the northern side, and they provided easy shore access. The sea met cliffs at all other places. A small island, Santa Clara, about one mile in length, stood off the southwest corner of Más á Tierra. I was told that there was a third island of the Fernández group, Más Afuera (Further Away), about ninety miles west. It was smaller and less inhabitable than Más á Tierra.

We saw no ships or people. There were goats on the mountain cliffs and seals and sea elephants in the bays and inlets, and of course there were all kinds of water fowl. The gunner whose leg had been crushed was not doing well, and the Capitán wanted to get him and the injured deckhand to Valparaiso. But Capitán Avila also wanted to replenish the ship with fresh water from the stream feeding Cumberland Bay. It being late in the afternoon, he decided we would anchor for the night and leave in the morning.

As we moved into the bay under one lone sail, the boats already lowered to help tow, I was amazed to see that elephant seals covered the beach all around us. Large bellowing males were fighting interlopers who tried to sneak in among the females who were sunning themselves while keeping an eye on their adventurous young. Snorts and hisses carried easily across the water, and the collective noise of the teeming beasts made for a raucous din. Their bodies were so packed together that it seemed as if anyone going ashore would have to walk across their backs. As the ship was positioned at its anchoring spot, Carlos took me down to my cabin.

"Abbie, you will have to sneak ashore tonight while everyone is asleep."

"But how can I do that?"

"You will have to swim. You can make the half cable's length, can't you?"

"Yes, but aren't there sailors on watch?"

"I will help you. There will probably be only one lookout, and he'll be aft. You can slip over the side up forward with a rope ladder that I will put down for you. There is only a half moon tonight, but I think you will be able to see well enough."

"But what about my clothes and the gun and all the things you said you would provide?"

"They will be in a small canvas punt that you will tow behind you. The punt is buoyant and will tow easily. The waves are slight, and everything is packed to stay dry unless you overturn it. It will be at the bottom of the rope ladder waiting for you. Tie the line around your upper arms."

"Nobody will hear me swimming?"

"Not with all the racket the seals make. They don't get much quieter at night."

"But how can I get through them?"

"You will just have to push between them. Only the bull males are dangerous. And you can move faster than they can."

"Oh, God. And what about the punt? What do I do with that when I get ashore?"

"You take out the sticks and fold the ends to the middle and tie them. There are straps to sling it on your back like a pack. It's heavy, but I'm sure you can manage. The canvas will be of use later in making a rain cover. The only thing to watch for is the camp of sailors who went ashore to sleep. I will keep an eye out after supper to see where they are located, and you can strike out in a different direction."

"And where do I hide?"

"Go up into the vegetation a ways and then bed down. There are blankets in your bundle. Then at first light, move further into the forest, keeping a watch out to the ship. When the anchor has been weighed and the boats are up, then come down to the edge of the bay and be conspicuous, but don't wave. They should see you but not think you want them to come back."

"But won't they stop and come after me anyway?"

"No, because I will give Capitán Avila a letter I found in your cabin from you addressed to him. It says that you want to live on the island alone and not go to Chile. You ask him not to come back for you."

"Do you think he will go along with that?"

"There's a gcod chance. He wants to get his sick men to Valparaiso. Why should he waste time on a crazy inglesa? But if they do come back, you have the map showing how to get to the little cave on the other side of the island. Leave for it immediately if you see a boat being lowered. That cave cannot be seen unless one knows exactly where it is. They will never find it."

So here it was, the key step in the Southern Dreams plan. I wondered if I could pull it off without mishap. I realized I could foil the plan simply by refusing to go. I could stay on the ship and go to Valparaiso. But what then? Nobody in Valparaiso would even know about me. It would create a major incident. They might think me some kind of spy. I could be jailed or enslaved. It would be too much of a gamble to count on Bitterroot rescuing me. No, there was no backing out now. Bitterroot had been damn clever.

After supper I went to my cabin and tried to sleep. Carlos was to wake me around two a.m. with a soft rap on the door. My sleep was fitful. I kept listening for the knock, and when it finally came, I was tired. I sneaked up on deck with Carlos, and following his hand motions, moved quietly to the forward quarter where the rope ladder was fastened in the moon shadow of the foremast. Carlos was right about the noise from the seals. Didn't they ever sleep? I slipped off my shoes and then shook the extended hand of Carlos.

"Goodbye and good luck, Abbie," he whispered.

"Goodbye, Carlos. Thanks for everything. I'll see you when I see you, I guess."

"Yes. Go now."

It was a strangely stiff parting, but I didn't have time to think about it. At the bottom of the ladder I could see the punt. It was about four feet in length and shaped like a pregnant kayak. I climbed down, managed to stuff my shoes into the punt, undid its line and slipped into the chilly water. Still holding the bottom of the rope ladder, I snaked the line around my upper arms and tied a knot. The punt would follow me at a distance of about ten feet, far enough to keep away from my kicking feet. After a quick upward look and wave at Carlos, I pushed off from the barnacle-laden hull and started a slow dog paddle toward the beach.

It was farther than I expected, and my arms became heavy. I could feel the tug of the punt bobbing behind me. The grunts and snorts of the seals became loud. Then I heard the surf. The breaking waves were small, but probably big enough to overturn the punt. I went in slowly, saw where the break line was, then swam fast with all my remaining strength to beat the breaker forming behind me. When my feet hit bottom I strode in backwards to keep watch over the punt. Once safely beyond the broken wave I turned to see where I should climb up the beach.

Suddenly there was a deep roar right in front of me. My heart nearly stopped. The towering form of a bull elephant seal, mouth wide open, tusks flashing, the hideous growth on his nose shaking, was rushing straight for me. Water flew in all directions as his five hundred or so pounds slammed into the surf. I thought it was all over. Some way, I mobilized despite the panic that gripped me. I dived to my right. My feet were hit by his chest, which flipped them up, forcing my head down in the sand under water. Then I felt a sharp pain around my shoulders. It was the line to the punt. I pushed my head up out of the foam and saw the beast behind me about where the punt should be. I grabbed the line, but it was limp. The cord had parted. Suddenly there was something coming out of the water toward me. I recoiled, but then realized it was the overturned punt. I grabbed the end of it just as I saw the beast spin surprisingly fast and start for me again. I ran as fast as one can run in knee-deep water, pulling the punt behind me. The bull was gaining on me until he hit sand and slowed to my pace. I had no time to think. I ran straight up toward the pack of light-colored bodies ahead, pulling the punt like a sled. Please let them all be asleep, I prayed.

They weren't asleep. They had been watching the action and now let out warning bellows. But to my surprise, they moved away from me as fast as their flipper-like feet allowed, creating a passage that I could weave through like a tailback. Not even the rocks hurting my feet slowed me. Soon I was beyond them. I was able to climb over a dirt embankment and, with some effort, to hoist the punt, still dripping water, over with me. I lay down, exhausted. Only after several heaving minutes did I realize I must get away from that exposed position. What if the sailors at the camp came my way? I retrieved and put on my shoes, removed the broken sticks from the punt, folded and tied it, and hoisted it on my back. It was all I could do to not cry out as the straps hit the raw spots on my shoulders caused by the punt's cord. Remembering that I should angle to the right, I trudged up the hillside, my body chilling from my wet clothes, the pack feeling like a chunk of lead.

It was dark in the thicket of trees and bushes. I moved slowly, trying not to run into branches or stumble on the uneven ground. After I had gone a ways I found a large tree with some fairly smooth grass nearby. I was thankful to find that not all of the contents in the pack were wet. I got out of my wet clothes and wrapped myself in two mostly dry wool blankets and curled up on the ground. At some point I must have stopped shivering and slept.

There was dew on my hair and eyebrows when I awoke in the gray predawn light. The weather was humid and balmy. I did not care enough to worry about being discovered and I allowed myself to doze off again, awaking a second time to sunlight shooting through the branches from behind the easterly hills of Más á Tierra. I could hear the sounds of human activity above the noise of the sea elephant colony. I dressed in the driest clothes I could find and cautiously made my way down to the edge of the thicket. *La Santa Rosa* was alive with sailors getting her ready to sail. Already a breeze was coming into the bay. Then I noticed a boat full of men and gear being rowed to the ship from shore. I looked south and saw that the camp that had been set up the evening before had disappeared except for a couple of wooden boxes and firewood laying about.

No sooner had the boat been shipped than the clinking sound of the chain on the anchor windlass could be heard. They planned to sail her out of the anchorage. As soon as I saw the first sail go up, I walked down the hill to the edge of a point overlooking the bay. Several shouts went up, and I knew they had seen me. Would they come for me? They wouldn't want to slow the ship for fear of not making it safely out of the harbor. To my shock I saw them moving the smallest boat near the gunwale for lowering. Oh God, I would have to get to that cave. Where did I put the map? It was in the pack. Had it stayed dry? Would I be able to read it? My heart beat wildly.

There were shouts and waves. "Señora, Señora."

The boat was now in the water with three men in it, making for shore. The ship kept its sails up and its weigh on. I turned and ran up the hillside, not looking back. When I was well into the brush, I went behind a large bush and then peeked out through some branches. I heard shouting. Now I could see that the little boat had turned around and was heading back toward the ship, which had reduced sail so as to make it easier for the boat to catch up. The boat eventually made it, and the men climbed a rope ladder. The boat was hoisted and shipped on deck. More sails went up and *La Santa Rosa* picked up speed, turned, and headed easterly into the sun.

I sat down because my knees were shaking. A familiar fear came over me. It was the same fear I had experienced that first morning in Pelican

Bay when I realized that Bitterroot had left me there on Santa Cruz. Again I was alone on an island, left to my fate, like a marooned sailor. I was all by myself on a strange piece of land in the southern ocean—an island called Más á Tierra of Juan Fernández. A year ago I hadn't even known it existed. And yet, Bitterroot claimed, its name and mine would become famous. Capitán Avila would write in his log that the inglesa, Abigail Spence, abandoned ship and chose to live on Juan Fernández. With Carlos' help the log would find its way to London and thereby change the history of the New World. Could that be true? For the next year, all I had to do was survive physically and mentally. The former would be the easier.

I must have been depressed, for I went back to where I had spent the night and lay down again, wrapping myself in one of the blankets. I just wanted to hide from the day, from the noisy seals, from the birds that flitted and chirped. I dozed off and on for a couple of hours. One time I opened my eyes and saw a rat sniffing my pack. I jumped up and 'shooed' him away. "God, do I need this?" I didn't want to worry about it. I lay down and closed my eyes again.

Around midafternoon, I had hunger pains, but I didn't want to move. Then I thought about the rat. Its presence was, no doubt, a harbinger of the abysmal life to come. He probably smelled the food that Carlos packed. This finally motivated me to unpack the rolled up punt. It would be good to dry out the contents. Slowly I inventoried everything. There were a goodly number of items: a hand axe, a knife, a flintlock pistol and powder horn, a pan, a large pot, a cup, fork and spoon, one change of clothes, sandals, the alpaca coat, blankets, fishing line, fishhooks, rope, a small oil lamp, an oil container, flint and steel, nails, soap, a map of the island, a Bible, bread, wine, salt, pepper, tea, and two cloth sacks.

I sliced a piece from the loaf and ate it. I don't know why Carlos included the pistol. I didn't plan to kill seals, and I doubted I could get near the goats. I figured I would live mainly from seafood.

Now that I was up I realized my first task was to find a campsite. It would have to be near fresh water. I thought it would be good to be away from the bay just in case pirates arrived or the Spaniards came back.

Further inland there would be less noise from the seals and also there might not be rats that no doubt feasted on the remains of the sailor camps. I repacked the punt, tied it up tight, then left it dangling from a tree limb, hoping the rats would not get to it. I decided to hike up the valley in the direction of El Yunque, following the main stream that entered Cumberland Bay.

The water, a fast moving current, was crystal clear and delicious to the taste. It came down from the rain and mist that seemed to be constant conditions at the tops of the mountains. The lush vegetation became thicker as the valley became steeper, sweeping up the mountain side. I recognized a stand of Chonta palms that Carlos had described, their thin trunks with bamboolike rings reaching seventy to one hundred feet tall. At the top of this palm were long, thin, feather-shaped leaves hiding the cabbage fruit, which Carlos said looked like a white loaf of bread. Hanging down below the branches were the red berries, clustered like large bunches of grapes. I looked forward to trying this famous natural food of the island.

I found several nice meadows, one near a rock cliff. Any of these would have made a good campsite but for the strong wind that blew down from the mountains. I decided to go east over a ridge in hopes of finding a less windy spot. In the next narrow valley, which had a smaller stream, the wind was not as strong, and I found a rock abutment with an indentation where an overhang jutted out from the cliff. The air here was almost calm, and by fashioning the canvas in the right way, I could be protected from wind, sun, and rain. I followed the stream down toward the bay. Coming over a rise, I spotted six goats grazing in a meadow. They bolted, heading up the side of the cliff with amazing agility, stopping near the top to give me one last look before disappearing. How does one get close enough to shoot one of those?

This stream also flowed into Cumberland Bay, and I recognized my position once I was at the mouth. I could now skirt the bay, avoiding the seals on the beach, and get back fairly easily to where I had spent the night.

The pack was as I had left it, but for one thing—the flap seemed to be tied looser than I remembered. Could the rats have gotten into it? I hit the pack with the large walking stick I had picked up, but none came out. Perhaps my memory wasn't serving me well. Or, more probably, the wind had come up and tugged at it. I got it on my back and headed toward my new campsite, eager for another look at the water lilies in bloom at a pool of the stream just below the spot I had selected. Surprisingly, I found myself whistling. I realized that for the first time since Santa Cruz Island I had freedom.

The next priority was to get my camp in order. I made two trips back to the bay to get the boxes and some of the firewood left by the sailors. The large box became my table and the smaller one my chair. I made a fireplace out of rocks and after figuring out how to use the flint and stone with tiny wood flakes, soon had water going for tea. I filled the oil lamp and tested it. I knew that at some point I would have to boil fat from a seal to replenish my supply of lamp oil. I gathered up green leaves from a nearby grove of trees and laid these down as a mattress over which I made a bed of the blankets. The alpaca coat was my pillow. That night my dinner was tea and bread.

Was it God's plan that the only reading material I had was a Bible? Maybe I had asked for it, but I would have to be pretty bored before I cracked open the good book.

That night I thought about what to do the next day. I should try my luck at getting some of the plentiful lobster-sized crayfish, which the Spaniards called langosta. I might try to cut down a Chonta palm for the cabbage and berries or look for some of the other edibles native to the island such as turnips, black plums, or pimentos. I should try to get the canvas up and secured. Perhaps I should explore the island first to see if there were a better place to camp. I could leave my goods under the overturned boxes for protection from animals. I didn't sleep well that night. I kept hearing all kinds of strange sounds, but I woke up more rested than I had the previous morning.

The sounds of the night must have gotten to my unconscious fears because the first thing I did was learn how to load and fire the flintlock pistol. To my satisfaction it worked about as Carlos had said, the first time. There was a slight delayed reaction after I pulled the trigger before it went off. I inspected the tree I had targeted and, surprise, there was a hole where the ball had hit. My powder supply seemed sufficient, and there were about fifty balls of shot. I decided I would carry the pistol and its paraphernalia whenever I left camp. I chuckled as I remembered the several contributions I had made to organizations for handgun control. If my Reed friends could only see me now. But they would understand that at Juan Fernández in 1705, one could not be an anti-gun liberal.

I hiked down to the bay by a more easterly route and found another stream. To my delight I discovered a waterfall that dropped several feet into a large rock-encircled pool, just before it cascaded into the bay. The pool was a dark green color and bubbles from the foam floated across the surface. It was a perfect fresh water swimming hole, with an ocean view, no less. I maneuvered down past it to a rock that provided a seat just above the ocean waves sloshing against the rock wall. After shedding all but my underwear, I entered the water with one of the cloth bags tucked into my waistband. Paddling down several feet I came to the base of the underwater cliff. There I found so many langosta it was hard not to step on them. Some were huge. I tricked two medium sized ones into the bag and climbed back to the rock. I had two main dishes without needing a second dive. No, I certainly would not starve.

With the hunger demons conquered, I set off for the high ridge between El Yunque and the adjacent peak to the west. The elevation would afford me a good view of most of the island and suggest areas for exploration. It was a rather strenuous climb, and I was reminded that I needed to be in better shape. No doubt I would be in good form after a few months of hiking around my new kingdom. It was slightly misty on the ridge top, but still the view was magnificent. I could see Santa Clara Island and the many green valleys and gray rocky ridges of Más á Tierra. All this, with the blue of the ocean sparkling in the morning sun, made for a dazzling sight. The gestalt—sharp forms and vibrant colors—brought tears to my eyes.

I hiked westerly along the ridge, feeling fortunate to be in such a gorgeous place. It was as if I were the caretaker of a special garden. It was my island in the sun. Then, as I reached the highest point of the ridge, I suddenly saw a pile of wood—large branches and logs that had been axed into four to five foot lengths. And just beyond it were the ashes and charred remains of a fire in the middle of a circle of rocks. I looked around but there was nobody. The only sounds were the cries of seagulls circling in the air below, the distant growls of the seals and the swish of the wind that blew the wisps of mist slowly overhead. I approached the firebed slowly and reached down into the ashes. I felt warmth. Somebody had made a fire fairly recently. Could it have been the sailors from *La Santa Rosa*? Some had hiked inland to get the Chonta cabbage, but would they have gone all the way up here? There didn't seem time for them to have cut the wood. Why would they build a fire here? Why would anyone?

I felt a chill go through my body. Maybe a religious ceremony? There were reportedly no Indians on the island. The Polynesians had made it to

Easter Island, but apparently not this far west. A party site? Bitterroot had said nobody lived on the island. But Bitterroot had been wrong before. The most probable explanation, I decided, was that some *Santa Rosa* crew members had come up here with a load of wood late the night before last. I would not have known this because I was asleep.

I practiced loading the pistol, then continued on slowly, now being highly cautious and observant. After hiking along the crown of the ridge for a while, I found a gradual slope going down the other side and decided to follow this easy terrain into the western valley below. About an eighth mile from the top, vegetation began. The ground was wet, almost muddy, from the heavy moisture. Then it appeared, clear as the sun overhead. I avoided stepping on it so as not to disturb the detail. It was a footprint. Someone with a bare foot had left it. I inspected it carefully. The foot was slightly longer than mine and much wider. The arch was fallen. The heel had dug in. The person had strode down this slope, apparently not in the least bothered by the sharp pebbles and sticky bushes. It couldn't have been one of the *Santa Rosa's* sailors. They wore shoes.

Then my mind flashed to my pack. The flap had been tied looser when I had gone back for it. No rat had done that. The wind couldn't have done it. Only someone with fingers could have done it. *La Santa Rosa* and her sailors had been long gone by then. The explanation was obvious. There had to be another person on the island. And he—for I assumed it was a he—more than likely knew that I was here. Oh Lord. My legs began shaking.

I found a rock and sat down. I needed to think. The question was, who might this person be, and did he present any danger to me? Is this another of Bitterroot's cohorts? Is Bitterroot somehow checking up on me? At this point there seemed no way to know. The fact that this fellow had not taken anything from my pack, the gun in particular, might be a positive sign. The fact that he had not accosted me after the ship left might be a good sign. He would have had an easy opportunity while I was asleep last night or diving this morning. But if he were friendly, why hadn't he approached me to say hello? Could he be afraid of me? Maybe the Spaniards are his enemies and he thinks I'm with them.

My imagination was running away. I needed to get hold of myself. The issue now was, should I try to find this person, head on down into the valley where the footprint led, or go back and try to avoid contact? The latter didn't seem realistic. Sooner or later, on such a small island, we were bound to meet.

Out of the corner of my eye I detected a movement up on the ridge. I quickly slid down behind the rock and looked up. A goat. A young ram. He shook his head and then trotted off. I moved off down the slope, alert, cautious and walking as quietly as I could. Now and then I looked back and all around. There was probably a stream in the middle of the valley. His camp, if he had one, was probably somewhere close to it. I decided to pick up the stream at a high point, near its headwaters, and follow it north, down to the ocean.

The sun was warm, and I was ready for a long drink when I found the stream. I had picked up several scratches from the bushes. I licked the wounds, remembering my experience with Biru. Following the stream downhill made for easier going. I came to several pretty meadows, one after another. At one point I was delighted with a large hawk that landed in front of me on the ground. I found a nice stand of Chonta palms, but as I got closer I discovered many stumps. Fifty or more of the trees had been felled. The hatchet marks meant only one thing. Human at work. If there was one thing our species was especially good at, it was environmental destruction. If hungry humans ever populated this island in numbers, the Chonta would probably not survive. And I, the liberal, would be guilty too. As Dostoyevsky said, everyone is guilty of everything.

I could hear elephant seals. The northern beach was not far away now. Then, looking down, I realized I was on a small path. I drew my gun from my waistband and loaded it, pointing it up so the ball would not fall out. Weapon in hand I followed the faint trail as it veered from the stream up over a rise and toward a cliff at the base of the mountain. Inching my way along I came to the edge of a clearing. There I could see a hut about half the size of a single car garage. Its roof was thatched with thick fiber. Goat skins hung over the door and over a small window opening on the side. The hut was built of thin vertical logs, the cracks stuffed with thatching. Next to it was a smaller hut, less than half the size with no standing room.

Goats were bleating. There was a small corral in which several were moving around out behind the hut. There were cats lying about, big ones. There was a firepit for cooking in front of the hut. Smoke rose from it.

Suddenly there was a blurred motion to my right, near the base of the cliff. A man with a rifle aimed directly at me had jumped out not more than twenty yards away. I cocked my pistol and pointed it at him, thinking that I had to fire when I saw smoke from his gun, not when I heard the sound. I tensed my body. This was it. This was Santayana's Truth. This bare-chested, bearded man with a rifle would hit me, and I with a pistol I had fired only once would probably miss him. I tried to stop my hand from shaking. Be poised. Take it like a man. I was on borrowed time anyway. Where was the smoke? Any instant now. He was refining his aim. I kept waiting. Surely we stood like that for a minute. One of the cats got up and lazily walked away. It was bizarre. I had the urge to laugh. Suddenly the man turned and ran behind the large hut and past the goat pen and was lost in the bushes. I was struck at how fast he moved, at how high his bare feet picked up as he ran. I turned and ran away too, back over the rise and up the path into the forest, the opposite direction. I didn't slow down until I was exhausted and had to rest. I lay down behind some trees at the edge of the second meadow I came to, trying to listen for footsteps in between my panting spells. My legs were numb.

Why hadn't he shot me? And why had he run? He was a European, not an Indian, that much was clear. He had goat skins around his waist and a goat skin hat. Why didn't he say something? Why didn't I? It was a close encounter of the craziest kind. Maybe he wanted to sneak up on me, to circle around so that he could shoot me without risking being shot.

"You're paranoid, Abbie."

I decided to get out of the valley and go back to my camp as quickly as I could. The faster I moved the less chance he could catch up. I went cross country up to the ridge where I had found the remains of the fire. I made very good time down the mountain, only to slow up over the next two ridges to my valley. My feet and legs ached. It was nearly dusk when I reached my camp. I came up on it carefully.

"Uh oh."

There was something on my table. It looked liked rolled up leaves. And there was a flower. I looked and listened carefully. Other than the sound of the stream, all was quiet. Everything else about the camp seemed to be as I had left it.

I approached slowly. The flower was beautiful It reminded me of a tiger lily, but it was larger. The color was lavender with black and yellow spots. I touched the package of leaves. They were wrapped around something heavy. I pulled them apart. Fresh meat, cut in several fillets. It had to be from the man, but how had he beaten me back to my camp? I pulled out the map and saw that the shortest distance from his camp to mine was directly east along the ocean cliffs. My route had been twice as long. I looked around, expecting him to be watching from behind a bush. There was nobody. Did I dare eat the meat? I inspected it closely.

Then I looked again at the flower. Could it be a gesture of welcome? I did not hesitate any longer. My stomach won. I barbecued the goat meat and ate it in the flickering light of the oil lamp. It was succulent. I decided to move my bedroll away from the camp that night as a precaution. For quite some time I stayed alert, listening for unfriendly sounds. Finally I drifted off.

Early the next morning I got up feeling chipper. I fished one of the langosta out of the bag I had submerged in the stream, twisted off the tail, and boiled it. That, some of the now stale bread, and hot tea, made my breakfast. I decided to get some Chonta cabbage and fruit for my lunch and wash my clothes. Then I would go find the man.

Chopping down the Chonta tree proved to be good exercise. The hatchet worked well. The only thing that bothered me was the noise—first from the chopping and then when the tree fell. Anyone this side of the divide would know where I was and what I was doing. I sampled the cabbage and berries and found them moist and pleasant to the taste. I packed them in a sack to carry. I gathered my clothes and the soap and headed to the pool.

How could I best coexist with this man? He didn't seem to be hostile or he wouldn't have brought me the meat and the flower—a rather civilized gesture. Certainly he might help me in some ways. But could he be hurtful? Sexually aggressive? The only way to know was to try to talk to him. But if he couldn't speak English or Spanish, that would be difficult. When I had finished washing, my arms had goosebumps from the cool water. I placed the clothes out on the grassy bank. I could hear the bull elephant seals in the distance.

"Heello. Heello."

I turned and looked up the cliff. The man was standing on a rock, looking down, smiling. His gun stock rested on the ground, the barrel in his hand. Had he just come or had he been watching me, that son-of-a-gun? He had probably gone to my camp and then, not finding me, come down this way. Did 'heello' mean he spoke English?

"Hello," I called, waving at the same time. "Do you speak English?"

He didn't reply but waved back and now started climbing down toward me. My heart started pounding, and my legs became weak. I picked up my pistol and tucked it in my waist band, but it was unloaded. If worse came to worst, I could run and dive into the bay. Soon he was standing about ten feet away. A faint musky odor came to my nostrils He was about my height, thin but heavily muscled. His forearms were particularly thick. His wide cheek bones were shiny with a deep tan that contrasted with the blond beard. His twisted moustache drooped around a firm mouth. The blue eyes had a sadness to them, even as they glinted in the sun. I guessed his age to be about thirty.

"I daub ask how wad ye came heer, lassie? Wha is your name, beGod?" He had taken a step forward.

"Please stay there," I said, holding up my hand. I had not fully understood him. He was Scottish, of all things.

"Nae, I wudna hurt. Wha is your name?"

"My name is Abbie Spence," I said slowly. "What is yours?"

"I be Alexander Selkirk aff the *Cinque Ports*."

"Have you been here long?" I asked, not understanding the last part of his sentence.

"Aye, lang." He shrugged, and the sinews on his bare shoulders rippled. "Nine months."

God, nearly a year, I thought. How could Bitterroot not have known that this Alexander Selkirk was here?

"Why d'ye leave the Spanish ship?" he asked. "Wha country be ye from?"

I wasn't ready for this. I should have been thinking what to say to this man. For some reason I didn't expect someone I'd have to converse with.

"I am from Virginia."

"Virginia? Virginie Colonie!" He smiled and nodded. "How d'ye came wi' the Spanish?"

"Well, it's a long story."

Then he sat down on a rock.

"I be pleasit t'hear."

And he sat there waiting. So I sat down, too.

"Well, Mr. Selkirk, I was with my parents and we went on board a ship for Jamaica. Jean LaRue, a pirate, captured us, and my parents were killed. Jean LaRue took me on board his ship and we went around Cape Horn to the South Sea. The Spanish captured us and sank the ship and killed LaRue and most of the crew. They allowed me to put ashore here because I did not want to go to Valparaiso. I did not want to become a slave or be put in prison. They probably thought I would not survive here."

He stared at me, either weighing my words or trying to understand them.

"Poor lass," he said quietly. Then his forehead wrinkled. "There sticks in my mind ane thing alsweel. How 'tis they wud gi'ye provisions?"

"I begged them for supplies. One sailor helped me. I sneaked ashore at night with a pack of things I needed. But they wouldn't give me food, except for bread and tea."

"Tea!" His face lit up. "Wud ye gi' me a cup o' tea?"

"Well, yes, sure. Don't you have tea?"

He shook his head. "Nie a year wud I hae tea."

"I will be happy to share some tea with you, Mr. Selkirk."

He smiled broadly. "God lave thee, lass. Ye be a blessen of the Laird."

Then he made a slight choking sound, put his head back and placed his palms together at his chest. His lips moved in whispers. He was praying. Tears began streaming out of the corners of his eyes. I felt suddenly touched, and my eyes watered. Was it just my offering to have tea with him? I thought he must be terribly lonely. I was pleased that he was religious. Maybe I would be safe with him.

I waited until he finished his praying, then I held up a finger.

"Before we have tea, please tell me one thing, Mr. Selkirk."

"Aye?" He wiped the tears away without shame.

"Why didn't you shoot me yesterday?"

"Me shoot?" He smiled, wistfully. "I believed ye were sent to kill me. But in my sites ye appear'd English, nae Spanish. I could'na fire."

I smiled at him. "I'm so glad. And by the way, thank you for the flower and the goat meat."

He nodded, now somewhat embarrassed.

"Let's go have some hot tea," I said. I picked up my things and headed off with Selkirk at my heels.

At my camp he quickly made a fire while I filled the pot with water and broke out the tea.

"Soon the ratten comen," he said as we waited for the water to boil.

"Ratten?"

He moved his hands to mime his meaning, and I caught on when he made the tail.

"Ye can move ower the ridge t' my hame. Tha cats keep away the ratten. It be safer we baith be togither."

"Uh, well, thank you Mr. Selkirk, but I think I will stay here."

He looked at me with surprise and then amusement. "Suit yoursel. Don' complain I did'na forwarn thee."

"Thank you for your kind offer."

I let him use my cup. When the tea was poured he immediately took a mouthful and savored it, making a pleasant sound in his throat. After he had swallowed it, he stood and raised his hands, looking skyward.

"Delightsome. Thank thee, Laird." He looked at me. "I could dare t' dance."

"Dance, Mr. Selkirk?" I wasn't sure what he had said.

Suddenly he moved away from the table and began singing and dancing a jig. His feet moved so fast I could hardly follow them with my eyes. He had a rather mischievous look, and I couldn't help laughing right along with his merriment. I missed the first verse but listened closely to the next one:

Oh merry blooms the hawthorne tree
And merry blooms the brier
And merry blooms the bracken bush
Whaur my true love doth appear:

She maks her bed and waits therein
And when I walk beside
She will rise up like a laverock
And her arms will open wide—

Oh start up and leap, man:
And never fall and weep, man:
Quick quick and rin, man:
The game will just begin, man—

Grinning, he sat back down as quickly as he had started and was scarcely breathing hard. I clapped spontaneously. He had a nice voice, too.

"That was wonderful, Mr. Selkirk. Do you dance a lot?"

He laughed. "Aye, most ever' day, dance and sang, after I pray and read the Haly Bible."

I smiled and nodded, then decided I should find out how he came to be on the island. It turned out to be a long story, more so than mine. Even though I did not understand it all, the gist was that he had marooned himself in October of last year, leaving his ship, the *Cinque Ports*, because he was angry with its master, Lieutenant Stradling. Stradling had apparently replaced the original captain who had died enroute. Selkirk had been the second officer and was worried about the condition of the ship's bottom and, along with most of the crew, had lost confidence in the new captain.

The *Cinque Ports* and its companion ship, the *St. George*, headed by the leader of the expedition, William Dampier, had left Kinsale, Ireland, in September of 1703. It was an English privateering enterprise. They had rounded the Horn and preyed on Spanish ships along the Peruvian coast, using Juan Fernández as a refuge.

Selkirk, who said he came from First on Forth, Scotland, was put ashore with only a few things. These were his clothes and bedding, his rifle and ammunition, some tobacco, a hatchet and knife, a kettle, nails, a Bible and some navigation books and instruments. He had been very sad for the first several months, losing weight because he did not eat well.

"How old are you, Mr. Selkirk?"

"I be bairn in 1676."

That made him 29. I then had to tell him my age.

"Ye be freshit."

I guessed this meant I looked younger than I was. He seemed impressed when I told him I was a teacher. I felt uncomfortable getting into the exchange of personal information as I wanted things to remain formal between us. So I decided we had talked enough. Our tea had long been consumed.

"Well, Mr. Selkirk," I said after standing up, "I very much enjoyed having tea with you. I now need to do some chores by myself. I want to thank you for coming by to see me. We will have to talk again another day."

He stood up and seemed saddened.

"I thank thee, Miss Spence, for the delightsome broo. I am pleasit to mak your acquaint. D'ye want me t'came again t'morrow?"

"No, not tomorrow. I will come visit you in two or three days. I'll look forward to seeing you then, Mr. Selkirk."

"Ane honour t'be sure. I bid ye fareweel."

And he nodded deeply—it was almost a bow—and moved off up the valley. I listened to his whistling until the notes faded.

I puttered around the camp, stuffing additional leaves into my bunk, restoring my supplies and scrubbing the boxes. My mind, of course, was on Selkirk. What was I going to do? Clearly I needed a better camp than this. It would be best to have a thatched hut like his that would keep out wind and rain from a storm. It certainly made a lot of sense for us to share resources and help each other. He might be the only person I would talk to for a year or so. So far, I liked him. He was charming, in fact. So why shouldn't I take up his offer to live at his camp?

I knew very well the answer to that. Because one thing might lead to another. He might be aggressive. No, at least for a while I had to keep distance between us. We should be friends, but not bosom buddies. So I resolved that I would look for another campsite away from the rats on this side of the ridge. I would visit him the day after tomorrow to learn how he constructed his hut. Once I knew how, I would build one by myself. When my separate camp was established, it would be easier to decide how often we would visit. Every third day was probably about right.

Off I went looking for another campsite. I tramped around the hillsides and valleys until my legs felt like they would fall off. On the afternoon of the second day I settled on a site next to the main stream feeding Cumberland Bay, but much higher than the sailor camp. It was a nice flat place among trees and not too windy. It was not visible from the bay, but it afforded a lookout in that direction from a small rise nearby. The trees would provide the limbs needed to build the hut.

The "ratten" had come the previous night. They chewed on my boxes, trying to get to the supplies inside. If they kept that up they would chew a hole through the wood. I needed to figure out a way to prevent that. Maybe it was the salt, pepper and tea they smelled. I could put these items somewhere else. Where? Hang them from a tree limb? It was worth a try. Or, maybe if I slept nearer the boxes the rats would not be so bold. But I couldn't stand the thought of them being near me. During my wanderings that day I tried to decide if Alexander Selkirk had subtly flirted with me. The lyrics of the song had been suggestive. But maybe it was just a typical Scottish ditty. His gorgeous eyes had definitely twinkled at me a few times. Or so it seemed. Why on earth were these thoughts going through my mind?

I had thought also about my decision to have a separate camp. The issue was well described by Kierkegaard more than a century ago. Or would be described by him more than a century from now. It was interesting how I knew things before their time. He pointed out that the self is a synthesis of opposing tendencies that always remain in opposition. One tendency is the need for self-assertion, to be oneself. The other is the need to be related to others, to have a role such as spouse, mother, student, and so on. Too much relatedness can create the threat of engulfment. To be totally independent creates loneliness and the feeling of not counting for anything. It is an existential paradox. One has to live with both tendencies. Keeping my own camp was exhibiting self-assertion; going over to his camp was expressing relatedness. Naturally I wanted both. But which did I want more?

I put the tea, salt, and pepper in a sack and hung it from a tree limb about fifty feet away. That night I was physically exhausted. I went to bed early, knowing I would need energy to move my camp the next day. I fell into a deep sleep. I must have dreamed. It was a bad one. Some large beasts were stalking me. I couldn't move. They kept getting closer and closer. Then one closed in on me, and I awoke screaming. He had bitten my toe. I heard them scurrying away through the leaves. My toe was in pain. I reached down and felt it. It was bloody. A rat had chewed on my foot! Oh God. What if it gets infected? Rats carry diseases such as bubonic plague transmitted from fleas. The ships are full of fleas and God knows what else. I could die from this. My mind was going wild. I jumped up limping and somehow lit my oil lamp and started a fire for hot water. I inspected my foot. The rat had bitten several times the toe next to the big one on my right foot. The wounds were small incisions. I washed the toe thoroughly with hot water and soap. Then I put on a clean sock.

What else could I do? There were no antiseptic medicines. I wondered if Selkirk had anything. But what? In this day and age there was nothing. Still, maybe it would be good to go see him. I had planned to do it anyway to see how to build the hut. I went back to bed, but stayed awake until dawn, fearing the rats would return. After a breakfast of Chonta cabbage, I set out, favoring my right foot. I had a small portion of tea leaves wrapped up in my pocket for a gift.

The direct way to his camp, skirting the seaward side of the ridge, was precarious at a few places where narrow ledges had to be traversed. With my tender foot I took particular care. Even so, in only two hours I reached a point just above his camp. I started to press on down, for I could see him in the goat pen. I heard his voice. He was singing. Then I noticed he was dancing with a goat, holding its front legs up while he and the goat pranced around each other. It was all I could do not to burst out laughing. When Selkirk's back was toward me I moved quietly down the slope, my hand over my mouth so as not to betray my presence.

Selkirk was doing a jig similar to the one I had witnessed at my camp. The goat's head was back, its eyes wide and wary as it picked up one hind hoof and then the other. I could now hear words sung out gaily in mellifluous baritone:

When I cam hame frae riden out
I fand my love in bed.
A minstrel harp hung on the rail
And a coat of the scarlet red.
"What man was here?" I speirt at her
And this is what she said
"Oh a dree dree dradie drumtie dree."

I moved up to the pen in stealth but the goat must have given some nervous signal for Selkirk dropped his partner like a hot potato and wheeled around, startled to find someone just a couple of feet away.

"O mi lassie, be God."

I started laughing. He began chuckling. Soon we were both laughing and tearing. Meanwhile, the goat limped off to the opposite side of the pen where the other goats watched us with uncertain curiosity.

"Why is that goat limping?" I asked when I finally composed myself.

"I brak baith their front legs so they canna' rin and jump the fence."

"Oh how cruel!"

He looked at me with surprise, then shrugged. "They be weel cared."

I gave him a searching look, but could find no guilt or remorse. He obviously found nothing wrong with maiming the animals. And why not? The goats were his food, first and foremost, and only pets for amusement until the time for their sacrifice. I climbed over the fence and went up to a small kid. It did not shy away, but nuzzled my hand for food. It made me think of the many times that my father had taken me to the Petting Pen at the Los Angeles Zoo. As a tot I had been afraid to feed the goats and sheep, fearing they would nibble my fingers by mistake. I usually threw the corn on the ground when the insatiable beasts trotted up.

I kneeled and hugged the little goat and looked back at Selkirk, feeling like a child again. But Selkirk wasn't my father. My father was gone. My mother, too, for all practical purposes.

"D'ye like her? I call her Angel. I gie her ower to ye."

"You will give her to me?"

"Aye."

"Then she will live as long as I'm here. I'd rather eat seafood."

Selkirk laughed. "Ye just brought her luck. May she bring ye luck alsweel."

"Thank you, Mr. Selkirk." I stroked Angel and she leaned into me. I loved her already. I fished the tea out of my pocket and held it out to Selkirk.

"Here, this is for you."

His eyes lit up. "Tea. O thank ye. It mak me most pleas'd." He put forward his hand and I took it. "Ane handfast o' friendship."

"Yes, we will be friends." I shook his hand firmly.

"Come," he said, pulling me forward beyond the pen. "Cast your eyen furth."

There across from his hut, twenty five feet away, stood the log frame of a new hut, to be the same size as his. Next to it were several freshly cut logs and a pile of thatching material.

"It weel be done the next day for thee, lass. With twae houses, this now be a village. I weel call it New Largo. That be where I was bairn." He grinned with satisfaction.

A strange feeling came over me. I dropped his hand and looked at him. I didn't know what to say. He could not help but see my unhappiness.

"Mr. Selkirk, I...was bit by a rat last night and wondered if I could have one of your cats to take back with me to keep the rats away."

"O, poor lass. Where waur ye bit?"

"On my toe." I pointed to my right foot.

"Let me look."

He sat down and took off my shoe and sock. I sat down while he inspected the wounds.

"It will heal alwright. Ane ratten chewed my toes alsweel. Nasty buggers."

I was disappointed when he let my foot go. He looked at me in a fatherly way as we sat together on the ground.

"I donna think my cats would gae w'ye. If ye stay heer, the ratten willna came. Be ye afraid to stay hear?" His gaze was serious. It made me uncomfortable.

I lowered my head, wishing I hadn't. "No, I'm not afraid." I lifted my eyes to his and saw the change of his expression from concern to warmth.

"Then pleas stay, Miss Abbie Spence."

I laughed at the formality. I looked into his soft eyes. A surge of good feeling came over me.

"OK, Mr. Alexander Selkirk. I'll stay. But I'll need to get my things from my camp."

"I waud help thee."

Don't ask me how I made that decision. Rats, cats, goats, huts, Selkirk, Kierkegaard—it all computed in my mind. The brain cells were primed in advance, I suppose. A wholly rational process completed beforehand. The emotions had nothing to do with it. Like hell.

We went to my camp and got my supplies and one of the boxes, which Selkirk tied on his back. He later went back for the other box, which he brought into New Largo just before sunset. His strength and stamina were truly impressive. I made my bed in the partially built hut. Selkirk got a kick out of this, kidding me that I would be safer there than out in the open. The animals would respect that I was in a hut-to-be. That evening he cooked goat meat, and I cooked langosta on his fire. He preferred goat meat because, he said, the ocean meat did not agree with his stomach. We also ate Chonta berries and had some vinegary wine in celebration of our new village. I was exhausted and crashed early with the help of the wine. As I went to sleep I felt a great sense of well-being, more than I had at any time before on my journey.

The next day we worked on the hut. He showed me how to stuff the thatching, which I did while he put up the logs. I helped him by holding some of the timbers as he nailed them in place. We worked hard all day, stopping only for lunch and for fifteen minutes of Bible reading by Selkirk. By the end of the day the hut was finished, and it was beautiful. He brought me one cured goatskin to hang over the door and said he would get me more later. I shuddered to think that the skins he meant were presently covering live bodies in the goat pen. After dinner he asked if I wanted to accompany him to the high ridge. Now that the Spanish were out of the area, he planned to set his signal fires again. Even though I was tired, it was a balmy moonlit evening and the hike sounded better than sitting alone in camp. Fortunately, my toe was no longer hurting.

Following Selkirk along the trail it occurred to me that a friendly ship might see the fire and come rescue us. That certainly would be counter to Bitterroot's plan. Did Bitterroot know in fact that no ship would show up at Juan Fernández until the English fleet he planned on? Well, he didn't know that Selkirk was here. So he probably didn't know about all the possible vessels in this region. If one came, would I embark on it with Selkirk?

I enjoyed watching Selkirk in front of me. The moon lit up his dancing muscles, and his body was most attractive. Earlier I had marveled at his coordination and prowess as he hoisted the logs, shoved them into place and knocked in the nails with the back of his hatchet. He had showed a temper, yelling and cursing when one of the logs had fallen from his grasp. Yet he was gentle and polite. I wondered what he thought of me. He had given no indication. He had taken my existence in stride, confident that we should be together in his camp, sharing and helping each other. And here we were, moving along in silence together, as if it were perfectly normal, as if we hadn't just met in this crazy place and nearly shot each other three days before.

It was cool on the ridge. A light wind was blowing. I felt goose bumps and wished I had brought my alpaca coat. Selkirk piled up some kindling and, producing a flint, soon had some twigs glowing. He slowly added larger and larger limbs. Before long we were backing away from the heat of a bonfire that darted and danced in the breeze. We sat down together and watched the flames, listening to the hisses of the damp wood, feeling the welcome heat on our bodies.

Selkirk felt like talking and told me of his life in Scotland.

"I have six braithers, all older. We be poor. I liked mi mither but mi father I fecht with. He wanted me to lairn shoemaking like him. I wanted to gae to sea."

"I can understand that." He explained that he had gotten into trouble with the local parish as a teen. He didn't say what for, but I gathered it was something embarrassing. He finally, with his mother's blessing, went to sea at nineteen. He was good at mathematics and learned navigation. On one of his return stays, he fought with his brothers and was rebuked one Sunday in front of the church congregation. That had convinced him to leave for good when the opportunity came.

"I sailed for Ireland in 1702. Captain Dampier chose me for his trip to the South Sea. And I be made sailing master of the *Cinque Ports*."

"That was the name of the ship?"

"Aye, the smaller of the two ships."

"Did you ever marry?"

"Nae. Never ane girlfriend and never ane whoor. I be confusit by the laydies."

I looked at him. He winked, but I sensed he was being truthful. I leaned in to him slightly, wanting to be close, wanting to touch this man who was so kind, so appealing. He put his arm around my shoulder. I felt electricity.

"Ye ha' said not much about yoursel yet. Please tell me yor hale story."

I had been prepared to discuss my Jamestown upbringing and I began talking about living on a farm with my parents. But as I talked neither of us seemed to be paying attention, for our bodies were communicating louder. I put my hand on his neck and he pulled me closer. The heat between us was suddenly greater than the fire. Nothing was said as we began hugging each other eagerly. Now we were embracing. It was a sensual explosion in slow motion. I was transported somewhere else. Now we were on the ground together. We locked, kissing, touching, pressing, entwining, rolling, panting. We were as two starved animals, suddenly allowed to feast. With the clouds casting moving shadows from the moon, the fire flickering and crackling, its flames licking and darting, we lost ourselves. Eventually we dozed in each others' arms.

Consciousness finally ebbed into a corner of my mind, and the ground, for which I had been so long oblivious, became hard and damp. I eased away from his warmth and sat up. Thankfully my clothes were still on. I looked down at Selkirk, prone and breathing contentedly. He was partially nude, the goatskins having fallen away. The glow from the fire's embers turned his body into bronze. The erstwhile steel muscles were now relaxed under the glistening skin. His lips held a smile like the Mona Lisa's and his tousled hair hung down to his nose. I combed his locks away from his face with my nails and bent and kissed his eyes. He awoke and squeezed my hands before looking at me deeply, somewhat fearfully.

"The fire has died down," I said softly.

"Aye," he murmured.

He rose slowly and rewrapped his goatskins around him.

"Should we go back home?"

"Hame. Aye."

Not another word was spoken except for the "Good nights" just before we went into our respective huts.

I had a difficult time sleeping. I remembered one summer when I was home from college and had to read several authors. I read, back-to-back, two of Colette's books, *Cheri* and *The Ripening Seed*, lyrical classics of French amorousness and sadness—what is called tristesse. They didn't do much for me. I had discussed them with my mother and Crystal, and we had had a big discussion about "surrender." For Colette, thinking about doing it, and who to do it with, was as much fun as actually doing it. The seduction and surrender, slow and exquisite, made all the difference. To my surprise, Mom and Crystal felt this was an important part of romance. I had had a hard time relating to it, and they had kidded me.

29

The hut kept the early morning light from me, and I slept until the meowing cats and bleating goats were too loud to ignore. I could hear Selkirk up and about, talking to the animals as he fed them. Mr. Alexander Selkirk, I said to myself. What would he have to say after our wild time on the ridge? What should I say? I was embarrassed. Maybe I shouldn't have come to live at Selkirk's camp. Of course, I could move back over the ridge. But why? What had happened last night was spontaneously wonderful. Why was I ashamed?

Selkirk was not around when I stepped outside. I ate some Chonta berries. A fire was crackling. I put up water for tea and sat down on a rock to wait for it and to begin a friendship with the big gray tomcat, Traitor, curled up next to the rock. He was licking his paws, having already eaten a ration of seal meat. Selkirk appeared from the direction of the stream, carrying a pot full of water. I waved but did not say anything. He seemed preoccupied. He put the water into the goat pen, then came over to me. I looked up, expecting a big smile, but found instead a stony expression.

"Good morning, Mr. Selkirk."

"Mornin' to ye, Miss Spence." He paused. "I wish to talk w' ye."

"Yes?"

"I pray'd to the Laird meist of the night. I be no Sanct, but I concludit we must go only one way."

Then he kneeled in front of me and took both my hands in his.

"Abigail Spence, I be asking ye to be my marriet wife. I do lave thee."

He had to be joking. I laughed, although somewhat nervously, I admit.

"Very good. That's a good one, Mr. Selkirk."

His expression did not change.

"Will ye marry me, Abbie?"

The man was serious.

"But we don't even know each other!"

"We know each other enow," he said, the first hint of a smile coming to his face.

"But there is nobody here...no minister, no church, no people. So why?"

"Na kirk is necessair. We can give our vows on ain Haly Bible. The mickle Laird will honour it intil we die. He told me so."

I felt suddenly lightheaded. I pulled my hands from his grasp. I looked at Selkirk in front of me, still on his knees, and I strangely felt for him. He obviously had been going through a lot during the night.

"Alexander, I am very flattered. This is just a great surprise to me, as you must know. I need time to think about it. Let me go off by myself for a while, and then I can come back and talk to you. Right now I cannot concentrate. Do you understand?" I reached out and touched his face.

He nodded, but with some disappointment.

"Thank you," I said with relief. "And...I want to thank you for last night. It was a lovely evening."

"Aye, that it was." Now he smiled.

Selkirk went hunting and I went fishing—he to the east side of the island, and I to the west. I picked up a langosta and carved it up for bait. I found a rocky cove protected from the surf and sat on a large boulder above a deep green pool. I tossed the line out, weighted by a nail, and finally allowed my churning feelings to express themselves in rational thought.

I realized first that as a religious man, Selkirk was acting honorably and predictably. For him, marriage was the only way. And, I allowed, he could be in love with me. I had always accepted the idea of love at first sight even though it had never happened to me. As for my own feelings, I was obviously attracted to him, infatuated even, but not in love. The beginnings were there, but a deep love—if I were to even accept the concept—would take much more time.

The issue was not whether we truly loved each other. Love would probably grow. So what was the problem? Was it the abnormal situation we were in? There weren't other men. He was it. For him I was the only female. We either stayed in his camp and became intimate or lived alone in separate camps. We couldn't be in proximity and maintain a platonic relationship. Neither of us were made that way. That was very clear after last night.

Intimacy was not really the difficulty. It was the nature of our commitment. It was the concept of "marriage." The real issue was the future and what "marriage" would mean to each of us. Given that I would be gone in a year or so, removed from him—and he could not be told that—I would necessarily deceive him if we married. Unless, of course, I were to stay in this time, go back to Scotland with him and be his wife.

"Oh c'mon, Abbie." That was out of the question.

So how on earth could I honorably respond to his proposal? How could I do the right thing?

I thought of the German philosopher, Immanuel Kant. He would argue that a sense of moral rightness and duty exists, a priori, in every human being. Rightness is rational. It is part of the fabric of the mind. The problem was how to get access to it. So somewhere hiding in my mind, according to Kant, was the right answer, the ethical thing to do. I just had to tease it out. I had only until the end of the day.

The jerk on my arm almost pulled me into the water. I paid out some line, tugging it slightly to make sure the fish stayed hooked. He began to tire after a while and I slowly brought him up. He was a big cod, black and white, with large eyes. The Spaniards called these bacalao. He would be good eating—a welcome change from the langosta. Without trying much, I had three large ones in my bag within two hours, having thrown a couple of smaller ones back. I took my time cleaning and filleting them. At camp I cooked a couple of the pieces for lunch. There was no sign of Selkirk. I put my bedding out in the sun and after that went to the stream and washed myself, my clothes and the one bedsheet I had. Enjoying the warmth of the day, I found a grassy place, sprawled out and snoozed.

When I walked into camp late in the day I found Selkirk skinning a male goat he had carried home on his back. The butchering process was bloody. The cats swarmed around nipping at the poor dead animal, Selkirk shooing them away. How he could get close to goats in the wild was beyond me. I figured he must have some sort of trap.

I got pans for the meat and helped him as much as I could in silence. He was practiced at it and finished fairly quickly. He took the carcass and offal and dumped them over a cliff into the ocean, while I kept the cats away from the fresh meat, which didn't turn out to be that much in quantity. Still we would be eating goat meat for the next several days, along with the bacalao.

That evening I put my clean bedsheet on the large box as a tablecloth. I picked some wild flowers and put them in a jar that Selkirk had found on the island. The bouquet became the centerpiece. I prepared the Chonta cabbage with pimento and toasted the last of the stale bread. Selkirk, after cleaning up at the stream, barbecued the tenderest pieces of the meat, using pepper generously. We each agreed that a quarter cup of the wine would be allowed for the occasion.

We chatted our way through the dinner, the best Selkirk had eaten since leaving Ireland, he claimed. We talked mostly about hunting and fishing and the goats and cats. I was surprised to learn that he caught the wild goats with his bare hands by running them down. This I would have to see to believe. When the sun had set and we had all but finished our dessert of wild blueberries, he lifted his wine cup to toast.

"Weel, Abbie, it was ane lang day, but a fine one. Heer's to ye, and heer's to our friendship. Ye can now tell me if I should say heers to ain thing more."

We both drank, and he looked at me expectantly, his eyes twinkling. I reached across the table and took his hand. It felt so warm and nice, I had to catch my breath.

"Alexander, I've given it a lot of thought today. I like you very much. I...I think I could fall in love with you. But everything is so sudden. So new. I agree that if we live together in this camp, the proper way is to be man and wife. But I don't know if marriage is right for both of us for the future—that is, when we leave the island."

"Oh Abbie..."

"Let me finish before you say anything. I have made up my mind. *Yes*. Yes, I will marry you, *but*...only for this time and place."

He grinned and then turned perplexed.

"Wha' d'ye mean by that, Abbie? Time and plaice."

"It means that if we ever go off the island, we would have to remarry in a church or civil ceremony in order to stay man and wife. Otherwise our marriage is not in force."

"But our aiths will be wi' God."

"I think God will understand."

He didn't say anything for a while, obviously thinking about my marriage condition.

"D'ye think this conditionit marriage will be honourable b'fore the Laird and Haly Ghaist?"

"Yes. If someone does not go to heaven because of it, I'm the one, not you."

Suddenly Selkirk roared with laughter.

"Ye be a delightsome lass, even if ye know Mephistophilis and Beelzebub." He came around the table and pulled me up into his arms. And there my heart melted quite a bit more.

We decided the ceremony would be at the fire site on the ridge in nine days. The reason for the delay was that I needed my period to be over, though I didn't tell Selkirk that. We also decided we would live in my hut, since it was fresh and clean. Somehow we managed to honor our singleness for the whole nine days. Selkirk was the strong one here. I came to appreciate that he believed deeply in the marriage crucible and did not want to take anything away from it. Those days before the sacred event went slowly.

Then the day came. We arose in the early morning darkness. We both dressed in goatskins so as to look alike. He put a rope around Angel's neck and put Traitor in a little basket he had woven out of reeds. They were going up with us to be witnesses. Selkirk carried Traitor, a blanket and the Bible. I trailed, carrying the wine bottle, some Chonta cabbage and cooked meat, and pulling little Angel. She could not jump, but she could hobble along surprisingly well. She seemed as excited as I.

We arrived at the fire site in the predawn light. The brightest stars were now fading. El Yunque looked like a huge black ship coming through the mists. Selkirk and I stood together, holding hands. Nervous tingles were going through me. Then the sun peeked up with white gold streaks jumping up in the sky. The brilliant white ball slowly rose above the horizon. It was so gorgeous I cried. Selkirk kissed my tears and soothed me, thinking I was sad. I told him it was because I was so happy. Angel, tied to a rock, stood looking at us like a little cherub. Traitor sat on his haunches, perplexed but waiting patiently. When the sun was a ways above the horizon, the ocean began to glint, the rays sparkling on the tops of the gentle waves, now showing hints of blue.

"Be ye ready?" he whispered.

"Yes, my love."

"Dear mickle Laird," Selkirk intoned with eyes closed, "we be standen heer aneath yor hev'n as our kirk, to take our marriage aiths wi' yor blessen. We hope and pray for yor help and lave and that our vows be pure b'fore thee. So now please hear and bless our marriage."

He held out his scuffed Bible with his left hand and put our right hands on it, his on top of mine.

Selkirk fixed his eyes on mine. "Abigail Spence, do ye tak me, Alexander Selkirk, t'be your proper and laving husband? Will thee lave, honour, and cherish me as I will thee?"

There was a lump in my throat. I cleared it as best I could.

"For this time and place, I do and I will."

He smiled and then nodded for me to now lead.

"Alexander Selkirk, do you take me, Abigail Spence, to be your proper and loving wife? And...will you help, honor, love, and cherish me as I will you?"

Selkirk squeezed my hand on top of the Bible.

"I dae and I will, Abbie."

We looked in each other's eyes for a long while. Finally he turned around to face Angel and Traitor. "If anybody hae raeson the two of us should nocht be marriet, let them spak now o' hold thaer tongues." Neither the goat nor the cat made a sound, but Traitor cocked his head.

Selkirk laughed. He then produced a beautiful, marble-like stone with swirled blue and orange colors, polished to a gem-like finish by the sea.

"Abbie, I gie thee this stone as ane token of our laving bond. With this, I thee wed."

I took it and then produced the clear, crystal-like red stone I had found, and pressed it into Selkirk's hand.

"Alexander, with this stone as a symbol of our love and marriage, I thee wed."

Then we faced each other holding hands and said in unison, "We are man and wife." We went together like magnets and kissed so deeply and so long that I lost touch with reality. I wanted to be swept down right then and there. But Selkirk reminded me that Angel and Traitor were watching and we should go ahead with the reception that was to follow the ceremony. This man had to be made of iron.

The blanket was put down and with the animals next to us, we broke out the Chonta, meat and wine. We all partook. Morsels of the cabbage went to Angel who gobbled them with little finesse. Traitor took the pieces of meat as avidly but at least showed some manners in chewing before swallowing. Selkirk and I washed down our shares with swigs from the wine bottle. The scene was a Titian painting.

The walk down to camp was buoyant but quiet. While Selkirk put

Angel in the pen I went into my hut, took the band off my hair, letting it fall, and quickly removed my goatskins and slipped under the cover. Selkirk soon came in, removed his coverings and got next to me. Our skin caught fire from the first touch. His arms went around me and pulled me further into the rising inferno. Breathlessly, inexorably we reenacted the wild night on the ridge. This time nothing was in the way and our love-making was physically exhausting but satiating.

The days that followed were magical. Selkirk and I worked together at our camp, went swimming, took hunting and fishing jaunts, and hiked around the island, finding wildflowers and seashells. He danced and sang for me and told me stories of his sailing adventures. I told him speculations on the future, such as the American colonies breaking away from England, at which he scoffed. We made love two or three times a day. It was an unbelievably romantic honeymoon, and my affection for him blossomed. I was a happily married woman, and felt this especially when he called me his "dairlin' wife." I even began to think that all of my prior tribulations in this painful odyssey were compensated by my new found love. Well, almost.

The only drawback, as expected, was abstaining during my fertile time. I discussed this with Selkirk and he agreed to the regimen, but it was difficult for both of us, particularly during one rainy period when we were cooped up in the hut for three days. We practiced the "interruptus" technique even though it made me nervous.

The days went by quickly. We began developing patterns. We included in our dinners dishes of both seafood and meat. One day we got a large turtle that came up on the beach. We had turtle meat and turtle soup for days. It was scrumptious. Every morning we went fishing, hunting, or hiking. We went up to light the fire on the ridge every other night. Selkirk even induced me to start reading the Bible so that we could be together in this. Every day after lunch we read quietly on our bed, each from our separate books. I skipped around, finding verses that pleased me. From Chapter One of the Song of Solomon I found:

> 13 A bundle of myrrh is my well beloved unto me; he shall lie all night betwixt my breasts.
>
> 14 My beloved is unto me as a cluster of camphire in the vineyards of Engedi.
>
> 15 Behold, thou art fair, my love; behold thou art fair; thou hast doves' eyes.
>
> 16 Behold, thou art fair, my beloved, yea, pleasant; also our bed is green.

In the afternoons we tended the garden or did chores around the camp. During all of our routines, we always took time to peer out to sea, searching for sails and checking for storms. But the sails did not come and the storms were few. The life was good and joy was complete. I had never experienced anything like it.

But balloons come down to earth. And the earth is a place where as ye sow, ye shall also reap. On Juan Fernández Island the seed had been sowed. I did not get my next period when it was due. I at first kept this to myself, hoping that I was just late. Perhaps my system was disturbed by all our lovemaking. After an anxious two weeks, I concluded it was not coming and I told Selkirk.

"Maybe your body be confusit. Maybe na worry," he said, shrugging.

"Maybe. But what if I am?"

"If ye be wi' child?"

"Yes."

"Weel, we must find naymes for the child."

He said it seriously. I was stunned.

"You mean you would want to have a child?"

"The good Laird decidit."

After all my concern and all the effort to follow the regimen, Selkirk seemed nonchalant about my being pregnant. It made me wonder if he had even tried to be careful. But the blame was not totally his. I, too, had not been completely careful.

"Well, I do not want a child."

He looked at me, surprised.

"If a child came, he be ane gift of our mickle Laird. We must accept and be pleasit."

"I'm going for a walk."

I went up to the first meadow and sat on a Chonta stump. The wind was blowing, whistling through the tall trees. I listened to it a long while, then began to chill. Maybe my body was "confusit." I should wait until the second month to see if my period would show. It might. I had missed periods before. I felt better and decided to go back.

When I returned to camp Selkirk came up and hugged me.

"I donna lak thee displeasit wi' me, Abbie."

I hugged him back, feeling bad that I had walked off.

During the next couple of weeks I would not make love with Selkirk. I knew he was upset with me, but he did not say anything. His spontaneity was gone, the twinkle in his eye missing. I tried to be as much a helpmate as I could, fixing meals, feeding the animals, keeping the fire stoked. When we were out collecting berries a week later, he tried to seduce me in the grass. It was tempting, but I was able to offer intimacy without the usual finale. My touch was warm and loving. After that some of the twinkle returned.

In the fourth week my anxiety rose as my biological showdown arrived. My mood was not helped by some nausea which I felt a couple of times. One by one the days came and went. But my period did not come. I seemed to feel a slight thickening in my tummy. On the day ending five weeks Selkirk found me crying in our hut. He did his best to comfort me. He was unhappy and bewildered.

"I am sure I'm pregnant, Alexander."

He nodded. "I lave thee, Abbie. I will tak care o' thee."

I knew he meant well, but his comment made me angry.

So, worst fear realized. At least there was some relief in ending the doubt. I had had plenty of time to think of what I would do if I were pregnant. Now it was time to get on with it. First, I would try to be alone so that Bitterrroot could contact me. He had promised to come get me if anything went wrong. I could still remember the conversation with him and Carlos in the hut in Panama. If Bitterroot were true to his word he would have no choice but to help. It was time to bail out of the Southern Dreams. But what if he weren't watching or listening? What if he chose not to come? I had a plan.

Selkirk did not want to let me out of his sight. I think he was suspicious of my new found composure. I assured him that everything would be fine, but he probably didn't believe it.

That night I woke up in the darkness. It was still and quiet outside except for the distant sounds of waves and elephant seals. I had been dreaming. My mother had been talking to me about how wonderful I had been as a baby. I had rosebud lips and a cute smile. When I was about to cry my lower lip would curl outward. Instead of crawling I had scooted. I was bowlegged and my first steps had looked so funny that she and my father had laughed, and I had cried.

It was a curious dream and it made me suddenly lonely. Selkirk was next to me snoring. I put my arms around him and snuggled. Slowly my fear subsided. I hadn't wanted to wake him, but I felt a rush of excitement when the snoring stopped. His hand reached behind him and met my thigh. I slowly doodled a pattern on his back with my fingernail. He made a low sound like some prehistoric beast awaking from hibernation. His hand moved roughly on my thigh, moving higher and higher until it found my femaleness, now hopelessly wet. I put my tongue on his neck and in his ear. It took no further time for him to realize that the honeymoon was on again. I had come to the conclusion that as long as I was paying the penalty for incautious love, I might as well get my money's worth. That night the goats and cats heard me.

In the morning Selkirk's eyes were sparkling. He decided to go hunting. The meat supply was low. He invited me to go with him, but I told him I wanted to fish for bacalao. I went to the southwest point of the island where I felt there was the least likelihood of Selkirk coming upon me. I found a secluded place behind a ridge so that I could not be seen from the high mountains. I even dropped my line in the water, but without bait. Fish were not the objective. A big reptile was. The question was, would Bitterroot be tuned in to me?

I sat on the ground. I closed my eyes and visualized Bitterroot in my mind. He was clearly there, smiling. Bitterroot, it's time to come for me. I'm in trouble. I need your help. I'm in a real fix. Please come. You promised you would. I'm waiting here. You must know my situation. So now is the time. The southwest point of Más á Tierra, nearest to Santa Clara. Please come. Please. Don't make me wait.

I opened my eyes. There was nobody. The only sound was the surf hitting the rocky shoreline below. It was strange not to hear the seals. But they made their homes on beaches, not under inhospitable cliffs. Still there was nothing. I decided to take a walk. Maybe it was time to look for the kind of half buried rock I could fall on. I picked my way along the edge of the cliff. I came upon the type of rock I had envisioned, a rounded surface protruding out of the ground. It would make a sharp but not piercing blow to my lower abdomen. I thought about how I would fall. It would be something like sepuku, the ancient Japanese art of falling on a sword. It would be horribly painful. But I would need to do it several times. Would it work? I had no idea.

As I stood there getting up my courage, I heard a rustle behind me. I turned and saw, about twenty yards away, a man standing in some low bushes. He waved at me, smiling. It was Bitterroot. We came to within a few feet of each other, not saying anything for several moments, just looking, expectant. Then he chuckled.

"Well, Abbie, you've not starved, I see."

"Hello, Gordon. Yes, I've had enough to eat. I'll say that. Thank you for coming. You knew I needed to see you, I guess."

"Aye. And your timing is perfect because I have wonderful news."

"I can go home?"

He laughed. "The news is that I had an audience with Queen Anne, herself. Her Highness is deeply interested in Juan Fernández Island and in launching an expedition. I told her about you, Abbie, and she is convinced that the English people, when they hear your story, will raise a clamor to save your honor and this island for the glory of England. She is eager to examine the Spanish captain's log, which will be arriving in London soon. She ordered her closest ministers to start advance preparations for the plan. Not only that, she looks forward to meeting you when you are brought to London. You will be invited to court. How about that, Abbie?"

He was bursting with triumph and glee.

"I am not going to London. I am going home, don't you remember?"

His grin did not lessen.

"What about Selkirk?" I said, now angry. "Does the queen want to meet him too?"

"Oh, her Highness isn't privy to him yet."

"But you are, I take it."

"Of course I know about Selkirk."

"And why didn't you tell me?"

Bitterroot laughed with embarrassment.

"Are ye two getting on?"

"Yes we are. Why didn't you tell me about him, Gordon?"

He shrugged. "I wasn't sure if Selkirk would still be here. There have been castaways on this island from time to time. He's a resourceful lad for a Scot."

"Gordon, I want to go home now."

"It's not time, lass. Ye must be found by the expedition. And ye must return to England on one of the ships to meet Queen Anne and her court. I promised her this. You are going to be celebrated. Thy arrival in London will spur the massive colonization effort needed. After you tour around England there will be waves of people leaving for settlements all over the Spanish Main, which will become the English Main. Don't ye understand? My God, woman! Any lady in the civilized world would give her eye teeth to have a triumphal audience at court."

"Gordon, I have to go home because I'm two months pregnant."

His mouth fell, but he couldn't keep the smile hidden.

"So, I guess you and this Selkirk are getting on," he said.

I had the urge to spit on him. Such an ass. But I knew I must hold my tongue.

"I cannot have the child. I need expert medical care. Take me to Los Angeles. Then I will come back here and meet the expedition. I promise."

He weighed my words, then shook his head slowly.

"Abbie, Abbie. If you were taken home, ye could change your mind on me. We both know that. But let's reason on this. You should birthe the child. It's wrong to stop a life. That baby will be a delight for thee. Bring the child to London. He will be the first Englishman born in the colony of Queen Anne Islands. You will be even more appreciated for that. But ye and Selkirk must marry—you can't bring back a bastard child. The expedition's captain can perform the ceremony on shipboard."

He was almost thinking out loud, looking beyond me.

"Aye, it will be glorious," he continued. "The expedition will find a family—man, woman and child—founders of Queen Anne Town, who hoisted the Union Jack for England, defying the Spaniards. By jove, it be a spanking tale."

"Gordon, I can't have the baby. I won't spend the rest of my life in eighteenth century England, Queen Anne or not. I'm not your slave. Don't you think I have plans for my life? Well I do have plans, and they are not in this backwater century."

"Plans?" His gravelly voice went up in pitch. "Plans? Ye moderns are something. Planning for the perfect life. Get married to the ideal person at the right time and have two perfect children. Plan a life of material success and find malaise, divorce, or suicide. That is no way to be, lass. This is life. This is real, for Christ's sake." He shook his head in disgust.

"No, this is unreal, Gordon. This is living in your fantasy. Pirates, kings, expeditions..."

"Abbie," he interrupted, stepping forward, pushing his finger against my collarbone, "be honest, damn thee. Alexander Selkirk, Scottish he be, is the finest man you'll ever meet, and that baby in you is as good as any baby you'll ever birthe. Just wait until that tyke sets eyes on the world. This is a fine place to be—a great moment in history. You are one lucky woman. Ye must be an idiot if ye cannot see it."

I began to cry. I don't know why. I didn't want to.

"Aye, cry. You need to cry, Abbie. I am not taking you back. You just straighten out. I'll see thee later."

I rubbed my eyes and looked up, but he was fading away in a strangely dark cloud. I began to wail. How could he leave me? The double crosser. He had promised. I sat down and sobbed my heart out.

When I could think again, I thought I must be crying because of the betrayal. He had done it yet again. I was one sad case to have believed him. But as I sat there with a fog coming in off the ocean I knew what had upset me. What had pierced my being was not so much that Bitterroot had left me here. It was what he had said about Selkirk. Bitterroot was right on one thing. Alexander was a fine man. I knew it. And the baby—why did he have to call it a tyke? In that instant it had become a person. When I finally dried up, I was exhausted and cold.

Somehow I got back to camp. Selkirk was not there. I went to bed and slept.

The men in my life—Bitterroot, Selkirk and Kant—had conspired against me. Conspire is not the right word. They influenced me, each in their own way, toward a decision. The combination was very powerful. The decision, which I made freely and solely during the next couple of days, was to let nature take its course. My own contribution to this decision was fear, which I openly admitted to myself—my fear of physical harm. It's strange but I could accept and even carry out, if need be, the ending of my life. But the pain of lingering injury and sickness was far worse in my mind. Falling on the rock was viscerally repellent to me. So through the forces of philosophy, authority, love and fear, I came to the decision to allow God's will, as it were, to unfold.

Once I did this I understood, perhaps for the first time in my life, the psychological benefit of turning things over to God. I didn't have to be in charge. I didn't have to fight my anxiety. I could just let things be. I forgot about the future and dwelled in the here and now. Because of that our honeymoon flowered again, as intense and rewarding as ever. As I swelled over the next few months our love swelled also. I began feeling protective—yes, motherly—toward the little tyke in me. Selkirk pampered me, and I basked in his tenderness. I particularly loved his enfolding me in his arms in bed at night, cradling my tummy.

Our life took on an idyllic monotony. We hunted, fished, gathered fruit and vegetables, chopped wood, set the fire on the ridge, made goatskin clothing, fed and played with the animals, and read the Bible. And of course we made love and talked a lot.

"Abbie, I want ye t'know the sin I carry."

"Tell me, Alexander."

"When I was a lad, anither boy and I were ketched without clothes in the kirk."

"Oh, Alexander, that is not a sin. That is boys being boys. I love you all the more for telling me."

I was secretly amused. Apparently in pre-Victorian Scotland, this was a major sin which was dealt with forcefully and publicly by the church fathers. Selkirk had been shamed. It seemed to have contributed to his becoming argumentative with males and not wanting to stay in his town. If those two dynamics had not come about, perhaps he would not have gone to sea and would not have fought with his captain. He would not have marooned himself on Juan Fernández Island. He and I would never have met.

The vagaries of historical circumstance are unfathomably profound. It is just such circumstances that Bitterroot wants to fool with, to interrupt, to revise. In so doing he would produce a social earthquake to remold the historical terrain during the next three hundred years of the New World. Bitterroot said it was wrong for me to stop my baby's life, but here he was, willing to stop millions of other lives and to create millions of new lives. If he were to succeed as planned, geopolitics, race and ethnic development, technology, ecology, art, literature—everything in Spanish America would be different. There would be different wars, different triumphs, different boundaries, different tragedies. There would be different works of art in the museums, different books in the libraries, different names on the tombstones.

If this happened, would it make any difference in a moral sense? Would God care? From a utilitarian philosophical viewpoint, would Jeremy Bentham care? Is it all just a wash? Still, how can Bitterroot be right about preserving my baby's life and also right about stopping so many other babies' lives? No, something was very wrong about all this. But why was I even worrying about it? I was enjoying being pregnant. I was leaving matters in God's hands.

As my due date came closer, we began to discuss the coming birth. Selkirk was uneasy for a time, but realized he would have to be my midwife. I appreciated the difficulty the role caused him. But as we talked about it I gained confidence that he would do all that I could expect. His moral support would be tops. The major problem was mine, of course. I would have to endure the labor and childbirth without any anesthetic or medical assistance. God forbid there should be complications. I decided my best preparation was to keep in good physical condition, which I did by hiking and hunting with Selkirk, and practicing Lamaze exercises, some of which I remembered from a girlfriend who had done them.

Along about my seventh month, my belly was big and round. My breasts were like large melons. I began to waddle, which slowed my hiking. Selkirk wanted me to stay in camp more, but I insisted on going with him. It was fortunate that I did.

Selkirk liked to hunt, even if he didn't need the food. He made a sport of catching the goats and marking them, and he caught them with his bare hands. The first time I saw him take off after a goat, running barefoot up the side of a hill, it was a marvel. I felt as if I were a spectator at an ancient Olympic event. The powerful legs, the surefootedness, the lithe and supple body were beautiful to watch. Like a cheetah on the Serangetti plain, Selkirk could run down his game in a short span, but could not succeed if he were seen coming from a distance. Catching a leg, he would jerk the beast to the ground and with a noose around its head, hold it down as he wrapped the legs like a cowboy with a dogie. The element of surprise was crucial. So we would sneak up the draws, and peak over the ridges, always downwind from the animals.

There was one large male that inhabited a ridge near El Yunque. Three times he had eluded Selkirk's charge. On this morning, I knew that's where we were headed. Selkirk was determined to best him. On recent trips I had tried to persuade Selkirk to stay in the low country where the rocks and the angle of incline were easier to traverse, but he was stubborn. It was now a grudge match with the big goat. My pointing out the danger of the sport and Selkirk's responsibilities as a husband and father-to-be fell on deaf ears. This, I saw, was the dark side of his adolescent character that at other times was so much fun.

We climbed up the eastern side of the ridge, staying as much in the bushes and trees as possible. When we came to the top, Selkirk crawled up to the lookout point to search the far side. Sure enough, the goat, which he had named Son of Yunque, was there, closer than before, but sunning himself much higher on the side of the cliff than usual. Selkirk motioned me up beside him and I gasped at the steepness of the slope that Selkirk would have to race up.

"It is too steep, Alexander. You cannot try that."

"I can rin over that. He's hie but close. This be an easy fecht. Stay heer, Abbie."

"Alexander, no," I hissed. "It's too dangerous. Please. If you love me you won't do it."

He looked at me strangely.

"I lave thee, Abbie. Shhh, now." He edged out and bent down as if getting into starting blocks. He adjusted the rope noose in his left hand.

"Alexander, please no," I said plaintively.

He was off. The goat spun and stared for a moment before jumping up the slope at an angle. Selkirk was closing, leaping from rock to rock. As he got within ten yards, the goat suddenly turned back the other way. Selkirk tried to turn up directly and head off the spooked animal. The rock face Selkirk tried to leap up was smooth and close to vertical, with only a few crevices to set a foot on. As the two closed Selkirk lunged and got one of the goat's legs. Suddenly Selkirk's feet lost their grip and in a blur he and the goat went tumbling down, cascading twenty feet to a large ledge. They landed together with a thud. The goat got up, groggy, then stumbled its way up the ridge. Except for the clicks of Son of Yunque's hoofs there was silence on the mountain before my scream shattered the air.

"Alexander, Alexander. Oh my God. Oh, please answer me. Are you hurt? Oh no."

I picked my way up to the ledge as quickly as I could. I shuddered as I saw the crumpled body of the man I loved. He was on his side. Blood was flowing out of a large gash on his forehead, running down his face and neck. I yelled at him but he didn't respond. I bent over him. Was his heart beating? Yes, but barely. Was he breathing? Yes, thank the Lord. He was unconscious, probably in shock. I didn't dare move him, afraid his neck or back was broken. I tore up my shirt to make a bandage for his head and I managed to stop the bleeding. I talked to him as I inspected his body. I found only abrasions, no broken bones. But there was blood in his mouth. Was it from an internal injury or just a cut in his mouth? I couldn't tell. I took off my alpaca coat and wrapped it around his torso. Oh, please be all right, Alexander. But he did not come to. After about twenty minutes I began to fear the worst.

Finally, after about an hour of my waiting and talking and praying, I heard a moan. Oh thank you, Lord. Selkirk could hear me. He tried to say something but couldn't get it out. Neurological damage? No, please, no. Then I heard it.

"Abbie."

"I'm right here, Alexander. Where do you hurt?"

"Back."

"Can you move your legs? Try to move each foot if you can."

I prayed. Please let them move.

His left foot moved slightly. The right one didn't move. But I saw muscles tensing in his right leg. The nerves were OK.

"Wonderful, Alexander. Wonderful. Now move your fingers."

Fingers moved on each hand. I felt like crying.

"Good. Very good." I kissed him on the cheek, and I saw a slight smile.

"Where on your back is the pain?"

"Bone. Tail bone."

I moved his buttocks and inspected the tail bone; there was a large bruise forming. He had obviously hit it badly. But that would heal.

"Alexander, can you roll over?"

He tried, but he couldn't.

"OK, just lie there. I'm going to go back to camp and get some blankets and food. Is that all right? You're going to be just fine. When I'm back, I'll stay with you until we can go back together. You're sure it's all right for me to go?"

"Be careful lass." He winked of all things. I kissed him on the cheek, then started down the ridge.

It took me quite a while to get down and back. It was late afternoon by the time I returned. I had blankets, several pieces of cooked fish and meat, Chonta cabbage, water and some cold broth. By the time I got it up the mountain, however much of the broth had spilled. But Selkirk took several mouthfuls. I was pleased that he kept it down. I put a blanket over him and put his head on another.

"Mony thanks, my lavely bride. Beelzebub nor my maker canna hav me for I belang to thee."

"Don't talk, Alexander. Just rest and get well."

I stayed with him all night, catnapping and checking him. He slept soundly for the most part. A few times he moaned. In the morning he could move his body slightly. He also had an appetite. Only then did I begin to believe he would make it.

On the third day, with my help, Selkirk was able to hobble back to camp. It was a several hour ordeal. I put him to bed immediately after a warm meal. I went down too, for I had little sleep on the cold rocky ledge.

I was exhausted and my bed felt wonderful.

That whole experience did something to me. I loved him even more, but I could not fully forgive how foolish his decision had been to risk going up that dangerous slope, despite my pleading. He had not thought or cared about what it would do to me to be here without him and to have to undergo childbirth alone. As the twinkle came back and he slowly healed, good as new, he said things to make me laugh. He knew he had hurt me and was trying hard to make up. But at breakfast one morning he vowed that he would get Son of El Yunque yet. For the first time I felt there was more than a 300 year gulf between us.

As my ninth month arrived I felt lethargic. Now I left camp only to fetch water from the stream. Selkirk hovered around, no longer hunting or setting the fire on the ridge. The baby was kicking frequently as if announcing its readiness. The strength of some of those knocks was astounding to me. Whether for this reason or others, my intuition said this was a boy. We picked names, Alexander Jr., if a boy—we would call him Alex—and Mary if a girl. Selkirk and I were as ready as we ever would be. And, as if nature were in tune, the first labor pain came on the exact day I had estimated to be my due date.

It happened in the late afternoon. The pains were far apart for several hours, but soon came faster and stronger. I knew that this was it. Mom and Dad, are you watching? I'll try to be brave. God, please make it a normal birth.

I lay on my bed. Selkirk was in and out of the hut, more nervous than I. All of our clothes, bedding and rags had been washed and cleaned. Selkirk had water ready to boil. The oil lamp was burning, casting long shadows.

Women friends of mine who had babies told me that labor was the worst kind of pain they had ever experienced. One hears this but until it happens it is just words. Now the pains were real; they were becoming fierce. I was a believer, a member of the club. Women down through the ages had borne babies and survived without drugs, without epidurals and without obstetricians. I was going to join my natural sisters and tough it out.

When the contractions were strong and fast I started my Lamaze breathing. The pain was so intense it was all I could do to keep the puffing going and not cry out. Selkirk kept encouraging words coming and wiped the sweat from my body. At one point I saw Traitor in the hut. Even he seemed sympathetic. But the pain went on and on, worse and worse. I thought I might become delirious. It seemed as if hours had passed since the start of my special breathing. I began not to care if I lived or died. Nature was a real bitch. Thank God for Selkirk. Without him I would have given up, I'm sure. Then...he said he could see the baby's head. Oh, what wonderful words! The baby was coming. This nightmare was going to be over. I pushed hard now at each contraction. I could have pushed a watermelon out. It was working. Suddenly Selkirk shouted. He was doing something down there. I pushed again as he instructed. And again. Then I heard the most beautiful sound in the world—my baby's cry.

"Abbie, a boy. A fine lad."

"Oh, Alexander."

The baby and I cried together. Selkirk wiped him off and cut and tied the umbilical cord. Then the tyke was put on my bosom, swaddled in an old, ragged shirt. I cuddled him gingerly. He was so tiny. Miniature hands. Blue eyes, just like his father's. He stopped crying. Maybe he sensed my heartbeat. I felt exhausted but wonderful. "Thank you, God."

In the middle of the night, after only an hour's sleep, little Alex woke me for the first feeding. His rooting reflex worked perfectly, and he found that big nipple as if he had practiced. He definitely had his father's genes. Before long we were in comfortable synchrony and except for it hurting until I toughened up—I enjoyed the breast feeding. I loved little Alex, and I loved the role of mother. I only wish I could have slept more.

I don't know when the depression set in exactly. Somewhere between the second and third day. There was no reason for it. Selkirk was helping with the baby, enjoying him in the unsure way that new fathers do, trying to allow me as much rest as possible. He brought me food and gave me a bath in bed. Still I began to feel horribly unhappy.

Little Alex's arrival no doubt had triggered my angst. He, my own flesh and blood, was the symbol of what was eating at me. It centered around one question: What on earth was happening to my life? I was mired in quicksand, inexorably sinking into an existence I did not want, did not plan for, but could not escape. My baby was sweet as candy. His father was a good man. But I could not see myself with them in Scotland or England living out my life in the 1700s. Such an existence would be suffocating. Oh Lord.

The Lord was part of my problem. I did not ask to fall in love, but I did. I did not ask to get pregnant, but I did. I had placed myself in the Lord's hands and my faith had seen me through. Through Selkirk's injury. Through the childbirth. I was given a beautiful, healthy child. What more could I have asked for? The problem was that after all of this good "fortune," here I was—stuck with it. Lord, what is the answer?

As the weeks went by, whenever I held or nursed little Alex, I would feel remorseful for these terrible thoughts. I should be thinking of what's good for him, not me. He needed my love and devotion. If it meant eighteenth century Scotland, then it did.

But the thoughts kept coming. They came when I made dinner, when we bathed in the stream, when I made goatskin booties, when we fished, when we gathered berries, and when I lay awake in bed next to Selkirk. And the thoughts took on more sinister dimensions. I began thinking of the Spanish towns and ports that would be attacked by the English expeditionary ships. I thought of all the men, women, and children who would be killed or maimed by cannon balls and grape shot. Bodies being run through with swords. People tortured. It was hideous. But what could be done? The expedition was already on its way if Bitterroot were to be believed. It would arrive any day. Couldn't I just go with the plan? Go to England with Selkirk and the baby, and then come back with them to settle in the New World? Why not? Yes...yes, I could do this. I would be with my baby and Selkirk. They mattered most. As acceptance slowly came, I began to feel better. And I began to wonder how Selkirk might feel about Southern Dreams.

"Alexander, honey, did you ever worry about the Spaniards you killed?" We were in bed, and I hoped he had not fallen off to sleep yet. I could not sleep.

"Na, the Wogs deserve t'be hangit. Ilk be nae good, includit the Pape."

"If the English had more ships and men over here, could they capture and hold the Spanish towns, and turn them into English settlements?"

"Aye. The Scots and English brang dread to the Spanish when they know we're comen. They rin awa'. There be nae better t' fecht than us. The Wogs be nae mair than a wet leaf blawn agin' the eyeball."

"If that's so, why haven't the English captured Spanish land and kept it?"

"We need more people to settle. Naebody comen to farm. Nae women for hames. It be nae enow to fecht."

Why don't English settlers come? Are they afraid?"

"Na, na. Nae enow money. Nae enow ships. Nae enow encouragement from the crown."

Selkirk's tone showed disgust, as if he had dealt with the subject before.

"Alexander, what if Queen Anne showed new interest in settling the shores of the Spanish Main and putting a colony on this island? What if she commissioned the ships? Would there be volunteers to come and settle?"

"Aye, many. But it would nocht succeedit outwith the Queen's auctority and riches. If she wud forgit about royal intrigues in France and Spain and tak more action o'er heer, this warld wud be turnen its lealty t' her and not to Spain."

"Would you be a settler over here, if given help?"

"Aye, in a minute. Abbie, wha questions be these?"

"Just curious, that's all."

I was surprised at how bellicose Selkirk was. He was almost as bad as Bitterroot. Wouldn't those two have a fine time together. He was so cocksure, it was scary. Bitterroot's Southern Dreams were not just one man's dreams.

The next morning as I was holding little Alex, stirring some soup, I watched Selkirk climb up on a rock and look out to sea. It was a constant ritual with him to search the horizon. One day soon he would see a sail. And then another and another. A fleet was on its way. How many ships would it be? Ten? Twenty? Wouldn't he be flabbergasted. He would be elated. He would introduce himself and me to the commander. Would he say Mrs. Alexander Selkirk? The officers would ooh and aah over Alex, Jr. But of course they would already know about me, Abigail Spence, the woman of Juan Fernández Island. They wouldn't know about Alexander Selkirk. He and the baby were their surprise.

A garrison would be set up. Any settlers that had come would begin staking out land for planting. Timbers would be cut for homes and barracks. Queen Anne Town would be founded at the edge of Cumberland Bay. The Union Jack would be flown. To Selkirk's surprise one of the ships would be readied to depart for England with the three of us on board. The captain would be under the Queen's orders to bring me to London immediately. It would be a heady scenario for Mr. Selkirk.

Two weeks later, about noon, I was introducing Alex, Jr., to Angel. My little goat had grown up, and I suspected she was pregnant. As a prospective mother she might be interested in meeting my baby, I thought. Little Alex was at the grasping stage and I thought he might like to try out his fingers on a goat ear. While both were using their senses on the other, Selkirk suddenly ran into camp, hollering.

"Sail ho! Sail ho! Abbie, come look dairlin'. A sail be standin' in. Wooah! Let her be any flag but Spanish."

I went up on the rock with him and peered out. The sail was little more than a speck on the horizon.

"How do you know it's coming here?"

"It's growing in size, methinks. Besides there be nae other land."

Selkirk retrieved his long gun and my pistol. He set about cleaning them and making sure they were working properly. To my surprise, he even fired both of them, using up two balls. The cats scattered in all directions and the goats panicked in the pen. Little Alex began crying.

"You didn't need to do that, did you?"

"If they be Spanish, we canna' throw stones. Our lives depen' on the guns."

Even though I felt this had to be the first ship of the expedition, there was the possibility it was not. It could be Spanish. I felt sorry I had questioned him. He was right. The men on this ship could be the enemy and we could be killed. Suddenly our island in the sun was clouded. I hugged little Alex to me. Our bucolic life might over.

As the sail drew closer and the hull and mast could be seen, the improbable revealed itself. It was a small, one masted open boat. Selkirk was relieved and disappointed at the same time—relieved that it was not large and able to carry an enemy of such numbers to overwhelm us and disappointed that it might be too small to take us away. I was perplexed. It could not be the expedition. So who was it? How could they be out here in such a small boat?

We watched it for quite a while. Now we could see a man in the stern, hand on the tiller. We didn't see others.

Selkirk jumped down off the rock. "He's going to Camberland. Let's gae ower the ridge to meet him."

"Me and the baby?"

"Aye."

That surprised me. Maybe Selkirk just wanted us near him to be sure we were under his protection. Either that or he might want two guns trained on whoever would come ashore. I bundled little Alex up in a carrying strap we had made. We went over the seaward route to Cumberland Bay, watching the small boat that Selkirk said looked like a ship's pinnace. It sailed far into the bay before the sail was dropped by the lone seaman. Selkirk and I stayed in the bushes so as not to be seen. The man dropped an anchor, then pulled on it to see that it had dug in. He worked in the boat for a few minutes, then hoisted and lowered into the water a dinghy so small it would have had difficulty carrying two people. The sailor then took two long guns and a bag and slowly rowed to shore. Selkirk wasn't at all happy about seeing the guns and had us remain well hidden. The man beached the dinghy and made his way through the elephant seals, unflinching. As he strode up the hillside toward us, the slightly swaggering walk seemed familiar. As he came closer, I realized I was looking at the unmistakable jaw, nose, and cheekbones of Mr. Gordon Bitterroot. I gasped and Selkirk looked over at me.

"Donna' worry. I'll tak care o' him."

I stood there, speechless, as Selkirk raised his gun and stepped forward out of the bushes about thirty yards from Bitterroot.

"Hold theer, sir. Put down thy guns."

Bitterroot looked at Selkirk, smiled broadly and set his guns on the ground. Selkirk approached him slowly, still sighting down the barrel.

"Are ye English?" Selkirk asked.

"Aye. I be Gordon Bitterroot, first mate off the bark, *Covenant*. And who might you be, sir?"

"I be Alexander Selkirk aff the *Cinque Ports*. I've been heer nigh on two yeers."

"I know of that ship. How glad I am to see thee," Bitterroot said, extending his hand. Selkirk lowered his gun and they shook hands warmly.

"Abbie," Selkirk called, motioning me toward him. "He's English."

I walked down to them, trying to keep composure. Little Alex was asleep in the sling, his head on my shoulder.

"Mr. Bitterroot, this be me wife, Abbie, and our baby."

Bitterroot looked at me knowingly and then smiled like a fox who had just eaten a chicken.

"How do you do, Mrs. Selkirk. That be a fine baby, I'm sure," he said, winking.

I nodded at him. "Hello, Mr. Bitterroot."

"Sae where be thy ship?" Selkirk asked.

"Heading for the coast of Peru, espying for prizes. The crew mutinied on us. Put poor Captain Small in irons and set me off in the boat only because they looked kindly on me." He shook his head, frowning. "I set off for Juan Fernandoes, not wanting to meet up with any Spanish. Took seven days and nights. I be mighty weary."

"O Laird, a mutiny."

"Aye. And when the Admiralty catches up to those blackguards, they'll be feeling manila around their necks, they will." He spat on the ground.

They continued talking, trading information on how they came to be here, seafaring people they both knew, ships they'd been on, ports they'd seen and so forth. Bitterroot was the consummate actor. I looked out to sea. I could not stand hearing his voice or seeing his face. My stomach turned sour as I realized then how easily I had fallen prey to his guile. I had hated his victorious look when Selkirk introduced me and little Alex. Bitterroot had to know that Selkirk was on the island when he put me here. He knew that I would fall for Selkirk. Somehow he knew or hoped I would have a baby. It was all part of the plan. What a total dupe I was. He had locked me into the Southern Dreams through Selkirk and my baby, and now there was no getting out. He knew I would not leave little Alex and Selkirk. How insidious. How Machiavellian. Though I had ranted about him in the past, I had never believed he was without some redeeming goodness. I finally had to accept how utterly unredeeming he was. Will Rogers had said he never met a man he didn't like. Well, he never met Gordon Bitterroot. This man was rotten to the core.

I looked at Selkirk. I could tell he was already charmed by Bitterroot. In just a few minutes, Selkirk was a Southern Dreams recruit and didn't even know it.

"Abbie, let's be walken hame. Mr. Bitterroot needs food and rest. He can hae the empty hut."

Bitterroot smiled at me. "I thank thee both for the hospitality."

When we got into camp, Bitterroot settled into Selkirk's old hut while Selkirk and I started cooking dinner. There was plenty of meat and langosta. When Selkirk went down to the stream for water, I went quickly to Bitterroot.

"Gordon, why did you come here like this?" I hissed.

"Because you, Selkirk, and the baby are in mortal danger. There be a Spanish vessel coming tomorrow. They want to see if you are still here. It be their plan to take you back to Valparaiso and put you on trial as a traitorous enemy."

"Oh my God." He was always getting me.

"We have to hold them off and make them leave before the expedition arrives. The first ship from England is due in a week. These Spanish banties are the only thing between us and success. Abbie, our Southern Dreams are coming true."

"How many men will be on the Spanish ship?" I asked, still in a daze.

"It's a small one. Maybe ten or twelve."

"Gordon, how on earth can three of us hold off that many?"

"I have a plan. Here comes Selkirk. We'll talk on the morrow."

"Mr. Bitterroot," Selkirk said, "ye must taste this. Ye hav'na tasted better water anywhaur in the warld. This island be a Blessen of God. And t'morrow will be anither greit day."

The sun came up on that next day and flooded Más á Tierra in brightness, bringing out all its colors—the greens, grays, browns, whites and blues of land and sea. The island sounds were loud—seabird squawks, seal roars and the crashes of ocean waves. I awoke anxious.

Selkirk and Bitterroot were already up and about. Little Alex was crying for his breakfast. I had slept fitfully during the night. Bitterroot's appearance had shattered my existence. The way of life of our tiny village could not continue. It would be ripped asunder by the Spanish attackers or displaced by the English settlers. Did it really matter which party brought about the demise?

I knew that Bitterroot had not come to save me. Or little Alex or Selkirk. He had come only to secure the Southern Dreams. The arrival of the English expedition and its mission of attacking mainland Spanish holdings were all that mattered. At one point in the night, I dreamed about the Nobel prize-winning novelist, Gabriel García Márquez. At Reed I had read his most famous work, *One Hundred Years of Solitude*, a timeless and boisterously poetic reflection of mankind's foibles and triumphs, as seen through several generations of the Buendía family. How could it be that this great man and this fine work might never exist? In my dream he and his books were sucked into a whirlpool of space, disappearing into the void. One might as well deprive the world of *Robinson Crusoe*.

"Mr. Bitterroot. Mr. Bitterroot." Selkirk was shouting from high up on the ridge.

I stepped outside the hut, little Alex still suckling at my breast. Bitterroot was climbing up the hillside toward Selkirk.

"Yor boat be gone," Selkirk shouted.

Both of them quickly disappeared, heading for Cumberland Bay.

At first I was alarmed. Perhaps the boat had dragged its anchor and run aground on the shore. But the more I thought about it the more I believed that the boat disappeared for a reason. If the Spanish were coming, it would be better for them not to see a boat at the anchorage. They should not be put on guard. Bitterroot probably sunk his boat. A small leak would have let in water enough to scuttle it during the night.

A couple of hours later Selkirk and Bitterroot came into camp.

"Abbie, there be anither vessel comen," Selkirk said.

"What country?" I asked, already knowing the answer.

"We don' know. Mr. Bitterroot think it be Spanish. Sae we be forwarnit to tak defense."

Bitterroot looked at me in earnest. "Abbie, can you shoot a long gun?

There's one for you and we'll need your help."

"I suppose I can. But what about little Alex?"

"You'll have to bring him and try to keep him quiet."

I looked at Selkirk questioningly.

"Abbie, I will tak the baby. I kin move fast with him. If this be the Spanish we dae or die t'day. Everthing be at stake, dairlin'."

As I listened to the feeling behind the words, tears came to my eyes. I loved this man. I squeezed little Alex closer to me.

"I know, Alexander."

He saw my tears and put his arms around me. I cried quietly, wishing Bitterroot was not there.

After placing little Alex in the sling on Selkirk's back, I grabbed my pistol and powder and put my marriage stone in my goatskin pocket for good luck. They carried the long guns, water, some food, and a blanket.

"Where is your boat, Bitterroot?" I asked when we reached a place up from the bay where they wanted to stop.

"It sprung a leak and sank. If our visitors are Spanish, that will be just as well. We've hidden the dinghy in the brush. Now let me explain my plan."

His strategy was to space ourselves out on the hillside overlooking the main landing place. We would stay hidden in the trees and bushes. By being spread out, we would seem to be more than three when we fired. We would let the boatload of sailors get close to the surf then we all would fire, trying to pick off as many as possible. If we were lucky, the boat would overturn in the waves and their powder would get wet. Any men making it to shore would be stranded without cover, making easy targets for our crossfire. Meanwhile, the men remaining on the ship would be unable to aid their companions on shore unless they had a second boat. Shooting from the ship would not be effective due to the distance. Having lost a large number already and thinking they were up against a sizable enemy force, they might hoist up the anchor and flee. This was typical of the Spaniards, according to Bitterroot. We could finish off those on the shore one by one.

"If they hae cannon on the ship?" Selkirk asked.

"They will be at anchor and unable to turn the ship to aim the cannon. Even if they can, they won't be able to see us in the trees. If cannonballs get close, we move."

We ate an early lunch, I nursed the baby, and we took our positions. Bitterroot was seaward, I was in the middle and Selkirk with little Alex was over toward the stream. My station was behind a rock. Soon the ship was close enough for us to make out detail, the most important being a Spanish flag flying from the mast. I could count nine men. There was one small cannon mounted on the foredeck. It seemed strange to me that it had all come down to this.

The ship dropped its foresail at the mouth of the bay and came in on mainsail alone. The breeze was light. I could see someone with an officer's hat on the afterdeck searching the island with a telescope. I kept hunched down behind the rock, keeping my flintlock rifle hidden. My pistol was in my pouch. The ship rounded up and the anchor splashed into the water. Over the sounds of the seals I could hear orders shouted. After the ship swung on its anchor, the mainsail was lowered and wrapped and tied. Now a long boat on the deck was unfastened and several of the men muscled it over the gunwale into the water. A rope ladder was dropped over the side, and one by one seven men went down into the boat.

I saw five rifles, several pistols, and some cutlasses. Two men manned oars, one on each side. There was waving and shouting as the boat was pushed away. It headed for a sandy place on the shore just below me.

The elephant seals became excited as the boat approached, bellowing and milling around. A large bull moved down to the water's edge facing the intruder. He stood tall and threatened to attack the strange beast coming toward his harem. One of the men raised up in the boat and fired his rifle. The bull shook his head several times, turned and moved a few feet, then slumped down. The rest of the seals scattered.

When Bitterroot waved a handkerchief, I placed my gun on top of the rock and sighted at one of the oarsmen. Even though the target was fairly close in range the shot would not be easy because the boat was moving up and down slightly in the waves.

A shot rang out from Bitterroot's direction. This was closely followed by one from Selkirk's direction. I beaded on the seaward sailor in the boat and squeezed. I must have hit him because he slumped backward just after my shot. Another man bent over him, and the boat began turning off course. Suddenly all hell broke loose as the boat went broadside into the surf. I could hear little Alex crying. Sailors jumped into water shouting and running to take cover at the bottom of the embankment. A couple fired pistols wildly. The two men on the ship were shouting and scurrying around on the deck. Another shot rang out from Bitterroot and a man in the boat tending his wounded companion screamed in agony and slipped over the edge into the water. The boat flipped in a large breaker. Selkirk fired and a man running up from the beach fell. I saw a man crawling along the beach beyond the embankment and I fired at him, but must have missed. I think I could have done better if it didn't take so long to load between shots.

Gunfire now came from the sailors at the embankment toward Bitterroot's position. Suddenly something big crashed into the brush next to me. Then there was a very loud sound. I looked out at the ship and saw smoke coming from the swivel gun on the bow of the ship. Bitterroot had not counted on facing such an weapon. I realized I was scared because my legs were shaking. So this is what war is like. I got down behind the rock and re-loaded. I heard Bitterroot and Selkirk fire again.

Little Alex would not stop crying. I wanted to comfort him but I had to let him suffer. "Baby, we just have to get through this." Again I faced up over the rock with my gun. I could see that the fire from the beach and the ship was now being directed at Bitterroot and Selkirk. I could see four sailors crouched at the embankment. They were vulnerable to the cross-fire. Suddenly, two ran up the hillside directly toward Bitterroot, pistols in hand. They had waited until he needed to re-load. He had a rifle and a pistol. Would he have kept one in reserve? Without thinking I ran toward Bitterroot. I could see the backs of the Spaniards moving through the brush in front of me. The nearer one must have heard me for he stopped and turned, peering my way. I fired the rifle from less than twenty yards and he fell, yelling. I could see the twisted pain on his young face. It was horrible. How could I be doing this?

I then heard shouting from Bitterroot's direction. I ran up toward him, pistol drawn, and then heard a shot. More shouting. Then another shot. As I got close I could see them locked together, then one was on the ground, not moving. The one still standing was Bitterroot. He was hopping on one leg. Had he been hit? Please, no.

"Gordon?"

"I'm here, lass."

I saw blood on his pantleg.

"Damn, that be close," He said. "But we have the Wogs now. Eeee yahhh. God save the Queen!"

We heard a shot from Selkirk's direction. Then there was a yell from the beach. We both looked out.

"Oh, oh." Bitterroot pointed.

I saw the two last seamen dashing away, cutlasses in hands, heading toward Selkirk. They had waited for his gun to be empty. I screamed.

"Gordon, Gordon. My baby! Do something."

He looked at me and shook his head slowly, grimacing. "There's nothing to do. Selkirk can probably outrun them, even with the baby. They only have cutlasses. The battle's decided. We've won. You and me, Abbie."

"You bastard." I lunged and knocked him to the ground, landing on him. I cocked the pistol in my right hand and held it away from his reach, pointing the barrel at his head.

"Do something to save them or I swear I will kill you!"

"Don't fire, Abbie. The powder will scorch ye." He looked at me, his lips curling upward. "I can't do anything for them. You are the important one."

I had seen the smirk one too many times. I had heard his crap once to often. I squeezed the trigger.

"No, Abbie..."

The flash hit my face and I felt a searing burn even as I began to move into the darkness, pulling away from that place. I was being transported once again. My ears were ringing from the explosion. As I moved into a smoky tunnel of swirling air I remember my face and eye in excruciating pain. I lost consciousness.

I don't know how long I slept. My face throbbed terribly. I couldn't open my right eye. There was something heavy on it. I opened my left eye slowly. I was on a cot, looking down at heavily trodden dirt. It was stiflingly hot and humid. I looked up and saw bronze bodies and heard strange language. Then I recognized the hut. I saw the Cacique and two of his men. Moving my head slightly, I saw Carlos. They were bending over the cot at the opposite wall. I watched as they moved their arms carefully, seriously, doing something. Carlos handed a knife out behind him to one of the men. There was blood on the blade. More talking and motions around the end of the cot. I heard a groan. Then I caught a glimpse between the moving bodies. I saw the tortured face of Bitterroot. Now they were wrapping a large poultice on his head and tying it with twine.

Then I remembered that I had pulled the trigger. I remembered the two Spaniards with cutlasses. And I remembered Alexander and my baby. I let out a scream. It turned into a mournful cry. Carlos was at my side, holding my hands.

"Abbie, Abbie. It's me, Carlos. I'm here. Don't worry." He stroked my arms and moved his hand gently on my face. I kept crying.

"Where's my baby? Where's Alexander?"

"They're safe. Don't worry."

"I must see them now. Where are they?"

"You can't see them now. You must rest. I have to help my father."

"Is he all right?" I asked softly.

"He was shot in the head. We had to remove the lead. I don't know how he made it out of there with you. He may not live."

My heart skipped. I had shot him. Please Gordon, don't die.

Carlos motioned to one of the men who brought me some sort of hot vegetable and fruit broth in a cup. It tasted bitter and sweet at the same time. It felt nice in my throat.

"Abbie, you have a nasty wound around your eye. But it will heal if you sleep. The drink will help, so take it all." Carlos helped lift the cup to my lips.

Soon I felt my self slipping into unconsciousness. There were voices. It was some sort of tribunal. I was being sentenced for the murder of three Spaniards and an Englishman. I looked out the window and saw a gallows. The hood was put over my head and...

It was dark when I stirred to consciousness again. I could hear the distant chatter of monkeys and Bitterroot's laborious snoring across the room. I looked out with my one good eye and saw Carlos on a mat on the floor next to his father. I had to relieve myself and quietly moved out of the hut, trying to pick my way to some bushes. I could hear the nearby creek. When I came out of the bushes, I saw Carlos outside near the doorway.

"Abbie, how do you feel?"

"Better. My eye doesn't throb as much. Tell me, have I lost my sight in that eye?"

"No, in another day it will be completely normal."

I let out a long breath.

"And Gordon?"

"I don't know. He wants to go to a modern hospital as soon as he gets some strength."

"You've talked with him?"

"Sí, but he is not fully in his right mind."

I hung my head, feeling guilty. Then I thought of Selkirk and little Alex.

"Carlos, where are Alexander and my baby?"

"Selkirk is on Más á Tierra. He's just fine."

"Is my baby OK too?"

Carlos looked at me with a pained expression.

"Abbie, you never were there. You never met Selkirk. You didn't have a baby."

I gasped. "What are you saying, Carlos?"

"We are back here at Panama, before you went on the ship to Juan Fernández. You are not going further. You will not stay in Panama with

Don Ramón's family. You will not board the warship, *Santa Rosa*, with me. You will not go to Más á Tierra."

I couldn't understand. I know I had my baby. I married Selkirk. I nursed him back to life on the cliffside when the goat fell on him. We fought the Spaniards.

"Abbie, don't worry. It will all be OK in a short while."

"Carlos, why did Gordon bring me back?"

"I don't know."

"Coming back ruined Southern Dreams...didn't it?"

"Yes."

The sun was beginning to send rays over the mountains to the east. Parrots and other birds began chattering. Carlos heard Bitterroot stirring and ducked back into the hut. As I stood there staring at the sunrise, my mind was on that far magical island—our little huts, my dancing Scotsman, and my cherub baby with the rosebud mouth. Why wasn't I with them? I reached into my pocket and grabbed the marriage stone. It was real. But the image in my mind wavered as if caught in the sun's heat. The beautiful picture began to fade, try as hard as I could to keep it. My body quivered. My bad eye tingled and my face had a strange sensation. The poultice fell off and my clothes were moving as I stood there in a daze. It was suddenly brighter. The sun was higher over the peaks.

I smoothed down the full length dress and readjusted the combs of gold and pearl in my freshly coiffed hair. I glanced down at my shiny black leather shoes. The mule snuffed and I looked at the wagon that would take us to Panama. I was nervous and I mentally rehearsed one more time the story of where I was from, to be convincing for the Panamanian officials. Carlos came out of the hut, wearing his white silk shirt, tight black pants, and matching black hat. He looked so handsome. Bitterroot followed him out, the poultice wrapped around his head. He was limping and looked much worse than I remembered.

"Are we leaving for Panama, now?" I asked.

"Aye, lass, come here. We're going, but not to Panama," he said softly. "Prepare thy mind, we're going away."

"Adiós Abbie," Carlos said, squeezing my hand. "Maybe I'll see you again some time."

"But why aren't we going to Panama?" I asked, rather bewildered. We had been talking about it, planning for it for the past couple of days.

"There's been an unexpected change in itinerary, let's just say. Prepare to go, lass." Bitterroot was speaking with difficulty.

I wasn't arguing about it. I felt the cool darkness come like it had before. There was a far off hollow sound as if wind were blowing in a canyon. I let myself relax.

It became suddenly light. Leaves brushed my face. I was on the ground. It was sunny but mild in temperature. I was in a row of Bird of Paradise. I stood up. An elderly man in a suit and tie was standing in front of me.

"Are you all right, young lady? That was a nasty fall. You should be careful about those hoses lying around." He helped me up.

"Yes, I'm fine. Thank you." I looked down. I had on the pollera dress. There was mud on it from the fall. My hair was in my face. I had only one shoe on.

"Do you work here?" he asked.

"Yes, can I help you?" It was strange. I felt like two people.

"Well, I want one of these Bird of Paradise."

"Yes, these are very popular. Which one do you like best?"

He selected a blooming one. As I lifted the can and carried it to the man's Ford Explorer, I realized I was exhausted. Bone weary. I put the plant on the floor of the back seat. Then I looked around, suddenly wondering why Bitterroot wasn't there. Where had he gone?

"OK, sir, just come with me to the front desk and we'll get this written up."

As we went up to the counter, my boss, Ron Shofner, looked at me like I was from outer space.

"Abbie, what the hell happened to you? Where did you get that outfit?"

"She had a bad fall in the yard," the customer said.

"I know I'm a mess, Ron. I have to go home and clean up. Do you mind if I take a couple of hours off?"

"No, go ahead, but first please wait on that lady over near the shade azaleas."

I went out to the auburn-haired customer stooping over a white azalea. She stood up and smiled at me.

"Abbie, well hello."

It was Claire.

"What a surprise. How are you, Claire?"

"It's good to see you, Abbie." She looked at my dress with a curious expression, but didn't say anything about it.

"Can I help you pick out some azaleas? We have some nice ones."

"Well, I'd like two white ones for a shady spot—an indoor atrium, actually."

I pulled out the two nicest ones, put them on a dolly, and took them inside to the cash register and then followed her out to her car.

"There you go, Claire. You picked a couple of good ones." She smiled slightly.

"Thank you, Abbie."

"Well thank you, Claire. Maybe we could have coffee some time."

"I'd like that. Actually, Abbie, we might be able to get together sooner. I came to ask you something. Cliff and Gordon are talking about a week's cruise to Santa Cruz. That's one of the big islands west of Ventura. They want the two of us to come along. If you go, so will I. But I don't want to be the only woman."

She looked at me quizzically and I realized I was being asked to go on the cruise. I had a vague sense of deja vu, but couldn't figure out why.

"You're looking for a fourth?" I asked.

"Would you come Abbie? I will go if you come too."

It sounded like a lot of fun, but for some reason I felt I shouldn't go. It was like one person in me wanted to go and another didn't. The two people couldn't survive.

"No, Claire, I will not be able to go to Santa Cruz."

Then something unreal happened. It felt like electrical voltage went through my head. My body quivered. Even the earth and sky seemed to shudder. When it became calm again, I was still standing there in front of Claire. But I felt a rush of excitement, as if my life was fantastically together, even though I was extremely tired.

"It is great seeing you Claire. Good luck with those azaleas."

She stood there with her mouth open as I walked back to the office.

My boss looked at me and laughed.

"Abbie, Halloween's over. Go home and get cleaned up."

Back at my apartment I took off the weird clothes. Where on earth did I get these? Then I found something in one of the pockets. It was a small polished rock, marble-like with swirled blue and orange colors. It was quite exquisite. As I turned it over in my hand, tears came. I realized that I was utterly exhausted. I showered, called the nursery to tell them I was sick and wouldn't be back for the rest of the day, and crawled in bed and slept.

For several days afterward I looked frequently at the mysterious rock. Each time I couldn't help from crying, although I didn't know why. On that next Saturday, I decided to show it to Bitterroot. I had nothing better to do. I hadn't seen him in a while. I could also stop at the cut-rate pharmacy that was near the bookstore. I needed a new supply of vitamins.

The front door of the bookstore was open but I didn't see anyone behind the counter or in the stacks. I knocked on the door to the back room and heard someone stir inside. The door was opened very slowly by Bitterroot, standing unsteadily with crutches. He looked bad. His head was freshly bandaged and there was a new looking cast on his leg. Deep circles under his eyes contrasted against the puffy face. He stared at me for a few long moments.

"Gordon, are you all right? What on earth happened?"

"Well, it be you." His voice was soft and gravelly. "How are you doing, me lass?

"I'm fine. But God, what happened to you?"

He shook his head slowly. A weak smile came. "I got shot in the leg and in me head."

"Oh no. Where? How?"

He eased down onto a stool.

"Well, we might just say that my head was in the wrong place." He then chuckled. "I had these Southern Dreams, you see, but my opponent thought otherwise. And she was formidable."

"She?"

"A woman who travelled with me. It was quite a long while ago. I don't expect you could place her. But what's that in your hand?"

I handed it to him. He inspected it and his eyes widened.

"It's a fine one. Agate. Polished by the sea. I'm surprised it came back with you."

"Gordon, I have no idea what you're talking about. Do you know where this stone came from?"

"From an island called Más á Tierra of the Juan Fernández group. I tell you what. If you'll trust me with it for a couple of weeks, I'll have it mounted with a chain so ye can wear it around your neck as a souvenir of something pretty special."

"That would be really nice, Gordon. Are you sure you can afford it?"

"It's the least I can do for ye."

"But how could you do it, being a basket case like this?"

"Well, two little balls of lead cannot stop me, by God. Although I admit, one of them kind of got to my brain." He chuckled and looked at me in a weird, knowing way.

And true to his word, in two weeks he called me and I went to the store. He handed me a package tied in an old London newspaper.

"Don't open it until you get home. And bye the bye, Abbie, what are your plans for the future?"

"I've been thinking I might go up to Portland. I've been in contact with one of my professors. He says I can be a teaching assistant for his course on the colonial history of the New World. For some reason that appeals to me. I really miss the Reed scene. I've come to realize I'm not getting any younger. So I'm thinking I might find somebody up there. You know, like start thinking about a family." I felt embarrassed.

"Mmm," he nodded.

"L.A.'s interesting, but I need an intellectual type. And Reed's got them."

"Mmm. Or you might like a blond, athletic seaman type."

Suddenly I began tearing.

"I don't know why I'm crying, Gordon. Why did you say that?"

"No reason."

"I'd like you to come up and visit, Gordon. There is the greatest dessert place near Reed. It's called Papa Haydn's. I think we need to sweeten you up."

He laughed vigorously then, and I felt good, having brought him some cheer.

"I'm beyond sweetening, lass, but I might enjoy sitting in on one of your New World classes. You will be a great teacher, Abbie. But don't think you are only an intellectual. There is more to ye than you know right now. Take my word. But you will find it out, I'm sure."

I looked at him, puzzled. Bitterroot didn't always make sense.

When I got home I unwrapped the package and found a handcrafted little wooden box. I pulled off the top and then gasped. The agate had been mounted in solid gold. The filigree design around the edge was hand done. The stone in its gold mount was absolutely stunning, and I began crying softly. I turned it over and saw it had been inscribed with tiny lettering in old English:

To Abbie Spence
Woman of Juan Fernández Island
Mrs. Alexander Selkirk
1706
Love, Gordon Bitterroot

My girlfriend Crystal had been right. Gordon Bitterroot was a total kook.

EPILOGUE

Alexander Selkirk lived on Juan Fernández Island for four years and four months. On February 1, 1709, the *Duke* and *Duchess*, privateering vessels of an expedition out of Bristol, England, arrived at Juan Fernández Island and found Selkirk. The *Duke* took him on board and departed the island on February 13 of that year. Heading west, the ship circumnavigated the world, took several prizes, and arrived in England on October 1, 17ll.

Selkirk's substantial prize money from the voyage, £800, allowed him to settle into an easy life. Several publications reported on Selkirk's existence on Juan Fernández Island, including the journals of Captain Woodes Rogers (Voyage Round the World, 1712) and the second in command on the *Duchess*, Captain Edward Cooke (Voyage to the South Sea and Round the World, 1711). In 1713 an interview with Selkirk by Richard Steele appeared in *The Englishman*.

Selkirk and his experience captured the imagination of the people of England. Daniel Defoe based the idea for his novel, *Robinson Crusoe*, on Selkirk's life at the island. The book was published in 1719, destined to become one of the most famous stories in history.

Selkirk settled down in his old home in Scotland and engaged in a number of amorous affairs. Later he married Frances Candis. There is no record of his having children. Selkirk died in 1721 as an officer aboard the *H.M.S. Weymouth*. In a pamphlet later published as a Selkirk memoir, he is reported to have exclaimed, "Oh my beloved island! I wish I had never left thee!"

In January, 1966, the Chilean government changed the name of Más á Tierra to Robinson Crusoe Island and that of Más Afuera to Andrew Selkirk Island.

Abigail Delgado, great granddaughter of Abbie Spence, graduated from Reed College with a degree in literature in 2068. She was invited to speak at her class graduation. Abbie attended the graduation ceremony in a wheelchair pushed by Gordon Bitterroot, who still looked to be about forty. Abbie was a happy woman nearing the end of her life.

The day after graduation, Abigail Delgado drove her great grandmother and Bitterroot to a cabin at NeahKahNie Beach on the Oregon coast. Abigail brought a tape recorder and a large supply of cassettes. That evening, after a pleasant dinner, they settled into comfortable furniture and Bitterroot began releasing in Abbie memories of her experiences between 1704 and 1706. Over the next several days, Abbie told the story of those lost years while the machine whirred and Bitterroot and Abigail listened.

In 2080, a ceremony was held on the eastern ridge leading from El Yunque mountain on Robinson Crusoe Island. Those in attendance included officials of the Chilean government, Gordon Bitterroot, and Abigail Delgado, who wore the blue and orange-colored stone willed to her by her great grandmother. The ceremony marked the official renaming of El Yunque to Abbie Spence mountain. As Abigail listened to the Spanish speakers she looked down at the vibrant colors of trees, rocks, beaches and ocean. Her eyes teared, it was so stunning.

Acknowledgements

I am indebted to many people who made contributions to the development or improvement of this book. Editor of Arch Grove Press, Julia Surtshin, was always there with supportive words, assistance with editing, and publishing expertise. Consulting editor Judith Searle reviewed an early draft and suggested areas for changes. Copy editor Susan Blackaby, a delight to work with, improved immensely the story's readability. Professor Ramón Araluce consulted on Spanish language usage. (Any errors are mine, not his.) Marine historian Herb Beals was a treasure trove of knowledge about the history of the west coast exploration. Other readers made comments resulting in beneficial changes. These included Dwight Sangrey, Chuck and Katie Riley, and bookstore owner Valerie Ryan. I also wish to thank Louise Nelson for her excellent advice and assistance, and June Shiigi who provided invaluable technical expertise preparing the final electronic book file. I am especially grateful for the existence and availability of the U.C.L.A. Research Library.

My deep appreciation also goes to people who offered me assistance early in my writing endeavors. Two people in the publishing business, Kenneth Atchity in Los Angeles and Donna Munker in New York, encouraged me to pursue fiction writing. Another in the Oregon publishing business, Eve Goodman, was ready with helpful pointers at various times. I especially wish to thank friends and family who offered encouragement along the way, including Linda Sessions, Rhoda Karubian, Louie Gast, George Sessions, Ruth and Jim Kent, Alfred Sessions, Phil Sachs, Charles Bird, and Hugh and Chris McIsaac. Finally, I am grateful for my daughter, Catherine Sessions, who gave me inspiration.

About the Author

Richard Sessions' fascination with west coast history began with childhood stories about his ancestors in historic California. A great grandfather came from Cornwall to California during the gold rush, and died bent over from a life in the mines. A great grandmother gave food to the notorious bandit, Joaquin Murietta, and later found a deer on her porch as repayment. The author's grandparents honeymooned to Yosemite Valley with a horse and buckboard; the horse died, the marriage survived. From such tales the author developed a keen interest in earlier times.

Like his parents and grandparents, Richard Sessions grew up in California's central valley. He attended Fresno State College, served several years as a naval intelligence officer, and then settled in southern California. He earned masters degrees from the University of Southern California and U.C.L.A., and served much of his career as a university research administrator in Los Angeles. An avid sailor, he has cruised in the Caribbean, sailed to Hawaii, and visited all of southern California's offshore islands. These adventures deepened his interest in the history and lore of the European exploration and settlement of the New World. He began writing fiction in the 1980s, and in 1990 moved to Oregon where he and his wife both work and write.

From a pre-publication review:

> A novel for historical fiction lovers and nautical buffs...this tale of a young woman literally taken back in time to the early 1700s...is an intellectual as well as entertaining story and would make a terrific movie.

BOOKVIEWS
Alan Caruba, Editor
Charter member, National Book Critics Circle